MAXWELL'S REVENGE

The position of Assistant Headteacher at Leighford High has become available, but Peter 'Mad Max' Maxwell has his hands full with his beloved Sixth Form – and as his fiancée, DS Jacquie Carpenter remarks, he also solves the odd murder... At the special lunch for prospective Assistant Headteachers, a mysterious sickness strikes the staff, and when a member of staff dies, Maxwell's hopes for a quiet term, followed by a quiet wedding, are swiftly shattered. The ever-enterprising Head of Sixth Form sets out to catch a killer, whilst juggling fatherhood, impending marriage and the sudden arrival of his mother-in-law to be!

MAXWELL'S REVENGE

MAXWELL'S REVENGE

by

M. J. Trow

Magna Large Print Books
Long Preston, North Yorkshire,
BD23 4ND, England.

British Library Cataloguing in Publication Data.

Trow, M. J.
  Maxwell's revenge.

  A catalogue record of this book is
  available from the British Library

  ISBN   978-0-7505-3108-5

First published in Great Britain in 2009 by Allison & Busby Ltd.

Copyright © 2009 by M. J. Trow

Cover illustration by arrangement with Allison & Busby Ltd.

The moral right of the author has been asserted

Published in Large Print 2009 by arrangement with
Allison & Busby Ltd.

Magna Large Print is an imprint of Library Magna Books Ltd.

Printed and bound in Great Britain by
T.J. (International) Ltd., Cornwall, PL28 8RW

Chapter One

The field was so silent that the sound of the grass growing was almost deafening. A late and lazy bumblebee mooched over the dusty clover, left long at the edges of the shaved green. A butterfly fanned its slightly ragged wings on a fading dog rose in the hedge. A fat, ripe blackberry finally lost its grip on the bramble and fell wetly to the ground. After a small pause, for health-and-safety reasons, a field mouse approached the dark pile of protein and delicately began to eat.

The sun was not exactly beating down, at this fag end of the summer heat. Its warmth was a friendly hug, not the passionate embrace of July and August. The light had an almost glutinous quality, as if it was too tired to do more than fall to the ground. There was no longer that feeling of a subliminal buzz as the ground took up the energy and gave it back in spades to the sky. The peace was perfect; summer was not so much dying as settling back in bed for a bit of a lie-in. Rumours of its demise were much exaggerated, mostly by the appallingly inept Meteorological Office.

Suddenly, the field mouse pricked up its ears, the butterfly poised its wings for flight and the bee concentrated for once. A distant muttering shook the ground on their microscopic level and fear was in the air. Even the grass stopped growing, its summer idyll abruptly at an end. Unwilling to leave its blackberry feast, the mouse turned its head, triangulating to detect the source of the noise. It was no good, it seemed to come from everywhere at once. With the noise came a smell which the mouse, though quite elderly at a whole twelve weeks old, had never experienced before. It made the little creature's nostrils wrinkle; it smelt of mushrooms, musty and dry, it smelt of flowers, every kind in the world all mixed up together, it smelt of creosote-oozing pine, of metal, of paper. It smelt of things which the mouse had no synapses to identify.

The muttering grew to a mighty rumbling. The sound of tapping heels and grumbling wheels. Of voices, raised in wordless greeting. The smell reached a crescendo of diesel, of leather, of pencils, of Lynx aftershave splashed on beardless faces. The mouse fled. The butterfly rose in the almost palpable current of warmer air given off by a thousand bodies. The bumblebee had buzzed off seconds before the tide burst on the close-mown grass.

Leighford High School was back in business for the Autumn Term. Let battle commence.

Chapter Two

Peter Maxwell opened the door of the fridge in the Sixth Form Common Room and recoiled in horror. He slammed it shut and leant against it, holding his hand out to prevent anyone else going near it.

'Who switched the fridge off last term?' he asked. 'And, perhaps more importantly, who left the piece of cheese in there? I only ask, because I think that person should now consider themselves the parent of the mutant creature that has grown up over the summer, parentless and friendless in the dark while we have been enjoying the sunshine. I think I saw something similar in Fellini's *The Cheese That Time Forgot*. Sir Anthony Hopkins was a *little* miscast in that one.'

'For goodness sake, Max.' Helen Maitland, his Number Two, brushed him aside with a sweep of an arm. 'Don't be so histrionic. I'm sure it's perfectly OK.' She was, after all, a Biology teacher. Her nickname among the students – The Fridge – gave her an extra empathy with all white goods. She swung open the door and slammed it shut with, if anything, even more alacrity than Maxwell had. 'Dear God,' she breathed. 'I've never seen cheese grow anything that colour before.'

Maxwell leant in close. 'I think it's got eyes,' he whispered. 'Three of them. One of them winked at me.' He looked furtively over his shoulder.

'What are we going to do?'

Helen took a deep breath and made an executive decision. 'Leave it,' she said briskly. 'One of the little darlings left it there. One of them can clear it out. Switch the fridge on at the wall,' and she did so with a flourish and the years of experience that being a Science teacher had given her, 'go into your office for our meeting and listen for the screams.'

He smiled at her and stood back to let her pass. 'Helen,' he said, falling into step behind her and, glancing at the sheer bulk that launched a thousand ships, told her, 'you are a jewel among women.'

'Yes,' she said, over her shoulder. 'I know.'

She had suffered the mad old fart for years, his Number Two, Straight and True. He was crusty, irascible, a Head of Sixth Form for all seasons. But he was Mad Max and she loved him just the same.

In his office, Maxwell filled the kettle from the bottle of water he kept for the purpose and brought out his stash of coffee makings from a bag. He always took the coffee rota on for the first month. That way, the shock of another year turning was slightly assuaged by decent coffee, real milk and a box of biscuits covered in proper chocolate, courtesy of Messrs Cadbury, not the chocolate-coloured substitute favoured by some of the less discerning and more cash-strapped younger staff. He blew in a couple of mugs to minimise the dust and then, seeing Helen's shudder of distaste, wiped hers out with a tea towel, newly bought from home and therefore spotless, as it would not be again until next September.

He unscrewed the top of the coffee jar and found that, as usual, Jacquie had been there before him and had stuck her finger through the foil seal. It was a little foible that had worried him at first, the psychologist that lurks in every teacher warning him that it was a bit of displacement activity that might have a dark meaning. But when she told him she just liked the sound of the little 'plunk' as the seal broke and the smell of coffee, never so perfect again and nothing like its taste, he just learnt to live with it. He spooned coffee into their mugs and poured on the boiling water. Helen held out her hand for her drink as if she had been crossing the Gobi desert all summer.

'Caffeine,' she murmured, taking a sip.

Maxwell looked at his watch. It was not yet nine o'clock. 'You're not that desperate yet, Helen, surely?'

She sighed and leant back. 'To tell you the truth, Max, I have been dreading today since ... well, since we broke up.'

'All summer? Helen, that's terrible. Did you go away at all?'

'Oh, yes. I had three weeks on a yacht touring the Greek Islands. Very nice. Lots of olives. Ouzo. Hot. Sunny.'

'Well, then.'

'Lots of time to think. About here.'

They took turns, these two, on Results Day. This year had been Maxwell's. He was there, milling among his ex-Year Thirteen, giving high-fives to successes and tea and sympathy to the bereft. One day, he'd ring those bastards in the

13

Exam Boards and tell them what he thought of their shitty little mark schemes that left such desolation in their wake.

Maxwell looked at her closely for the first time and saw that she was looking rather haggard. She was usually so bouncing, so healthy and fit that the look sat uncomfortably on her. 'What is it, apart from beginning-of-termitis?'

She looked down into her mug as if the answer lay in the dark coffee. 'Ummm, I applied for Dierdre's job.'

If Maxwell was surprised, he didn't let it show. 'Good for you. You'll be good at it.'

'But I'm not sure now.'

'Why not?'

'I just feel, oh, I don't know.' She blew outwards, a blast of coffee breath washing over Maxwell. 'Dead man's shoes. Dead woman's, perhaps I should say.'

'That's what all promotion is, Helen, in a way. As the cavalry officer's mess toast had it in the nineteenth century– "Here's to a bloody war and a sickly season".' He raised his mug in her direction. Dierdre Lessing's death earlier in the year had shocked the whole school, as death always does when it is violent. Teachers don't die, they just crawl into cupboards. Somehow, it was demeaning for the buttoned-up Dierdre, her life suddenly on show for the whole world courtesy of the red-top papers, exposed in all its seamy detail. Because of this, she had become someone of whom no one spoke, for fear that they would seem uncaring, desensitised to her lonely end. Maxwell understood Helen's sensitivity and

14

applauded it.

'Of course, but not so literally. Anyway,' she sipped her coffee again and gave herself a shake, 'I've decided to see Legs today and cancel it.'

'That would be a shame,' Maxwell said, but only paying lip service. He had spent years grooming Helen and she knew all his little ways. She kept out of his hair, he kept out of hers. When he was absent she seamlessly filled in the space. When she was absent he barely noticed. Perfect. On the other hand he was reminded again how ludicrous it was that the hapless, hopeless Headteacher who was James 'Legs' Diamond, had to be consulted on career moves at all. He'd left it too long. Dierdre's place should have been filled already. They should all have moved on.

She gave a little laugh and chugged back her coffee. 'No, Max, you can't kid me. I'm happy up here with you, where the wild things are. I'm not SLT corridor material. I'll go and tell him now,' and she left the room, resting her hand very briefly on his tweed-clad shoulder in mute thanks.

Maxwell glanced up at the clock. The term was considerably less than an hour old and already it had begun. He dunked his chocolate finger with care. Nothing worse than a mug half full of sludge to start the day. Whoever thought of a staggered start to this day, with Post-16 coming in at lunchtime, was nothing short of a genius. And Peter Maxwell was nothing short of a genius. He checked last term's film posters, reminding himself it was time he replaced them courtesy of a little man he knew in Wardour Street. Above his head, he was reassured to know that Buck Jones always gets his man in *McKenna of the Mounted*. Ginger Rogers was the *Lady in the Dark*, more or less where Helen Maitland was now, Maxwell supposed. And *The Long Riders* trotted beigely out of the Old West towards him, walking adverts for Driza-Bone. So he had to go by guesswork when he heard his office door open and close behind him.

'Sylv,' he cried, 'how the devil are you?'

'Max,' she said, coming round to sit in the chair recently vacated by Helen. 'How did you know it was me?'

'First day of term.' He lapsed into full Sherlock Holmes mode, with just a nod in the direction of Basil Rathbone. 'You've had just enough time to see the malingerers back to their classes and count the new pregnancies. Ah, "suddenly one summer". Then, you fancied some decent coffee. Decent coffee is reliably to be found in this office, first month of the year guaranteed, courtesy of Yours Truly. Ergo elk, you have come to see me, aintcha?' He had been honing his Catherine Tate take-off all summer, though it didn't sit well with residual Monty Python. It would take work and he still couldn't decide which was the funnier. 'Anyway, dearest, how can I help you?'

The School Nurse beamed at him. 'I came to give you this.' She handed him an envelope.

'What a coincidence,' he smiled back. 'I was waiting for an opportunity to give you this.' His envelope was almost identical, slightly smaller than usual and made of thick beige paper. 'Shall we synchronise openings?'

16

'Why not?' the nurse said. 'One, two, three ... open!'

They ripped back the flaps in perfect harmony, extracted the piece of card and read silently for a few seconds, Maxwell taking slightly fewer seconds than Sylvia Matthews what with his Cambridge degrees, Speed Reading City and Guilds etc, but, ever the gentleman, appearing to finish last.

She looked up, eyes sparkling. 'Oh, Max,' she said. 'It's perfect. You're a lucky man.'

'And so is Guy,' Maxwell said. 'Oh, God, they're not on the same day, are they?'

Sylvia's eyes widened and she looked in horror at the card. 'Oh, phew!' she said, clutching a hand to her chest. 'Yours is December 26th. Ours is the 29th. Oh, but does that mean you'll be away? On honeymoon?'

'No, we're not going away. Remember what happened to Good King Wenceslas when *he* went out on the Feast of Stephen? If it was up to Jacquie we would have just gone off and got married somewhere and not mentioned it, jumping over a stick, or something. But her mother got wind of it and went demented. Ummm, more demented, as I suppose I should get used to saying.'

'Pardon?' Sylvia was confused.

'Mother-in-law jokes. I had better start using them. Never had the need, before. Where's my Les Dawson Joke Book?' He looked up, to see Sylvia looking at him fondly, protectively. 'Don't worry, Sylv. I'm not being a brave little soldier. I'll never forget her, you know. It's just that I didn't have a mother-in-law in my previous in-

17

carnation; she had died years before.' No, Maxwell's first family, torn from him on a wet day, on a wet road, were not forgotten. Every day, when he looked at Jacquie and Nolan, or when he trod on some abandoned bit of banana, found leg hair in his razor, found the biscuit barrel empty and put carefully back in the cupboard with only the trail of crumbs to point to the culprit, every day he gave thanks for now and for then and the happiness both had brought him.

Sylvia smiled. That man always could read her mind. To hide her confusion she said, 'I always thought you'd get married on ... oh, I don't know, Balaclava Day, Trafalgar Day, something historical.'

'Bastille Day, that would have been a good one, but apparently there wasn't enough time to arrange the ten million bridesmaids and three miles of tulle by July, so we had to let that one go. In the end, we thought the Feast of Stephen might be nice. It was Jacquie's idea. She can't remember historical dates, but she said cold turkey would always remind us. Anyway, are you coming? We don't want to be on our own.'

'Max, the church will be packed. Of course we'll come. Are *you* coming to *ours?*'

'May I be a bridesmaid?'

'No.'

'Never mind, we'll still come.'

'But we'd like Nolan as a pageboy. Are you having him...?'

'God, no. The dragon – there I go again – wants him as a ring bearer, which all sounds a bit Tolkien to me. Anyway, Jacquie refused unless we

18

can have Metternich as well and her mother wasn't sure whether she was serious or not, so she backed off.'

Sylvia laughed and got up to go. 'She's perfect for you, Max.'

'Yes,' he said, quietly. 'She is.'

The years of unrequited love for this curmudgeon were behind Sylvia Matthews now. Time was ... but time always was and there was nothing to be done about it. She gave him a hug and they went their separate ways down the corridor to the background music of the bell for the first lesson of the year. Sylvia wistfully wondered whether it wasn't time for a new ringtone – perhaps something from the *Carnival of the Animals*. Maxwell didn't know what a ringtone was.

'Melanie,' she called to a disappearing rump. 'Why aren't you in your orthopaedic shoes? See me at break!'

'Milly! Molly! Mandy!' Maxwell yelled to the other end of the corridor. Ever since his primary school days he had always wanted to do that and today seemed as apt as any. It was not their fault that the boys in question were called James, Stanislas and Bradley, so they turned anyway as one man and waited to hear their fate. This was Mad Max, the great, the terrible. You didn't argue, you didn't mess. All you could do was look on his works and despair.

The long day passed, as even school days do. As Maxwell had predicted on the last day of the previous term, Chantelle Wiggins set a new record as the shortest-lived sixth-former on record, leav-

19

ing as she did at 12.07 precisely, having arrived at 11.45 and learnt that Dance was not an A-level subject at Leighford High and, even if it had been, would not alone be sufficient to get her into Oxford.

The staff meeting had begun at three o'clock sharp. The newly qualified teachers, looking younger and more newly qualified this year than ever before, had stood and introduced themselves and the business of the term was begun. Lois was a Business Studies teacher; Malcolm taught Maths; Ronaldo was a Spanish assistant, but everyone knew he'd just been taken on for his footballing skills. Maxwell was sitting as usual, an offshoot of the back-row element at the very front of the assembled staff, ready to fight the good fight whenever necessary, but particularly when Legs Diamond was the adversary. Mostly, the droning updates passed him by, the need for IEPs, the Assessment for Learning programme, the rather debatable notion that Every Child Matters; but Dierdre Lessing's name brought him to full consciousness with a start.

'As we all know, since Dierdre's unfortunate ... er...'

'Death,' Maxwell said clearly.

'Yes, thank you, Max.' James Diamond could waffle for England. He put the bland into blandishments and his skills more or less ended there. 'Yes, since her... Since... We have been without an assistant Headmistress. The advertisement went into the Times Educational Supplement at the end of last term, and over the holidays Bernard and I have compiled a shortlist. We have whittled it down to three...'

'From?' Maxwell asked.

'Pardon?' Diamond had been dreading this meeting for weeks. Maxwell was always at his sharpest at this time of the year, having been resting his irritating synapses over the summer. The last chance he'd had to demolish his Headmaster was GCSE Results Day, two and a half weeks ago. How he'd missed it.

'Whittled, Headmaster,' Maxwell said. 'Whittled to three. From how many? Ten? Twenty? Two hundred?'

'Four, actually,' Diamond said, tersely. 'Senior posts are hard to fill, these days.'

'Right,' Maxwell beamed, not at all surprised to hear that. 'Carry on.'

Diamond bridled. 'I beg your pardon?' There were limits, even for Legs.

'Where are my manners?' Maxwell asked, rhetorically, clicking his tongue. 'Carry on, Headmaster.' He beamed and closed his eyes, the better to snatch bad grammar and illogicalities out of the air.

'What was I saying?' Diamond appealed to his secretary, though probably not to anyone else, as she sat, as always, at his right hand.

'Hmm?' the woman asked. 'I'm sorry, Mr Diamond. I wasn't listening, I'm afraid. This isn't a minuted meeting, is it?' She looked momentarily frantic, her expression that of a passenger on an express train who has just seen her station flash past.

'Oh, don't bother,' Diamond said, testily. Roll on Christmas. 'I remember ... Dierdre's replacement. The interviews are to take place the day after tomorrow, Thursday. There will be a light lunch provided in the staff section of the dining hall, so that you can all meet the candidates.' He glared at the soccer hearties lounging at the back. 'If you could hold your department in check, Mr Massie, I would be so glad. Three sandwiches are adequate for anyone and the normal lunch menu will be available as usual to fill up any corners.'

The massed muscle of the PE department managed to look both huge and affronted at the same time. Their brain cells rattled. There was muttering and an outbreak of miming the eating of one tiny sandwich. This was followed by muffled laughter. The Newly Qualified Teachers looked horrified. Was this the Professional Conduct they had been told to maintain, the subject of a lecture every third Thursday?

Diamond had learnt over the years to let the staff room settle down in its own time. When the shuffling had reached the minimum possible, he began again. 'Obviously, this early in the term, there are not too many notices. Departments have their SEN register for the new Year Seven. I've asked Subject Leaders for the usual results breakdown and Bernard will be number crunching by Friday. So if anyone has anything to add, now is the time.' He looked out over the sea of faces and sighed inwardly. They were all so young, these days. If he'd had any culture at all, he'd feel like war-weary Stanhope in *Journey's End* welcoming the green boys to the killing fields. He was beginning to have panic attacks when addressing serried ranks in case he was giving the Sixth Form his prepared speech for the staff and vice versa. There was not so much as an eyebrow quivering out there and thank goodness. He dismissed the meeting and reached behind him for his jacket. If he was quick, he might avoid being grabbed by...

'Headmaster,' Maxwell's voice sounded as though it was actually inside his head, slicing through what passed for his brain. 'Could I have a moment of your time?'

'Not really, Max, no,' Diamond said without turning round.

'No problem. I'll just leave this in your office, then.'

Diamond spun round. What game was this? Maxwell never backed down. He stood like an ox in the furrow. He would never be the first to blink. His eyes met the man's smile first and then travelled down to the envelope in his hand. His resignation! Oh, frabjous day!

Maxwell was still smiling and the envelope was still being proffered. He wondered sometimes how Diamond had ever got this job. He sometimes seemed very slow on the uptake. 'It's a wedding invitation, Headmaster,' he said, hoping to give his man a hint.

'Oh.' Even Diamond could tell that that response was a little dour. 'I mean, thank you so much, Max. Congratulations. I assume it is for *your* wedding? Ha ha.'

'Nolan is a little young as yet, Headmaster. But as soon as he names the day you will, naturally, be a guest of honour.'

'What? Oh, yes, ha ha. Yes.' Diamond took the envelope and waved it roguishly at Maxwell.

'Well, as I say, congratulations, Max. Um. Well, I must be away.' And he was off, like a rat up a pipe.

Sylvia joined Maxwell. 'What was that about?' she asked him.

'I just gave him a wedding invite. You'd have thought I was giving him arsenic.'

'Perhaps he thought it was your resignation,' she laughed.

Maxwell looked thoughtful. 'You may well be right, Sylv. But I'm not sure I intend to give him the satisfaction. I'll see him out, you see if I don't.' It was pure Victor Meldrew at his most waspish.

'Does Jacquie know you intend to stay here until you are ninety?' Sylvia asked.

'Until next year? Oh, she knows about that. It's the fact that I'm staying till I'm a hundred she's not ready for.' He smiled at her. 'Good night, Sylv. See you tomorrow.'

He made his way out to the bike sheds for what seemed like the millionth time, when in fact it could have been no more than the nine thousandth or so. He breathed in the smell of new-mown grass and sun-warmed tarmac and thought again that the fresh air at the end of the first day back at school was the sweetest air in the world. So he was in quite a good mood as he swung round the corner of the Science building to be hit square amidships by a trolley laden with boxes.

He went down under reams of recycled copier paper like a ton of bricks. He lay there, winded, and looked up to try and see what had happened. A face looked at him over the edge of the trolley. It looked like an extra from a *Lord of the Rings* film – wispy beard, deep-set, beady eyes and all.

'Oliver Lessing!' Maxwell wheezed, when he was able. 'What are you doing here?'

'Volunteering,' Lessing spat. 'County delivery service. Look at what you've done. That paper is all bent now, thanks to you.'

'Lucky you,' Maxwell said, hauling himself up using the trolley for support. 'You'll excuse me if I don't help you. I appear to have done something to my back.'

'You should look where you're going,' snapped the old man. 'This school isn't what it was since my poor Dierdre went.'

Maxwell almost felt pity for him. He was a really horrible man, with no one to love now his niece was gone. But then the horrible old git ran over his toe with his trolley and his sympathy withered on the vine – which gave it something in common with Oliver Lessing.

Chapter Three

Maxwell was thoughtful as he pedalled White Surrey home. The bike was beginning to show its years; this one really had been made by Walter Raleigh. There was a persistent though quiet click with every revolution of the wheels which had become a subliminal speedometer in the recesses of Maxwell's brain. The brakes came with their own built-in alarm and many was the pedestrian who had collapsed panting on the pavement, watching in panic as Maxwell sailed past, waving his apology as he slowed, noisily and just a bit too late. The saddle had been given expert attention during the holidays. It was one thing for a bike to give off random noises. Incipient castration was not a fault with which Maxwell cared to become familiar.

The start of term at Leighford High was always a mystery and a wonder. The wish list of Post-16 students which Maxwell compiled in his head in quiet moments in the watches of the night never quite materialised. The high-flyers went elsewhere, to the Martin Bormann comprehensive down the road; the low-flyers, flying so low they went under any bar he could set, turned up in vast numbers. There were always a few staff missing; in previous years they had included the lottery winner, the one with all those knives in his back; the rather mousey woman from Art who had married a Masai warrior and was living in his hut, on the proceeds of the donation from the *Mail on Sunday;* and any number of men and women now living quiet lives courtesy of Eli Lilly and his little pills. But none had left a hole so gaping as had Dierdre Lessing. True, she had been gone for almost two terms already. But somehow, the beginning of a year flagged up changes like these and Maxwell missed her, in his way. When he tired of baiting Diamond, she had always been there, snake-hair coiling in the winds that shook her world. When Bernard Ryan came out with an especially banal banality, she had always backed it up with just a little bit more. Like Archimedes, Maxwell needed a long enough lever to move his world. And Dierdre had been his lever. When Maxwell opened his mouth to speak, she was the fool everyone heard. And yet, he found himself thinking, she wasn't such a bad old stick. Oh, God! He was turning into his granny.

Never mind. Had he not been bowling down the slight incline that led into Columbine he would have rubbed his hands together. Her replacement might be fun. And not necessarily in a good way – fun in a good way was no fun at all.

He stowed White Surrey neatly in the garage. He didn't have to be neat – the inside of the garage at 38 Columbine was a car virgin. Until he met Jacquie, Maxwell had no recourse to cars and over the years the garage walls seemed to have thickened out, with layers of Notes To Self, bent hammers (used for unblocking drains), bent screwdrivers (used for opening paint) and bent saws (Maxwell himself couldn't understand that one, but they were bent nonetheless) and there was no room even for Jacquie's tiny Ka.

The door from the garage into the hall had long ago healed up, so he had to go outside again to get into the house. Humming almost silently to himself, he put his key in the lock and as he turned it a voice, at the same time both raucous and virtually inaudible, came from the level of his elbow. It was as if a mouse had laryngitis. Without turning, he answered it.

'Mrs Troubridge. Hello.' Beaming, he turned to her, doffing his shapeless tweed hat. 'How is Miss Troubridge?'

His neighbour sniffed. 'I really couldn't say,' she said, giving herself the kind of all-over body shake that a wet dog would do. 'She's on holiday somewhere and as yet has not honoured me with a postcard.'

'Well, I'm sure it's on its way,' he placated. 'You know what the post is like.'

'Indeed I do,' said the old lady. She raised a small claw holding a sheaf of envelopes. Almost all were open, or at least severely mauled. 'The postman put these through my door by mistake.'

He took them from her, but warily. 'What are they?'

'Well,' she said, 'mostly replies from people you have invited to the wedding. They can all come, except your cousin, Jennifer, is it? Hmm. She will be away over Christmas. There's a statement of your pension as of this December 31st. I must say, it's very generous, Mr Maxwell. I had no idea. And some junk mail. I didn't open that; it's such a waste of time and paper, isn't it?'

28

He stood there mutely, holding the scraps of paper. 'But, and I know you won't mind my asking you this, Mrs Troubridge, but why did you open the ones you did open?'

She looked up at him, aghast. She had always assumed he was moderately intelligent and indeed, if the salary hinted at in the envelope marked 'Strictly Confidential' was anything to go by, he was certainly paid as though he was. And yet, here he stood, asking yet another silly question. 'Because they seemed quite interesting, Mr Maxwell,' she said, as though speaking to a child.

'Indeed. But they don't have your name on, Mrs Troubridge, do they?'

She cocked her head at him, an interrogative eyebrow raised. Had she been Kaylie-Louanne from Nine Zed Queue she would have shifted her gum to the other side of her mouth and muttered 'Whatev*ah*.' The effect was identical and the meaning exactly the same. So, his response was the same also.

He looked down at her, shrugged one shoulder, turned on his heel and went into his house, all in the time it took him to say one word. 'Random.' He closed the door gently in her face and stood just inside, riffling through his post. She was right. Invitation replies and a pension statement. She was wrong on the generosity, though. What Gordon Brown's government proposed to buy him off with wouldn't pay for Surrey's oil. That's what you get when you have a Chancellor of the Exchequer called Darling – familiarity breeding contempt.

Metternich was waiting at the top of the stairs, in a furry, black-and-white sort of way, rather testily waving his tail. He took a half-hearted swipe as Maxwell passed and then tried his usual murder attempt; his theory was that he would be deemed innocent when the man was found at the bottom of the stairs, trouser cuffs dusted with cat hair. What could be more natural than a fond pet weaving in and out of his master's ankles of an evening? There again, he seemed to remember the Old Duffer warning him once that they used to put animals on trial in the Middle Ages – and hang them. But that was the Middle Ages – Maxwell was *far* older than that. But, yet again, Maxwell's nifty footwork foiled him and he curled up to wait for Jacquie, although she usually protected herself by hiding behind The Boy.

Maxwell and Jacquie had had surprises before in their lives, living happily together day on day being one of the biggest. But none had been as huge as the amazing discovery that Metternich loved Nolan with every fibre of his evil feline being, and didn't seem to want to eat him at all. From the time Jacquie had brought the little bundle home from the Maternity Unit, it had been protection at first sight.

The house was silent, apart from a slight drip from the kitchen tap and the hum of the fridge. It had been a long day, the longest of the year, though only perhaps for an old teacher, climbing into the harness of the Autumn Term for one more time. He sat down in his favourite chair, lay back and just rested his eyes.

He was still resting them when all hell broke loose on his lap. He leapt awake just as Nolan shared his ice cream with him by the time-honoured method of ramming it up his nose. Maxwell's eyes swam into focus as Jacquie and Nolan both doubled up with laughter and skipped away into the kitchen. Another conspiracy. At least, in theory.

'Hello, dears,' he said, wiping the drips from his chin with his handkerchief. 'Good day?'

Nolan came running back, his latest *oeuvre* from Nursery Art Class clutched in a rather sticky hand. It depicted a cow, or at least it may have been a cow, had it not been for the rather numerous legs. Alongside it stood a man in bright blue, with what looked like a house on his head. Maxwell smiled encouragingly. 'That's lovely, mate,' he said, giving the boy a hug. It was a generic response but hadn't let him down thus far.

'Sodjer,' Nolan announced.

Maxwell bridled. 'Jacquie,' he called. 'Did you check out that nursery? He seems to be picking up some bad language.'

Jacquie was in the room like a shot, holding the kettle aloft. 'What? What did he say?' She bent down. 'What did you say, darling?' she asked the little boy.

He looked at her rather sternly and smoothed out his paper. He turned to his father and adopted a sterner tone. For the second time that day, Maxwell was addressed as if he were a backward child. '*Sodjer!*' Nolan said. 'Daddy's *sodjer!*' Maxwell felt his eyes fill with unbidden tears and couldn't look at Jacquie, who he knew would

31

have the same problem.

He pulled his son to him and kissed the top of his head. He got another small dose of ice cream as a bonus. 'Soldier,' he whispered.

Jacquie coughed and said, her voice a little croaky, but with a laugh there somewhere, 'So, that proves it. He's not the milkman's after all.'

'So,' Jacquie said, kicking off her sandals with a sigh and putting her feet up in Maxwell's lap. 'How did it go today?'

'Usual,' Maxwell said. 'Loads of kids we didn't want back. Loads of *staff* we didn't want back. Building not finished. Loads of children posing as NQTs.'

'Same old, same old.'

'As you say. Oh, Sylv and Guy are getting married in December.' Jacquie went to sit up, but he pushed her gently back. 'Not the same day as us, the following Saturday.'

'That's good. We must reply. Are you a brides-maid?'

'No, but they want Nole as pageboy.'

'How sweet. Shall we let him?'

'As long as he can dress as a hussar.'

'I'm not sure he'll settle for anything else.' She smiled at him. 'Wasn't that lovely? His picture.'

'I can sometimes hardly believe my luck, you know,' he said, stroking her ankle.

'We're lucky too,' she said. 'And I must say, it's been nice to have such a lovely quiet summer, just a bit of planning...'

He looked at her disbelievingly. 'A *bit* of planning? A *bit* of planning? Are you having a laugh?

There hasn't been a day without a call from your mo–'

The phone rang, perfectly on cue. They looked at each other in horror. How many more details did the woman need to confirm? It was still nearly four months before the wedding and she already knew the shade of napkins for the reception.

'Well, answer it,' he said.

'No, you answer it.'

'No, you. It's *your* mother.'

'How do you know? It might be for you.'

'I recognise the ring.'

'It always sounds like that.'

'No,' Maxwell insisted. 'It's shriller.'

With a sigh, Jacquie reached for the phone. 'Hello? Oh, hello, Helen.' Triumphantly, she held the phone out to Maxwell. 'It's for you. Helen.'

'Don't call me Helen,' he muttered and took the handset from her. 'Dear heart, how can I help you?'

Helen's voice came loud and clear down the phone line, through Maxwell's head and out into the room. Jacquie could hear it as a disembodied squeak, but she could get the sense of it, crouched as she was on the arm of Maxwell's chair. 'I've decided, Max. I've definitely withdrawn my application.'

'How many does that leave in the field, then, Helen? Legs mentioned three.'

'Well,' came the squeak, 'that's what decided me, in fact. The ignorant pig didn't even include me in that number. I checked. Apparently, he didn't think I counted, quickly altered to didn't think I would want people to know before the day.'

33

Maxwell chuckled. 'Good Lord, Helen. You've known the man for almost as long as I have. Surely that didn't surprise you.'

'Surprise, no. Annoy, yes, as a matter of fact. Anyway, I thought I'd let you know, as we had chatted this morning.'

'Thanks,' he said. 'I think you've made the right decision, if only for selfish reasons. But you're far too normal to go and live in SLT-land.'

She chuckled in return. 'Thanks, Max. See you tomorrow.'

'Yes. *A bientôt.*'

'With bells on. Bye.'

He looked up at Jacquie. 'Well, that's great. Helen isn't going for Dierdre's job.'

'I gathered that,' Jacquie said, going back to her own seat. 'Something about Legs.'

'Yes. He told us this afternoon there were three candidates and in fact Helen made it four. He was just being his usual crass self, but it made her make the right decision. At least, it's good for me, but she would have done a good job, I think.'

'Well, of course she would, but she would have hated it, surely?'

Maxwell leant back, hands behind his head. 'Yes, very likely. Anyway, we now just have the three candidates in the frame – sandwiches at one o'clock in the dining room.'

'When?'

'Ummm – day after tomorrow. It will be the usual: curly sandwiches for us, a few rather more elegant bits for the SLT and the candidates slightly to one side.'

She laughed. 'Come on, Max. Even County Hall

34

aren't that cheap. Surely the food is for everyone.'

'By no means,' he said. 'Legs has already warned the entire PE department to hold back. One sandwich is enough for anyone and the usual turkey twizzlers are available to fill up the little corners. Any scraps go to the school cat – begging your pardon, Count,' he called to the snoring black and white heap in the corner, 'and the cleaners, probably in that order.'

'I'll pack you a goodie bag to take in with you.'

He clapped his hands. 'Yes, please. Egg sandwiches, please, *with* cress, easy on the mayo. No, make it salad cream. A packet of crisps – cheese and onion, so as to make myself extra charming when introduced to the candidates to date...' He paused as Jacquie dutifully hummed a few bars of 'Mrs Robinson', an ancient song her beloved had told her about. '...and a bottle of Orangina, for the burping.'

'No problem,' she said. 'It will be good practice for when Nole goes on school trips.'

'Aah,' he said, sitting up and steepling his fingers. 'School trips call for specialised packing. Can you still buy nasty plastic duffle bags with drawstrings? All the aforementioned, but *plus* a banana, rather old and black, for squashing into the inside of his bag and stinking out the bus; an orange, but the sort you can't peel without spraying everyone in sight and, finally, some really brightly coloured chewy sweets, so that he and his friends will bounce hysterically off walls all day long.' He smiled at her and added, 'And do you know what the best bit of all that will be?'

'Go on.'

35

'It will be some other poor sod who will have to take that trip because I will be ... da da da da da da daaaaaaaaaaaaaaaaaa ... retired.'

'But you're only a hundred,' she cried in mock alarm. 'Surely you aren't thinking of retiring yet!'

He looked at her fondly and then spoke more seriously than usual. 'I'm thinking about it, yes. I'm getting a bit long in the tooth for this game. Just getting to the mezzanine floor takes its toll. My left leg fell off this morning and all I'd done was cough. The little buggers seem to get more obstreperous every day, barrack-room lawyers to a man, and I'd quite like to live my life sur-rounded by nice people, for a change. You, Nole and, to a lesser extent, Metternich.'

She looked almost as shocked as she felt. The age gap was only something other people noticed. Sometimes she felt as if she had two two-year-olds in her care, and now, out of the blue, he had made an old-person remark. Her foundations rocked a little. 'Won't you be bored?'

'Probably. In which case, I'll look for something else to do. Work in B and Q. Give old ladies a lift to the hospital on my crossbar. Garden.'

'Solve crimes,' she said, a trifle stiffly.

'A spot of that, possibly. But only if asked, naturally.'

'Huh.'

He had often wondered how a policewoman could get so much meaning into such a small sound. How could 'huh' mean 'you must be joking, since when have you waited to be asked, you've even risked my career with your meddling, almost died half a dozen times, been arrested, beaten up and who knows what, yeah right' and so much more? 'If I'm not working, I probably won't even have any solving to do. Anyway, I've always preferred the word sleuthing. It's so first conjugation, isn't it? I sleuth, you sleuth, he, she or it sleuths.'

Jacquie opened her mouth to say something much more than 'huh' but he was saved by the bell. And this time, it really was her mother.

It was twelve of the clock when Peter Maxwell finally put down his paintbrush. Above him, through the skylight, the silent stars of September shone down, over the sleeping little town at the end of the season.

He pulled the gold-laced pillbox cap off his barbed-wire hair and hung it on its hook.

'You should take that to the *Antiques Roadshow*,' somebody had suggested. 'They're at the Winter Gardens in November.' The problem was Fiona Bruce might assume that Maxwell himself was the antique and it was just not possible to put a price on him. *Flog It* had connotations of a vicious and even perverted past. *Cash in the Attic?* Well, no one got into *this* particular attic, the one where Maxwell sat now in his modelling chair, except Nolan (accompanied), Jacquie (by appointment) ... oh, and...

'Metternich!' It wasn't often that the Great Man used the surname. Only when needs must and the interminable flea-catching out of the corner of his eye drove Maxwell to distraction. 'Come on, then. I told you I'd be asking questions later. Who's this one?'

The black and white beast raised his elegant head and looked at the pieces of white plastic scattered in front of his Master. How the hell was he supposed to know? He hadn't even been listening when Maxwell had reeled off the facts. And he'd been putting these bits of plastic together now for so long, Metternich had lost the will to live.

Maxwell waited. As usual, nothing. If any number of Nine Ex Eight had been so stubbornly defiant, he'd have shot them.

'This one, Count,' the great modeller under the skylight told him again, 'is Cornet Fiennes Wykeham Martin, as you can tell from his jacket, an officer in Her Majesty's 4th Light Dragoons. His mummy was a daughter of Lord Cornwallis – you know, the Johnny who surrendered to the Americans at Yorktown.'

Metternich didn't.

'He was Lord Paget's Adjutant in the Charge of the Light Brigade – Martin, that is, not Cornwallis – do keep up, Count. Poor bugger, having survived the Charge, died from a brain abscess, almost certainly triggered by a fall from his horse. Life's something of a bitch, isn't it?'

Metternich yawned. He hardly needed the Master to tell him that. Anyway, he had places to be. The Old Duffer would switch off the modelling lamp any minute, but not before placing the partly stuck, partly unpainted Adjutant at the right elbow of Lord Paget on the huge diorama of plastic soldiers that filled the rest of the room. Then he'd totter downstairs and check on The Boy before hitting the hay with that woman. Well, *he* could be as boring as he liked. Metternich stretched and slunk off down the stairs, like the silent killer he was. What would it be tonight? Vole-au-vent perhaps?

Chapter Four

Maxwell had always had a thing about Wednesdays. In all the years he had been teaching, it had always been the day with the worst timetable; the day with the most boring meetings. Its one saving grace had been that it was Roast Day. The menu never varied, summer and winter. Two slices of grey meat, identified only by the accompaniments; mint sauce, lamb, obviously; Yorkshire pudding, beef. Stuffing was more of a challenge. With apple sauce, then it was pork, without, chicken. The *pièce de resistance*, though, and Maxwell had found this had come down through the years unchanged, had been about a gallon of gravy and the best roast potatoes this side of the Pecos.

So, on a Wednesday at 12.30 he was very easy to find. At the head of the queue, plate in hand and large piece of absorbent paper ready tucked into his shirt collar. On this particular Wednesday, he was even easier to find than usual, because of the noise.

'There's no *what*, Freda?' he was yelling at a hapless school cook, or defroster, as she would more accurately be called.

'No Roast,' Freda said, in as unthreatening a tone as possible. She had been taught by Mad Max Maxwell and she still had the nightmares. 'The menu's changed.'

40

Maxwell's eyes blazed and he looked from left to right. 'I'm going to track down and kill that bloody Jamie Oliver,' he promised the delighted queue of kids forming behind him.

'Yeah, go on, sir. He's a wanker.' Normally, Maxwell would have admonished the child for his language, but not this time.

'It's cutbacks,' Freda told him, not sure whether that was a good or a bad thing to say.

'*Cutbacks?* Do they want the entire child population of Leighford to die of starvation? Where will they be without their Roast? Look at this lot,' he turned to the queue again, 'climbing the walls because of sticky sweets and fizzy pop. Limbs twisted with rickets, teeth down to their gums. Oh, no, wait, that's me.'

That would be a bad thing, then. 'The take-up was falling and it was expensive buying the meat.' She smiled up at him, hopefully, like she used to on Friday afternoons in his History lessons. It hadn't worked then, either. He fixed her with a glare. 'There was wastage.'

He took a deep breath. 'I see. I'm sorry, Freda. It's not your fault.' He turned a lighthouse smile on the assembled school. 'I'm sure the options you have prepared for us are totally delicious.'

She smiled encouragingly, but didn't speak.

He leant nearer. 'What are they?'

'What are what?' Yep. Friday afternoon History. The Corn Laws; the causes of the First World War. It had all been one to Freda. Silence.

'The delicious options.'

She pointed anxiously with her spoon. 'Baked Mediterranean vegetables with vegan cheese.

41

Gluten-free tortilla wrap. Coley à la king. And to follow, dairy-free rice pudding with sugar-free jam garnish.' She looked up. He was still there, leaning forward, one eyebrow raised expectantly. 'Or fruit,' she finished, desperately.

'Lovely. What's in the wrap?'

She brightened up. 'There are two choices for the contents of the wrap,' she said. 'Either baked Mediterranean vegetables with vegan cheese, or coley à la king.'

'That would be just the one choice, then,' Maxwell corrected her.

'No,' she felt on firm ground here. The Old Bugger hadn't, after all, taught her English. 'Two. Baked Medit–'

'Exactly. *A* choice between those lovely comestibles. *Two* options. But not two choices. However, this isn't keeping the queue moving, is it? I think I'll have ... hmm...' His eye was suddenly caught by a row of small glass dishes filled with pink goo lined up on a counter at the back of the kitchen.

'Come along, Mr Maxwell!' Ben Holton, the Head of Science, thundered from further back in the queue. 'Some of us have lessons to prepare.'

Maxwell stared back at the man in total disbelief. 'And I'm a Seventh-day Adventist,' he admitted, before turning back to Freda. 'I'll have one of those. Prawn cocktail, is it?'

She turned her head. 'Oh, sorry, Mr Maxwell,' she said. 'They're for tomorrow. You know, for the special lunch.'

He sighed. Special lunch was right, if they were going to stay out on the side for much longer. He didn't much like prawns anyway. He knew when he was beaten. 'I'll have an apple and a banana, then, Freda, please.'

She cast her eyes down and almost whispered, 'I'm sorry, Mr Maxwell.' She was beginning to feel that that was her only line. 'County cutbacks. Only one piece of fruit per person.'

'Just the banana, then,' he said and, taking it, made his way back to his office. He hoped that Jacquie wasn't joking about his goodie bag for Thursday.

And, good policewoman that she was, she had not been joking. There it sat on the work surface in the kitchen, everything beautifully wrapped in its own plastic bag (don't tell the *Daily Mail)*, sealed with tape. Closer examination revealed the bags to be evidence bags, and Maxwell sent up a fervent prayer that they were not second-hand, Bernard Spilsbury and Keith Simpson for the use of. He cycled off towards Leighford High School, a little anachronistic bubble in the hurly-burly of Leighford's early morning. Purring over the Flyover, clicking past the Dam, skirting the eternal roadworks at Asda and on to the yellow-brick road. He swung out of the saddle and lashed Surrey to a bollard, prior to trotting up the stairs and stowing his little package in the fridge in his office.

He was making his way to his Lesson One, British History with Year Thirteen; learning objective: 'was Gladstone really a pervert? – a good deed in a basically naughty world', when he heard the not too dulcet tones of Bernard Ryan

43

call his name. His nerve endings fired like light-ning. He usually ignored Ryan, just as a matter of course; the man was essentially something you scraped off your shoe. But this morning he was likely to be showing round the candidates and Maxwell was, if nothing else, a polite and gentle man; he wouldn't deliberately snub a lady. Not yet, at least. Let her get the job first. He spun on his heel, smiling in readiness.

'Mr Ryan. How may I help you?'

Ryan walked towards him, against the flow of backpack-toting children, all resolutely ignoring the polite, reasonable, pinko-liberal requests on the walls to keep to the left. There was a tinge of grey about Bernard Ryan these days. Less of the Young Turk and more of the old turkey. He had increasingly the air of a Deputy Head who had left it ten years too late to float any higher in the cesspool of modern education. In tow Ryan had three women, clearly the candidates, if only by virtue of the fact they were each wearing a version of the same clothes: crisp white shirt, dark suit, with skirt of a sensible length and smart shoes, clearly cripplingly uncomfortable. They also wore the same smile, with the same strained quality found on any lips that had been in Bernard Ryan's presence for more than half an hour.

'Max, may I introduce the candidates for Dier ... for the post of Assistant Headteacher?' He ushered them forward, one by one, as best he could in the press of bodies. The woman nearest to him had a face like a Botticelli angel. It was hard to estimate her age, but Maxwell guessed it was more than was immediately obvious. Her mouth, though delicately drawn, looked obstinate. Her eyes were intelligent, though baby-blue. She would take watching. 'Miss Mackenzie,' he placed his hand in the small of her back and pushed her forward just a tad. 'May I introduce Peter Maxwell, Head of Sixth Form and,' he broke off with a little laugh, 'our longest-serving member of staff.'

Maxwell shook her hand. 'Miss Mackenzie. It's very nice to meet you.' She was ripped from his grasp as a gangling youth with a larger than normal pack on his back hit her amidships. He bowed slightly towards her and yelled, 'Bloxham! Get back here this minute.' The boy froze like a special film effect. It shouldn't have been possible for a person to balance on one toe like that. Billy Elliot would have been proud. He slowly turned and inched back to confront Maxwell. 'First of all, apologise to this lady at once.'

The boy dipped his acne and muttered ''m sorry, miss.'

'Well, not gracefully done, but it will do as we are pressed for time. Now go and sign in as late and then go and report to Mrs Maitland. At lunchtime, come and see me and we will arrange something along the lines of a detention, but more like the cat-o'-nine-tails you actually deserve.'

The boy's head snapped up. 'Oh, but sir...'

'Come on, Bloxham. Even you can't have too many detentions yet. We've only been back three days. See me at 12.30. Don't be late. Don't knock anyone else over.'

With a final injured glance, the boy was gone.

45

Ryan tugged down the hem of his jacket and cleared his throat. He reached for the second woman but before he could touch her she had frozen him with a basilisk glare. She stepped forward under her own steam and grasped Maxwell's hand in a grip of iron. 'Smollett!' she snapped. It sounded like an order, but Maxwell hadn't smolled anything for years and was just about to say so when she explained herself a bit more. 'Fiona Smollett,' she said. 'Liked the way you dealt with that. Good man.' She dropped his hand and stepped back. He almost saluted but managed to stop himself just in time. Save for the different scale, she would have been at home in Maxwell's attic with the assembled Six Hundred. She was so perfectly groomed her hair looked painted on to her skull and her neat suit wasn't just for interviews, that was clear; it was for all time. A suit for all seasons. Her pyjamas were probably identical to it with, just possibly, a small embroidered teddy bear on one pocket, to relieve the gloom. A black teddy, obviously, with a black ribbon round its neck. A black teddy called Adolf. Maxwell's arm felt chilly and he flexed his fingers to bring some life back.

'Thank you, Fiona,' he smiled.

'I prefer Miss Smollett.'

'Of course,' Maxwell nodded. 'So do I.' He snatched a glance under his brows at Bernard Ryan, but he looked like a rabbit caught in the headlights. CVs are wonderful things, aren't they? They never prepare you for the truth. The corridor was largely empty of children now and the silence was palpable. 'Well, Bernard,' he said and inclined his head to the other Candidate.

Ryan visibly jumped and said, 'Oh, sorry. Miles away. Yes, Max, may I introduce you to Mrs Bevell. She comes to us from Littlehampton. You may have met her at courses or whatnot.' The Deputy Head remembered who he was speaking to; Maxwell was not the natural choice for sending on courses. He annoyed too many people, and also people often seemed to get killed. But he could hardly introduce him to the woman in those terms.

Maxwell rose, as always, to the occasion. 'I don't think I've had the pleasure,' he smiled and metaphorically doffed his hat. The poor woman was startlingly ugly, more especially so when standing next to the porcelain-pretty Miss Mackenzie. Still, live and let live was one of his many mottoes. Thank goodness the discrimination laws were so tight these days. Thou shalt not discriminate on the grounds of age, sex, creed, sexual orientation or the ability to stop clocks and turn milk.

'How patronising,' she hissed, the words wafting to him on charnel house breath of staggering awfulness.

He came nearer to rudeness than was usual with him and, mouth breathing to minimise the stench, he nodded to them all and almost ran down the corridor to his class.

The questions began almost as soon as he was through the door.

'Are they the ones to replace Miss Lessing, sir?'

'Ain't she ugly, sir, that big one?'

'Yeah, sir, she won't get the job, will she?'

'Cor, I don't half mind that little one. Which one do you fancy, sir?'

'We've been all right, sir. Why do we need to replace Miss Lessing?'

'Why aren't you Headteacher, sir?'

Maxwell used a technique honed on the north face of Mrs B, cleaner, gossip and misunderstander par excellence; he took each question one at a time and let them dig the bones out as best they could. 'Yes. That's rather unpleasant, Mike, but essentially accurate. I'd like to think not, but you didn't hear that from me. You won't catch me that way, Tess, and I'm glad to see you have that orientation uncertainty settled at last. Good question. And again, good question; too sensible, I like to think. Now then, since this is the first time I have seen you in your A2 incarnation, let's get the textbooks given out.'

The class looked around aimlessly but couldn't see any books.

He noticed their puzzlement. 'First test safely passed; there are no textbooks. Cutbacks. So, let's see – who knows anything about Gladstone? That's apart from me, of course.'

Paul Bloxham waited with his heart in his mouth outside Maxwell's office, sharp at 12.30. He wasn't really worried; he knew that Maxwell wasn't a vindictive man, but his punishments were justly famous for their ingenuity. There was a story, apocryphal, but Paul Bloxham didn't know that, that Mad Max had once made a kid from Year Eight lick the whole library clean

48

because she had spilt crisp crumbs on the floor. The other rumour was that he had made another kid clean his bike with a Q-tip. That one was actually true. So it was with moderate trepidation that he heard the Great Man's bouncy tread come along the corridor behind him.

'Hello there, Paul,' Maxwell said brightly. 'Nicely on time. I like that. Punctuality is the politeness of princes, you know.'

Bloxham nodded. It was a race memory, handed down from child to child, that it was best to agree with the mad old sod.

'Come in, come in. I'm just going to have my lunch. You don't mind, do you?' He motioned the boy to a seat and took a bag out of the fridge. 'Do you like egg sandwiches?'

'Not really.'

'They've got cress in them. Made with salad cream, really nice. Ambrosia of the gods.'

The boy still looked doubtful. 'They're not from the canteen, are they?'

'Good Lord, no. I brought them from home.'

The lad had to agree they did look rather nice. Cut from corner to corner, really posh and on nice-looking bread. He nodded. 'I will have a bit, sir, if it's all right.'

Maxwell proffered the paper plate and the boy took a quarter and bit into it.

''S lovely,' he muttered, mouth full.

'I'll tell the missus,' Maxwell beamed. 'She makes a good sandwich.'

Like most of the school, Bloxham was confused by Maxwell's domestic arrangements. How an old fart like him had managed to snaffle a cracker

49

like Jacquie was beyond them, as it was occasionally beyond the man himself. Bloxham had seen her out in the town with the Great Man occasionally and had debated with his oppos whether she was his daughter or his bit on the side. Only Jacquie seemed to think the relationship quite normal. Sandwich eaten, Bloxham just sat there. He was offered a crisp, which he took. One of those fancy ones, caramelised onion and camembert, aka cheese and onion, but very nice all the same. He declined the swig of Orangina, to Maxwell's relief.

'OK then, Paul, off you bugger,' said Maxwell, standing up and brushing the crumbs off his lap. 'I've got a lunch to go to. Thanks for your company.'

Bloxham was confused. 'Is that it, sir?'

'Yes, yes indeed. Sitting quietly for a bit, that's what you need. You're all knees and elbows, lad, you need to slow down, think who you might be knocking over. Count to ten a bit more often. Especially in Maths.' He ushered the lad into the corridor and watched him with a smile as he half galloped, half slunk away. 'Now,' he rubbed his hands together, 'time for some fun, I think,' and, suitably full of decent grub, he made his way to the dining room to watch everyone else gannetting away on one sandwich each and a prawn cocktail for the VIPs. 'What larks.'

The dining room at Leighford High was a game of two halves. The Formica tables and benches of the students' end gave way seamlessly to Formica tables and chairs for the staff. Many of the chairs had at least one rubber foot missing off a leg, but never four, as that would have given a stability which would encourage staff to linger, and that would never do. The roiling mass on the student side was thinning out now as Maxwell arrived and he made his way through them to the staff end, where pleasantries were being exchanged as far as possible around a faceful of Brie-and-cranberry sandwich. The caterers had gone a little mad; a whole summer of no school functions to service had given the head chef time on his hands in which to conjure up fresh horrors. In fact, Leighford had been spared his worst excesses. Tottingleigh Infants were appointing a new Head on this very day and they were at this same moment enjoying, should that be the word, the delights of Thai chicken and pineapple on rye. The Brie sandwiches had been made well in advance, as was the caterers' way, and to Maxwell's initial horror it looked as if everyone was tucking into a piece of raw meat, due to cranberry ooze. The favoured few were spooning down the prawn cocktails from the day before. The candidates were struggling with the shell-on prawn on the top, holding a glass and a fork at the same time. Some race memory of interview technique had convinced them that shelling the darned thing and eating it neatly would somehow stand them in good stead. Only Miss Mackenzie had opted to stash her prawn behind a dusty spider plant and say no more about it.

Maxwell, comfortably full with egg, cress and crisps, was not drawn to the sandwiches, and the prawn cocktails had all been spoken for. He

51

picked up a jelly with fruit in, set in a waxed paper bowl. He had had a weakness for them since he was three and went to his first birthday party. The flavour – sugar and a fruit not yet invented – had never changed and the texture of the bits encapsulated in the goo was still that of cardboard and plasticine. Nevertheless, he spooned it in with relish.

'Max,' hissed Sylvia at his elbow. 'Where have you been? This do is dying on its feet.'

'I didn't realise I was the Turn,' he said. 'What would you like? "Hiawatha" or "The Boy I Love Is Up in the Gallery"? I've been having lunch upstairs and a chat with one of Leighford's characters.' He looked round. 'I don't seem to be missing much.'

'Just the paint drying. They aren't a very inspiring bunch, are they?'

'Sylv, don't be pass-remarkative. I'm sure they're all lovely women, in their own ways. Incidentally, shouldn't there have been a token man among them? I mean, I know "Senior Mistress" is no longer an acceptable term, but the job's the same – girls' welfare. In these PC times, you'd think...'

Sylvia wasn't rising to it. 'The angelic-looking one is a bit scary. People who look like that are rarely as nice as they seem.'

'Mind like a razor, I suspect. Puts me in mind of Reese Witherspoon. She scared the shit out of Matthew Broderick in *Election* and Ms Mackenzie scares the shit out of me. Ms Smollett?'

'Miss. Miss Smollett. She has a certain military charm, perhaps, for those so inclined.'

'Miss – and you're right, a definite Miss – Whiplash. Without the sex appeal. But, I suspect, *with* the whip.'

She poked him with her spoon. She had only eaten the jelly and had left the cardboard and plasticine alone. 'Max, don't. If she gets the job, I'll never be able to look her in the face. What about Miss Bevell?'

'Mrs, extraordinarily enough. And that's Be*vell*, by the way, like Ra*vel*, he of the *Boléro*. If it *was* Bevell, of course, she'd have the edge. But I didn't get a close look; her breath could strip paint.'

'You noticed that. I found myself looking to see if I had stepped in something.'

'No, Sylv. My money is on angel-face. She is ruthless, mark my words. The only trouble is that Legs might be on a bit of a reverse-psychology thing. We all *expect* him to be a sucker for a pretty face, so he'll go with one of the others. And if he did, it could go either way. But I think he will expect us to expect that and so, to confuse us, he will go with his natural first choice.'

Sylvia Matthews was confused already. She tried to work it out on her fingers, but failed. In the end, she admitted as much. 'I'm sorry, Max, I've forgotten what the first choice was.'

He handed her his bowl with a magnanimous gesture. 'Sylv, the one who will get the job is–'

'Miss Mackenzie!' someone shouted. The cry was almost simultaneous with a crash of breaking glass and tumbling cutlery. Maxwell and Sylvia turned in the direction of the noise in time to see Legs Diamond jack-knife in pain and crash to the

53

floor, taking Bernard Ryan with him. After that, there was chaos; it was hard to tell who was actually lying on the floor and who was kneeling there to help them. Some people who had keeled over had pulled others with them in their attempts to stay upright. Helen Maitland was lying under Mrs Bevell, her head averted and her leg at a rather unnatural angle.

Sylvia went into first-aid mode in a second, leaving Maxwell to stand aghast for several more, before he too was down among the bodies, sorting wheat from chaff, sheep from goats, the sick from the injured or merely curious.

It was no place for the squeamish. In the crush of the fallen, it soon became obvious that they fell into two basic categories: those who were vomiting uncontrollably and those who were being vomited on. Sylvia, using skills most people would rather be without, quickly sorted them into these groups and tended those who had clearly eaten something that disagreed with them very badly indeed. Amongst the wounded were Helen Maitland, who had taken the full weight of Mrs Bevell as the woman fell, and clearly had a broken leg. Being the stalwart she was she had quietly put herself in as comfortable a position as she could under the circumstances and contented herself with screaming at anyone coming too near, shock coursing through her body. She, Sylvia decided, would keep. One of the PE staff had gashed his head badly on some broken glass and one of the secretaries had fainted. They could all just get over it on their own; she knew that more serious casualties were among the vomiting. She gestured

Maxwell over.

'Max.' She whispered. 'There's something very odd here. Poisoning, I think.'

'I'm not too surprised,' he said. 'Those prawn cocktails were made and out on the counter yesterday lunchtime. Salmonella, I'll warrant.'

'No,' Sylvia said, brooking no argument. 'There's not a bug alive can make everybody sick at the same moment and so quickly. If it was a stomach bug, the first we would know would be when they didn't come in tomorrow. No, this is poison. Get rid of any lingering kids. Dial 999.' She looked down into the face of Legs Diamond, which moments before had been creased in pain. It was smooth now, no expression. He was totally unconscious and barely breathing. She met Maxwell's eyes. 'Do it, Max. People are dying here.'

Maxwell scrambled to his feet and ran from the dining room, shepherding frightened children ahead of him. He was a public schoolboy, for God's sake. You should see him in a shipwreck. Staff behind him were recovering from the initial shock and were marshalling what thoughts they had and attending their friends and colleagues who were still on the ground. The place looked like a battlefield and sounded like one: groans and sobs, overlaid with soothing voices.

'On yer bikes, everybody.' Maxwell was an oasis of calm in a sea of chaos. 'Nothing to see here. Please step away from the dining room. And if I see any of today's events on anybody's phone cameras, just remember, I know where you all live.'

A kind of peace began to reign.

Then, suddenly, a scream which went up everyone's spine like broken glass. A new teacher from the Business department leapt to her feet, her knuckles in her mouth. 'Oh, God, she's dead!' She looked wildly about her and screamed again. 'She's dead. Somebody help! She's dead.'

Sylvia raised her head and caught the eye of Paul Moss, kneeling at Helen Maitland's side. 'Paul, go and calm her down, would you? Helen, you'll be OK.' All the woman could do was nod and even that sent arrows of pain through her body. She'd wanted a rest, but not like this. 'Paul.' Sylvia called him and he turned. 'Get her away and then see whoever she's talking about. They're probably just passed out, like the Head.'

'OK, Sylvia.' Paul was a re-enactor at the weekends, and he *was* Head of History, when all was said and done. He played with soldiers like Maxwell did, only his were life-size and tended to run bayonets through themselves with monotonous regularity. He was a pretty good first-aider. 'Come on, dear,' he said, putting his arm round the girl. He might learn her name in time, but now wasn't the moment for niceties. 'Off you go and sit down. I'll deal with this.'

The girl wouldn't move; panic had her rooted to the spot. In a whisper that spoke of the child she still almost was, she said, 'She's dead. I know she's dead.'

'No, I'm sure she's not,' but Paul Moss was no longer as certain as he looked. The NQT was pointing at her Head of Department, a very nice woman with whom he had exchanged possibly three words in the whole time she had been at the

56

school. She lay on her side, her arms folded across her stomach. Her head was arched back in a very uncomfortable looking way, with her face half-turned to the floor. Her head was pillowed in a pool of vomit and her mouth was still streaked with strings of spit. In all, she did not present a very pretty picture and she certainly wouldn't have stayed like that had she had an option.

Pushing the girl to the edge of the dwindling crowd, he bent down and touched the woman's shoulder lightly. She rolled over on to her back, but her expression did not change. She lay there, staring at the ceiling, her sightless eyes half rolled up into her head. Paul Moss had been a History teacher for years – he had taught war, death and destruction with equanimity. And yet he had never stared death in the face until now. After a brief pause while the shock sank in, he did what he always did in an emergency. He lifted his head and shouted, 'Max! Over here!'

'He's calling 999,' someone offered.

'No, I'm not. I'm here.' The kids were beyond the dining hall doors now, jabbering excitedly, peering in, but Mad Max had told them the handles were electrified now and that was good enough. No one touched them. And, like a guardian angel, the man was standing over him, taking him by the shoulder and moving him aside. 'What is it, Paul?'

Paul Moss shook his head. 'I ... I think she's dead, Max,' he said.

Maxwell looked down at the woman's face and put his arm round his Head of Department. There was no way to make this easier. 'Yes, Paul.

57

She is, I'm afraid.' He turned him away from the sight. 'Go over there and talk to Sophie. She looks in a bit of a state.'

'Sophie? Is that her name? OK.' Like most people in the middle of a nightmare, Paul Moss clung to facts. Sophie. Right. He would talk to Sophie. It didn't dawn on him to wonder how the hell Mad Max knew her name. This was a guy who called his wife-to-be woman policeman. Paul walked off like a zombie.

Maxwell knelt down and felt for a pulse in the woman's neck. There was none, as he knew there wouldn't be, but he had to be sure. He took off his jacket and covered her face; he knelt there for a moment with his head bowed before he got back to his feet.

'Max, was that a prayer?' A member of the Religious Studies department was looking at him with big eyes.

'No, Nicola. I don't pray. But everyone deserves a bit of dignity and poor Mel had little enough, at the end.'

The teacher looked down at the shrouded figure. 'Oh, God, I didn't know. That's Mel? But she can't be dead! She's only young.'

'There's no sell-by date on a person, sadly,' Maxwell said, looking round for Sylvia.

'But she was so nice.'

'Again, no guarantees. God moves in a mysterious way, as I am sure you have told many a class.'

'I only teach comparative religions, but I dare say you're right. Look, Max, I'll stay with her. You go and see if you can do anything for anyone else.'

He looked down at her, only a kid, really, and scared to death. But she couldn't leave a nice, youngish woman alone there, under his jacket, dead on the floor. He held her close for a moment and then was off, weaving his way through the thinning field of victims, to where Sylvia was still bent over Legs Diamond, now neatly stowed in the approved Red Cross recovery position. She looked up when she recognised the cavalry-twilled legs approaching, with the cycle-clip crease still visible.

'Are they on their way?' she asked, her anxiety giving her voice an unaccustomed tremor.

'Yes,' he said, crouching down. 'I didn't know how many casualties, so I just said for them to send as many ambulances as they could muster.'

'Good call,' she said. She looked over her shoulder. 'At first estimate, we've got ten down, some poisoned, some hurt. Helen has broken her leg. Tom has cracked his head open and I think may be concussed. Bernard and L...' she stopped herself. '...I mean, James, have collapsed.' It didn't seem right to call him by his nickname when he was lying, barely breathing, with his head in her lap. 'All the candidates seem to be down and in a pretty bad way. Anyone else?'

'Yes,' Maxwell said quietly. 'Mel Forman from Business is dead.'

Sylvia looked at him, suddenly pale. 'Dead?' she repeated. 'Are you sure?'

He nodded.

'Max, this is serious. I know I *said* poison, but I was hoping it was just a dodgy prawn, all the same.'

59

'I'm hoping that as well, Sylv, but I agree with your first gut reaction, if you'll excuse the phrase. It's too quick for food poisoning. This is chemical poisoning, though whether deliberate or accidental remains to be seen.'

'You've called the police, I suppose?'

'Yes. I tried Jacquie, but her phone isn't responding. I left a message at the station for her, but it's in the hands of the 999 people to get the police here.'

'God, Max! Try her again. If she hears about this before she gets your message, she'll be frantic.'

Maxwell looked at her and knew she was right. It wasn't often he dropped the ball on this kind of thing, but how often had he been surrounded by the dead and dying in quite these numbers? He had turned to leave the room when, without warning, Bernard Ryan heaved himself up onto one elbow and, with what looked like the last of his strength, threw up all over Maxwell's feet. The Deputy Head looked up at Maxwell, for whom he rarely had a civil word and whispered thickly, 'Max, help me, please.' And, always a gentleman, Maxwell did.

Chapter Five

Henry Hall was taking advantage of a miraculously quiet Thursday lunchtime to catch up with his paperwork. He had been on holiday in August, a very unusual occurrence about which he was in two minds. He loved his wife, no doubt about it, but over the years they had got used to not seeing each other much; in all the family holidays they had booked, he had probably managed to be present at about three. Work had always intervened, so he wasn't much bothered where she booked, because he was unlikely to be sharing the cosy cottage/farmhouse/family tent or whatever the case may be. This summer, though, fate had caught up with him and he had endured, while Margaret had enjoyed, a fortnight learning to do watercolours in a mountain retreat in the Algarve.

Never mind, he thought, that was all behind him and, apart from a line of recalcitrant cadmium red under the nail of his ring finger, it was all but forgotten. The paperwork was a pleasant change, but was getting boring, so he was pleased when his phone rang.

'Hall.'

'Guv, this is an odd one. We need you a.s.a.p. at Leighford High.' It was Bob Davies, sounding rather more uncertain than his usual style.

'Leighford High? Bob, can't you deal with this one? You know how I hate to–'

'Mix it with Maxwell? Yeah, guv. I can't stand the bugger myself. Only, this sounds quite serious. People throwing up, poison, they say.'

'People throwing up, Bob? Surely, that's more a job for the School Nurse, isn't it? Or the paramedics, at the outside.'

'But, guv.' Davies sounded like a wheedling child. 'Poison, guv.'

'Who says it's poison? Who rang this in? It could be some kid.'

'No, guv. It's kosher. An adult rang it in.'

'Who?'

'Umm, hang on. I'll have to put you down.' There was a clunk as the phone went down on a desk and a distant sound of rustling paper. 'Sorry, guv. Can't find it. But I know they've sent four ambulances.'

Hall tapped his pen on the desk and came to a decision. 'Right, this is what we'll do. Send a car, because if it is a hoax, we'll need to investigate. If, when they get there it is, as you so colourfully say, kosher, they can radio for help. Would that be OK with you?'

'I'll go, shall I, guv?'

Hall sighed. 'Yes, if you like. Where's Jacquie? Perhaps this is one for her?'

'She's on split shift today, guv. She'll be back in about half an hour.'

'That will be fine, Bob. I don't feel that a bunch of kids throwing up their lunch is really one for us, but if you want to go, then wait for Jacquie and then you can *both* go.'

Silence on the other end of the phone.

'Bob? Will that be OK? Wait for Jacquie?'

'Oh, all right, guv. Only...'

'Yes,' Hall appeased. 'Poison. I know. I look forward to being proved wrong.' He put the phone down with a sigh and picked up his pen. Where was he? He hated it when someone interrupted his train of thought. Quotas. Community Policing. Peter Hitchens was asking awkward questions again. His phone rang.

'*Yes!*'

'Guv? This is a bad line, sorry. It's Jacquie.'

'I know who you are, Jacquie. What do you want?'

'Bo ... rang me and ... now. Shall ... or what?'

'I'm sorry, Jacquie. I can only hear one word in ten. Can you ring me back when you have a better signal?'

'...uv. I'm in ... co's. Really ... nal here. Bob ... want?'

'Jacquie. I can't hear you. I'm putting the phone down.' And he did.

At the other end of the line, Jacquie looked at her phone in fury. First Maxwell had tried to ring her and, failing to get through, hadn't left a message. She hated it when he did that. Then Bob Davies had rung her and, on a really bad line, seemed to be asking her to come in early. Then Henry Hall had hung up on her. Plus, she was in a ten million mile queue in Tesco's, with a trolley full of extremely perishable food and half an hour to buy it, get it home and get back to the nick. It wasn't going to happen, she told herself, and abandoned her trolley by the time-honoured system of quietly sidling away and then running like hell to the car. Her instinct was telling her

63

that, although the odds on Maxwell's call and Davies's call being connected were astronomically long, she would be a fool to disregard the coincidence. She didn't hear the Security Chappie ask her, 'Is everything all right, madam?'

Once in the car park with a five-bar signal, she rang Leighford High. The irritating list of numbers she might want seemed to take longer than usual to roll out. No, she didn't want Student Services, or the Site Manager or a chance to comment on the new interactive website. Post 16 she did want, because that's where they kept Peter Maxwell, but it was lunchtime and the chances were he wouldn't be there. Pressing zero for reception got her nowhere. The hairs on the back of her neck began to rise. The Thingees on the Front Desk ran a tight ship and there was always someone on the switchboard. Ringing off, she punched in Davies's number. After two rings, it went to answerphone.

'Hi. Bob Davies here. In line with police and government guidelines I have switched my phone off whilst driving. Please leave a message after the tone, and when I am safely parked I will get back to you. Beeeeeeeeeeep.'

'Bob, it's Jacquie. I'm on my way in. Don't quite know what's going on. See you in about five.' She hung up and turned the ignition key in one movement and was soon heading for the police station. As she approached a junction, just before the town centre, she noticed traffic pulled in to the side. Then she heard the sirens and sat amazed as no fewer than four ambulances streaked past. She tried not to worry that they were heading in the direction of Leighford High. They were heading in the direction of lots of places, after all: the Sea Front, Littlehampton, Portsmouth. She sat helpless in the traffic jam they left in their wake, drumming her fingers on the wheel. When she got to the junction, her hesitation was fractional; she indicated left, not right into the centre of town, and was soon in hot pursuit of the ambulances. If they turned off before the school, she told herself, or if they went right past, she would turn round and only be a few minutes later at the nick. And, anyway, she reasoned with herself, she was still on her break between shifts. She could do what she liked for another twenty minutes.

As she got to the crest of the hill just before the school, she looked into the distance to see if she could catch a glimpse of the ambulances. There was no sign. They must really have been going flat out, she tried to reason with herself. Even so, while convincing herself they were halfway to Littlehampton by now, she still slowed down at the school gates. The flashing lights were slowing to a halt and the sirens were on their last drawn-out wail. The paramedics were jumping down from their cabs in blurs of green overalls and hurrying inside. Neat groups of children were scattered over the playing fields, each one shepherded and comforted by at least one adult, sobbing little girls and big, tough, hard men trying not to cry. She looked frantically for the one comforting adult she had come to find; there was no sign.

There was nowhere to park. The car park was a

perennial complaint at Leighford High; too many indulged and affluent Sixth Formers with cars meant there were never any spaces and now, with four ambulances blocking her path, there was nowhere to go, so she just abandoned the Ka, jumping out and trying not to run. She hadn't gone more than a few paces when she heard an engine behind her and, looking round, saw Bob Davies jumping out of his car, abandoned like hers, forming a motley queue.

'Bob!' she called. 'What's happening?'

'I'm not sure,' he said, as he drew level. 'Someone rang in that someone had been poisoned at the school. I was going to wait for you; Henry said I should, but the more I thought about it, the more I thought that if they were sending four ambulances it had to be genuine, so I just came along. But why are you here?'

'Gut reaction,' she muttered. 'Come on,' and she turned back to the school entrance and broke into a barely controlled trot.

He drew alongside her and they clattered up the steps together, arriving at the doors just as the first pair of paramedics came out, wheeling James Diamond trussed up on a gurney. Jacquie bent over him and turned to Bob Davies.

'My God. It's the Headmaster,' she gasped, automatically calling him the polite version of the term Peter Maxwell habitually used. She looked up at the paramedic bringing up the rear. 'Leighford CID,' she snapped, making no real attempt to flash her ID. 'What's going on here?'

'Dunno,' he shrugged. 'About ten down, we reckon. A couple of injuries, but mostly some

66

form of very serious poisoning. One dead.' He tossed his head back. 'Coming out next.'

She looked past him and, as her eyes focused, almost passed out. The body on the gurney was covered with a red blanket, pulled up over the head and tucked firmly in at the sides, as if, somehow, the body beneath it could still stage an escape attempt. It looked oddly small and pathetic, trussed up like that. Over the legs, folded tidily, as if its owner might still need it, was a tweed jacket. It had seen better days. Jacquie knew without looking that there were leather patches on the elbows. That there was a red pen and a black pen in the breast pocket. That there was a photo of her son in the battered wallet in the right-hand side pocket. And older photos, too, of a smiling mother and daughter, long dead. She knew that in the left-hand pocket there were two cycle clips. She knew that it was Maxwell's jacket and she folded neatly to the ground, as her world tumbled around her in ruins.

'Look out,' cried the rear paramedic. 'Looks like another one.'

'No, no,' Davies said, pushing round the feet of the body; the gurney was almost filling the doorway. 'We've only just got here. She's fainted.' He bent down to Jacquie; she was already coming to. 'Leighford CID,' he said to the paramedic. 'Her partner works here. She's a bit overwrought.' And he hissed under his breath, 'For fuck's sake. This is all we need.'

Jacquie was struggling to sit up. She grabbed Davies's hand. 'Bob,' she whispered, through lips as dry as dust. 'Bob, that's Max's jacket.'

He straightened up to see. He wouldn't know Maxwell's jacket if it bit him on the leg, but he could tell that she was serious and, fair enough, if he had to name anyone who would wear a worn-out tweed thing like that, Maxwell's name would be top of the list. He put a restraining hand on her shoulder. 'Don't get up,' he said. 'Take your time.' Over her head, he gestured to the man at the rear of the gurney to pull back the blanket. He peered over and saw a woman's face, chalk white and vomit smeared, turned away from him, as if sorry to be causing any trouble.

He bent back down to Jacquie. 'It's OK, Jacquie,' he said quietly. 'It's not Max.'

'But ... but, his jacket?'

'His jacket, but not him. Come on, up you come. We'll go and see what's what through there, if you're up to it.' Women!

She scrambled to her feet, and swayed into his arms. 'Ooh, feeling a bit woozy.' She looked up into his eyes. 'Is it really not him?'

'Really. It's not something I'm likely to lie about, is it?' he asked her, quite reasonably. 'It's not as if you wouldn't find out eventually.' He smiled at her as convincingly as he could and patted her back. 'Come on, let's do this, Jacquie. Because it is someone's loved one, even if it isn't yours.'

Tears sprang into her eyes at the mild rebuke and she turned to go through the foyer into the school building proper. The red plastic chairs ranged along one wall of the foyer were filled with the walking wounded. A woman in kitchen uniform was saying, over and over, that she had

68

eaten one. Paul Moss was trying to tell her that she was going to be all right, but she wasn't listening. Some of the staff had just been unable to cope with the panic and were sitting with their heads between their knees. They were mostly men, but Jacquie wasn't in the mood to joke about that, scoring off Davies as she normally would. She looked them over quickly and, although she knew almost all of them, none was Maxwell. Not that she would have expected to see him feeling sorry for himself like that. So, that must mean he was still with the others, the eight remaining 'down' in the words of the paramedic.

Another gurney was coming through. This one bore Helen Maitland, her leg strapped between two boards. 'Oh, Jacquie,' she called. 'Thank goodness you're here. It's bedlam in there.' She gestured behind her into the dining hall. 'Someone poisoned the buffet.'

Jacquie was confused. 'But...' she pointed at the woman's leg.

'Oh, I know,' Helen said. 'One of the candidates fell over and pulled me down with her.' She caught Jacquie's look. 'She's a very big woman. I fell awkwardly and broke my leg. Tom from PE has gashed his head really badly, and a few others fainted. Diamond is in a really bad way. All the candidates are out of it. Bernard Ryan is ill as well, but not unconscious.'

Jacquie cleared her throat and tried to pitch her voice the low side of hysterical. 'Max?'

'In there, covered in sick, but don't worry. It's someone else's. He and Sylvia are the heroes of the hour, Jacquie. But, why don't you go

69

through? He'll be glad to see you.' She twisted round as best she could and spoke to the gurney-pusher. 'Off you go, my man, and don't spare the horses. Aren't you supposed to give people lots of brandy at times like these?' The paramedic tried to look as if he had never heard that one before and bent his back to the task.

''Bye, Helen,' Jacquie said. 'We'll be in to see you this evening, if that's OK.'

'Ooh, please. Don't bring grapes, though. I prefer crisps.' And then, a second thought, 'Actually, don't bring anything.'

'OK. See you later.' Davies was going through the swing doors ahead of her into the dining hall. All the kids had now been cleared out of the building and the detective's shoes squeaked on the still-polished floor. Jacquie caught up with him as the doors began to swing closed. On the other side of them, calm was beginning to return. The paramedics from the third and fourth ambulances had spread out among the fallen and were assessing them where they lay. Although no more were dead, everyone who had eaten whatever it was was either unconscious or close to it. Sylvia and Maxwell were kneeling together over the prone form of Bernard Ryan. He was groaning and every now and again leaning over and trying to be sick. Sylvia was patting him consolingly. Jacquie walked over to them, putting on her professional demeanour, though her heart was hammering in her ribs. 'Max, Sylvia, thank goodness you're all right.'

Maxwell looked up at the sound of her voice and clambered to his feet. 'I won't hug you,

70

heart. I seem to be covered in sick. Just like the Light Brigade at Varna. Of course, that was cholera. Christ knows what this is.'

'Max,' she said. 'I was so worried.'

'I left a message,' he said. 'With the desk sergeant.'

'You might as well have told the cat. Not *our* cat, of course,' she said. 'He always passes things on. I mean the station cat.' Her lip trembled. 'I was just so worried, when I got here. Ambulances. Dead bodies with your jacket on them.' Regardless of vomit traces she hugged him tight.

'Sssh,' he said, rocking her and stroking her hair. 'Sssh, I'm all right. Thanks to your egg and cress.'

She pulled away and became professional again. 'It was in the food, then, you think?'

Sylvia stood up. Bernard Ryan had drifted off again, but was about to be loaded up and taken away by a paramedic. She flexed her knees and leant against a table. 'I'm getting a bit old for this lark,' she said, smiling at Jacquie. 'Yes, we've pinned it down to the prawn cocktail, we think.'

'That explains that, then,' Jacquie said. Too many loose ends at this stage could be a disaster.

'Explains what?'

'A woman in the foyer was saying she had eaten one. Oh, but that means it can't be the prawn cocktail...'

Maxwell dismissed Freda with a wave. 'She's been eating council leftovers for years. She's probably immune to any poison yet invented. Anyway, the buffet was a general free-for-all, but the cocktails were only for SLT and candidates.

There were a few spare and Mel from Business took one for herself and one for her TA. However, the teaching assistant is allergic, so Mel polished them both off, rather than put the spare one back.'

'How do you know all this?'

Maxwell coughed discreetly. 'Just asked a few questions, used my eyes, Heart of Midlothian,' he said. 'It did people good to chat while we were sorting out the walking wounded from the ... well, the others. Mel had laughed about her cocktails, because Diamond had made a big thing about the PE department being greedy, but apparently she said there was no one like a Business Studies teacher when it came to getting a deal.' He looked more sombre than the story seemed to warrant.

'Is it Mel who died?' she asked him, hand on his arm.

'Yes,' he said. 'She died really quickly. She collapsed so fast that no one really had a moment to get to her. Diamond and the rest were throwing up and sort of drooling and behaving oddly before they went down, but she just fell over and died. Sylv realised straight away it was poison – it was all too quick just to be a bad prawn.'

Davies had moved to the door and was taking names as people were either wheeled or walked away. Now only Jacquie, Maxwell and Sylvia were left and he joined them. Jacquie introduced him to the nurse and he brightened.

'A professional. Brilliant. Can I ask you to give me a statement straight away, Mrs Matthews, while the memory is clear?'

'Wait, Bob,' Jacquie said. 'I think it would be

72

best if you interview Mr Maxwell and I will interview Sylvia. Just to keep it a bit more professional, do you get my drift? But before that, we need samples. Are SOCO on their way?'

'I've called it in,' Davies said, 'and they're on their way.' He looked at Maxwell. 'All we have to do is swab Mr Maxwell, and I think that would more or less do it.'

Maxwell looked down at himself ruefully. 'I do feel a bit ... grubby,' he said. 'Do you mind if I find something else to wear, have a shower perhaps?'

'Well...' Davies had no mind to help Maxwell feel more comfortable.

'What if the poison can seep in, through his pores,' Sylvia put in her four-pennyworth. 'After all, we don't know what it is and you don't want that on your conscience, surely, Mr Davies.'

'Could it?' he asked her, as the nearest thing to an expert he had handy.

She shrugged. 'Who knows? And I must say, I could do with a change of clothing myself. It's easy for me, I have my home clothes in my office.' She turned to Maxwell. 'What are you going to wear, Max?'

'I'll see if the PE Department can kit me out in a little Lycra number, or failing that, there's always the Drama Club costume collection. I'll find something. I've always fancied that glitzy concoction they made for Herod in *Superstar* a few years back.' He raised an eyebrow at Davies. 'May I?'

Davies sighed. 'Knock yourself out,' he said, hopefully. 'I'll find us a couple of offices,' he said

73

to Jacquie. 'I'll see you when you've finished scrubbing Mr Maxwell's back,' and he turned on his heel and left, keeping his dignity by a whisker as he nearly slipped in a pool of something indescribable.

'Bitter,' mused Sylvia.

'Wanker,' replied Jacquie, and Sylvia bowed to her better judgement and went off to change.

Chapter Six

Jacquie caught up with Davies outside Diamond's office. The school was strangely quiet, now that all the sirens had gone. The kids were being taken inside, class by class, to be signed out and sent home. There wasn't time to send a letter with them and anyway, what could it have said? The governors were the lucky ones. They had been poised to attend the interviews in the afternoon and now they were being contacted to take the brunt of the media piranha-tank frenzy as the news broke generally. By the time all the kids were home and the garbled half-truths had been semi-digested by shocked parents, the story would involve at least three armed gunmen, a pride of man-eating lions and a Viking funeral pyre afloat on the swimming pool, so the phone calls would be fun at least. Both Thingees, morning and after-noon Receptionists, braced themselves.

'Bob,' Jacquie said quietly. 'Do you have some sort of problem with Max?'

'No,' he said truculently. 'No more than anyone else.'

'Only, you seem to be a little bit rude, all things considered. He and Sylvia kept things ticking over in there, while they waited for help to arrive. Who knows, they may have saved lives.'

'Yeah, yeah,' Davies said. 'Course they did. Man on white horse, everyone step aside. Mighty

Mouse is here to save the day. Oh, yeah.'

Jacquie took a step back. 'I don't often threaten this, Bob, and I've never actually done it. But when we get back to the station, I will be putting in a complaint to Henry about your attitude today. Here we are, riding a breaking wave that could still drown us if a kid starts feeling icky, and you are letting personal prejudices hamper the investigation. Meanwhile, I'll interview Sylvia Matthews in the Head's office. I will also ring the nick and get a squad car to come and collect Mr Maxwell. Henry can interview him there.'

'I'm doing that interview,' Davies shouted. 'Don't try and sideline me, Jacquie. I get enough of that at the nick, Jacquie this, Jacquie that.' He stood at bay, red in the face and ready for action.

'That's enough.' Jacquie grabbed a startled Paul Moss by the arm as he tried to sneak past without listening. 'Mr Moss, I want you as a witness to this conversation.'

'Oh, umm, Jacquie, I don't think so...' he stammered. 'Police business, I expect, isn't it?'

'It was,' Jacquie said. 'But now it's personal. I am relieving Detective Sergeant Davies from his duties at this crime scene, the reason being that his attitude is not conducive to the professional coverage of the site. If he refuses to leave of his own free will, I would like you to go and phone this number,' she passed him a card, 'and speak directly to DCI Henry Hall.'

They stood there, a triptych of tension. Jacquie still had hold of the card which was also in Paul Moss's grasp. Davies stood with feet apart, knees locked, aggression in every pore, staring at them both. Then, the tension broke.

'Fuck you,' Davies spat. 'You'll be sorry, Jacquie,' and he stormed out, knocking a Year Seven to the ground in the doorway.

Picking the child up and dusting her down perfunctorily, Paul Moss said mildly, 'Nice chap. Are you all right, Annie?' It was the kid's second day at her new school. Teachers chucking up and falling over. Policemen knocking her about. Could it get any more exciting? Junior school was never like this.

'The best,' muttered Jacquie as Annie ran for the Great Outdoors. 'Sorry you had to see that, Mr Moss.' Like all teachers' WAGs, she automatically reverted to formality when a student was around. 'May we talk in private?'

'Of course. I suppose we could use Diamond's office,' Paul said. 'He won't be there at the moment, that's for sure,' and he headed that way.

'Perfect. I'm interviewing Sylvia in there shortly. But with that little contretemps, things need to change and I don't have time to make it happen. Could I ask you to help?'

'Of course.' He opened the door to the Head-teacher's office. Inside, it had an unreal feel. Not only was the school on the other side of the door almost silent, the last few students having finally gone home or shoplifting, whichever was the more tempting, but the room itself seemed to be holding its breath. The chair was pushed back from the desk and a pen lay on a pad, abandoned as the time for lunch had come round. Diamond's coat hung on the back of the door, his car keys were tumbled on the desk. Jacquie and Paul felt like voyeurs, looking in on the private life of a man who was in no position to complain. In fact, the police person inside Jacquie was shouting it may even be a potential crime scene, if he died. She shook herself free of that thought. No point in meeting trouble halfway; she knew that if trouble wanted to meet you, it would wait in a doorway and jump out at you when you were least expecting it. She walked purposefully behind the desk and moved the pen and pad aside. She pulled up the chair and sat down.

'Right, Paul. Oh, have a seat.'

He was looking round. He turned to her with a shudder. 'This feels peculiar,' he said. He normally sat in that chair once a year, when having to explain his decidedly average GCSE results to the Headteacher. In fact, he was due there next week.

'Murder makes everything peculiar,' she replied and watched his face drain of colour.

'Murder? I think we all assumed ... oh, I don't know. A bad prawn?'

'I think it would have to be a very bad prawn, don't you, Paul? A prawn with a sub-machine gun, for example. A member of staff is dead already and many others have been whisked off to the General, sirens going.'

He looked ashen and finally subsided into a chair. Then, 'What do you want me to do?'

'I want you to ring Henry Hall, as I asked. As soon as you've done that, I'd like you to find Max and warn him he will be going to the nick for his interview, nothing serious but DS Davies is no longer available.'

'Is that what you call it?'

'For now. Who knows, by tonight it might be me on gardening leave. We'll cross that bridge when we come to it. Then, unless you have urgent teacherly things to do, I'd be grateful if you could sit down and try to jot down your recollections of where everyone was in the few minutes before the first person collapsed, and any impressions you got. We'll be asking everyone to do this, but Max always says that historians make the best witnesses.'

'So...?'

'So, you're a historian, Paul, aren't you?'

'Yes, of course. But not like Max.'

'I know that, Paul. Just do your best.' She hadn't meant to be condescending; it just came out that way. A bit like Jack Shaffer's words in Maxwell's favourite Western – 'Tell him no man should be ashamed of being beaten by Shane.' It was just how it was. And Paul Moss knew it, too. He stood up to leave and the door behind him flew open and caught him a nasty one on the back. 'Ow.'

Thingee Two stood in the doorway, her hand to her mouth. 'Oh, I'm sorry, Mr Moss. I was look-ing for Mr Maxwell. Is he in here?' She looked around, aimlessly, as if he was perhaps on a shelf, or under the desk.

'No,' Jacquie said. 'He's getting changed. Can we help you?'

Thingee was in a cleft stick. She knew that Jacquie was Maxwell's Other Half, as the Ladies of the Office had it, but never knew what to call her. She settled for nothing and spoke to Paul

Moss instead. 'Oh, Mr Moss, it's just that we've had County Hall on the phone. It's about, well, you know, all the stuff that happened at lunch.'

'Yes,' Paul said. 'I thought they'd be involved sooner or later. What did they want? They don't think it's Mr Maxwell's fault, surely?'

'Oh, no,' said the girl. 'Not at all. They've looked through their records and found that Mr Maxwell is the senior teacher not ... umm, ill.'

Paul Moss thought about it for a moment. 'Yes, I suppose he is. So what?'

'Well,' said Thingee, looking round with big eyes. 'That means that he's the Headteacher.' She wasn't ready for the reaction her words got, as Paul and Jacquie collapsed in helpless laughter. She backed out of the door and raced back to her office, where telephones rang off their hooks and people were a bit more normal.

Chapter Seven

'I'm what?' Maxwell, scrubbed and smelling sweetly of Timotei and Dove, stood looking rather dumbfounded. He had never really thought of himself as Headmaster material and it was true that, wearing lilac tracksuit bottoms in size Absolutely Tiny and an orange tracksuit top in size Simply Enormous, he didn't look like it either.

Jacquie wiped her eyes and coughed to regain her composure. 'The Headmaster. Acting, of course.'

'Of course. I can act being a Headmaster, no problem. Damn sight better than Legs, anyway. I think my style will be something like John Gielgud in *Forty Years On*. Puzzled, but well meaning. With just a threat of Robert Newton as Dr Arnold.' A strange light came into his eye. 'I wonder whether I will have full powers?'

Paul looked askance at Jacquie.

'You're embarrassing Paul, Max,' she chided him, still smiling.

'No, no, not *those* powers. I mean full Headmasterly powers. Hiring. Firing. Expulsion. Ordering things.'

Paul Moss shrugged. 'I should think you'll have at least day-to-day powers; ordering, obviously.' He looked at his department member and smiled. 'Firing, only when necessary, I should hope. Remember who your friends are.'

Jacquie gave a final chuckle. 'Well, dearest,' she said, pecking him on the cheek. 'Well done on your sudden elevation. May I use your office to interview Sylvia, Acting Headmaster?'

'Why don't you do it in here...? Oh, I see. Ha, yes, of course you may. I'll get off to the nick then. Can you give me a lift, Paul?'

'There's a car coming for you,' the Head of History said. 'I rang earlier.'

'A car?' Maxwell grinned. 'I like the sound of that. Will it be a stretch limo, do you think? Or a Roller.' The distant sound of a dying siren came filtering through from the drive at the front of the school.

'Sounds like a squad car,' Jacquie said. 'And from the sound of the siren, I suspect that Davies has put the boot in with his cronies already. Never mind. Off you go and interview Henry.'

'Isn't he interviewing me?'

'To begin with, I expect,' she said wryly. 'I'll see you later. I promised Helen we'd pop by.'

'All right, snookums, see you later. And, Jacquie, I'll see you at home.' The bonhomie was lost on Paul Moss. He flung open the door and was almost punched in the face by a police driver, hand raised to knock on the door. 'Don't worry, officer, I'll come quietly.' And out he went.

'That'll be the day,' Paul and Jacquie said in unison.

'I heard that,' came his plaintive cry as the door swung shut and peace came briefly to the Acting Headteacher's Office.

Jacquie smiled at Paul Moss. 'If you should

happen to bump into Sylvia, could you get her to come in here?' she asked. 'If it's not for a minute or two, that would be good. I still have residual tremors from seeing Max's jacket across the feet of a dead body.'

He patted her shoulder and left.

The squad car driver had indeed been briefed, if inaccurately, by Davies. He bundled Maxwell unceremoniously into the back seat, doing that thing policemen do with people's heads to avoid allegations of brutality later, and set off at a blistering pace for the nick. As instructed, he took the most twisting route the RAC could devise and Maxwell was black and blue, as well as orange and lilac, by the time they reached Leighford Police Station, where Henry Hall waited in his eyrie.

Maxwell was bustled through reception and into Interview Room One, a setting with which he was very familiar, having spent a good few hours in it, over the years. He waited patiently, drumming his fingers on the scarred table top, testimony for future archaeologists to a strange, probably totemic habit which involved making small random burns on the Formica, but which had clearly fallen into disuse for some reason, lost to time, in the mid Noughties. He was mulling over this scenario when the door opened and an apologetic head poked itself round the door.

'Mr Hall apologises, Mr Maxwell, for the misunderstanding, but would you like to come with me up to his office?' The police person looked about six and had curls and big blue eyes like Shirley Temple, but Maxwell had learnt from his own beautiful and ingenuous Jacquie that appearances could be so very deceptive. He merely doffed his missing hat, gathered up the folds of his Simply Enormous top and followed her meekly. If she found his dress at all eccentric, like a well-trained police person she gave no sign.

As they turned a corner in the top landing, they were met by a scarlet-faced Bob Davies, who shouldered them aside and slammed out down the emergency stairs, relabelled by some wag 'Smokers This Way'.

'Excuse us,' Maxwell called after him. He really didn't care what Bob Davies thought of him, but he objected to his treatment of a female colleague. Political Correctness was not one of Maxwell's hobbies, but once a public schoolboy, always a public schoolboy, and rudeness was never left unremarked or, if possible, un-punished.

'Don't worry about me,' said his guide. 'Davies is an ignorant pig and we just ignore it. He's a bit of a dinosaur. Watches too much *Life on Mars*.'

Brontosaurus Maxwell decided she meant one of the meat eaters and let it go. Leaning round him she pushed open Hall's door. 'Mr Maxwell, sir,' she said and ushered him in.

Hall stood up and waved Maxwell to a chair. Maxwell was unused to such relative civility even from the ever-urbane Henry Hall and the surprise must have shown on his face.

'Thank you for the invitation,' Hall began.

'The...? Oh, the invi*tation!* You're welcome of

course, Henry. And the family, of course. We've decided on the more the merrier since Jacquie's mother seems intent on inviting everyone we've ever queued behind in Sainsbury's. Oh,' he added hurriedly, 'not that you fall into that category, of course. You've interrogated me under caution too many times for that to apply. Which brings me,' he said, half standing and trying to make the tracksuit bottoms conform a little more to his needs by hauling at the crotch, 'which brings me – do excuse me, by the way, Henry, there wasn't much on offer in the Lost Property Cupboard – to our business in hand. Do you have any news of the people at the hospital?'

As always, Maxwell had caught Henry Hall on the back foot. The eyes gave nothing away behind the dead lenses of his specs. 'Ermm, we have had a bulletin, yes.' If Maxwell hadn't known Henry Hall so well, he would have suspected an attempt at a John Major impression, but no, that was just his usual voice. 'There is no change at the moment, and they are trying to find out the poison so that they can administer an antidote, should there be one.' He looked down at a piece of paper on his desk. 'Let me see, yes, Mr Diamond is still unconscious, but has stabilised and is not on any form of support.' Maxwell knew that Mr Diamond *always* needed support, but now was not the time to be flippant. 'Mr Ryan is rather more serious and is in ICU being helped with his breathing. Who else...? Yes, a Mrs Bevell is also on ICU but the effects of the poison have been superseded by a pneumothorax, whatever that might be.'

'I believe it means that she has a damaged chest in some way. Air is leaking in and so the lungs can't inflate properly.'

Hall looked up from his bit of paper and adjusted his glasses. 'Mr Maxwell,' he said flatly, 'will you ever cease to amaze me?'

'I sincerely hope not, Henry. I just happen to know because I tested Jacquie on her first aid and that happened to crop up. But the question remains, however did she get one of those from being poisoned?'

'I don't know, but I think I'll ask.' Hall reached behind him and pulled a dog-eared phone number list off the wall, sending a drawing pin pinging into oblivion. He leafed through it and finally found the number he needed and punched it in to the phone. He looked vaguely through Maxwell as he waited for an answer. 'Hello? Yes, may I speak to the senior nurse, please? Oh, is she? Well, perhaps you can help me. It's DCI Hall here, Leighford CID. I am enquiring about injuries sustained by a...' He shuffled his papers and found the name, 'Mrs Bevell.' He listened for a moment, then said, 'Yes, but we don't know how that happened, when it seems to be a case of poisoning. Oh, how unfortunate. Yes, thank you.' He put the phone down and almost smiled. But then again, no. Henry Hall never did that.

'What caused it, then?' Maxwell was agog. 'Was it an additional attempt? Should we be looking at the people in the dining hall?'

'No,' Hall said. 'Apparently, Mrs Bevell needed CPR and when the paramedic tried, he found that it was beyond him.'

'That's dreadful. Wasn't he trained or something?' Maxwell's high horse was whinnying close at hand.

'No. Her breath was so bad that he just couldn't do it. Following guidelines, he did chest compression and broke two ribs. One turned inwards and caused the pneumothorax. She hasn't said much, the poison is still in her system and also, of course, she has assisted breathing, but she has mentioned that she will be suing.'

Maxwell nodded. 'I have met the lady. I'll be a witness. For the paramedic.'

'That bad?'

'At least. What about the others?'

'Miss Mackenzie and Miss Smollett are in recovery, but expected to be in for some time. Mrs Maitland has a broken leg – she's going down to theatre shortly. A couple of bumped heads going home soon...' He tapped the papers and looked up. 'That's it.'

'That's it?' Maxwell was appalled. 'I'm appalled, Henry, that you can say that. People hospitalised, unconscious, one person dead. Surely, you don't usually deal with these sorts of numbers. It's like the Blitz all over again.'

Hall had the grace to look shamefaced, if only slightly. The war was something his mother had told him about. 'It seems major, Mr Maxwell,' Hall still found that any other form of address stuck in his throat, 'but we still don't know whether this is deliberate or accidental.'

'I don't see how it can be accidental,' Maxwell said. 'They went down like ninepins.'

'That's why we need to speak to you,' Hall said.

'As an experienced, if you don't mind the term, observer of wrongdoing, we thought ... that is, *I* thought, that you might be able to give us some insight.'

Remembering Bob Davies's expression on the landing, Maxwell hazarded a guess. 'I assume Sergeant Davies doesn't think I can help.'

'Sergeant Davies thinks you *did* it, Mr Maxwell,' Hall said, cutting to the chase. 'He *always* thinks you did it. That's why he is suspended from now until his review board.'

Maxwell rocked back in his chair and was immediately sorry as his tracksuit bottoms bit deeper. 'That's rather draconian of you, isn't it, Henry?'

Hall steepled his fingers and looked at the man before him. In his motley, he hardly seemed someone in which to confide. But Hall knew that the mind was razor-sharp, the intuition honed on the same stone, and that his compassion was sometimes his only weakness. He decided to confide in him. 'He has a bit of a problem with you, Mr Maxwell,' he said, then paused. 'Before I go on, I need hardly say that this is confidential?'

Maxwell waved him on with the flap of a sleeve, some ten inches beyond the end of his fingers. As Acting Headmaster, it was body language he would have to employ more often from now on.

'He has been a problem for some time and has had counselling for his attitude to women. Jacquie in particular seems to get under his skin, and the fact that you and she are a couple seems only to make it worse. He came into my office straight from Leighford High, ranting about

Jacquie and unprofessional behaviour, which I knew at once was not likely to be true. He sent the police driver to get you, inadequately briefed, so that you were treated like a suspect. He arranged for you to be left in an Interview Room. But basically, he is a loose cannon, so intent on promotion that he has made it impossible by his behaviour. So please don't worry about him in this investigation.'

'Henry,' Maxwell said, 'I have to think of Jacquie here. If it makes a problem for her...'

'Mr Maxwell,' Hall said patiently, 'If I had a pound for every time you have brought Jacquie to the edge of suspension I would be a rich man, so don't let's say things we clearly don't mean. This subject is closed. Now, please tell me what your impressions were in the dining hall when the collapses began.'

'Well, firstly, I didn't eat there,' Maxwell said. 'Not really. I had a jelly thing with what they claim to be fruit in it. My main lunch was sandwiches from home.'

'Why?'

'I like sandwiches from home. Egg, as it happens.'

'No, I mean, why, when senior staff seemed to be involved, were you not included?'

How long had Hall got, Maxwell wondered, when both of them had a murder on their hands, to even begin to understand the subtle knifings of staffroom politics? Maxwell was a maverick, a misfit. He stepped aside for no man and made no concessions. The Powers That Be never invited such people willingly to their junkets. 'I was,' was

89

all he settled for, 'although I am not part of the SLT.'

'But I understand from Leighford High that you are Acting Headteacher.'

'News travels fast. I am, but only, like Bruce Willis, because I am the oldest man standing.'

'So why did you not join the others for the buffet?'

'So I am a suspect?' Maxwell leant back and regretted it all over again.

'No, but I just want to get the picture straight.'

'Well, firstly, I hate these pseudo-elegant things at school. They use outside caterers who are average at best, frankly deranged at their worst. If I tell you that the sandwiches were cranberry and Brie, heavy on the cranberry, I think you will get the general gist.'

Hall, who, like Maxwell, preferred his sandwiches to be the kind that evoked nursery school memories, shuddered slightly.

'Secondly, I had, as it happens, seen the prawn cocktail jobbies laid out on a counter in the kitchen the day before, when I failed to have my Roast Lunch. I'm not much of a stickler for food hygiene, Henry. If I find a faded M&M down the sofa, that M&M is mine, believe me. I put it down to having parents who had known rationing. But even I am none too keen on the thought of seafood lurking around at room temperature for all of twenty-four hours. At least. That can't be right. Plus, they were being delivered by a man who I believe to be a raving maniac. He is Oliver Lessing, uncle of Dierdre; you probably have a file on him this thick.' He held up his hands, about two feet apart. Hall shook his head, but made a note. 'And, I believe that the redoubtable Freda, dinner person of this parish, had one of the cocktails and is living yet.'

Hall brightened. 'But even so, we might still be looking at very severe food poisoning, mightn't we?' His eyes were hopeful and Maxwell would have liked nothing better than to have been able to cheer him up. But that just wasn't possible.

'Sorry to rain on your parade, Henry, old thing. My very good friend Sylvia Matthews who is the School Nurse, you may remember, says that it couldn't possibly hit that hard and that fast, even the kind of horrible things that prawns carry. No, it has to be poison.'

Hall deflated and said, 'You can't blame me for hoping, Mr Maxwell. The thought of a deranged random poisoner running around isn't exactly music to a policeman's ears.'

'Or to the ears of anyone who indulges in food from time to time,' agreed Maxwell. 'To continue. I came down from my office and helped myself to a jelly. I was talking to Sylvia and weighing up the chances of each candidate. There was the usual background hum of conversation, the click of texting, the sound of healthy food being shoved down behind radiators. And that's just from the staff. The kids were obviously much noisier.'

'Wait a minute.' Henry Hall held up a hand. 'The students were there? I didn't know that.'

'Well, not there as in mixed with the staff. There is a staff section where we can have our lunches, if not in peace then at least without having to watch Nine Zed eat pizzas with their

91

collective mouths open. It's like watching banks of tumble dryers at the launderette. Anyway, where was I?'

Hall spread his hands. Who knew?

'Ah, yes. There was just the usual background noise when suddenly someone shouted out. And then there was the noise of someone falling, you know, bringing plates and stuff down with them.'

'In that order?' Hall asked.

Maxwell closed his eyes and waved his hands in front of him, trying to reconstruct the scene. His lids flew open and his dark eyes focused on Hall. 'I have to admit, Henry, and this is something I don't have much call to say, but I have to admit I don't really know. I suppose the nearest I can come is that they were almost simultaneous. Then, everyone seemed to be falling over and being sick. But I can be a little more accurate here, if your stomach is up to it.'

'Mr Maxwell, just take it as read that my stomach is at least as strong as the next man's, if not almost certainly stronger.'

'Of course, how silly of me. You must have seen much worse sights than a load of teachers being sick. Well, it seemed as if there was more than one thing going on. There were some people lying on the ground and being sick. That's very awkward; I don't know if you've ever tried it, but to be sick efficiently, you need to be sort of arched over. Think hangover and you'll see I'm right. These people didn't seem able to do that, they were all floppy and just being sick as best they could, if you see what I'm trying to convey.'

'Yes,' Hall said, scribbling notes on a pad in

front of him.

'Then there were those who were being sick just because others were being sick. Some teachers get their vomit level adjusted on the first day of the job, others never get used to it. No doubt my colleagues in the Infant Sector are more hardened than my oppos, bum-wiping and so on. They were leaning over in the usual way. Added to that, there were a few injuries, people knocked flying by the ones who fell over. My number two, Helen Maitland, is one of those.'

Hall put down his pen. 'Can you remember who belonged to which of the first two categories?' he asked.

Maxwell paused for thought again. 'Oddly enough, Henry, I can. The first group were exclusively the ones now in hospital or dead. The others all recovered after a moment and helped with the kids or the ill and injured.' He tapped his forefinger on his chin a few times as he checked back in his memory. Then he looked up at Hall again. 'Yes, I'm absolutely sure I'm right.'

'And the first group, they all were members of the SLT or candidates?'

'Not quite. Because I wasn't there, there was a cocktail left over, possibly a couple if Legs Diamond had been generous enough to slightly overcater. Mel Forman from Business...'

'...the dead woman?'

'Yes. She took one for herself and one for her teaching assistant but ate them both because the girl couldn't eat prawn. I also noticed that Miss Mackenzie hadn't eaten her shell-on prawn garnish.'

'I don't think that's too important – she was the first one down.'

'That's true,' agreed Maxwell. 'But she's not as seriously ill as most of the others now.'

'Neither is Miss Smollett.'

'Indeed, but I'd say Miss Smollett is a much tougher cookie than Miss Mackenzie, who looks like a Botticelli angel who a puff of wind could blow away. Perhaps she was more susceptible to the poison so it took less to affect her.'

'True,' pondered Hall. 'When we find out what the poison is we'll know, perhaps.'

'I think I may know what the poison is,' offered Maxwell.

Hall reached in behind his blank lenses and rubbed his eyes. From behind his hands he said plaintively, 'Mr Maxwell. Could you outline your credentials as a toxicologist?'

Maxwell gave a rueful smile. 'Please, Henry. Does no policeman ever learn from history? I either know it or can blag it, as you have found down the long arches of the years. It happens that this is one of those things I know. We teach Crime and Punishment as a GCSE module and poisoners are criminals, as you were doubtless taught at Hendon. William Palmer, Dr Pritchard, Graham Young. I could go on.'

'OK then,' said Hall. 'I'll go with this for now.'

'Well, having thought it through, with the falling down, the vomiting, the total collapse and, of course, sadly, the rapid death, I can only conclude aconite.'

'Aconite? A little old-fashioned, isn't it?'

'Yes. But also very easy to get hold of if you

94

don't mind having poisonous plants in your garden. Wolfsbane is a handsome plant and, incredibly, available from garden centres. We had some in the back of a border until Nolan started walking and we rooted it out. You have to be thorough, because the roots go down to bloody Australia, and of course you have to be careful not to get the sap on your hands just before you eat your restorative ginger nut.'

'I'd still like to wait for confirmation, if you don't mind.'

Maxwell bowed, but carefully.

Hall's phone rang and he snatched it up. 'Hall. Yes.' He covered the mouthpiece and quietly said, 'Lab,' to Maxwell. Into the receiver he said, 'That was quick. Uh huh. Uh huh. Thank you.' He looked up at Maxwell. 'I mustn't keep you. I'll arrange a car to take you home. I expect you'd like to change, wouldn't you?'

'Love to,' said Maxwell, standing up gingerly. 'What did the lab have to say?'

'I'm not sure I can tell you that at this stage, Mr Maxwell,' said Hall, primly.

'Aconite then,' said Maxwell.

'Or a derivative,' said Hall, flatly. He shuffled some papers and then looked up. 'Don't let me keep you.' He reached for his phone and Maxwell, dismissed, left the room. Once outside he couldn't resist a small chuckle of triumph as he made his way down to reception. He didn't lose sight of the large picture: people were ill, people were very possibly dying, one person was dead. But at least he was right.

Chapter Eight

Jacquie sat quietly behind Maxwell's new desk and practised some yogic breathing, interspersed with sobs. It had been bad timing for her. Maxwell had inadvertently let out a small intimation of mortality with his flippant talk of retirement, and the jacket over the legs of a dead person had put the tin lid firmly on her fears and given it a twist to keep it in place.

The fact that he hadn't broken but had, as usual, bounced at this latest crisis had soothed her, but she was still shaken. Like every frightened child at Leighford High, she wanted Maxwell to mend it and make it right. Failing Maxwell, she wanted Sylvia Matthews. There was a gentle tap at the door and the nurse popped her head round.

'Jacquie?' she said. 'Are you ready for me yet?'

With a final sniff, Detective Sergeant Jacqueline Carpenter replaced frightened Jacquie. 'Come in, Sylv.' She beckoned her in and opened her notebook.

Sylvia kicked the door open wider to negotiate through it with the tray she was carrying. 'I thought you would probably like some coffee.'

Jacquie eyed it dubiously. 'Er ... don't think I'm ungrateful, but where is it from, exactly?'

Sylvia chuckled. 'Max's secret stash,' she said.

The policewoman breathed a sigh of relief.

'That's OK, then. I'd love one. I don't remember having lunch and I must say I don't really fancy any now.'

'I know what you mean,' said Sylvia, deftly being mother. She handed a mug over the desk. 'Careful where you put it down. Max doesn't want rings on his furniture.' She gave a little laugh. 'I wish it wasn't like this, Jacquie, but I think we have the right Head at last.'

'That's very sweet of you, Sylv, but I don't think it's really Max's thing, you know, this kind of admin post. He likes to get in amongst stuff, not just chair meetings and make phone calls. What he'd really like to do is lead a cavalry charge, but there would be bound to be health and safety implications.'

Sylvia chuckled. 'I totally agree,' she said, sipping her coffee. 'That's why he's the right man. Whoever said being a Head meant not getting in amongst stuff? He might make it hands on again, even if only briefly. These kids will be lucky to see a real leader for once. Who knows, even if he's only Head for a while, he might make a lasting difference to Leighford High.'

'That would be nice,' Jacquie said, with the air of someone putting a full stop to a conversation. 'Now, Sylv, I'm afraid I'm going to have to interview you about the events of this lunchtime.' She clicked her pen open and looked hopefully at the woman opposite. When nothing happened, she tried again. 'What if you start from the beginning of the lunch break?' she said, helpfully.

'Jacquie,' Sylvia eventually said. 'I'm not used to this. I just can't do it.'

'What's the problem?' she said. 'Do you want me to ask you questions, to prompt you or something? Or do you find it distressing?'

'It was distressing, yes,' she replied. 'But it isn't that. I found I went onto autopilot, really. The training just kicked in. I know I didn't do anything wrong, because that would have broken the flow, but as to what order things happened in, or anything like that, I'm afraid I won't be a help. And I don't want to give you my version as I have reconstructed it. It is bound to be hopelessly inaccurate.'

Jacquie put down her pen and rubbed her eyes. This was all she needed. She looked up. 'What can you remember?'

'Eating a jelly with Max. You coming in. Between, just a lot of vomit and crying. Sorry. Ask any medical person and if they're honest they'll say the same.'

'Sylv, there's no need to shield anyone.'

'I'm not. Please, Jacquie, it's what I remember. Nothing.'

'Well,' the policewoman pushed herself back from the desk. 'That's it, then. Thanks for coming in.' She moved towards the door, shepherding Sylvia Matthews ahead of her. 'Are you off home now?'

'Yes,' she said. 'When I've checked the loos and things; I sometimes find the occasional lost soul in the girls' changing room.'

'I'll come with you,' offered Jacquie.

'Really,' smiled Sylvia. 'There's no need. I just do it to satisfy myself all is well.'

'I like to do that too,' said Jacquie, and fell into

step alongside the nurse.

The first stop was the boys' cloakroom, off the main foyer. At first, Jacquie thought that something horrendous had happened in there. The smell was a bizarre compound of the warm fudgey smell given off by socks worn too long on sweaty adolescent feet, armpit, cheap deodorant, baked beans *after* digestion, and ammonia. This was undercut by the rather unexpected smell of mock leather and wood, from the brand new, granny-bought school bags and newly scraped-down floors. It would be all of a week before the bags became Tesco bags or the anonymous grey holdalls sold in sports shops throughout the known universe. The whole was enough to make anyone's eyes water and Jacquie wiped hers with her sleeve. She glanced at Sylvia who had not reacted.

As they backed into the foyer again, Jacquie still trying not to breathe, Sylvia remarked casually, 'How they can still find cleaners with the olfactory functions of a gnat, I can't imagine. I really only go in there in the first week of term. After that, the smell is too bad.' Although Sylvia Matthews had been close to Maxwell for many years, Jacquie had still to learn her expressions. Did that face mean what the words did, or was it some ironic comment? Jacquie just couldn't be sure.

'Right,' Sylvia said, 'the girls cloakroom. Abandon hope all ye who enter here.' Jacquie held her breath in readiness, but there was no need. It smelt of talcum powder and shampoo. But it was so untidy that it was totally impossible to see the floor. Lockers spewed their contents everywhere and for some reason a blouse was hanging from a light fitting.

'Don't touch anything,' she hissed to Sylvia. 'I'll see if SOCO are still in the building.'

Sylvia looked at her in surprise. 'Whatever for?' she asked, mildly.

'Well, look around you, Sylv,' Jacquie said. 'The place has clearly been ransacked.'

Sylvia laughed and patted Jacquie on the arm. 'No, no, Jacquie,' she smiled. 'This is the *girls'* cloakroom. It always looks like this. Except for about thirty seconds on the first day of term, and in the holidays when the little dears aren't here.'

'But, it's ... it's disgusting.' Jacquie was almost lost for words. 'How can they leave it like this?'

Sylvia surprised Jacquie by giving her a hug. 'Welcome to Leighford High,' she smiled. 'The skull beneath the skin, as Max calls it.'

'Yes,' said Jacquie. 'I expect he does. But that's because he doesn't do the cleaning.'

'He does occasionally offer to use a broom in a rather unconventional way,' Sylvia said, 'but I don't expect he means it. Anyway, nothing to see here, as your American counterparts say. I'm for home, I think. Are you done here?' She pulled open one half of the double doors leading out into the foyer and stepped through. Jacquie turned to take one last look at the chaos that lay behind, so she didn't see in detail what happened next. Sylvia Matthews just crashed back into the cloakroom and sent them both flying. Jacquie's head hit the floor and bounced. If it hadn't been for a pile of discarded gym kit, she would have been knocked cold. As it was, she was merely winded and was on her feet almost as soon as she hit the ground. Sylvia, burdened with more years than Jacquie, clambered up in a rather less gainly fashion but was out in the foyer only seconds behind her, to see the doors to the outside still swinging behind a running figure.

Jacquie gave chase but hadn't a hope of catching up. She settled for standing still on the top step and trying to commit to memory a detailed picture of the man, if man it was. The person was small, wiry and was wearing a hooded anorak in a dirty green. It appeared to be wearing trousers rather than jeans and shoes rather than trainers. Trying to avoid jumping to conclusions, Jacquie nonetheless concluded that this was not a youngster. But who else would behave that way? She decided to call the runner 'he' simply because that was the impression she got; the run was neat and methodical, but the strides weren't very long. He wasn't particularly fit, she thought, but didn't seem to be running out of steam, so averagely active. He was carrying a bag which chinked as he ran. He turned out of the drive and was gone. Jacquie ran into the dining hall and grabbed a walkie-talkie from a startled SOCO and patched herself through to Henry Hall.

'Guv,' she said. 'I think we need more bodies here. Mrs Matthews has just been attacked, although I think by accident. I think the man who did it has made away with some evidence.'

The SOCO men looked up as one. Then, one broke ranks and rushed to the serving counter. He looked round at the others. 'Oh, bugger,' he said. 'She's fucking right as well. Some wanker has stolen the cocktail dishes off of the side.'

Jacquie addressed the walkie-talkie. 'Did you hear that, guv?'

Hall's sigh echoed round the cavernous room. 'Yes, Jacquie. I'm on my way – if only to remind my team of the need for modified language in a public place.'

She broke the connection and looked around the assembled white suits. They were un-characteristically silent. The pounding hearts and dry throats thudded and scraped in the quiet-ness. A devil took hold of Jacquie. 'Now, sit down at the tables, boys,' she said. 'Backs straight. No talking. You're all in detention.' She turned on her heel and was almost through the door before the first expletive hurtled after her.

Sylvia was sitting on a bench outside, rubbing her elbow and ruefully examining a gash on her leg. She had not been as lucky as Jacquie, with her handy gym kit pillow to land on. She had landed half on a bench and was battered and bruised. Also, Jacquie's knee had caught her in the small of the back and she could feel it stiffening up as she sat there.

'Are you all right, Sylvia?' Jacquie said, sitting beside her. 'Do you want to go to the hospital?'

Sylvia shuddered. 'God, no,' she said and tried a small smile. 'I hate those places. MRSA. C. difficile. E. coli. I'll be all right. I just need a nice hot bath and a lie-down and I'll be right as rain.' She turned. 'Are you all right? I landed on you, didn't I?'

'A bit,' Jacquie said. 'I think I must have hurt

102

you with my knee. But I bounced on the piles of crap those girls had kindly left on the floor, so don't worry. Henry Hall's on his way.'

'Why?' Sylvia was wide-eyed. 'Just because some bloody kid gave me a shove?'

'That was no kid,' Jacquie said. 'That was a man, and not a youngster at that. He was wearing quite expensive clothes and didn't run like a young person. He was over fifty, I'd say, or if not, then not used to running. He was carrying a bag.'

Sylvia waited for the punchline.

'It had the prawn cocktail dishes in it. The SOCO guys had left them lined up on the counter. He must have crept in and just taken them.'

'Why would he do that?' Sylvia asked.

'Because, Nurse Matthews, you were just knocked over by our murderer, unless I seriously miss my guess.'

And, with no fuss or preamble, Sylvia Matthews, SRN, slid gracefully off the bench and onto the ground in her first faint in living memory. What would Miss Nightingale have said?

'So I didn't really know what to do,' said Jacquie, snuggling up to Maxwell when the day was finally done. 'The designated First Aider was lying at my feet in a heap. So I put her in the recovery position and yelled for help. Then one of the SOCOs came out in all his white stuff and leant over her. She woke up, saw him, passed out again. She's not really cut out for crime.'

'I think you're right there,' Maxwell agreed. 'Blood, gore, various body bits, which I hope never to have more than a passing acquaintance with, being presented to her day in and day out. But a little brush with a murderer and she goes to pieces. Tcha.'

'Tcha?' Jacquie rose up on an elbow and looked at him. 'Nobody says "Tcha".'

'I do and I'm proud of it. I'll say it again. Tcha! It's a sort of Wodehousian, Thirties thing, but I sense it's making a comeback.'

She prodded him in the ribs and wriggled down into the pillows to prepare for sleep. 'Sleep, now,' she said, gave a huge sigh and went off, just like that. Maxwell lay there amazed, as he always did. Was it a police thing? A female thing? How on earth did she do that? He rolled over and tried to put the day's events out of his mind. He counted, in his head, the squadrons in the Light Brigade at Balaclava. He listed their commanding officers. He began to list their...

Someone was pulling his hair. It really hurt, but not as much as the exploratory finger up his nose. A bright light was shining in his eyes.

'God,' he muttered. 'I've been abducted by aliens.'

He forced open one eye and found that he was face-to-face with Nolan. 'Dada? Brekkie.'

Maxwell tried to ungum his mouth. To make time, he gently disentangled his son's fingers from his hair and unplugged his finger from his right nostril. He planted a kiss on the boy's nose and struggled upright. He glanced behind him. Jacquie's side of the bed was empty. 'Where's Mummy?' he asked the boy.

'Mummy ha gone,' Nolan said. He sounded so precise that Maxwell half expected him to produce a Post-it note with the details.

'When?' he asked and then stopped. This lovely boy, bright as a button and twice as cute, was pretty good on where the biscuits were, how far he could push Metternich before the animal moved out and which Hoob was which, if indeed anyone knew. But time was something that happened to other people. For some bizarre spatial reason, Maxwell had been twelve before he could tell the time and he quite understood. He picked the child up and they went into the kitchen to get breakfast. The cooker clock, a tad more forthcoming than his son, told Maxwell that it was seven-thirty. So Jacquie had gone out earlier than usual. He hadn't heard the phone, but that was no guide; he often didn't. He stepped deftly over a lurking Metternich and perched Nolan on the worktop. He raised an interrogative eyebrow at him.

'Pops!' the little one shouted.

'Coco Pops it is,' agreed Maxwell. He glanced down at Metternich. 'Coco Pops?' The cat's disdain was palpable and he showed Maxwell a clean pair of heels as he sped off down the stairs. Maxwell looked at his son who shrugged his shoulders and spread his arms, palms uppermost; a facsimile in miniature of his mother that made his father laugh out loud. The boy's lip quivered for a moment and then he laughed too. A chip off each block, and no mistake.

As they sat together in companionable silence, watching the apparent acid trip that was the Night Garden, Maxwell began to wonder, ever so slightly, if he should find out where his wife-to-be had gone. As if in answer, the phone began to ring.

'Hello?'

'Max? Is that you?' Jacquie asked, puzzled.

'Who were you expecting?'

'Well, no "War Room"? No "Piccadilly Circus"? No "Bedlam"?'

'All of the above, obviously. But I didn't know who it might be.'

'Max, it's quarter to eight in the morning. Who else might it be?'

'Your kidnapper?'

'Hmm, all right, sorry. I should have left a note, but I had to dash. I'm at the hospital. Someone had another go at Mrs Bevell last night.'

'My God!' Maxwell nearly dropped his Coco Pops. 'Is she... I mean, did they...?'

'Succeed? No. But obviously, she is very scared and also she did take in a bit of the poison, so is back in intensive care big time. She is now planning to sue the paramedic and also Leighford General.'

'I hope she makes a bundle.'

There was another silence. 'Max, are you sure it's you? First answering the phone like a sane person and then applauding the blame culture. I'm in shock.'

'No, no. Blame culture be buggered. I just mean that if she wins, she won't need the job, so we won't have her at Leighford High.'

'Thank goodness. You had me worried, there. Anyway, the reason I rang was to check you were up, firstly.'

'No trouble. The time bomb that is your son

106

was primed and ready to go at seven-thirty.'

'Good. Also, I managed to get one of the mums from nursery to pick him up at around eight-fifteen. Are you all right with that? Will you be ready?'

Maxwell looked down at his son. If there was a category in the *Guinness Book of Records* for how many Coco Pops could be embedded in one child's hair, then Nolan was a contender. 'Ready? Aye, ready. We'll be fine. We're all ready and dressed as a matter of fact.'

'My word,' Jacquie said, with scarcely a trace of irony showing through. 'In that case, my work is done. I'll either see you tonight or let you know what's going on. Oh, and Max, just one thing.'

'Yes?'

'The only way to get Coco Pops out of his hair is to rinse them out. If you try combing, they just squash further in. Bye.' And she was gone.

Slowly replacing the phone, Maxwell asked Nolan, 'Did you see when she put the cameras in place? Do you know where they are, eh, little man?' And he scooped him up, all chocolately, and took him off for a bit of a rinse, careful all the time to keep him at arm's length.

Leighford High School didn't look any different on that Friday morning. The dining hall was cordoned off with stripey police tape and the kids were a little subdued, but most staff agreed that that was a definite plus. Maxwell, Acting Head-teacher, decided against a special assembly. He opted for a staff meeting instead. He stood at the

107

front of the room, and waited patiently for the staff to settle down. He cleared his throat quietly and the room was still. So this was what power felt like from the front. He took a deep breath and waited for the comments from the old geezer sitting at the front. Oh, but hang on, he *was* that old geezer, so no point in waiting.

He consciously copied Herr Hitler at the Berlin Sportpalast at his first big rally as Chancellor. He glowered left and right, but mostly right, and slicked down his hair, which sprang back immediately. Then he folded his arms until all the shuffling had stopped.

All eyes were on him now – aged shits like Ben Holton, the Head of Science who was at school with Isaac Newton. Crawling toadies like Philippa Parses, distraught that poor Mr Diamond was no longer at the helm. And a goodly smattering of his old gang – Sally Greenhow of Special Needs, Paul Moss of the History Department, both Thingees from reception – rubbed shoulders with bright young things newly appointed by Legs Diamond; NQTs as green as grass who would be mown down by the withering fire of Year Eleven.

'As of this morning,' he said, no longer thinking in German, 'our Lords and Masters at County Hall have decreed that, as a temporary measure, I shall be Acting Headteacher of Leighford High School.'

Whoops and cheers all round, followed by laughter. Some were genuinely delighted. Some were hysterical. Some would not know what hit them.

'This has been ratified by the Chair of Governors – and it's nice to have the furniture on our side, isn't it, boys?'

Philippa Parses could not sit there and take all this. 'Is this flippancy going to continue?' she snapped.

There was a silence. All eyes were on Maxwell.

'I will attribute that remark to the fact that you are still in shock after the events of yesterday, Pippa,' he said quietly. 'If you wish to apply for compassionate leave...' he peered at her more closely, 'or early retirement, I shall be only too happy to consider it. In the meantime, I have a school to run. Can I or can I not count on your support?'

Philippa wanted the floor to swallow her, but it wasn't going to oblige. She lost eye contact and muttered a rather feeble, 'Yes.'

'Good,' said Maxwell, 'Now, people, to business...'

Jacquie sat at the bedside of Mrs Bevell and listlessly flicked one more time through a very old copy of *Hello*. The corners had worn off with use, so it was not possible to tell exactly how old the issue was, but Jacquie gave a wild guess at 1990 as there was coverage of Ulrika Johnson's first marriage and Jacquie felt for her as she stood there next to Mr Right.

Mrs Bevell was mercifully unconscious, as were all the Leighford staff, current and potential, who surrounded her, swathed in white sheets and punctuated by tubing. It was an eerie feeling, a little like being on the set of a real, honest-to-

God sci-fi movie or that one with Genevieve Bujold where Richard Widmark is up to no good in cryogenic skullduggery. Even the world of *Hello* was a welcome link with reality.

She had interviewed the night nurses as they went off, standing in a smoke-wreathed group at the cigarette-end-carpeted spot just outside the hospital gates where they were no longer thanked for not smoking. They all agreed that they had seen nothing unusual that night, no furtive figures, no syringes left on bedside tables, no cries or screams to break the rhythm of assisted breathing. No, the Senior Night Sister had said, taking one last desperate drag and throwing aside the filter, the only odd thing had been Mrs Bevell's relapse into unconsciousness.

The others agreed, with varying degrees of thankfulness at the woman's sudden silence. Jacquie had noted their names and gone on to interview the patients.

But answer came there none. Those who could be wakened were not to be wakened. The others were well and truly unconscious. Only Miss Mackenzie was back on an ordinary ward, and she was now under twenty-four-hour guard. Helen Maitland was in an orthopaedic ward, leg in plaster and still more or less as happy as a clam on pain killers. The stunned, bruised and otherwise knocked-about members of staff had gone home hours before to relive their moment of glory by not being mentioned at all on the local news bulletin.

So Jacquie sat there, quietly leafing.

There came a croaking noise from the bed and

Jacquie looked up and threw down her magazine. She leant forward and then hurriedly drew back. Having a tube down her throat and nothing to eat for the best part of twenty-four hours had done nothing to improve Mrs Bevell's almost terminal halitosis. 'What happened?' asked the woman, as best she could through all the hardware. 'Where did that doctor go?'

'Doctor?' Jacquie said and reached for her notepad. As far as she knew, only nurses had been present when the woman had relapsed.

Mrs Bevell licked her lips and tried to be more precise. 'Doctor. Consultant, I think. Gave tablet.'

'Consultant? Had you seen him already?'

'No.' The reply was as sharp as the woman could make it. Broken ribs and poisoning weren't going to make her gentle on the stupid. And everyone but her was stupid, that much was clear, and she'd known it all her life.

'How did you know he was a consultant, then?' Jacquie asked, quite reasonably.

Mrs Bevell's eyes began to close, but before she drifted away to a dreamland where everyone did as she told them with no argument, she muttered just one word. 'Old.'

'Old? Mrs Bevell, did you say old? Mrs Bevell?' Jacquie resisted the urge to shake her awake. The sister, leaving her glass-fronted fastness, was beginning to come her way.

'Can we help you?' the nurse said frostily in Jacquie's ear.

Ah, the royal we. How Jacquie had missed it since her days in ante-natal. She turned. 'If you

111

can wake her up, that would help.' She forced herself to be polite.

'Sorry.' The nurse almost smiled. 'I'm afraid she's sedated. I'm surprised she woke up at all.'

'She's a very determined woman,' Jacquie replied. 'Perhaps you can help in another way, then. She spoke of a consultant who came to see her in the night.'

The nurse snorted derisively. 'A consultant? In the night? Are you nuts? They're strictly daytime. A registrar, perhaps? A houseman? But they usually only come when we call them and we had no need to do that.'

Jacquie gestured at the full beds. 'These people seem quite ill,' she said.

'They are, but they are also quite stable. We didn't need to do anything except check signs regularly and they are all doing OK. In fact, apart from Mr Ryan, they are all improving. Most of them will be on open wards by the weekend.'

'So who could it have been, then?' Jacquie asked.

'I have no idea. Could she have imagined it? Is she an imaginative woman?'

'No one knows her. She's not from round here. She was only down for an interview. The school have been trying to contact her family, but there doesn't seem to be anyone at home.'

The nurse snorted again. 'They've probably been down here, trying to kill her.' She gave the unconscious woman a poisonous look. 'I know I would.'

Jacquie smiled. That seemed to fit with everyone else's opinion. 'I think he was real. He gave her a tablet.'

'Well, there you are, then,' said the nurse. 'She wouldn't have drugs by mouth. We'd add it to her drip.'

'Thank you,' said Jacquie, making a note. 'Look, I need to make a call. Can you watch her for a moment? No one, absolutely no one, is to go near any of these people, is that all right?'

The nurse shrugged. 'I've got nowhere to go,' she said. 'I'll watch them from in here if you think it's necessary.'

'I do,' said Jacquie and went into the nurses' station to the phone. She stood there, tapping her fingers on the desk as she waited for a reply. The nurse's rather more up-to-date copy of *Hello* – spookily featuring Ulrika Johnson standing next to Mr Right – lay open on the desk. So, she didn't spend every second watching her charges after all, thought Jacquie. If the night staff were the same, then anyone could have come in, as long as they were quiet and were ready with an excuse if challenged. A picture was emerging, though, of someone...

'Hall.' He had finally answered his phone.

'It's Jacquie here, guv. I'm at the hospital. I've managed to have a word with Mrs Bevell.'

'Well done. And?' Hall wasn't wasting words today. He was a man down and the paperwork on that fact alone could keep him busy until dooms-day.

'And she isn't saying much, but what she did say was interesting.' Jacquie knew her man too well to pause for a reaction, so she ploughed on. 'Apparently, an old man gave her a tablet.'

'That's it?'

'Ermm, yes, guv. But that fits with the person that Sylvia and I saw yesterday, the one who took the cocktail glasses. He looked old, well, ol*der*, we thought.'

Jacquie sensed rather than heard Hall take off his glasses, rub his eyes and sigh. 'Well, it cuts it down a bit, I suppose. Come back to the station, Jacquie. We need to discuss this Bob Davies business.'

Jacquie's heart rose into her mouth. She knew she needed to address it, the constant carping, the unprofessional behaviour, but at the end of the day it was the man's career they were messing with and she wasn't sure she was comfortable with that. 'OK, guv. I've just got to make sure everyone from Leighford High is under perman-ent watch, then I'll be on my way.'

'You really think they're still at risk. Not just Mrs Bevell?'

'Why just her?'

'Well, we've been doing a bit of brainstorming here and the consensus is that the poisoner was after one person and didn't mind poisoning a whole lot of people, just to get that one. It's not unknown.'

In an Agatha Christie, perhaps, thought Jacquie, but she said, 'Well, it's certainly a theory, guv. I'll be back soon,' and hung up. She made sure that the nurse knew how important it was that she put aside her magazine and actually watched the patients, not just for medical prob-lems, but for the approach of any dodgy old men, even actual consultants. She checked on the

114

other wards to make sure the same was happening throughout the hospital, wherever a Leighford High teacher might be languishing. This was more than slightly embarrassing for the lab technician who had hoped that the lancing of his gluteal boil might remain his secret, but better safe than sorry.

Finally, she got to the car park, removed the parking ticket from under her windscreen and explained to the attendant where it might end up if he didn't cancel it. She got into the car and checked her phone. Three messages. One from Maxwell, one from Henry and one withheld. She dialled 1571 and listened.

'Hello, Immortal Beloved. Me here, speaking after the beep. This Headmaster lark is like falling off a log. I've done a bit of light ordering and a bit of light ordering around. Everyone here would really appreciate a bit of an update, if that's possible. The hospital is being cagey as usual, although we did get some detail about a boil. Can that be right? At any event, heart, can you get back to me? Just ask for the Headteacher. They won't know what Headmaster means. Acting,' and he broke into a flurry of Sir John Gielgud and gales of laughter, before ringing off. She obediently pressed two to save for thirty days. She always saved his messages; a little superstition of her own. She pressed one.

'Jacquie.' Hall as always sounded peremptory. 'Don't come back. Go to Leighford High. There seems to be a bit of a problem there. Let me know how it goes.' No laughter. No Gielgud. Same old. Same old.

Her heart in her mouth for the second time in two days, she rammed the car into gear and broke every speed limit to get to Leighford High.

Chapter Nine

This time there was only one ambulance waiting outside on the drive, with a bored-looking paramedic sitting on the back step, flicking some desultory ash from the end of his cigarette. He looked up as she flung herself out of her car.

'Hello again,' he said. 'We can't keep meeting like this.'

She stood looking down at him as she skidded to a halt. 'I assume,' she said, somewhat haughtily, 'that there is no actual emergency this time.'

He stood up, grinding out his dog-end with an ambulance-service issue boot. 'Not as such.' He blew out the final lungful of smoke and immediately popped a mint in to his mouth to replace it. 'Some bloke ate something and it made him sick. Bit of overreaction in my opinion, but there we are. Better safe than sorry.'

'So you weren't needed, then?' she asked, her heart slowing to normal speed.

'Well, my mate's just checking the geezer over. Just in case. For the record, you might say. But no, no real damage done. He was offered some snack thing by a kid and just went down as if he was poleaxed, by all accounts. The kids went mental and rushed off to get somebody. Well, they would, wouldn't they, after yesterday? They called us. And you, by the looks. Anaphylactic shock, y'ask me.'

The long technical word from his mouth was so unexpected that Jacquie just nodded and went up the steps into the foyer. The other paramedic was there, talking to Maxwell who was in full Headmaster mode, thumbs in braces, bow tie perky, interested expression firmly pinned in place; no idea of education at all.

'So, no harm done,' he was saying as she got into earshot. 'It was a mini sausage roll, apparently, that a child offered him. We're thinking he may be allergic, but I gather you've kept the pack just in case. When the plods get here, could you hand it over?'

Maxwell looked aghast and then, seeing Jacquie from the corner of his eye, amused. He turned. 'Ah,' he said. 'Plod, my dear.' The paramedic looked momentarily confused, then blushed. 'This gentleman was just talking about you. He has given into my care a pack of mini sausage rolls, innocently proffered to Paul Moss by a grateful pupil this morning, just before break. To say it disagreed with him would be an understatement.' He turned to the paramedic, who was trying to creep away. 'Wouldn't you say?'

'Sick as a dog,' the man agreed. 'And I suspect he will then go on to shit like a racehorse, as it makes its way through ... as we say in our business.'

'What an entrancing picture,' smiled Maxwell. 'Don't let us keep you.' Then, to Jacquie, 'It was Paul. Some perfectly nice child in his Year Nine class this morning gave him one of those evil pasteurised, keep-at-room-temperature-for-a-whole-lifetime-and-still-not-catch-botulism

118

sausage rolls they sell in train stations and the like. You know, "Best Before the Great Exhibition" sort of thing. We can't use the dining room until the tape comes down, so we had a delivery of a whole lot of processed stuff for keeping starvation at bay until we can get the parents mobilised on the packed lunch front. Most of them were ahead of us, in fact, but this little dear, at the centre of things when couch potatoes gather, had bought a few packs to keep the wolf from the door. She had so enjoyed her lesson on the dissolution of the monasteries that she shared her bounty with Paul. With the results that our friend in green conjured up so beautifully.'

'Where is Paul?' she asked. 'And where is the pack of sausage rolls?'

'Paul is in my office, my real office, I mean, the one with the dead spider plant and the film posters. What *is* that supposed to be, by the way?' He was talking rhetorically, really, pointing to a particularly awful print that Mr Diamond thought was Art. 'The sausage rolls are in a drawer in my desk. I didn't want someone accidentally snacking on them.'

She patted his arm. 'You make such a good policeman,' she said.

'Well, after that fiasco with the cocktail glasses yesterday, I thought I had better. And I can't use my other office. Mr Bevell is in there.'

She stared at him. 'Mr Bevell has turned up?'

'Yes. Rather unpleasant individual, turned up this morning. Looks like a weasel in a wizened sort of way. Apparently, he intends to sue.'

'Sue? Who?'

'You sound like a huntsman. Or an owl. Us. The County. For as much as he can get. Dereliction of care, or so he says. He has the number of one of those buy-one-get-one-free solicitors.'

'A what?'

'No, I don't mean that. I mean, no win, no fee.'

'You mean he did that before he visited his wife?'

'Don't be silly, heart face. No, he did that before he came here shouting the odds. He hasn't been to see his wife yet.'

'Aren't people odd?' she muttered, half to herself. 'Look, Max, I've got to do a bit of serious multitasking here. Can you give me a hand?'

'I'll try. But I'm more comfortable with just tasking, if that's all the same to you.'

'Can you ring Henry and tell him what is going on, in broad terms? I need to see Paul, collect the sausage rolls in an evidence bag and get them to the lab, then see Mr Bevell.'

'I'll deal with Mr Bevell, sweetie,' he said. 'He's not as bad as all that. I can cope with the nasty man.'

'No, Max, you don't understand. I'm going to have to take him with me to the station.'

'And add wrongful arrest to his list? They'll be living in tax exile if this goes on.'

'I'll explain later. Meanwhile, can you just give Henry a buzz? I'll pop up and see Paul.'

'I bow to your judgement, oh great and powerful Oz,' Maxwell said, scrunching down to improve his Munchkin impersonation.

'I should think so too,' she said, making for the stairs. The Headmaster's wife must, of course, be above suspicion.

Paul Moss was lying on Max's LEA-issue corner unit and therefore probably looked rather worse than he was, although doubled up seemed to be his position of choice. He was a pale green, not an unattractive shade in its own right, but not really designed to go on a face. He turned his head slightly when Jacquie crept in.

'Hello, Jacquie.' He was so quiet, it was almost as if he mimed the greeting.

'Hello, Paul.' Jacquie sat on the end of the seat, moving his feet slightly to do so. She preferred to keep away from the business end where vomit was concerned. 'How are you feeling now?'

'Better. I've been sick and ... you know. But Sylvia gave me something and I think the worst is over.'

'That's good,' she said, patting his knee. And I hope you're right, she thought, bearing in mind where I'm sitting. She was glad, too, that Sylvia Matthews seemed to be back to her old self, but she didn't say so. Paul was a little too pre-occupied at the moment. 'Can you tell me what happened? I'm sorry to bother you right now, but I need to know the child's name and whether this kind of prank is in character.'

'Prank?' In his enfeebled way, Paul Moss was totally outraged. 'Prank? A bit more than a prank, Jacquie, surely?'

'Well,' she looked down at him. She couldn't describe the colour he was now. It was a kind of enraged purple with green highlights. There was no easy way to say this. 'Well, you're not actually *dead*, are you, Paul? Or even close, as far as I can see. I think that this may just be one of those things. An unfortunate coincidence.' She got up hurriedly as his colour deepened. 'But I will take the offending rolls to the lab, and if you could just let Max know the kid's name, that would be lovely.'

Paul Moss was beginning to scramble to his feet, a desperate look on his face. She moved so as not to be between him and the door as he made a dive in its direction.

'I won't keep you,' she called after him, then, more quietly, 'I suspect this may be more than man-diarrhoea, but you ain't been poisoned to kill you, my dear.' She riffled through the drawers in Maxwell's erstwhile desk and found the sausage rolls in a large Manila envelope labelled 'Sausage rolls. Please do not touch' in an Acting-Headmasterly hand. She put the whole thing into an evidence bag and signed and dated the fold. Then she took herself back downstairs, before the racehorse returned to the couch to suffer some more.

Down in his temporary office, Maxwell was coping with Mr Bevell, although he was privately thinking that perhaps coping was rather an overstatement. He was as wizened as his wife was expansive, half her girth and nowhere near her height, but in all other respects they were the same. The threats of their lawsuits, which Maxwell had inevitably named 'sewage', were multiplying to the point that the Acting Headmaster was hard-pressed to think of anything to say. So far, his commiserations had been threatened with a suit for emotional distress. His offer of a cup of coffee had been greeted with threats of suing for damage to life and lip because it was hot. The drips from the bottom of the cup had permanently damaged the man's trousers. And these were Countryman's, not any old rubbish.

When Jacquie tapped on the door, he jotted down a note of the time.

Maxwell was finally forced into speech. 'Mr Bevell, the lady who has just entered is my wife-to-be. Why did you just write down the time?'

'Just in case I should suffer post-traumatic stress some time in the future. A shock like a knock on the door in my condition could be serious.'

'So the note is a kind of pre-traumatic stress insurance, is it?' said Maxwell, a rather testy tone creeping in to his voice.

Jacquie hastened to interrupt. 'Mr Bevell? May I offer my–'

'No. You may not. If he accepts condolences or apologies, it may impact on any payout in the future. That's according to Miss Grabbit from the no win, no fee solicitors, Ambulance and Chaser,' cut in Maxwell. 'Did you say you wanted to take Mr Bevell down to the station, dear one? Let me get him his coat.'

Jacquie was quite silenced by this sudden desire of Maxwell's to get the man off his property. She thought quickly. 'I'll have to call a car,' she said. 'Unless, of course, Mr Bevell is in his own vehicle?'

'I came by train,' he said. 'My guaranteed seat

was, of course, not available, but rest assured they will be hearing from my solicitors. A man in my situation...'

'Yes, yes indeed,' agreed Maxwell, appearing behind the man with a coat. 'Very difficult for you. Policeperson Carpenter will call a squad car to take you in comfort to the police station. Don't worry, they do that thing where they pat your head to make sure you don't bump it accidentally on the roof. I will just take you out to our specially designed visitors' waiting room, which has passed all tests, both Health and Safety, it also has a current fire certificate and no less than three fire extinguishers. You'll be quite safe there,' and he ushered the man out, beaming broadly, much as Legs Diamond used to do.

Jacquie stood waiting, looking down at her shoes as she rocked gently from heel to toe. She smiled gently to herself and hummed a little tune. When Maxwell came back in she gave him a silent hug of comfort. 'A difficult gentleman,' she said, her voice deliberately without inflection.

Maxwell threw himself into the chair behind Diamond's desk. 'I can honestly say,' he said, 'that I have never met a man who made me want to kill him quite so much. Or so soon. Or so horribly. Slowly. Painfully. Enjoy him at the station, won't you?'

'Ooh!' Jacquie reached for the phone. 'I must call that car,' and she quickly did so.

'I assumed you would take him in yourself,' Maxwell remarked.

'What? And get sued for having a loose sweet wrapper in the car? He might get too hot. Or too

124

cold. How can you live like that?'

'Very comfortably, I would imagine. The reason we couldn't reach him was that he was having a short break at a hotel. He was rather disappointed that he had to stay in an independent, but the Bevells are banned by all the chains, because they keep suing them. And, before you ask, he hasn't got a mobile phone because there isn't a provider who will deal with them. No car insurer will insure them either, and the trains are becoming a bit tricky. But it's a living.'

'You mean ... that's how they make their money? By suing people?'

'Apparently. Although, it often doesn't come to that, because lots of companies just pay out to save the bother. They had to get a cat, because one of the deals was free cat food for life and they didn't want to waste it. The man's a menace.'

'Do you think that *he* might have done the poisoning?'

Maxwell looked thoughtful, then regretful. 'No matter how much I would like to say yes, I don't think that he'd go that far. And not being local, there would be the logistics. No, he's a nasty piece of work, but he didn't do this.'

'What about the attempt on his wife last night?'

'Hmm, possibly. But still, I think, no.' He suddenly banged the desk and sat up straight. 'Damn it, Jacquie, this sue-everybody culture makes me angry. When I was young, you accepted that the aftermath would inevitably follow the math. It didn't have to be anyone's fault.'

She leant over and kissed his empurpling brow. 'Calm down, darling. You'll go off pop.'

He subsided, but ungraciously. 'Well,' he muttered. He looked like Nolan, with his lip stuck truculently out and she suddenly didn't want to leave him. She wanted to stay tucked up in the office with him, while nasty things happened and other people picked up the pieces. But she knew it wasn't possible.

She turned to the door, saying, 'I've got to go, Max. I'll wait with the horrible sod while the car comes, then I'll be off. See you tonight, but I'm not sure what time. Well done with the Coco Pops, by the way.'

'What Coco Pops?'

'At a guess, the friends of the one peeking out from behind your lapel. He always manages to hide one at the last moment, the little rascal. I interviewed a suspected burglar once with one in my eyebrow. It's good for breaking the ice.' She blew him a kiss and was gone.

Maxwell extricated the lurking cereal and balanced it on the end of his finger. 'I wondered where you had gone,' he said to it, before popping it into his mouth. He had decided to stick to food brought from home for the moment. He picked up the phone and buzzed for Thingee One.

'Yes, Mr Maxwell?'

'Thingee, old thing. Has woman policeman Carpenter taken Mr Bevell off the premises?'

'Just going, Mr Maxwell.'

'Excellent. I shall count to ten so they are well and truly gone and then I will be out of the office for a few minutes, while I check on Mr Moss.'

'Yes, Mr Maxwell. I'll hold your calls.'

126

'Hold my calls? How many are you expecting?'

There was a pause. 'Well, there have been thirty-seven so far today, Mr Maxwell. You are the Headteacher, after all.'

'Thirty-seven? I haven't taken that many, surely?'

'No, Mr Maxwell. I have dealt with them, mostly. But I just have to, you know, say "I'll hold your calls". Otherwise you won't know that I'm, well, that I'm...'

'I know. Holding my calls. Thank you, Thingee, you're a diamond; no offence.'

'No, Mr Maxwell,' and he could hear the smile in her voice, 'none taken.' And she rang off. She shook her head indulgently. Mad old bugger, but it beat being condescended to by Diamond. He didn't use her name either, but that was because he couldn't remember it. Maxwell could *remember*, he just *preferred* Thingee and that was all right with her.

Chapter Ten

Jacquie's Ka and the squad car arrived at Leighford nick almost neck and neck. Mr Bevell clambered out from the back seat, already jotting down a few crimes against humanity to which he had been exposed in the short drive from the school.

She deliberately avoided making eye contact with him and scurried up the steps and used the back stairs to Henry Hall's office. She knocked gently.

'Yes?' Henry Hall in full curmudgeon mode replied from inside.

She stuck her head round the door and said, 'Mr Bevell, guv. He's downstairs.'

'He can wait,' Hall said. 'Fill me in on what's been going on. It seems to me that this poisoner of ours is all over town. At the hospital, and now again at Leighford High.'

'Well, guv, it might not be in that order.' Jacquie found a chair.

'By which you mean...?'

'The tablet that Mrs Bevell was given was certainly administered by an unknown assailant in the early hours. The sausage roll was certainly eaten this morning at the school, but may have been tampered with at any juncture. It had been in storage at the warehouse for months, possibly years.'

'Don't exaggerate,' Hall snapped. Oddly for a man of his generation, he had a thing about sell-by dates and food tampering and it was all beginning to get to him. 'Sausage rolls aren't stored for years.'

'These are. They are pasteurised and vacuum-packed to last for virtually ever on a shelf. Once they are opened, they have a normal shelf life, but before that they could be older than the child who buys them.'

'They sound disgusting.'

'I would imagine they are. Paul Moss certainly thinks so. He took one bite and was immediately sick. He has had diarrhoea since then as well. I have the pack of rolls with me and I'll get them to the lab as soon as I can.'

'Did anyone else eat one?'

'I gather that the little girl who gave Mr Moss his treat had eaten about half of the contents, guv.'

'Is she all right?'

'As ninepence. I know kids have cast-iron stomachs, but I think she would have shown some symptoms, at the very least a bit of a gippy tummy.'

'How could just one elderly sausage roll be poisoned in a pack, the rest of which being apparently all right?'

'I don't know, guv. The lab will tell us, I'm sure.'

Hall looked at his sergeant, less convinced than she was. 'Do you have any of the one he had?'

'No, guv, sorry. He managed to make it to the loo to be sick and ... er ... flushed. Same with the...' she looked at her boss. 'Well, you know. So we don't have anything. Unless there is another dodgy one still in the bag.'

'Let's hope so,' said Hall, sipping his tea. 'So,' he steepled his fingers and flashed his blank lenses at her, 'what about Mr Bevell?'

'Oh, guv,' she said, eyes rolling ceilingward. 'How long have you got? He's suing everyone and everything in sight. He is making notes as we speak, no doubt, and is planning a class action against the entire county. I always thought those ads about Deeply Unpleasant Lawyers For You were designed to fill airspace. Mr Bevell was at a hotel overnight, the Excelsior in Reading, so he has no alibi as such. He could have left the place at any time. He travelled the remaining distance by train, so again, nothing he can rely on in court. He is almost the most unpleasant person I have ever met, and yet no, I don't think he tried to kill his wife.'

She filled him in on the details of the Bevells' nice little earner. 'What is it you do, Mr Bevell?' 'I'm a professional shit.' 'Nice one.' Hall looked thoughtful.

'Do you think he might have just intended to make her ill?' he asked, hopefully.

'I suppose that's possible. But it's a risk and also, without a car or local knowledge, almost impossible, I'd say. The lads are still checking the taxi rank but nothing so far. Physically, he fits quite well with whoever it was stole the glasses yesterday, but again, I don't think he could have been in the area and then back at the hotel with no car.'

'Are we sure he doesn't have a car?'

'Apparently they can't get insurance.'

Hall leant back in his chair and blinked rapidly. 'Jacquie, are you saying that this man can't be a murderer because he can't challenge Churchill?' Hall didn't try the take-off of the advert's jowly dog; he left such things to those who could, like Peter Maxwell. 'If someone has murder in mind, I don't suppose a bit of driving without insurance would bother him much.'

'Guv, as a rule, I would agree. But you've got to meet him to understand. The man is a total one-off. Obsessive, but not in a good way.' She looked at him quickly to see if he had recognised the small dig at his pedantic ways. Her luck was in; he had either not noticed it or had decided not to care. She decided to make her escape while the going was good and got to her feet. 'Anyway, these sausage rolls aren't getting any fresher. I'll get them down to the lab boys, shall I?'

'You don't have to take them yourself. Put them in the internal mail.'

'I want them to get there some day soon. I'll take them. It's no trouble. It's only Chichester.'

'As long as you're sure. Don't you want to interview Mr Bevell?'

Her merry laughter as she left his office rang in his ears, and he had to take that as a clue. 'I'll call that a no, then, shall I?' he muttered, picking up the phone. 'Hello? Desk? Is Mr Bevell in an interview room yet?'

The phone squawked at him indignantly.

'I see. Well, I'm not sure you can be sued as an individual if you are doing your designated job.'

131

The squawking got louder.

'As long as you just *want* to give him a smacking, Bill, but don't actually do it, I'm sure it will be fine. I will be down in ten minutes.'

Squawk.

'All right. I'll try and make it five.'

Henry Hall sat back in his chair and tried to calm his rebellious stomach. He'd never been bothered this way before, but unbidden pictures rose in his mind of sausage rolls older than his children, lurking in greening piles in a warehouse, ready to swamp the town. Of langoustines, Marie Rose sauce dripping pinkly from their twitching feelers, lurching down Leighford High Street, calling in shrill, deep-sea voices for revenge. He shook himself, took one more sustaining sip of his cooling tea and went down to meet Mr Bevell, possible murderer, serial suer and all-round unpleasant person. Another day, another dollar.

Maxwell crept into his office and peered over the back of the corner unit to see how his Head of Department was doing. Paul Moss lay in a sweaty heap and he wasn't the sweetest smelling thing Maxwell had had in his office, although he was far from being the worst. But he was asleep and, as Maxwell's granny had always been fond of pointing out, sleep was a great healer. Although nowhere near as great as penicillin, Maxwell's rather more prosaic granddad had always rejoined. And that great knitter, William Shakespeare, had said that it was also a dab hand when it came to ravelling sleeves of care. And Anne

132

Hathaway, or whichever bloke Shakespeare was sleeping with at the time, would probably have tutted in disgust; what, after all, did he know?

The Head of Sixth Form-cum-Acting Headmaster crept back into the corridor and closed the door behind him with infinite softness. He was just leaning on the wall finishing a warning note requesting silence when a noise exploded in his head. Mrs B, cleaner and all-round nosey person, was abroad with mop and bucket.

'Ooh, Mr Maxwell, I hear you been elevatored. 'Bout time, if you ask my opinion. 'Ow's Mr Moss, poor little bleeder? He don't deserve that. I very nearly didn't come in this morning, all that poisoning, you don't know what's in the air, do you? It could still be floating about. I'm surprised these kids are here. If I was their mother I'd keep 'em at home, where I knew what they was eating, wouldn't you, Mr Maxwell?'

'Ooh, Mrs B, I hardly know where to start. Let's see, now.' Maxwell had an uncanny ability to answer Mrs B in the order of her questions, statements or general whiffle. His mind was largely elsewhere today, but he thought he might give it a shot. 'Yes, I have. It is and I don't. He's asleep, hence,' and he fished out a piece of fluffy Blu-tack from his pocket and affixed his note, 'this note saying just that. Umm, where was I? Yes. Didn't you? Indeed you don't. It could, but I doubt it. Are you? Best thing, and I would, should I find myself the mother of approximately one thousand kids.' He beamed. Another full house, nothing left out. And the list had been longer and more tortuous than usual. 'Anyway,

Mrs B, if you could refrain from hoovering while Mr Moss is having a rest, I would be grateful. I'll be downstairs in Mr Diamond's office if you want me.' He looked at her sternly. 'Quiet, now. He's asleep. Sshh.'

'I ain't senile, Mr Maxwell. I ain't got short-term memory loss. I know he's asleep,' she said, her feelings clearly hurt.

Maxwell was contrite. 'I'm sorry, of course you do. What was I thinking?' And he went off down the corridor, feeling a little ashamed of himself. Of course the woman knew how to behave. She wasn't an idiot. Two blameless girls from Year Thirteen came towards him, speaking quietly, heads together, no doubt locked into a deep discussion on Bismarck's motives in the Congress of Berlin. Their little bepumped feet made nary a sound on the corridor floor. He knew what would happen and turned to prevent it, but he was too late.

'Oy!' came the eldritch screech. 'Be quiet. Mr Moss is trying to sleep.'

Maxwell sensed rather than heard the small desperate whimper from the Head of History, curled up in his office. He hesitated for a moment, then did the Acting-Headmasterly thing. He went down to his Other Office and rang Sylvia Matthews' number. Delegation; that was the name of the game and it sorted out men from boys.

Jacquie drove to Chichester and hardly noticed how she got there. This case was a bugger and for once she couldn't seem to see the wood for the trees. It would be foolish to say that Maxwell's involvement had shaken her; Maxwell was always involved sooner or later, usually sooner. But this case had infiltrated his life in a way that she thought could soon get out of control. When you couldn't trust your food, what could you trust? Maxwell could have told her all this was commonplace in the Good Old Days. Unscrupulous retailers mixed chalk with flour, painted fish to make them look fresher, sold slabs of crawling meat. For such things were vindaloo and tandoori invented. But that was then and this was now. A doctored prawn cocktail was relatively unthreatening; all you need do is avoid prepared food. But a random sausage roll in a package bought in a school canteen? An innocent if not terribly appetising piece of snack food had turned out to be an instrument of, if not death, then at least grievous bodily harm. What next? Milk? Eggs? Bread? Water, even? She remembered the case of the Tesco blackmailer, who had terrorised a town by tampering with food. But his reign had been short-lived and he had tipped his hand. He wanted money, pure and simple. But this case was different and she couldn't get a handle on it. There'd been no demands, no proud boasting by some deranged member of the Save the Unborn Gay Whale Lobby. Nothing.

She drove into the car park of the forensic lab tucked discreetly away behind the Pallant and parked. She grabbed her evidence bag of sausage rolls from the back seat. She shouldered the door open and decided to climb the stairs rather than take the lift. This gave her more time to repeat the mantra that everyone who trod that way repeated over and over. 'Please don't let it be Angus. Please don't let it be Angus. Please don't let it be Angus.'

But, as was almost always the case, it was Angus. Angus was a master of the flexitime and could bend it, not just like Beckham, but like Doctor Who himself. Today, he was his own locum and therefore getting double time as himself because it was bank-holiday lieu time and also time and a half as his own replacement. A nice little earner, as he was wont to remark, acknowledging all the time his undying gratitude to Einstein and his continuum.

Jacquie sighed when she saw him. His laconic voice on the end of the phone was enough to make most police personnel turn to the Prozac. Face-to-face, he was even harder to take and when he stood up his head seemed to reach the ceiling. 'Hello, Angus. I have a bit of a rush job, here.'

He shifted his gum to the other side of his mouth, ever the professional. 'Yeah?'

'Yes. It's a suspected poisoning.'

'Dunnit.'

'Pardon?'

'Dunnit, en' I? Yesterday. Phoned results to Hall. Aconite.'

'Or a derivative, yes,' Jacquie agreed. 'But this is another case of poisoning.'

'Dunnit.'

'What?' Her patience was wearing thin.

'Blood test on that woman what had the tablet. Same. Aconite.'

'No. Angus, listen to me. This is not something

136

you have done. This is a bag of sausage rolls from Leighford High School, one of which poisoned a member of staff. This morning.' She looked for some spark of intelligence in his eyes. 'Today.'

He picked up the evidence bag, opened it and shook out the contents onto his counter. 'I hate these,' he remarked. 'They sell them down our all-night garage. I had some last night. They're 'orrible.'

Jacquie knew she shouldn't, but she asked anyway. 'Why did you eat them, then?'

'Munchies.'

Well, that explained part of his personality anyway. 'Right. Well, these were bought today in the school canteen and the thing is that they came from the same place the prawn cocktails did, though obviously packaged, not prepared by the chefs there.'

'Chefs. Ha. That's a laugh. Frozen prawns and ready-made sauce. Not exactly cordon-bleeding-bleu, is it?'

'Well, no. But the difference is that the prawn cocktails...'

'...had been put together by hand, yes I know. Whereas the poison in these rolls had been injected.'

'How on earth could you know that?' she asked. Angus had hidden depths, although she didn't care to plumb them.

He held up the bag. 'Hole,' he said.

She peered at it. 'It's tiny,' she said.

'Course it is. Needle, ennit?'

'Um, yes, I suppose it is. But how do you know it isn't just a hole?'

137

'Be*cause*,' said Angus, as though speaking to a slow child, 'be*cause* if you look, there is a kind of raised rim, yes, can you see it? A bit like a really tiny volcano? Yeah?' He sounded almost enthusiastic in his use of the aptly named moronic interrogative.

'Yes,' Jacquie said, adjusting the distance to suit her eyes. 'Yes, I can.'

'So,' Angus said, triumphantly, 'that's where the needle went in, pushing the plastic, stretching it a little bit and then, when it was pulled out,' and he mimed the movements as he spoke, 'it pulled that little frill out with it. So, unless a weevil or something shot out like a bullet, then it was a hypodermic. In. And out.'

'Angus. You're a marvel,' said Jacquie, fingers crossed behind her back.

He looked down and blushed slightly. 'I know,' he agreed. 'Now then, I'll see if I can find out what the poison was, but don't hang around, it might take me a few minutes. Ha ha.'

Jacquie smiled at him and meant it. She left him her card in case he had mislaid the last one and left the lab. Angus picked up the sausage rolls and went over to the fume cupboard. Triple and a half time and a few quiet minutes with Jacquie Carpenter. Days didn't get much better than this.

The Headmastering lark was turning out to be a bit more work than Maxwell had envisaged. Diamond was not brilliant academically and now, Maxwell thought to himself as he ploughed through mounds of paperwork, he understood

138

why. An intelligent man, skating along the sharp white cutting edge of original thought, would put a ball through his brain after less than a day of this. It was that most irritating of tasks, both boring and difficult. It needed full attention, but to the most mind-numbingly boring subject matter. Time sheets. EMA approval. Memos from days before seemed almost poignant: little billets-doux from Bernard Ryan, with pencilled notes in their margins in Diamond's pernickety hand. Of one thing, though, Maxwell approved. Despite huge pressure from the Paperless Office Company, Diamond had not yet gone totally over to the death knell of civilised behaviour, the endless email.

Maxwell was conscientious in everything he did, be it solving murders, teaching History or being the Acting Headmaster. So he tried not to give in, but then came the memo which made him throw in the towel. An email, printed out despite the County exhortation to save paper, from Bernard Ryan, bore the pencilled comment – 'Yes, Bernard. That is the elephant in the room. JD.'

'That's it!' cried Maxwell. 'I can't stand any more.' He walked to the inner door which led to the office suite and stuck his head round it. 'Michelle!' he yelled. 'Michelle!'

Diamond's secretary came running. 'Yes, Mr Maxwell?' She was finding being the Great Man's secretary rather strange. There seemed to be both less and more to do. Less running to and fro with coffee. More spelling mistakes to correct in her own typing.

'I'm off home. Tell me, does Mr Diamond have *all* his emails printed out?'

'Oh, yes, Mr Maxwell. In triplicate.'

'Triplicate?' Maxwell was not a byword where environmentalists gathered, but he did want there to be a planet for his son to grow up on. Or in, as the case may be. 'I hesitate to ask, but really, why on earth does he do that?'

'One for file.'

'Yes.' He supposed there had to be a paper trail, especially with the standard of IT at Leighford High. After all, had Herr Hitler faced trial at Nuremburg, he would have got off precisely because there *was* no paper trail. What Holocaust?

'One for his personal file.'

'Hmm. That sounds a bit like duplication to me, Michelle. And the third?'

She went a little pink. 'To be quite honest, Mr Maxwell, I can never remember and I don't like to ask Mr Diamond. So I just make the copy, keep it for a while and then...' Her voice died away.

'And then?' Maxwell tried to sound managerial.

'I shred it.'

He tried not to overreact. 'Shred it? But isn't that a terrible waste?'

She brightened up. 'Oh, no, Mr Maxwell. It doesn't go to waste. It goes as bedding for the school hamster.'

He sighed and reached for his coat. He would have to have a word with Ben Holton, the Head of Science, who was clearly running some sort of health spa for rodents in the bowels of his laboratories. 'Bye-bye, Michelle. Have a good weekend now, y'hear?' It was a perfect Beverley Hillbillies but, as Michelle was too young to remember that, largely wasted. Maxwell jammed on his hat and moved towards the outer door, rummaging in his pocket for his cycle clips.

Michelle appeared in the doorway from her office. 'I'm going to see Mr Diamond this evening, Mr Maxwell. Any message?'

He turned, something scathing on his lips. But she looked so anxious to please, so willing, that all he said was, 'Yes. Tell him get well soon.' He walked into the foyer and added under his breath, 'Really *really* soon. Now, where did I leave my bike?'

As Maxwell smoothly took the curve of Columbine in his stride, something struck him as rather odd. A car, not a Ka, was pulled up at the kerb and it seemed to have attracted a small but significant crowd, composed of Mrs Troubridge, a rather unpleasant dog-walking woman who tramped the roads in all weathers accompanied only by a disgruntled Peke and a bag of doggie-detritus, the rather nice woman from over the road and, almost inevitably, Mrs B. As the squeal of Surrey's brakes announced Maxwell's presence, they turned as one woman to stare at him.

Mrs B broke the silence first. 'See, I said 'e'd be along in a minute.' She was proud of how well she knew her man.

'That poor little mite,' said the dog walker. 'Someone should be informed.'

'He would have been perfectly happy with me, wouldn't you, Nolan?' Mrs Troubridge crooned.

141

'I often babysit.'

'Then they should be ashamed,' snapped the dog walker. 'You must be nearly a hundred.'

'I *beg* your pardon,' Mrs Troubridge began, 'I'll have you know...'

Maxwell swung his leg over Surrey's crossbar and came to an elegant stop, more by luck than judgement. He had often ended up in the fuchsias. 'What seems to be the trouble?'

The door of the car opened and Nolan's voice added to the din. 'Daddy,' he carolled. 'Dad-deeeeee.'

'Hello, mate,' Maxwell said, reaching in and ruffling the boy's hair. 'I'll be with you in a moment, but these ladies seem to have a problem.' In best teacher style, he had singled out the troublemaker and spun round to face her. The dog walker took a step backward. She had heard he was mad. 'What, I repeat, seems to be the trouble?' His smile could have turned milk.

'Um, well, I was passing,' she stuttered. 'This child, it appears, had been left on the doorstep.'

'What?' came a voice from the car. 'Nolan, pet, go to Daddy. I must just get out and speak to the silly lady.' Sarah, the owner of Nolan's nursery, erupted like a force of nature from the driver's side. 'Mr Maxwell, I simply brought Nolan home. I know you usually pick him up on a Friday, but Jacquie had explained about things at the school, so when you didn't come, I just brought him here. This woman,' she raked the dog walker with a basilisk glare, 'seems to have got the wrong end of a very strange stick.'

'Well, I'm sorry, I'm sure,' said the dog walker

and stalked off, nose in the air, Peke at her heels.

'She's a nasty piece of work,' said the nice woman from over the road. 'She lets her dog do its business wherever it wants, you know. It's disgusting. That scooper she carries is just for effect.'

The conversation looked set to become a marathon and Maxwell just wanted to take his son and get indoors. To be civil, he asked Sarah in. To his annoyance, she accepted. But before they went inside, he asked Mrs B what she was doing there, Friday not being her day for doing for him.

'I do up the road on a Friday, Mr Maxwell. Mrs Briggs, you know, her with the leg. She can't do the rough.'

Mrs Troubridge bridled. She had heard otherwise. It was reputedly the smooth that got the better of Mrs Briggs.

'So, and you'll forgive me for asking so bluntly, what are you doing actually *here*, outside Number 38, as opposed to being in the general vicinity?'

Mrs B leant in, carefully angling her cigarette end away from the little boy now clinging to Maxwell's leg. 'I was just bein' nosey, Mr M.'

Faced with such devastating honesty and economy of speech from his cleaning lady, Maxwell could only raise an eyebrow and usher his son and his minder in through the door.

Upstairs in the sitting room, Nolan toddled off to persecute Metternich in front of the television. Maxwell and Sarah decamped to the kitchen. She was a good-looking woman in a children's institution sort of way, a slightly wonky Doris

143

Day. Only dark. And no freckles. 'I'm sorry about that, Sarah,' he said, filling the kettle at the sink. 'To be honest, I forgot it was Friday, what with one thing and another.'

'Don't give it another thought, Mr Maxwell,' the woman said, patting his hand. She had always been led to believe that teachers *never* forgot it was Friday. 'This happens all the time, honestly. I'm sorry about the crowd. They just seemed to appear from nowhere.'

'Yes,' he smiled ruefully. 'They tend to do that here in 1984-land. I think they hide under the hedge. But still, Sarah, they were right...' He was interrupted by the phone ringing. 'Hello? Bedlam.'

Jacquie's voice was warm with relief. 'Oh, Max. Thank goodness. You're home. I thought you might have forgotten Nole and everything, what with the poisoning and whatnot.'

'Well, yes, about that...'

Her voice rose to a shriek. 'What? Don't tell me you haven't got him.'

'Not exactly. Look, sweetness, we'll have to have a chat about what to do about this. Until he can reach the keyhole by himself, that is. Sarah brought him home, but it's not really the answer. Mrs Troubridge is too slow for him nowadays and anyway, he's almost as tall as she is.' He looked up and saw Sarah dissolve into giggles.

Jacquie sighed. 'There's only one answer, Max. I'm sorry.'

'We can't sell him, Jacquie. I don't think eBay allows people these days. Not after there was all that fuss.'

'Be serious. I mean that, while you're Acting Head, we'll have to have my mother to stay.'

'Hell's teeth!' wailed Maxwell. 'Not the Wedding Planner?'

'The same. Now, be good boys and I'll be home as soon as I can. With news, I hope, of sausage rolls.'

'And cabbages and kings,' added Maxwell. 'Don't think you can sweet talk me with forensics, woman policeman. There's got to be some sort of deal in this.'

'There is,' Jacquie said. 'Social services don't get to grab the kid. Kisses to Nole and say a big thank you to Sarah for me. Is that the kettle I can hear? Bye-bye.' And she rang off.

Sarah smiled in the embarrassed way that people do when they have overheard a phone conversation. She looked around aimlessly and said, 'What a nice house.' She accompanied the remark with a nervous laugh.

Maxwell poured some water into the teapot and swilled it round, then spooned in the tea. He brought the kettle back up to the boil and added it to the pot.

'I do like to see tea made properly,' the woman said. 'So many people just use a tea bag in a mug.'

He smiled grimly. 'I'm just limbering up,' he said, 'for the visit of Jacquie's mother. We'll have to dust off the doilies and get out the guest soaps. And if you are wondering why we have such things, it is because she has bombarded us with them and their ilk ever since we decided to get married. The fact that we have lived in our own

145

houses for a total of over forty years and have enough stuff to stock a shop seems to have passed her by. We're going to have a bottom drawer and like it.' He peered into the pot and replaced the lid. He looked up. 'Is that brewed, do you think?'

'I haven't a clue. I usually just use a mug and a tea bag.'

He laughed. 'Me too. Let's risk it.' He poured a little. 'Looks all right. Anyway, where was I? Yes, Jacquie's mother. She has planned this wedding about twenty times and that's just so far. She has had Nolan as everything from ring bearer to vicar. The top number for bridesmaids was twelve, but Jacquie beat her down on that.'

'I must say, Mr Maxwell, your ... wife-, er, to-be seems to have a very strong character.'

'Oh yes, that she has. But, and here's the thing, where did she get it from? Not her father, that's for sure, who just died quietly at some point, not wanting to be any trouble and desperate, no doubt, to escape from the wrath of Khan. She means well, of course, Jacquie's mother I mean, not Jacquie.' He sipped his tea. 'It's all right, isn't it? But hardly worth the bits.' He spat out an errant leaf. 'But she is just so single-minded over the wedding plans that I doubt she will ever remember to pick up Nolan either.'

The nursery nurse looked serious. 'Is she able to drive at all?' she asked. 'I think what I mean is, is she an elderly lady, your mother-in-law-to-be?'

Maxwell hooted with laughter. 'Oh yes,' he said, laughing so hard he had to put down his cup. 'Definitely. She's a whole six months older than I am, and I don't let her forget it, oh dearie me, no.'

The woman blushed.

'Please,' he said, leading her through into the sitting room, where Nolan was wrapped round the cat, watching *The Weakest Link*. Either of them was smarter than Anne Robinson. 'Don't think she's not capable of looking after Nole. She's brilliant with him. Although he finds her a bit tiring. You know how you can scare children with tales of the bogey man?'

She nodded.

'We don't need that here. Just mention G-R-A-N-N-Y,' he spelt it out in a half whisper, 'and he's as good as gold. Watch this. Nole?' The little boy turned his head and smiled widely, sensing a party piece coming up.

''Es, daddy?'

'Where's Granny?'

The boy's eyes widened and he looked momentarily frantic.

'Don't worry,' Maxwell soothed him. 'Daddy's just teasing.' He turned to Sarah and said, comfortingly, 'He loves her to bits, as the saying goes. He just needs a bit of warning of her arrival, as do we all.'

'Well, I'm glad to have had some as well, Mr Maxwell. What does she look like, so we'll know her when she picks up Nolan?'

'Hmm, well,' Maxwell pulled his lip thoughtfully. He reached down and scooped up his boy and, inadvertently, his cat, who promptly bit him on the leg. 'Let's think. She looks very like Jacquie, I suppose. But ... bigger. In all directions. You know Jacquie's eyes? Soft and lovely.'

147

Sarah smiled politely.

'Well, they are, take it from me. Like his.' He pointed at Nolan. 'Well, her mother's are the same colour, but like gimlets. And really close together. Think *The Dark Crystal*...' He appeared to be gathering himself together for a minute description, but Sarah had places to be.

'Well, I'm sure we'll know from Nolan's reaction. But even so, it would be good if one of you could introduce her to us, you know, on the first day.'

'I'm sure one of us will,' said Maxwell, silently delegating that one onto Jacquie.

'I'll be off then,' the woman said. 'We can see if the crowd has dispersed.'

'It never completely disperses,' said Maxwell, in a resigned tone. 'It just alters in size and personnel.' He got up, hitching Nolan on to one hip. 'I really can't thank you enough, Sarah, for bringing Nole home.'

'You're welcome,' she said, patting the little boy's cheek. 'See you next week, poppet,' she said.

'And Nolan as well,' added his father, with a chuckle.

With another nervous laugh, she went down the stairs and let herself out. He was just the same as when she had been to Leighford High: mad. At least he hadn't remembered her and her disastrous showing at A Level.

Maxwell watched her go from the sitting room window. It was funny, he thought to himself, how those kids never changed; though she was less like Doris Day than she used to be. She hadn't had much of a sense of humour when she had been at school, either. Although, as he remembered it, she had needed one when her exam results came out.

He turned to face the other men of the family, both staring at him balefully. The news about Granny's visit was out now, and he knew there would be tears before bedtime. Metternich already had secret plans to lie across staircases in the dark.

In the shop on the corner, the lights flashed twice to warn lingering shoppers that the late of 'Eight till Late' had come. The till girls slid down from their stools and flexed their arms, reaching for their coats on the hooks behind them. The owner stood in the doorway that separated one little kingdom from the other. He was probably the last retailer in the Western world to live over the shop. He liked to get upstairs on the stroke of nine, to tuck up his children and eat a civilised meal with his wife before coming back down to check the till rolls against the actual contents and make up the newspaper boys' bags, as far as he could, with magazines which he could take from stock. He was a conscientious, if unimaginative man, the sort of bloke who, along with the rest of the nation, had beaten Napoleon.

So it would have surprised him very much had he found the man, dressed in black like a ninja and with a balaclava pulled down over his face, who was crouching in the space between the wall and the freezer where he usually stored the toilet rolls.

The ninja heard the front door close behind the

149

women as they gabbled out into freedom and then the lights went out and stayed out. It wasn't totally dark, but it was dark enough for what he needed to do. He crept out from his hiding place, and stood rubbing his knee where it had seized up in the cramped space. Then, he reached into his pocket and brought out a small bottle with a rubber bulb on the stopper. Keeping low and taking pains to be quiet, he moved slowly around the little store, placing a drop here, a drop there from his bottle, on bread, on cakes, in milk and orange juice. This was a cut-price store; anyone finding a seal broken or top loosened would put it down to yet another corner being cut, nothing more sinister than careless packaging. Finally, his bottle was empty. Now, all he had to do was wait. He settled back down in his hiding place and savoured an undoctored doughnut he had selected. Then he dozed off.

He was woken by the shopkeeper coming down the stairs and into the shop, snapping on the lights, suddenly bright and neon-strip. He knew that he had very few minutes now, as a window of opportunity. He massaged his dodgy knee in readiness for what had to be a quick manoeuvre. He heard the man open the door and grunt appreciatively. The early editions of the various local papers had been delivered outside. Now came the clever bit.

The man had propped open the door to make carrying in the piles of papers easier. He had picked up a huge stack of the Leighford Advertiser and was carrying it, legs splayed with the effort, to the back of the shop where the newspaper boys' bags were waiting. While he was struggling to get round a teetering tower of cut-price tins without bringing the whole edifice crashing down, the ninja slipped from his hidey-hole and broke into a crouching run, round the bread counter and off into the night. He didn't stop running until he was round several corners. He was both out of breath and safe.

Back in the shop, the owner counted out the papers and magazines. The till rolls and the contents matched to the penny. A happy man, he chose two nice-looking Eccles cakes from the display on the counter and made his way upstairs.

Chapter Eleven

Maxwell dug Jacquie in the ribs. 'Phone,' he muttered, half asleep.

'Who?' she asked. 'Who d'ya want me to phone?' She snuggled back into the pillow and pulled the duvet over her head.

'No, no.' He shook her. 'It is the phone. Ringing.'

'Answer it, then,' she said, indistinctly. 'It might be for you.'

'Don't be a twerp, dear heart. I'm a teacher. We only work thirty-nine weeks in the year, the conscientious ones, that is,' he said, acerbically. 'It's bound to be for you. You're a police person. 24/7.'

'You're a Headmaster,' she reminded him.

'It's Saturday,' muttered Mister Answer-For-Everything.

'Only just.'

She reached out and grabbed the shrilling thing and jammed it to her ear. 'Yes. Carpenter.'

'Is it the walrus?' Maxwell asked facetiously, turning his back. She kicked him as she sat bolt upright.

'Where?' She scrabbled for the pad habitually on her bedside table for times like these. 'What, both of them? Did you mention children? Is someone...? Oh, a neighbour. Is that OK? I'll be right there. Thanks for calling, Josh. Yes, thanks. Bye.'

'Was it for me?' Maxwell muttered.

'It was for me,' she said, so seriously that he unwound from the covers and looked her in the face by the faint light from her reading lamp.

'What was it?' he asked.

'There's been another poisoning. Like Paul Moss, instant vomiting, no collapse as such, but both the victims are very ill.'

'Any connection to Leighford High?'

'Well, in a way. The eldest two kids from the family go there.' She was hopping round the bedroom, trying to avoid getting both legs down one leg hole in her knickers. 'It's a couple from a shop down near the Sea Front. A sort of corner thing, open all hours. Apparently,' she pulled a brush through her hair, 'he usually takes a treat up after they close, for their supper, you know. Obviously, they waited until bedtime, a couple of Eccles cakes to eat with their cocoa. One bite was enough. We have the remainder, on its way to the lab, now. The couple are in hospital.' She leant over and gave him a kiss. 'Name of Barlow.'

Maxwell knew the girl. She was in his top set Year Nine History, a sweet little thing, all eyes and braces. 'How bad are they?'

'Just in for observation, really. But, even so, our poisoner seems to have widened his net. These were not wrapped items, not from the same wholesaler. It seems he's on the loose.'

'I wish I could come with you,' he said. 'I was there at the beginning of all this, don't forget.'

'I would gladly take you with me, Sherlock.' Fully dressed now, she looked down at him as he sat up in bed. 'But there's a little matter of Nolan to consider.'

'True. Although...' he brightened.

She raised a hand. 'No, Max. I know he sleeps like a log. I know he is terribly interested in crime. But he's not coming, and that's flat. What's he going to do? You go high, I go low, we use Nole to batter the door down?'

He sagged and looked pathetic, despite the idea having merit.

'Don't do that, Max. My decision is final. However,' she patted his cheek, 'once Mother is here, you'll be able to hop in the car with me and come and annoy the police again. Just like the old days.'

'Good Lord,' Maxwell said, in frank amazement. 'You've found the silver lining in the cloud.'

'There always is one, beloved,' she said. 'Just like round every fly you'll find ointment. Night, night. See you in the morning.' And she snapped out the light and was gone.

Maxwell lay awake and listened as her Ka accelerated over the hill away from Columbine, making for the Flyover in the still watches of the night. He was fully awake now and his brain was whirring. He tossed and turned and finally got up and crept along the landing and up the stairs to his attic.

He patted the gold-laced pillbox on the top of his hair and switched on his modeller's lamp, sticking and painting, for the use of. Mentally awake he may have been, but his eyes were light years behind his little grey cells and anyway, horse furniture for the 4th Lights was a bitch without real daylight. The lambswool effect alone could take years. Cornet Fiennes Martin would have to wait until after tomorrow's – oops, today's – shopping expedition up the Asda Limpopo.

At least the stars twinkling in the heavens beyond his skylight gave him the incentive to ponder the nature of the universe. Random nibbles had made sure that Maxwell was in his own heaven, yet all was not quite right with the world.

He crossed his legs on the modelling table, careful to avoid the Cornet's not-yet-shakoed head and rested his own on the cradle of his hands. What had he got? Poison. He rummaged in the database of his historian's brain. William Palmer, Neill Cream. Doctors to a man. Graham Young, the St Albans poisoner, who had used the all-but-untraceable thallium. HH Crippen who had signed his own name and address for the hyoscine that killed his wife. A dentist. Herbert Armstrong, slaughtering wife and attempting to slaughter rival in the sleepy little town of Hay-on-Wye long before it became one huge bookshop. Solicitor. But they were all men. Traditionally, Maxwell told himself, poison was a woman's weapon; it had that at-a-distance thing about it, that sense of dispassion and remoteness. Adelaide Bartlett, Florences Bravo and Maybrick – with wives like that, who needed enemies?

Judging from the varying symptoms, he couldn't help thinking that there were two sorts of poison in use in Leighford. Why? Doesn't a poisoner find one that works and stick to it? Was

155

there a supply problem? And where does it come from? Aconite. Aconite. He had a book on it somewhere. It was folkloric, one of those ancient remedies the cunning women used to kill or cure before they invented the NHS. They called it monkshood in some parts of the country, elsewhere blue rocket or wolfsbane. Old Doc Lamson had used it to kill his brother-in-law in 1881 (Maxwell remembered the case well) – the poor lad took five hours to die in agony. Lamson's wife got the £1500 inheritance. *Cherchez la femme* after all.

'Then,' Maxwell found himself talking to the cat, although Metternich was on his third vole of the night, by now somewhere beyond the shrubbery of Number 16, 'we have the administration thereof. We have produce from a County store. We have pre-packed: the sausage roll. We have "freshly made" – note the use of the speech marks. We have stuff open to the elements on a shelf: viz and to wit the prawn comestibles. And now, we have something nasty in the corner shop – details to follow.

'And then, and this is the bitch of course, we have the Leighford High Connection. The first outbreak hits the school like the St Valentine's Day massacre without machine guns and the second is like unto it, only smaller: dear old Paul Moss.'

Maxwell could almost see in the lamplight the grizzled head of his old black and white sparring partner lift at that point, catching his drift before he did. 'A kid?' Maxwell asked the silent Light Brigade. Not a man answered, too preoccupied

156

as they were with the ride of horrors they were about to undergo. 'A kid has it in for Legs Diamond and Bernard Ryan? Of course. Who hasn't? But the candidates for the job? Was that it? Some general pedagogodium – hatred of teachers? Far-fetched even by the standards of the misfits who lurk in the very corner of Leighford High? And who, in their right mind, would have it in for sweet Paul Moss?' A coldness spread over Maxwell like a clammy morning. 'But we're not talking about right minds here, are we, children?'

Maxwell uncrossed his legs, old crusader that he was. Such operations took longer than they used to and he didn't want to risk waking Nolan by crashing back inelegantly on the boy's ceiling. Sylvia, of course, had bumped into Chummy. Or at least, a potential Chummy. Not a kid, she said, but old. Frail. Creaking. Some geriatric wanderer of the night, but out and about in broad daylight. He reminded himself that the school's Site Manager had told all and sundry that the CCTV was on the blink at the moment; all they could hope for was endless reruns of July 28th. Very like Sky TV, really, Maxwell mused.

What about Bevell? Silly name that reminded Maxwell of a screwdriver or something else with a similar edge. What if the other poisonings were mere red herrings? That Mrs Bevell was the actual target? Why go to the lengths of waiting until she got to the interview, chancing his arm in a hostile environment? All right, so he didn't want to shit on his own doorstep; understandable. But shitting on somebody else's was equally fraught with mild peril. *If* he was determined, *if* he was lucky, he had the opportunity. *If* he brought the poison with him, he had the means. But the motive? Is it really worth going down for life to get a few thousand quid in compensation? Perhaps it is; people kill for mobiles, trainers, laffs. It is, after all, Maxwell told himself, a mad world, my masters.

And talking of motivation ... blackmail? Agenda? Mother of God, great circles of logic or lack of it were beginning to rotate slowly over Maxwell's head. It was more than time to go back to bed.

As he switched off the light, he heard a distant cat flap bang. He silently counted the seconds as the great beast slid, like fluid night, up the stairs. A slight pause outside His Boy's room to check that all was well. Then the pounce and the bounce as he landed on the end of Maxwell's bed. With a questioning chirrup he nudged his master's knee.

'Forget it,' muttered Maxwell. 'If you think I'm going over it all again, you're much mistaken.' And he turned over and went to sleep.

There seemed to be someone banging. Maxwell craned his neck to see the time on the bedside clock. Seven-thirty. Why was someone banging at seven-thirty on a Saturday morning? Surely, Mrs Troubridge had given up the DIY after all the trouble with the Gas Board that time. He swung his legs over the side of the bed and fumbled with one foot for a missing slipper. Nolan had started a counterpoint to the banging, a half-furious, half-frightened wail. Get used to it, kid. It's good training for University Halls of Residence, circa 2022. Maxwell went to his bedroom first and scooped him up from his bed. Nolan was very proud of being in a bed and had not yet sussed that in fact it was his cot with the sides off. But random banging which woke him up was still not on his list of acceptable stuff, so he was red-faced and tear-streaked. Maxwell kissed a hot, wet cheek and tucked him under one arm. He ticked the boxes off in his head. Box one: get Boy. Box two: avoid cat sleeping on top stair. 'Nice try, Count, me old Bucko,' he hissed. Box three: find out who was making that appalling din.

The banging was reaching a crescendo as he flung open the door. He and Nolan both gave the same involuntary start as they faced Jacquie's mother, in glorious Technicolor, standing there on the doorstep alongside the most enormous suitcase either of them had ever seen.

'Hello, Granny's little man,' she crooned, kissing Nolan's by now hot, wet and snotty cheek. 'Don't be upset, poppet. Granny's here.' She fixed Maxwell with the gimlet eye. 'Really, Peter, do you not know better than to let him cry himself into this state? Too busy with your books, I suppose.' She stood on the step. 'Are you going to bring in my cases?'

Maxwell looked frantically this way and that. 'Cases?' No, it was no good; he could only see the one.

'The others are in the boot of the car.'

'The others. Well, yes, I'd be delighted. May I get dressed, first?'

159

She looked him up and down and then scanned the road outside. 'It's not very busy, Peter, and it's a lovely morning. I'm sure you'll be all right in your pyjamas.'

'Will you take Nolan, then, so I can carry them? Otherwise...' But she was gone, up the stairs and into the kitchen, from where the Maxwell men could hear appalled clucking. They looked at each other. 'OK, my little bloke,' Maxwell said to his son. 'If you pick up the cases, I can carry you and we'll cut out the middleman. What do you say?'

Nolan's wide eyes and the thumb quietly inching its way into his mouth were answer enough. Post-traumatic stress disorder. Maxwell knew the symptoms well. You didn't need the Gulf War. You just needed to meet Jacquie's mother of a morning.

'Enough said, fella. I'll take you upstairs and then come back for the cases. Since she is happy that the road is empty, then we'll assume there are no hidden burglars, shall we?' He hitched the boy up his side a bit more and toiled up the stairs. 'I'm just popping Nole back in bed for a minute,' he called into the kitchen. 'Then I'll bring your cases in.'

There was no reply, but Maxwell had learnt that that did not necessarily mean assent. Jacquie's mother, after all, had no real understanding of English jurisprudence. But since there seemed to be no argument either, he went back down the stairs and, some ten or fifteen increasingly breathless minutes later, had her cases stowed in the spare room, his son installed on his play mat in the sitting room and his mother-in-law-to-be provided with a large cup of tea and a biscuit. And it was still only ten to eight.

She sipped her tea and nodded approvingly. 'Nice cup of tea, Peter,' she said.

'I wish you'd call me Max,' he said. 'I hardly know who you are talking to when you call me Peter. Even my own mother only used it when she was cross with me.'

'What did she call you, then?'

'A variety of endearments, probably too embarrassing to discuss now. But I've been Max to everyone for so many years that I hardly answer to anything else.'

'Well, I'll try,' she said. 'After all,' and she tried to keep the incredulity from creeping into her voice, 'you are marrying my daughter.'

'Indeed I am,' Maxwell said. 'And very lucky I am, too.'

'Where is she, by the way?' Jacquie's mother looked aimlessly around, as if hoping to spot her daughter lurking somewhere. 'I didn't see her car.' She'd caught sight of the ghastly paintwork, however. Corn in morning. Uggh.

'No, she was called out in the night. It's this poisoning case she's working on. There was another incident and she had to dash off.' Maxwell looked more closely at her. She had stopped sipping her tea and was looking at it in horror. 'Not *everything* is poisoned, Mrs Carpenter. Certainly not this tea. The bags have been on the shelf for weeks and the poisoning only started the day before yesterday.' Even as he said it, Maxwell

161

could hardly believe his ears. So much had happened in just two days, it seemed like months.

'If I am to call you Max, Max,' she smiled over the rim of her cup and for a moment she looked so like Jacquie that Maxwell did a double take, 'you must call me ... well, what do you want to call me? Not Mum, surely?'

'Would you mind if I didn't?' Maxwell asked. 'It's an age thing, really. Can't I just call you by your name?'

'Like you, I've never used it much. Jacquie's father always called me "Darling" or something similar. Having you call me "Betty" makes me feel I'm at work.'

At that moment Nolan, with the perfect timing he had inherited from his father, turned from his toys and, with a grin, pointed at his grandmother and said, very clearly, 'Ninja!'

'My word,' she said. 'What a compliment!'

'And what a brilliant name,' Maxwell laughed. 'Ninja it is, although I will try to stick to Betty in public. People might not understand.'

So Jacquie walked in on a happy family scene; not the one with the blood and feathers she had been imagining all the way up the stairs, having seen her mother's car at the kerb. 'Hello, chaps,' she said, kissing her men. 'Hello, Mum. You must have set off early.' She made a small grimace over her mother's head at Maxwell. It spoke volumes, but it came from the one labelled 'Love You – Sorry' on the spine.

'Not at all, dear,' her mother said, giving her daughter a cheek to kiss. 'We've had a lovely time.' She drew back and gave Jacquie a shrewd glance. 'You look tired.'

'Well, I would do,' Jacquie said, testily. 'I've been up since midnight. And I didn't get to bed till eleven.'

Maxwell stood up and went over to her. 'Nice cuppa tea?' he asked.

'No, thanks. Not even a horrible one. I just want to get a quick shower and then a lie-down.' She looked at her mother. 'Mum, do you mind? I'm pooped.'

'Of course you are, dear,' her mother said. 'Look, I'll give Nolan his breakfast while you two have a chat and then Max can settle you down, can't you, dear? What does he have, something like groats or rusk?'

While Jacquie digested the 'Max' and the 'dear', Maxwell explained that actually the only cereal to pass her grandson's lips at the moment was Coco Pops. And the trick with giving him those was to stand well clear and have a friend check you over before you next went out in public. Before she could launch into the cereals given to babies in her day, when that nice Mr Asquith was at Number Ten, Maxwell and Jacquie had made a break for the stairs and freedom.

While Jacquie had her shower, Maxwell got the guest room ready. That meant moving the huge stack of books from the floor. At least that gave him a chance to look up a few old friends. Schama. Tawney. Trevor-Roper. Even JH Elliott lay in the pile. They all found their historical way into the wardrobe while Maxwell removed the Metternich hair which had woven itself into a facsimile of the great beast on the foot of the

163

duvet. When he heard the water switch off, he went back into their bedroom and closed the door. Jacquie emerged from the bathroom in a waft of steam and lay on the bed with an arm over her eyes. He poked her on the leg.

'Oy. Sleeping Beauty. Can you stay awake for a minute longer? I'm agog.'

'Hello, Gog,' she muttered. 'What do you want to know?'

'Means. Motive. Opportunity.'

'Whether they are still alive?'

'That too, of course.' There was a pause. 'Poor people. I hope they are all right.'

'Don't overdo it.' She sat up and arranged the pillows behind her back. 'As a matter of fact, they are fine. They are staying in until tomorrow for rest and recuperation. The children are at an undisclosed location in case it was targeted, but we don't think it is.'

There was a pause.

'It was the Eccles cake, by the way.'

'That makes sense. I never liked them ever since I realised they were named after a Goon. Anything else in the shop got at?'

'Oh, don't. That's a huge task. I've never seen so many extra SOCOs drafted in. They've had to strip the shop and test everything: every wrapper, every cap, every bun and loaf. It will take days. Angus is totting up the overtime as we speak.'

Maxwell chuckled. He had heard about Angus. 'Do they have the poison, yet?'

'They haven't pinned it down, but it isn't anything meant to be fatal, we don't think. It is an emetic of some kind and, of course, could be

164

dangerous in someone very old, very young or already ill. But really, it isn't that important. The poisoner seems to have turned from precise targets to random ones and that's the worry. He–'

'...or she,' chipped in Maxwell.

Jacquie looked doubtful. 'Yes, or she, but it was a man who pushed Sylv over.'

Maxwell shrugged. 'Go on.'

'He, the poisoner, could have laced every shop in Leighford with noxious substances by now. He wouldn't have had to put it in many things. It could just slumber away in freezer cabinets for days, weeks, months until someone buys it, then uses it. Imagine, if he has contaminated something like a pack of dried mushrooms, a Pot Noodle, something you buy against the day. It could be next year before it gets used.'

They sat for a moment in a shared and silent ponder. 'But, fragrant one,' Maxwell said, 'that sets us a bit of a problem, surely.'

'What, another? As if we didn't have enough already. What is it?'

'Well, at first, we thought it was someone who had targeted the school. Then we thought it was Mr Bevell. Now it's random. And possibly a bit of a time bomb. Why would anyone want to poison randomly over what could become years? Isn't gain the only motive left? And no one has asked for money or made contact with the police in any shape or form.'

'It hasn't been long, Max. Only two days.'

'So I keep telling myself. What do we do, then? Just wait and see? I think you'll find that the good burghers of Leighford won't do that. Excuse the

165

pun. The school didn't have half the kids it should have on Friday. As soon as this latest little bit of fun gets into the news, the schools will be empty, the shops as well. People feel very strongly about food. It's deep in those lizard brains we still carry in our heads; it's a nurture thing, a trust thing. Giving food is love; parents don't risk poisoning their kids. What you put in your mouth isn't supposed to kill you. The phrase is to die *for*, not *of*. Most people carry enough food for a week or so, if not more, in cupboards and freezers. I think those stores will get a bit of an airing in the next few days.'

Jacquie looked at him, through sleepy eyes. 'Are you serious? The town will grind to a halt?'

'Trust me on this one, heart. An historian is never wrong. Want to start a panic? Stand by the bread counter in Asda and shout "I hear there's a bread shortage" and you'll be killed in the stampede. Death by housewife. *This* historian can tell, too, that you are nearly asleep. Snuggle down now, and have a kip. Ninja and I will see to Nole.'

'Hmmm,' she said, sleepily. 'I think I will close my eyes for a...' She sat up suddenly. 'Ninja?'

But all she heard in reply was a chuckle and his soft footsteps on the stairs.

Downstairs in the dining room, a small battle was being waged and at this early stage it was hard to tell who was winning. Nolan seemed to have the upper hand; he had after all got his Coco Pops. But Nolan's grandmother had a secret weapon. In order to be his grandmother she first had been his mother's mother and that role had taught her

166

much. She had learnt negotiating skills that would put most SWAT teams to shame. Move over, Kevin Spacey. So she had introduced to the breakfast table some slices of wholemeal toast which she had spread with organic marmalade. She was eating them with extravagant enjoyment and Nolan's interest was piqued. His spooning was automatic but lacked its usual enthusiasm. Maxwell noted with amusement that he had hardly any cereal in his hair and absolutely none up his nose. This woman would take watching. Who could tell what she might think of next? Straight bananas? The Boy chewing his food forty times?

He sat down next to his son. 'Nice brekker?' he asked, in a casual tone.

'Mmm,' said the boy, still watching his chewing grandparent.

Maxwell smiled at his mother-in-law-to-be. 'Clever Ninja,' he remarked.

'If you say so,' she smiled. 'Toast?' She pushed the plate towards him.

Maxwell toyed with raising a glass to someone like 'The King Over the Water' or 'The Little Gentleman in Velvet', but only Nole would get it, so he settled for a feeble, 'No thanks. I know that wholemeal toast tastes like the burnt remains of a budgie cage bottom. But keep up the good work; I think Nolan might be fooled.'

There was a silence, broken only by Nolan's spoon clinking on the bowl. Then Maxwell spoke again; this time there was no humour in his voice, no room for doubt.

'Betty. Sorry to be so formal, but this is serious.

If you take Nolan out for a walk, or a drive, please don't buy him any food or drink. Take everything with you. Take a flask for yourself as well.'

'But surely, Max,' she said. 'Something like an ice cream? Or a bottle of juice?'

'No,' he said. 'Nothing is safe. A perfectly innocent couple were poisoned last night by an Eccles cake from their own shop. The police haven't found out yet what the poison is; in fact, they are referring to it as a noxious substance, which to me sounds worse than plain old arsenic or strychnine, but there you are.'

'Are they going to be all right?' Betty asked anxiously.

'Yes, I believe so. But at Leighford High School someone died and others are in a very serious condition. A teacher was given something horrible yesterday; he's all right now, but feeling pretty ropey, Jacquie says. There was another attempt on one of the original victims in the hospital. But now it seems to have become much wider, more random. And so that's why I'm saying, don't let Nole have anything to eat outside. It will need planning; the child is like a dustbin. Take crisps, biscuits, juice boxes. Pack as though you are going on a safari even if you just go to the end of the road. I don't want you to be driven by his yelling to buy him something.'

'Give me a bit of credit,' she bridled. 'I have brought up a child, you know.'

'Yes,' Maxwell said gravely. 'And may I congratulate you on an excellent job. But that was a while ago now, I'm sure she wouldn't mind me saying, and I can't imagine that Jacquie had a

168

pair of lungs on her like his, and although I grant you she is a very determined woman, she has passed on the stubborn gene times ten to her son.'

Betty looked at him, head cocked on one side. 'I wonder where the other nine parts came from,' she remarked to no one in particular. Then, she swept the plates and mugs up and carried them into the kitchen. 'Don't worry,' she said. 'I'll guard him with my life.'

'I know you will,' he said, and bent to kiss his little boy's head. 'I know you will.' But, alone in that house, he knew that, sometimes, even your best isn't good enough. That the wet road, the speeding car, the innocent bar of chocolate, can rob you of all you love.

Saturday lunchtime came and went. Jacquie's store cupboard was perhaps not quite as well stocked as Delia Smith's, but it beat Old Mother Hubbard's into a cocked hat. She and her mother calculated that, as long as ravening hordes did not descend on them, they were good for a fortnight, give or take. It might get a bit boring towards the end, but as long as they paced themselves on the pasta, it should all go well. They wouldn't have to do a General Gordon and kill their favourite camel. Metternich, now, might be different... And by then, well, the poisoner would be caught or they would all decamp to Grandma's house or shop at a distant Tesco, far from Leighford.

A siege mentality had descended on 38 Columbine. Maxwell felt like singing a few

169

wartime standards from his Vera Lynn Songbook and had indeed let fall a few platitudes about planting carrots for the night fighters, joining the parson in parsnips and listening to Lord Haw Haw on the wireless, until silenced by Jacquie. Nolan's car seat had been relocated in Ninja's car, with only one pinched thumb and a small amount of language calculated to make a mother-in-law-to-be bridle, and he and his grandmother had driven off for a bracing walk along the Dam. Maxwell had seen them off with a tightened throat and a sick feeling in the pit of his stomach. He knew she would look after him. He knew she wouldn't let him eat anything. He had told her so many times how important it was that she had finally told him rather tersely that, although his son was not a Gremlin, she didn't intend to feed him, before or after midnight.

As they waved them off, Jacquie and Maxwell held hands so hard it hurt.

'He'll be all right,' she whispered. 'Don't worry.'

He gave her a hug. 'I can't promise that,' he said. 'But I promise I'll try not to run up to the Dam and follow them to make sure.'

'That's good enough for me,' she said. 'Now, I have a bit of a surprise for you.'

'Ooh, goodie. I assume it isn't coffee and cake at our favourite rendezvous?'

'Better. It's coffee and a biscuit in Henry Hall's office. I rang him at home before I came down from my nap. I told him what you said, about the food panics and how it might all go. He wants to have a chat with you, see if you might be able to see a connection between all these different cases. He doesn't want to face the fact that we may have a mass poisoner on the loose, but he can't ignore it.'

'Henry Hall wants to see me? Again? I thought I annoyed him enough on Thursday.'

'Apparently not. You must be slipping.'

'Second time lucky, then. Is there a set time? Do I have time to do my hair?'

'Max. Stop taking the piss. But you might want to put some shoes on. After that strange ensemble you were wearing last time, we want to try and make a good impression, don't you think?'

Maxwell looked down at his feet. He was wearing the slippers given him by the Ninja last Christmas, and he agreed that mules made to look like pints of Guinness perhaps didn't give the impression of coherent intelligence that he wanted to convey. He held a finger in the air and trotted back into the house. He came back a few minutes later, suitably shod and twirling Jacquie's car keys round his finger.

'Off we go, then,' he said, hopping into the car. He bent round to click shut his seat belt and could scarcely prevent a small scream of alarm when he straightened up to find Mrs Troubridge's face pressed against his window. He rolled it down, stretching her cheek in a disconcerting George A Romero moment as he did so.

'Mr Maxwell,' Mrs Troubridge trilled. 'I couldn't help noticing that dear little Nolan was taken away just now. Social Services can be so interfering, can't they?'

'Pardon?' Maxwell was, as was so frequently the

171

case, completely flummoxed by the old bat's thought processes.

'That rather boot-faced woman who took Nolan away. Social Services, had it written all over her. I knew that woman with the dog was going to ring them. After he was abandoned yesterday, you know.'

Jacquie leant across Maxwell and said curtly, 'My mother, Mrs Troubridge. Nolan's granny. Come to stay for a while. And if the woman with the dog has so much as picked up her phone, she will be so sorry. If she doesn't disinfect the entire pavement every time her dog farts, I'll have her up for fouling, just see if I don't. Sorry, must go.' And she pressed the window button and they watched in horror as her face rose up pressed to the glass. The memory of the eye disappearing behind spare cheek until she broke away with a faint plop would revisit them in the watches of the night for years. 'Mad old bat,' she muttered, reading Maxwell's mind as she slammed the Ka into gear. 'Social Services, indeed.' She drove in silence for a while, then, 'Boot-faced. Hah!'

Maxwell knew better than to speak. It was an odd conundrum that, although Jacquie looked like her mother, the features that they shared had been distributed in different ways. On Jacquie, they were attractive, open, regular and downright gorgeous. On her mother, they had come to-gether to resemble a boot. Nature could be cruel. He stifled a small smile. No point in antagonising her. He had a long way to go and must be steady.

Chapter Twelve

Henry Hall was rather undecided about weekends. On the one hand, he didn't have to go to work. On the other hand, if he stayed at home he would be roped in to painting something, digging something or going off on what Margaret called 'a lovely long ramble' with another couple who seemed to wear seven-league boots as a matter of course. So, when work called, he didn't really mind. Alice had the IQ of a lamp base and Norman sold insurance; nuff said. He usually had to put up with token resistance at home, but this time his wife almost shoved him out of the door. That lizard brain that Maxwell had identified was working overtime already in Margaret's head. Contaminated food was the start of the end of the world and her man could stop it in his tracks. Superman. Mighty Mouse. The Incredible Hulk. He stirred his coffee moodily and raised the mug to his lips. As he took his first sip, his heart skipped a beat and he waited to see if it would manage another. All was well – for a start, he could tell by a strange old-damp-shoe taste at the back of his throat that the coffee had been in the canteen for more years than he could tell.

He needed his caffeine at the moment. He was at least one man down, with Bob Davies suspended, and it was hard to make the rota work without him. The man may be a menace to many sections of polite society, but at least he was a name to put in the box. And pressing forward with his case wasn't going to be easy. There was no reply from his landline or mobile and the ex-Mrs Davies was not much help; as far as she was concerned he was too near if he was on Mars, coming, as she did, from Venus. He plied his eraser again as he discovered he had used one person three times in one time slot. He knew most of them could manage two, but three *was* pushing it a bit. As though to save him from himself, there was a tap on the door.

'Yes?' he called. It wasn't like him, but he was feeling a bit jittery. The place was too quiet; he wasn't used to it.

Jacquie's head popped round the door. 'Are you free to see us, guv?' she asked.

'Come in, come in,' he waved a hand to encourage her further. As a rule, he would run a mile from asking Maxwell anything, but this case didn't seem to hang together by his reckoning. And yet, the chances of random poisonings being unrelated just seemed to be off the scale of probability. 'Have a seat. Coffee?'

'Is it old?' asked Maxwell, suspiciously.

Hall peered into his mug. 'Judging by the oily sheen, I should say ... very.'

'I'll have some, then,' the Great Man said. 'It's become my new diet. I will accept old food, as in, known to the donor for some while, only.'

'That will be a little self-limiting, as time goes by, surely,' Jacquie piped up.

'Distant food, then, that will be the next level,' Maxwell said, placidly. 'Followed by, and heaven

174

forfend, foreign food.'

'I never had you down for a picky eater,' Hall said. 'I'm sure I remember Jacquie mentioning Chinese takeaways.'

'Indeed,' Maxwell smiled. 'Chinese, Indian, Thai, Korean, Mexican. Even, on one memorable occasion, Mongolian. That one gave a whole new meaning to the term "yak!" I can tell you. But the thing about all these takeaways is they were taken away from venues within about two miles from my home. No, when I say *foreign* food, I mean, food from not round here. Not *local*, you might say.' His League of Gentlemen expression, though fleeting, made Henry Hall jump perceptibly. He found himself staring into Maxwell's nostrils, wondering if he'd ever leave.

'Guv, Max is serious. I think we ought to get ready for panic.'

Hall pushed himself away from his desk and got up to look out of his window. The view took in a corner of the High Street. He turned back to them and gestured. 'The crowds down there don't look like an angry mob. They are just doing their shopping in the usual way. Picking over the oranges on the market stall, but looking for juicy ones, not needle marks.'

'That's today,' Maxwell said. 'But wait until the news of the poisoned Eccles cakes gets out and it will be like a ghost town, I promise you.' He had a year or two on Henry Hall; Maxwell remembered *Panic in the Streets*. Hell, he remembered the run on the banks in 1797.

Hall sat back down and pulled his chair up to his desk. He took up a pen and turned to a clean

175

page on his pad. 'Let's assume you are right then; not about the panic, I don't buy that, but about a random poisoner. How are we going to deal with him or her and why has it started now?'

'Why not now?' Maxwell came right back at him. 'I don't think we're talking full moon or anything. I think the Leighford High poisonings began it and for some reason it has continued.'

'What are your views on Mr Bevell?'

Maxwell shuddered. 'Nasty gent. The sort you boys used to be allowed to give a good smacking in the good old days. But not our man.'

Hall sighed. 'I agree. We've had to let him go. He's at the hospital now, I believe, guarding his wife and making notes. Apparently, he is allergic to the flowers belonging to Miss Mackenzie in the next bed and is planning a lawsuit for emotional distress. Interflora could soon be a thing of the past.'

'How heart-warming,' Jacquie said. 'I didn't see him for many minutes, but he seems a real diamond geezer.'

'Salt of the earth,' agreed Maxwell. 'But, talking of geezers, how are the rest of the staff? I suppose I should visit them, in my Acting capacity.'

'What?' Jacquie chuckled. 'Like the Prince of Wales does when there's been a train crash?'

'Similar. More like comforts for the troops, but I get your drift,' Maxwell replied.

Hall turned back a page in his notepad. 'Not much change, really. Mr Ryan is still in a bad way. They say they may be looking at permanent liver damage in his case, although it's early to be sure. James Diamond is back on the main ward, but still on drips and things. Miss Mackenzie and Mrs Bevell are on the main ward, side by side, as I said. Miss Smollett, having done quite well, is giving cause for concern, but in her case they think it may be a hospital bug, C. difficile or something suitably horrific. Helen...' he looked down his list, 'Maitland is sitting up as best she can on traction and giving the nurses a pretty hard time, from what I can gather. Apparently, one of them offered her a Zimmer frame to take home with her.'

Maxwell and Jacquie both pursed their lips and shook their heads. 'Not a good idea,' said Jacquie.

'I gather not.' Hall's face had not changed. 'Is that everyone?'

Maxwell counted on his fingers. 'Yes. Mrs Bevell must have the constitution of an ox, if she's back on the ward. She had another dose, didn't she, on Thursday night?'

'Yes, she did. But it didn't contain much and, of course, she was still on the antidote, so it really hardly touched the sides. As soon as she was well enough, we had her moved. It was easier to keep an eye on her on the main ward.'

'How did Mr Bevell take to that?'

'Well, I think he has cut a few noughts off his compensation claim, but he does, amazingly, seem glad she is getting better.'

'So,' Maxwell said. 'Let's recap. It isn't Bevell.'

There was a long pause, filled with the faint sound of the shoppers and traffic in the street below.

'Yes?' Jacquie prompted.

'That's it,' Maxwell said. 'Apart from you, me

177

and Henry here, it could be absolutely anyone.'

Henry Hall sat so still he looked frozen, his lenses reflecting the ceiling looked opaque with condensation or frost. Then, one finger on his right hand started to drum lightly on the top of his desk. As if the movement had galvanised him into action, he suddenly leant forward. He grimaced, like the shine on the barrel of a gun. 'Well, both of you. Thank you for coming in. Jacquie, if I could see you first thing on Monday, that would be good. Mr Maxwell,' he stuck out his hand, 'thanks.'

Maxwell didn't move. 'Just because I don't actually know in detail who it is, it doesn't mean I don't have some ideas.'

Hall sat back down. 'Oh?'

'Well, it's quite easy to get to quite a short list or, to be more accurate, a list of lists, all of them short.'

Hall pulled his pad back into the centre of the table. He hated working with Maxwell. He was Adrian Monk, Jessica Fletcher and Jane Marple all rolled into one. Except that he wasn't reading from a script and he was madder than any of them. 'Go on.'

Maxwell cleared his throat and pushed back his chair. 'May I walk about? It's how I think best.'

That would be the Monk in him coming out. Hall had to stop watching daytime television. 'Help yourself.'

'Firstly, we need to know if there is anyone with a grudge against Leighford High, specifically. On that list, we need to put any staff who have left under a cloud, any pupils who have done likewise

178

or who, perhaps, hold us responsible for bad results, bad university choices, all that kind of thing.'

'Are we listing these people?' Henry asked, nearly as aware as Maxwell that he was talking telephone book proportions.

'No, we're listing the lists, Henry. Please try and keep up.'

Jacquie winced; the men in her life at each other's throats she could live without.

'Then, we need to juggle that list in two directions – narrow it to people who might have grudges, personal or professional, against anyone senior at Leighford High, and expand it to cover any of the interviewees. That would include exes, would-be exes, neighbours from hell, pupils again, but more focused. You might have people who are owed money, or who owe money. Black-mail victims, though that is a bit Agatha Christie. All right so far?' Hall and Jacquie nodded. 'Good.'

Maxwell was circling the room. 'Before we spread our wings over the poisoned shopkeepers, we check down the categories and give them a tick for likely and a cross for unlikely, when looked at across the board. So, we have the grudges against the school in general. Now, obviously, they could run into hundreds, but we would soon sort out the likely psychopaths from the unlikely perfectly pleasant members of society. I could probably do that off the top of my head in very few minutes, but I don't think I need to, because of the poisoning of Mrs Bevell in Leighford General.'

'I see,' Hall was getting the hang of this. 'Someone with a grudge against the school would have targeted Diamond or Ryan, not Mrs Bevell.'

'Correct. Unless they wanted to make the school look bad, rather than personally injure someone from there.'

'True, but unlikely. What was the code for that, again?'

'It should be a cross,' said Jacquie, 'but I think it should be a cross in brackets.'

'Fair point,' said Maxwell. 'So that brings us to the second category so far, which is a personal grudge. Now, this is more difficult, because obviously, we don't know who they are, as we don't know all the personal ins and outs of the people involved. Your people will no doubt be on this already, Henry. But what I would say here is that the list of people intended to be victims may be larger, or even completely different, from the people hurt or killed. A prawn cocktail is not a weapon known for its deadly aim. For this one, Henry, I think you will have to send out a whole load of coppers door to door and be ready for lies.'

Hall made a cryptic note in the margin. Grannies and eggs.

'The next category goes off on one slightly. The murderer, who, by the way, may not have intended to be a murderer at all, may have just been firing a warning shot. It may have been the opening ceremony for his little spree.'

Hall looked up. 'That sounds quite likely,' he remarked.

'And if it is,' Jacquie said, 'Sylvia and I should put our heads together for a description of the

180

person who stole those glasses. It's the only concrete thing we have. If Mr and Mrs Barlow and the victims at the school show any names or places, clubs or things like that, in common, then we more or less have our murderer on a plate. If not...'

Hall raised an eyebrow.

'If not, then I'm sorry, Henry, we're back to intuition and luck.'

'But, if you think the thing was targeted like that, why do you also expect a panic and more poisoning?'

'That's the thing, isn't it?' Maxwell came back to his seat and sat down, lacing his fingers over his midriff and looking between the two police people. 'I think he's got to like it.'

On Hall's desk, the phone rang. 'Excuse me,' he said and picked it up. 'Hall. Yes, they're here. Which one?' He held out the phone to Jacquie. 'Your mother?'

Jacquie looked quizzically at Maxwell and took the receiver from her boss. 'Mum?' The men saw her face darken and she seemed to stop breathing. 'Where are you? Have you phoned the paramedics? Well, we'll go straight there, then.' She handed the phone back to Henry Hall and took a deep breath. 'That was Mum,' she said, rather redundantly. 'She was taking Nolan for a walk on the Dam when she met some other walkers. They got chatting and ... one of them must have given Nolan something, because suddenly, he was being sick. They're on the way to A&E.' She reached for her bag and fumbled in it for her keys.

Maxwell and Henry were both on their feet.

181

Maxwell put his arms round her and held her tight. Henry was more practical.

'I'll drive you,' he said. 'You're in no state,' and he shepherded them in front of him to the stairs. Sometimes, thought Maxwell in a small, calm side road in his head, you could really tell why Henry is where he is. Then the mad traffic of panic took over and he let himself be taken where he needed to be: with his little boy.

Henry Hall was just the sort of driver they needed at that moment. Economical with mad screaming gear changes and gestures at idiots who shouldn't be on the road, very generous with taking the lights at amber and cutting up dithering shoppers. The siren was tucked away in his glove compartment, but he decided to keep that in abeyance; he didn't want to freak out the couple sitting white-faced in his back seat any more than he had to. He was a father, but he didn't have to be to understand how they were feeling. The pool of sick despair in the pits of their stomachs which drowned any little bits of hope that they might be able to conjure up; wanting to get to the hospital in a second, whilst not wanting to get there at all. This was Schrödinger's cat made real. While they weren't there with the boy he was possibly all right. When they got there, they would know the news and, if it was bad, it would be real. If they had had the time to catch his eye in the rear-view mirror they would have seen the real Henry Hall for the very first time, with feelings showing behind those eyes.

Soon, either too soon or not soon enough

depending on the point of view, they were slowing and stopping under the canopy of the A&E at Leighford General. Jacquie and Maxwell, showing a turn of speed that Hall could not have expected, were out of the car and in through the double doors before he even had the handbrake on. Other mortals would then have gone off to park. Henry Hall just left the car where it was, flashing his badge at the rapidly approaching jobsworth porter, stopping him in his tracks. Just one of the little perks of office he secretly enjoyed.

He found Maxwell and Jacquie talking earnestly to a woman in the waiting area. Even here, the indefinable smell of a Third World hospital hit his nostrils. Any day now they'd empty the vending machines of anything vaguely tasty and bad for you, and the picture of abject misery would be complete. The woman was wringing her hands and Hall didn't need to be told who she was. He was seeing into the future of Jacquie's face if, in the intervening years, someone took his sergeant's face and gave it a hard squeeze. Add a jaundiced view of life, mix in a little venom and misery and you ended up with Jacquie's mother.

'Guv, Henry, this is my mother,' Jacquie was saying. The niceties, he thought, wryly, even at a time like this. Ever the professional. He caught Maxwell's eye and took the woman by the elbow.

'Mrs Carpenter,' he said. 'Let's just sit over here for a moment and let Max and Jacquie see how Nolan is. You've had a shock. Have you got a cup of tea?'

The woman shook her head miserably.

'Would you like one?'

She made a gesture as if to push him away. 'No! I've got a flask. I'm not to have anything outside. I'm not to let Nolan...' and she subsided in floods of tears.

He patted her shoulder, in a patently foreign gesture. 'There, there,' he said, as if surprised at himself. 'Let's get you a drink of water.'

She looked up and was about to speak.

'From the tap. I'll let it run for a while. Don't worry.' He went off to get it and she slumped over, her hands between her knees in total despair.

A nurse in pale blue came scurrying out from behind a pair of double doors beyond the waiting room.

'Mr and Mrs Carpenter?' she asked.

'More or less,' Maxwell said.

'Would you like to come this way? Nolan wants his mummy.' She caught the look on Maxwell's face. 'Oh, and his daddy, of course,' she smiled. She held out an arm and ushered them through. 'Come on. This way.'

They were taken into a curtained-off cubicle, where their little one sat on what looked like an acre of trolley, a waffle-woven blanket over his chubby knees. His curls were clinging damply to his forehead and his eyes were wide in a white face. He held out his arms to parents in general and they flew into them, kneeling on the chairs helpfully placed on either side. When they let him go enough for him to speak, he said, 'Mummy. Dadda. Nolan has be sick.' He pulled a sad face.

Jacquie brushed the hair back from his forehead and kissed it gently. 'You are such a brave boy,' she said, wetting him with her tears. 'Do

184

you feel better now?'

He beckoned her closer and whispered in her ear, 'Want to poo.'

'Oh, sweetie,' she said and gave him a hug. She turned to the nurse. 'He needs the loo,' she said. 'Where is it?'

The nurse smiled at her and shrugged her shoulders regretfully. 'Well, it's right here, I'm afraid. Because we have been told he may have been given something, we will have to save ... samples ... until we know what it was. Sorry. He has refused to use a bedpan, claiming, and quite rightly, to be a big boy now. But I'm sure you can explain.'

Maxwell had been standing mutely by the side of the trolley. He didn't dare speak because he knew his voice would let him down. He had been in another world, the tunnel where past and present meet, since the phone call. Even now that he could see and feel his little boy, clearly hardly the worse for his adventure, he was still feeling as if he had been through the mill. But now, his teaching skills were called for and he bent down to his son.

'Now, my little bloke,' he said, 'I know you don't want to poo in here, because you are a bit big for that. But, you know how it is, NHS cutbacks and whatnot, this hospital doesn't have any toilets!' He clicked his tongue and raised his eyebrow. 'Now, what do you think about that?'

'Hum!' Nolan said, and clicked his tongue in reply. 'Is it the guv'ment, Dadda?'

'Too right, old mate,' said Maxwell. 'So, could you stretch a point and use the potty thing, just

185

this once?'

The little boy gave a theatrical sigh. 'O-kaaay,' he said and looked up at the nurse. 'But you go. I want my Mummy.'

'Fair enough,' the woman said, utterly unaware that Charles II used to go, loudly and lavishly, in front of a dozen or so courtiers, and went out through the curtain, followed by Maxwell. She turned to him. 'What a lovely child,' she said. 'Very bright.'

'Just as well, or we would have thrown him back,' Maxwell said with just a touch of his usual self. He saw her expression. 'Just joking,' he added, hurriedly. 'We would have been quite happy with anything; we're just extra pleased with what we have.'

She nodded and hurried off to get the baby bedpan, feeling grateful that she hadn't made any gaffes along the lines of calling him Granddad.

He poked his head back round the curtain. 'I'll go and talk to the others,' he said to Jacquie. 'Give me a call when you want me.'

'Yes,' said Jacquie, not turning round. She didn't want to take her eyes off the boy in case, like the cat i' the adage, he turned into the other possibility. 'See you in a minute.'

Maxwell smiled and ducked back out into the corridor. He went out into the waiting area and saw the unlikely sight of Henry Hall sitting with his mother-in-law-to-be, murmuring what were almost certainly platitudes, but kindly ones. As he approached, he could tell that his first impression was right.

'...very strong at that age,' Henry was saying. 'I

remember when mine were small, they were always eating things and they've all grown up well and strong.' He looked up gratefully as Maxwell came up to them and took a seat on the other side of the dejected woman. 'How is he?' he asked and leant back, as if handing over the reins.

'He's been sick,' he said. 'He is now, rather reluctantly, using a bedpan. He refused to go before Jacquie arrived, because he doesn't use potties any more, now he is a big boy.' He stopped for a moment and ducked his head. His boy was even rather lovely when pooing and how many people were there in the world of whom you could say *that?* 'The nurse said they are having to save everything, because of his having been giving something potentially harmful.'

Betty indulged herself in another round of crying, which had strangely not increased the general boot-ness of her face, but it was now a wet, scarlet boot.

'Now, now,' Hall said, by now almost on automatic. He leant down and spoke to her as if she was a rather dim child. 'Will you be all right here if we go over there a minute and have a talk?'

She snuffled in reply and Hall decided to take that as a yes.

He and Maxwell got up slowly and moved away, glancing back at her from time to time. They moved with that sideways, bent-over shuffle peculiar to people uncertain as to whether they should be standing up at all. Eventually, with a final look over their shoulders, they straightened up and moved off into the corner by the fish tank, obligatory furnishing feature of casualty departments the world over, complete with one strange black fish suckered to the glass and a moth-eaten guppy.

'She's taken it badly,' Hall remarked.

Maxwell took a deep breath. 'Empathy is my middle name, Henry. I sometimes wonder what my parents could have been thinking.' Hall looked up, glad to hear the old Maxwell back. This was the best proof that the little lad was not too poorly. 'But even I am having trouble feeling sorry for her, being Jacquie's mother notwithstanding. She had one simple task – to take Nolan for a walk and not let him eat anything. All right, I suppose that is two simple tasks; but they are *very* simple, I think you'll agree. She managed the walk, which was pretty much optional as to how it was achieved. But she didn't manage the other part, not even slightly. In another time, I'd have hacked her to pieces, à la the hound Gelert. As it is, I still may sue.'

Hall waited while the other man vented his spleen, using his policeman's nose to tell when to butt in. 'I agree, Max, but even so...'

'I'm still venting, Henry,' Maxwell said crisply. 'Wait your turn. She's only here to so-called help with Nolan and in less than half an hour she proved she couldn't look after the cat. In fact, I won't *let* her look after the cat and he is getting on for the most self-sufficient cat I know. I expect she was wandering along, gassing with some hearty walking type and not even looking down to see what Nole was up to–'

'I will have to interrupt you, Max, and I'm sorry. You've clearly had a horrible shock and what with ... well, what happened before, it is hitting you hard.' Henry Hall knew about Maxwell's first family and felt for him as everyone who has been lucky enough to love and not lose must. 'But I don't think you can blame Betty entirely. For a start, Nolan is by way of being pretty much his own man and I applaud you both for that. The only thing that makes him different from the two of you in your treatment of him is that he is smaller. So he doesn't take kindly to being given orders. Betty, on the other hand, seems to be an ordering sort of woman, if I may presume to make a judgement, having only seen her crying and weeping.'

'Yes,' Maxwell conceded. 'That's a very fair summation, Henry. You're obviously not a Detective Chief Inspector for nothing. However, I miss your thrust on this one.'

'All I'm saying is, don't be too hard on her. I expect she told Nolan not to take anything from anyone. He's used to being asked to consider not taking anything from anyone for reasons a, b and c. Do you see what I'm getting at?'

Maxwell looked thoughtful. 'Yes, Henry. I do. You're right. Too much democracy. Logic. Tears before bedtime.' Then the frightened father took over again, 'But, for God's sake, Henry! Even so...'

Hall put a heavy hand on Maxwell's shoulder. 'I'm going to have to question him, Max.'

'Who? Nole? But he's just a baby, Henry! There must be laws covering this sort of thing. Ask Betty.'

'And she will be ... how much help, on a scale

of one to ten? I'd rather go with the kid.'

Maxwell considered. 'All right. Ask Nolan. But only when we get him home. And only with us there.'

'And I will leave my handcuffs at the nick. Look, he knows me. I think he quite likes me.' The DCI almost chuckled. 'He tries to take my glasses off.'

No wonder, thought Maxwell. Like the rest of us, he wonders if you've got eyes behind there.

'Nothing he says will stand up, so don't worry about video links to court or anything else. I just think that we might get the only partial description from him that we have at the moment. Sylvia's old running man is a start, but hardly comprehensive. Betty says they were all dressed for walking in shorts and things. All ages, both sexes. In other words, a perfect cross section of the population. So if Nolan noticed anything, anything at all, like a funny nose or a missing tooth, the sort of thing you might expect from the son of a policewoman and a raving lunatic, then it will help.' Payback time.

Maxwell was shocked. Henry Hall had almost been amusing. It was nearly as scary as the rest of the afternoon's experiences put together. He made a decision and hoped Jacquie would agree. 'Yes, Henry. That will be fine. Come over this evening, when we have him back home.'

Hall looked over his shoulder. 'I think you'll have him home before then. Look behind you.'

Jacquie had come through the double doors with a smiling Nolan in her arms. He was a little pale, but smiling broadly. He gave a laconic wave to his father. 'Hi, Dadda.' He looked across at his grandmother, who had jumped to her feet but not gone forward to meet her daughter and grandson. Jacquie gave a lightning glance at Maxwell and then went straight to her mother.

'Can you just hold Nole for a minute, Mum,' she said and handed the rather reluctant toddler into her arms. It was the most difficult thing she had ever done, and possibly the best. Maxwell and Hall went to join them, united in silent admiration for their favourite woman policeman.

She turned to Maxwell with a smile to light up his life. 'His poo was quite normal,' she said happily, adding automatically, 'sorry, guv. The doctor thinks he perhaps just ate a fly or something. I'm not so sure. He was given a lolly by a man, he says. I told him he shouldn't have taken it, but he says the man had been talking to Ninja, so that he thought it would be all right.'

'Ninja?' Hall was confused.

'Betty,' said Maxwell in an aside. 'If I thought I could begin to explain, I would.'

Jacquie touched Hall's sleeve. 'We'll need a lift home, I'm afraid, guv. Is that OK?'

'Of course,' he said, his eyes still on Nolan. 'Look, Jacquie, is it all right if I come in with you when we get back to your house and just ... well, ask Nolan a few questions?'

'What?' Jacquie looked fit to bite him.

'I think he should, darling,' said Maxwell, cringing inside as he spoke. He knew what her reaction would be and here it came now.

'What?' she said again. 'Max, are you insane? He's just a baby.'

'Granted,' Maxwell said. 'Well, I think he would prefer the word "boy". But, yes, he is young for this, but he knows Henry. He tries to take his glasses,' he said, he hoped winningly. 'He may be the only witness.'

'There's my mother,' she said, truculently.

There was a silence.

She gave in all at once. 'Yes, Henry,' she said, wearily. 'You can come in. But only for a short while. I think we all need a quiet evening, just the three of us...'

'Four,' said Maxwell, with a sigh.

'Oh, yes, four of us, to get over this.'

'Understood,' said Hall, briskly. 'We'll get someone from the nick to bring your car home. That will save you a journey in tomorrow.'

'I'm rostered tomorrow,' Jacquie said.

Henry Hall was a kind man at heart. He didn't consider the hours of work it would take him to replace her with a policeman who didn't exist. He just said, 'I've rearranged it. Take all the time you need.'

'Henry, I could kiss you.'

It was only because it was Maxwell speaking that Hall did not allow it. Just this once.

Chapter Thirteen

It was nice to be home. Ninja, boot polish touched up suitably, was making tea in the kitchen. Nolan sat in state on the sofa, with Metternich spread defensively across his lap. Nobody would have given his Boy a lolly if he'd been there. Only a parent could see how the afternoon had affected the lad. He had hold of Metternich's right ear between the finger and thumb of his right hand. The middle fingers of the other hand were firmly in his mouth. He kept nudging Jacquie and Maxwell with a bare toe every once in a while, as if to check they were still there, sitting on the floor on either side of his makeshift throne. Henry Hall sat opposite him, on the pouffe that usually held either his father's feet or his cat.

'Nole,' Maxwell said quietly, 'Mr Hall would like to ask you a few questions about this afternoon. Is that all right, mate?'

Nolan turned his eyes without moving his head and regarded his father solemnly. He let go of his sucked fingers for long enough to murmur, 'S'all right, Dadda.'

'Right. Now, if the questions make you worried or sad, you must just say so and you can stop.'

'Is like a quiz?'

Hall raised an eyebrow at Jacquie.

'Yes, poppet. A quiz.'

'You do quizzes?' the policeman asked Max-

193

well, the tone of amazement unmistakeable.

'Well, yes. Nothing hard. Colours. Teletubbies. The role of the lumpenproletariat in Hegel's dialectic. That sort of thing.'

Hall knew his man by this time. So he knew that it was a possibility that one of those was a joke. 'Right.' He turned to Nolan. 'So, Nolan, like Mummy says, this is a quiz.'

'Awright,' Nolan said around his fingers.

'Take your fingers out, poppet,' Jacquie said, 'or Mr Hall might not hear what you say.'

He looked at her with big eyes and for a moment she just wanted to grab him and take him upstairs to wrap in blankets and look after him while she had breath. But, right now, there was a killer to catch. He slowly let his fingers drop out of his mouth and wiped them dry on the cat. He turned his big eyes on Henry. 'OK,' he said. 'Numb'one.'

Henry got the idea. 'Nolan,' he said. 'Question number one. Did a man or a lady speak to you when you were walking with Granny today?'

'I wen' with Ninja for a walk,' Nolan offered.

'I'll give you a point for that,' Henry said. One small thumb went up in the air. 'Did a man or lady speak to you when you were walking with Granny?'

'Ninja talk to some men.' A smile crept over his face and he giggled. 'They were funny men.'

'That's another point,' said Henry. Maxwell and Jacquie could only watch in amazement. Was this the bland Henry Hall they knew and sort of liked? He seemed quite human. 'Why were they funny, Nolan?' he asked.

194

The little boy squirmed with the pleasure of remembrance. 'They were funny,' he said again and pointed to his legs. 'They had trousis like Nolan.'

'Shorts,' said Jacquie. 'Mum said they were walkers.'

'Right.' Hall turned his attention back to Nolan who was beginning to lose interest. 'Did a funny man speak to you, Nolan?'

'No.'

'No? Not at all?'

'He gived me a lolly.'

The adults' heads went up as they sniffed a clue at the waterhole.

'Good boy. Two points for that!' With care and muttering under his breath, Nolan triumphantly displayed all four fingers and his thumb. So what if he had inherited his father's maths acumen? The child was being helpful and Hall went with it. 'Did you eat the lolly?'

Nolan pulled a face and shook his head. 'No.'

'What?' It was like Greek choral speaking – every adult voice in the room raised in query.

He looked from his mother to his father, then back to Henry Hall. He leant forward as if to impart a secret. He dropped his voice, almost to a whisper. 'It was hobble. Yeuch.' He shook his head and did a whole body shudder.

Everyone held their breath as Henry Hall asked the 64,000 dollar question. 'What did you do with the lolly, Nolan?'

The little boy threw himself sideways, convulsed with laughter, much to the annoyance of Metternich who had only put up with the shud-

195

dering out of laziness. With a snicker of annoyance he left the sofa, via Henry Hall's knee.

'Ow,' the policeman said, absently. What were a few flesh wounds when he might be on the verge of a breakthrough? 'Go on, Nolan, you can tell me.'

Nolan shook his head solemnly, then his expression brightened. 'I tell *Dadda*,' he said. 'I whipser.' Maxwell leant forward, as did Hall.

'Don't bother,' Jacquie advised quietly. 'Whipsering is a little ad hoc at the moment.' And indeed, Maxwell looked poised for sudden flight as he leant there against his little one's mouth.

And sure enough, they heard clearly, through Maxwell's head like a buzz saw. 'I put it in Ninja's handbag.' Then he beamed around the room. 'Have Nolan won the prize?'

Henry Hall leant forward and tickled the boy's toes. 'You certainly have, Nolan. What do you usually get?'

'Hmm.' The boy put a finger theatrically to his chin. 'What do userly get, Mummy?'

Jacquie looked at Henry Hall. 'Well, we usually leave it to the quizmaster, don't we?' It was usually a sweet of some kind, but that didn't seem appropriate somehow. 'A small toy, perhaps?'

Nolan looked Hall in the eye and repeated, 'A small toy, haps?' with a tilt of the head.

'Well, I'll tell you what,' Hall said. 'I have given Mummy some days off to spend with you, Nolan, so I'll give her some money and she can take you shopping on Monday and you can choose something nice.'

'Thank you,' said Nolan and suddenly uncoiled

from his seat and wound his arms round Henry's neck. The smell of that small neck and the damp kiss on his cheek was the best thank you Henry Hall had had in years. He stood up, wearing Nolan like an exotic necklace, then handed him gently back to Maxwell. Jacquie had turned her back and was surreptitiously wiping her eyes.

'Take care of him, Max,' said Henry. Then, tipping his head at Jacquie, 'Of both of them.'

'Will do, Henry. Um, I've something to ask you. Can I see you out?' And hefting Nolan up onto one hip for comfort, he led the way out onto the landing.

Jacquie sat curled up in the corner of the sofa, letting relief wash over her. There was a clink of cups and her mother was there with a tray of tea.

'Sorry to take such a long time,' she said. 'It took me a minute to find everything. I like to use cups and saucers in the afternoon, rather than mugs.'

Jacquie lifted her head. 'I've got cups and saucers?' she asked in amazement.

'Well,' her mother pursed her lips and looked a trifle disapproving, 'there were some in the cupboard, at the back.' The unspoken corollary was that they belonged to Maxwell, left over from another life, one that had mostly happened while Jacquie was at junior school.

'Oh, there's all sorts of stuff in there if you look,' she replied. There was no good trying to argue this one; it would always be there in the background. Her mother seemed to resent the fact that neither she nor Jacquie could ever know everything about Maxwell, and not because he hid it on purpose. It was just that it takes time to tell a person every single thing that has ever happened. Just filling each other in on the day they were still in often took until the wee small hours of the next one, let alone what happened in June of 1967.

'Has Mr Hall gone?'

'Yes. He needed to get back to the nick to rearrange the rota and make a few notes.' Jacquie sipped her tea.

'Didn't he want to question me at all?' Her mother looked hopeful. 'He is such a gentleman, don't you think? I had no idea from what you'd said.'

Jacquie mulled that one over. Yes, on sober reflection, he was quite a gent, in that he, like Maxwell, tended to treat everyone the same. It was just that he treated everyone as if they were another potential number in the police computer; Maxwell treated everyone as if they were sentient human beings until it was proved otherwise. Henry must have really pulled out all the stops to impress her mother. Finally, she said, 'Yes. I could have much worse for a boss, that's certain.'

Her mother leant forward and touched her knee. 'Are you all right, dear? Only, this afternoon has been a bit eventful, hasn't it?'

Jacquie's tea did a vertical take-off. 'Eventful? *Eventful?* Please, mother, don't get me started! You took Nolan for a simple walk, with simple instructions. We end up in A&E. If he wasn't so picky about what he eats, we could be now mourning our son. So don't give me eventful.' Her voice rose to a scream. 'I don't know why I even thought you could do this. I needed help and what did I get? Well?'

The buzz of male voices on the landing had stopped, Jacquie's screaming had stopped. Had a pin chosen that moment to drop, they would all have heard it. Instead, Maxwell and Nolan came through the door, bouncing horse-riding style from the head of the stairs.

'Hello?' Maxwell said, innocence personified. 'What have we here, Nole? Mummy and Ninja. Well, ladies,' he raked them with a warning glance, 'Nolan has just remarked that he is feeling a bit peckish but he doesn't want any sweeties, or any of Ninja's toast.' He looked at his mother-in-law-to-be and smiled. 'Nole and I agree about wholemeal toast, Ninja, if that's OK. We did win the war, after all. He wants...' he jiggled the boy up and down, 'he wants... Well, Nole, what's it to be?'

'Dippy and egg,' he crowed, with his arms in the air, then, more seriously, 'not Ninja toast vo. Dadda toast!'

'White bread rules,' Maxwell said. 'Play nicely, girls, while we cook,' and off they rode, the Lone Ranger and Silver to the life, into the kitchen, where crashing noises almost immediately began.

Neither of the women spoke for a moment. It was inevitable that the elder would break the silence first. 'I told him not to speak to anyone. I told him not to take anything from anyone.' It sounded pathetic even as it left her mouth.

'How old do you think he is, Mum? He's a *little,*

199

tiny boy for God's sake.'

'Yes, but ... he just seems so grown up.' She grabbed for Jacquie's hand. 'I just got talking. They were nice people. Walkers, you know, serious ones with maps and everything. I don't know round here and I just thought,' she sobbed and had to pause, 'I just thought they could tell us a nice walk, that's all.' She looked up through tear-filled eyes. 'I didn't think any of them would hurt him. They...' her voice fell to a whisper, 'they were just some nice people, Jacquie.' She put her head in her hands and cried.

Her daughter reached over and patted her knee. Hugs were not on the menu just yet. 'No one said that the murderer would be wearing a badge, Mum. That's why Max said *no* food out, *no* sweeties from anyone. We're not health food loonies as you must have spotted already. We just can't trust anyone. Any of us.'

Ninja gave a sniff and blew her nose for good measure. 'Have you wondered why Nolan got the lolly?' As a way of shifting both blame and attention from her, she had hit on a cracker of a theory.

'I beg your pardon?' Jacquie was aghast. 'What do you mean?' A cold hand clutched her heart.

'Well, the place was crowded out this afternoon. The weather is lovely, and some of the posher schools are still on holiday, plus the Saga louts like me who take holidays a bit later. There was practically a queue for the kissing gate at the car park end. There were children everywhere with mums, dads, grannies, you name it. But *Nolan* was the one who got the lolly. Statistically, as I'm sure a colleague of Max's could prove quite easily, it is ridiculous.'

Jacquie had gone white. 'It was deliberate,' she whispered. 'The poisoner singled out Nolan. He tried to kill *my* baby. Not anyone's, but *mine*.'

'Or Max's,' her mother added. To her, that was the more obvious version. Her daughter was a policewoman, true, but, put it how you liked, Maxwell was rather high profile and more than a bit annoying. Especially if you happened to be a criminal. Or a student. Ex-student. Colleague. Ex-colleague. The list could go on and on.

Jacquie didn't know where to run. To her husband and son. To Henry Hall. To a dark cupboard under the stairs. In the end, she compromised. She called Maxwell into the sitting room. She phoned Henry Hall. The call was transferred to the front desk.

'Leighford Police. How can I help you?'

She knew the voice. 'Bill. It's Jacquie. Is DCI Hall in the building? I mean, he's just left mine. But is he back yet?'

'He's just gone home.' The desk sergeant couldn't sound more disinterested if he tried.

'Thanks, I'll ring him there.'

Meanwhile, Maxwell and Nolan had come in and were standing hand in hand in front of her. 'Yes, ma'am?' Maxwell asked. 'You rang? Only, Nole's egg will get hard.'

'Mum,' Jacquie said. 'Could you take over the egg? Go with Ninja, poppet and have your egg. Mummy will be in in a minute.'

Her mother took him by the hand and they went out to the kitchen, Nolan generally laying

201

down the law on how to cut soldiers. He was taking no risks on her toast skills. He was with his father on the bottom of budgie cage properties of wholemeal, even if he didn't yet know what the old man was talking about.

Maxwell sat on the sofa and turned to face his wife-to-be. 'What is it? You're as white as a sheet, woman.'

'Mum has just said something which has really shaken me.'

'She's moving in?' He made the sign of the cross.

'No, worse than that.'

Maxwell bridled in mock horror. 'There's nothing worse than that, dear heart, so don't play me false.' He toyed for a moment with reaching, with a palsied hand, for the Southern Comfort. 'What did she say that could be so bad?'

'She said,' she dipped her head and summoned up all her policepersonly skills of control, 'she said why did *Nolan* get the lolly? Why, with all the kids and other people there, did it get given to him?' She watched his face with care. It became impassive while he weighed up the possibilities.

'There are two, or perhaps more ways of looking at this,' he said at last. 'The first, of course, is why shouldn't he get the lolly? He's a cute kid. If I was going to give a random lolly to someone, I would most probably choose him rather than some snaggle-toothed, snotty-nosed tyke. He's just more attractive. Although, since it seemed to have been doctored with something nasty, you'd have to be a bit warped to give it to the cute one. However, I digress. Another is that there was

202

more than one lolly. We don't know what happened to other kids. Why should we? Not every granny would scream like a steam whistle and take her grandchild to casualty. Some of them wouldn't even bother to hold its hair while it threw up. Then there is the possibility, which can't be discounted until we hear back from the lab, that the lolly is totally harmless and Nole is allergic to cyanomothprooferphilicophilos or whatever the thing is coloured with. And then, finally...' He paused and she filled in the gap.

'And then, finally, is the possibility that some warped sod gave it to him because they knew who he was.'

Maxwell compressed his lips and nodded. 'I agree, Watson, that there is always that possibility.' They sat in silence for a moment, holding hands. Then, Maxwell said, 'Have you phoned Henry?'

'He's on his way home.'

'Look, let's have something to eat and then, when Nole is in bed and your mother is thumbing through *What Bride Already?* or whatever her current reading matter is, we'll ring him and see what he thinks.' He lifted her chin with a finger and made her look into his eyes. 'Is that a good idea or is that a good idea?'

She smiled wanly.

'Well, madam. An answer if you please, or I'll take me horsewhip to you, you strumpet.' It was, all in all, an excellent Nigel Davenport playing George III circa 1979 and it was unfortunate that Ninja came in at that moment, but Maxwell's timing was so rarely out that he allowed himself

203

that one little mistake. He turned at her intake of breath. 'Has he finished his dippies?' Butter wouldn't melt in his mouth.

She pulled herself together. Her poor baby; why had she never said anything? 'Yes. He's having a nice yoghurt.'

'Nice yoghurt?' Maxwell was perplexed. 'Surely, they haven't invented those, have they? About time. Well, I'll take over now, Ninj. Have a sit down and chat to Jacquie. Aren't there wedding plans to discuss?' He beetled out of the room, knowing he would pay later, but it was worth it just to hear Jacquie's little whimper as her mother pulled out the tablecloth swatches from her bag.

'Hello, Nole,' she heard him say, 'yoghurt face mask, that's the ticket. What say we go and have a bath?'

Betty Carpenter didn't see much of her grandchild and her head turned at the sound of that. 'Oh, Jacquie. That sounds so sweet. Can I bath him tonight?'

'Be my guest,' said Jacquie. 'But take a big sponge. When Max says "we" he does mean it quite literally.'

Her mother blushed and Jacquie could have kicked herself. Maxwell could take it and it would perhaps have taken buttonholes off the conversational menu, if only for a while.

Chapter Fourteen

Nolan was tucked up in bed, sweetly smelling and chatting over the day's events with his teddy and Metternich. Although her mother had protested loudly over the cat's presence in Nolan's bedroom, Jacquie had been firm. Metternich was not allowed in there as a matter of course, only when he and Nolan had stuff to discuss and, if ever there was a cat who wouldn't sleep on a child's face, then that cat was the Count. *Far* too uncomfortable. The nose, for one thing, would be bound to stick in somewhere and the dribble would mat his coat. So, the cat stayed.

Maxwell, meanwhile, no less sweetly smelling, was ensconced in his favourite chair and half watching the news. He liked this time of day and even the addition of Jacquie's mother couldn't spoil it. The architect had played a blinder on 38 Columbine. The evening sun slanted in through the windows of the first-floor sitting room and gilded the walls and ceiling with mellow light and warmth. At this point of the year, where summer slid slowly into autumn, and the sun was lower in the sky, it fell on Maxwell's chair and he knew how birds must feel, taking a sunbath. He let his inner lizard out to bask on his favourite rock. The hum of conversation from the kitchen, the faint witterings of Nolan through the monitor, all wove together and he was on the verge of sleep.

Then, suddenly and with no preamble, he was upright and kneeling in front of the television. 'Quick, Jacquie, quick. Come here,' he called. 'Quickleeeeee.'

'Good heavens, Max,' she began, crashing through the door. 'Whatever is ... oh, my God. It's Henry.'

And Henry it was, the DCI talking to camera outside a building that looked horribly like Leighford General. Maxwell had been woken by the sound of his voice.

'No, I'm sorry,' he was saying in his bland way. 'I'm afraid I cannot comment at the moment, except to say that everyone should keep calm. There is no need to panic. There have been a few isolated instances of gastric symptoms which we are currently treating as suspicious, but we have no positive proof that there is a poisoner at loose in Leighford.'

'Ooh, Henry Hall,' breathed Maxwell. 'I hope your fingers are well and truly crossed.'

'What has happened?' Jacquie said. 'How come the media are on to it? Why is he outside the hospital?'

'To be on the safe side, however,' Hall was saying, as if this was the most sensible remark in the world and by no means likely to cause panic and mayhem, 'if anyone is concerned, it is advisable that for the moment, only food bought more than four days ago, or tinned items, should be used.'

This statement met with a barrage of questions from the cluster of pressmen and women around the DCI.

'One at a time, please,' Hall said. 'In fact, I

would prefer to just answer one more question before I go back inside. Yes.' He pointed. 'You. One question.'

'DCI Hall,' the cubbest of reporters said. 'What alerted you to the fact that there might be a pattern of poisoning in Leighford?'

Hall looked at him for what seemed, in television terms, an eternity. Dead air. Finally, he swallowed and said, 'Well, there had been previous incidents of which we were suspicious, including an incident with a child this afternoon which we were in the early stages of investigating. But,' and here Henry Hall did a scary thing and took off his glasses, polishing them on a spotless handkerchief, 'when I got home this evening, I found my wife in a state of collapse. Beside her was the remains of cake which she had bought the day before. So,' he said, in that same, bland voice, 'if you could, as I said earlier, let me go back inside to be with my wife, I would be very grateful. Thank you.' The blank lenses, polished to perfection, shone once in the lights of the cameras and he turned and disappeared through the doors of the hospital.

Maxwell sat back on his heels, exhaling for what felt like the first time in hours. Jacquie looked as if she was a small roadside-dwelling mammal caught in the headlights of an oncoming pantechnicon.

'Max,' she said finally, 'what can we do?'

'Nothing,' he said. 'It has to be Henry's call, precious. If he needs us, he'll let us know. I expect his boys are still home, aren't they, or at least not back at college yet? Come here,' he held

207

out an arm and she subsided into it. 'He'll call, don't you worry.'

'But poor Margaret,' she said. 'I wonder how bad she is?'

'I can't make it out,' Maxwell said. 'Why did she collapse, not throw up or...?'

'Die? I don't know. Chummy must be using different things.' She hated herself for using Max's Fifties terminology, but somehow it went with the territory. 'Max,' she said, pulling away and looking up into his face. 'How many different poisons could you name?'

'Sweetheart,' he said, with a smile. 'Look more carefully. To whom are you speaking? Is it a member of the public? No. Is it even a police person, completely immersed in traffic law and ethnic amelioration but little else? Nope, wrong again. 'Tis I, Peter Maxwell, doyen of crime and particularly murder, horrible for preference. I know poisons from the Middle Ages. I know thallium, I know strychnine, I know how to give your arse a nick. Ask someone else.'

'All right,' she said, hutching herself back into her favourite sofa corner. 'Then answer me this. How do you go about *getting* poison?'

'Well,' he tossed an insouciant head, 'clearly, the great white way, the internet.'

'Aha,' she said. 'Gotcha. Because you, Peter Maxwell, couldn't do that if you tried all day.'

'Well, ha and I raise you that gotcha. I can, so there.'

'I think that the internet as a source of dodgy things is very overrated. I agree that you could get Viagra and its ilk until the cows come home.

208

There are sites with recipes for bombs and all sorts of things. But, as an amateur, and I think we agree that is what our man is, you can't just put "arsenic" in a web search and come up with a shopping site where all you have to do is choose your poison, as the saying apparently goes, add it to your cart and check out securely using Paypal.'

'Well,' he had to agree and was also mightily glad she hadn't called his bluff, 'you may be right. But if you have even a small knowledge of chemistry, I'm sure you can conjure up all sorts of dodgy stuff. I have never knowingly accepted so much as a Jammie Dodger from our very own Head of Science, for example. Take cyanide ... no, I'm sure I can phrase that much better ... in the case of cyanide, it is very simply made. It is also used routinely in pathology labs in various tests. Technicians have died of it, in the past. And aconite, the first one used. Do you remember...?'

'The wolfsbane, yes I do. But surely, even with the plant growing in the garden, it doesn't just become poison by picking it?'

'Oh yes,' said another voice. Ninja was standing in the doorway, drying her hands on a tea towel. She perched on the edge of a chair. 'Some plants that we routinely have in the garden are deadly poisonous. Oh, my goodness, have you got rid of that wolfsbane at the back of the border?' She looked poised for flight as if she would go and hack it down at once.

'Yes, Mum, we got rid of it before Nole could even walk. The roots went down to Australia.'

'Well, yes,' she said, settling in to her subject. 'It is related to horseradish and the roots are very long, I know.' She chuckled. 'Daddy and I had to do exactly the same in our garden when you were small. There was nearly a disaster, though. He had been digging and digging and then hacked at the root with a sort of billhook thing. He got the sap all over his hands and then stopped for lunch and ate a sandwich. We weren't so safety conscious in those days.'

'Those days?' Jacquie said, affronted. 'How old am I, Mum?'

Maxwell pointed at her. 'Welcome to the age of "In Those Days",' he said. 'It's all downhill from here, believe me.'

'No,' Ninja said, flapping her tea towel at him. 'We weren't, though, Max, were we?'

Jacquie threw him a glance and a kiss. It was a generation thing.

'Anyway, Daddy ate his sandwich and licked the mayonnaise off his fingers.'

'Gosh,' Jacquie said, 'had mayonnaise been invented then?'

'Shush,' her mother said. 'This is important, isn't it? I just heard on the radio in the kitchen about poor Mrs Hall. She's quite poorly, I think. Anyway, where was I?'

Maxwell, honed on the granite face of Mrs B, was ready with the answer. 'Many ... no, sorry, some plants that we routinely have in the garden are deadly poisonous.'

Ninja looked at Jacquie. 'How does he do that?'

'I have no idea,' she replied. 'Useful, though, isn't it?'

'Well,' the woman said, drawing herself up a little, 'I hope his brain doesn't fill up or anything.

210

Then where would we be?'

'Oh, don't worry,' said Maxwell. 'I give it a good scrub out every night. Don't I, thing? Don't I, thing?'

Ignoring him, she began again. 'Some plants that we routinely have in the garden are deadly poisonous. Wolfsbane, as we said, is very *very* poisonous, with no need to do anything to it at all. The roots of Kaffir lily are very poisonous too, but you'd have to do something with those, to concentrate the nasty stuff, I can't remember what it's called.' She mused for a moment. 'Anyway, it's very nasty and causes collapse, sickness, you get very drooly, if you know what I mean and,' she pursed her lips, 'you know.' She nudged a distant elbow at Jacquie and nodded.

'You get the shits,' Jacquie explained.

'There's no need for that kind of language, Jacqueline, but yes, Max, she's right.'

'Thank you for the translation,' he said. 'We'll take it as read next time. If there is a next time?' He looked questioningly at Ninja. 'Are there more?'

'Loads,' she said with relish. 'I can't remember them all and, of course, some of the poisonous ones are really quite rare, so you just don't find them outside a botanical garden. But, hold on, here's one I remember. Hydrangea.'

'We've got those as well,' Jacquie said. 'And Mrs Troubridge's garden is awash with them.'

'Well,' said her mother, 'it's the leaves and buds with those, I think, but if you ate enough you would sink into a coma. Let's see ... oh, yes, there's the Swiss Cheese plant. Do you remember Jacquie, when you lived with ... oh, you know, nice boy, what was his name? Anyway,' she hurried on with a glance at her daughter's face, 'he had a huge one, do you remember?'

Jacquie just raised an admonishing finger to Maxwell without even meeting his eye. He subsided without speaking.

'It sat on the dining table, if memory serves. Well, that contains calcium oxalate, that I *do* know. It causes loss of voice. Then you get to the really nasty ones.'

'Ninja, I must interrupt here,' Maxwell said. 'How the hell do you *know* all this?'

She smiled at Jacquie, the smile all daughters know. It is used in the application of A-Level guilt, but can be taken on to degree level in extreme cases. Jacquie's mother had nothing less than a doctorate. 'I spend a lot of time on my own, Max,' she leant forward with a martyred smile. 'I am a member of the Women's Institute, the Townswomen's Guild, the Soroptimists, the Stitch and Bitch Club and, of course, the Royal Horticultural Society. And before you ask, it was the WI that had the lecture on poisonous plants. I *always* make notes.'

Maxwell threw her a look that contained at least some admiration. She was not his favourite woman, never would be, but there were certain points at which they very nearly met.

'Max?' She closed her eyes and held out her hand to him.

He chuckled. 'Then you get to the really nasty ones,' he said.

She smiled at Jacquie. 'So clever,' she murmured. 'Anyway, to get on, because I'm sure Henry will be phoning soon.'

'Hope so,' muttered Jacquie.

'Then you get to the really nasty ones. I can't remember many of those but the two I *can* remember are really quite horrid. There's the Jerusalem cherry – do you remember, Jacquie, Granny Carpenter used to give me one each Christmas and it was dead by New Year? Anyway, Max, I'm not sure whether you're familiar with it, but it is a member of the deadly nightshade family and the fruit is very poisonous, causes abdominal pain, vomiting and all the rest. I can't remember what the poison is called.'

'Solanocapsine,' Maxwell offered. He'd been to a good school.

'No, dear, stop making it up,' she admonished. 'Then there's oleander, which is such a pretty plant and that one really scared us, I can tell you. Every single piece of it is poisonous and can kill you. Even, and this is the bit I think is very sneaky of it, even the smoke if you put it on a bonfire.'

There was a silence as her list of horticultural horror stopped.

'So,' Jacquie said at last, 'basically, darling heart, you are right and I am wrong. You can get poison very easily on the net. Just type in Thompson and Morgan or Suttons Seeds and you're away.'

'It certainly looks that way,' Maxwell said, standing up. 'Ninja, dear, can you do us a favour? Can you babysit Nole this evening?'

Jacquie's eyes widened and she also stood up.

'Don't you think...?'

'I don't expect there'll be random walking parties in here, do you, my little cabbage?' He turned to his mother-in-law-to-be. 'Would you like Mrs Troubridge in here for company? I'm sure you'll get on like houses on fire.'

'Max, how thoughtful. I would love that. And thank you both *so* much for letting me mind Nolan after ... well, you know. But might Mrs Troubridge not be busy already? It is Saturday night.'

A whole range of late-night activities flashed through Maxwell's brain: pole dancing at Big Willie's; sniffing lighter fluid on the Flyover with half of Leighford High; standing on the corner of Knocking Shop Lane earning her last five bob.

Jacquie shook her head as if she was reading his mind. 'I wouldn't be at all surprised to find her waiting for our call, Mum. I'll just go and see, shall I?' She went to the top of the stairs and crouched down slightly so that she could see through the frosted glass of the front door, one floor below. Sure enough, she could see the faint outline of Mrs Troubridge's elbow, pruning, pruning, always pruning the hedge between their houses.

She trotted down the stairs and opened the door a crack. 'Mrs T, do you fancy an evening in with my mother? We're going out.'

'Your mother, dear? I didn't know your mother was here.'

'Gosh, didn't you? Well, I did tell you this afternoon.' Jacquie's heart dropped. Perhaps this wasn't one of Max's better ideas. 'You know,' she added. 'Boot-faced?'

Mrs Troubridge laughed the girlish trill which had won her Mr Troubridge all those years ago from under her sister's nose. 'My dear, I will have my little joke, you know. I'll just pop back indoors and powder my nose and I'll be right along.'

Jacquie climbed the stairs and stuck her head round the sitting room door. 'She's on her way. Have fun now, Mum. Open a bottle. Let down your hair. Oh, and, can we borrow your car? Henry was supposed to get mine sent back but I suppose, what with one thing and another, he forgot.'

'Of course, dear. The keys are in my bag on the landing.'

Maxwell sketched a wave as he went out to join her on said landing. 'Just remember Thelma and Louise and make sure you behave.' He closed the door.

'Which one is which?' Jacquie giggled.

'Hard to say,' he said and handed her a jacket. Although the nights were still warm, there was a slight Septembral dampness in the air. 'Let's go and see Nole, and I suppose we'd better move the Count.'

They crept up the stairs and peeped round the door. They had no chance of moving the cat, who was stretched out alongside his Boy, who had an arm firmly round his neck. The great beast had one paw protectively on the child's chest and, old warrior that he was, one eye permanently and disconcertingly half open.

'Let's hope that neither of them checks on the

215

chaps,' whispered Maxwell as they crept back down the stairs. 'They'll freak out.'

Jacquie did a very creditable impression of her mother, 'Darling, that animal will sleep on his face. He'll get fleas.'

Maxwell was outraged, but his Mrs Troubridge was immaculate. 'As if my boy would give anyone fleas. The idea!' And he almost threw out a 'tcha' again, but thought better of it. They crept right on past the sitting room door and down the stairs. The real Mrs Troubridge was waiting on the step, about to ring the bell.

'Just go on up, Mrs Troubridge,' Maxwell bowed low and ushered her in. 'Mrs Carpenter is all set to open a bottle.'

'Oh,' Mrs Troubridge pitched her voice low. 'Is she a drinker, my dear? What a worry for you. It probably explains the...' she waved a hand vaguely in front of her face, '...expression.' She patted Jacquie's hand. 'Off you go, you youngsters. Well, Mr Maxwell, I know you won't mind me saying, youngster and Mr Maxwell. I'll look after her. Have a nice time, now.'

Wearing the usual expressions of those who had tangled with the weird and wonderful world of Troubridge, they got in the car and drove away.

'Where are we going, Max?' Jacquie asked, at her first T-junction. Her mother's Peugeot was a bit of a bitch until you knew how to handle it; bit like its owner, really. 'Left or right would be enough information right now, if you are still undecided. But be quick, because I have a bus on my tail.'

'Hmm?' Maxwell looked up and glanced

behind him. 'Oh, sorry. Miles away. Make it left. That will do as well as any other direction.'

'You don't mind me saying that this seems a little random, do you? Am I right in assuming we're not just out for a drive to get away from the wedding planning? To watch the branches stir across the moon at Grantchester?'

Maxwell smiled. So she *had* been taking in the snatches of his favourite poem that he lobbed into the conversation from time to time. He made no comment, of course; he'd rather die than let her know he was impressed.

'Well, that was part of it, of course. But, no, I had a bit of a think in the bath. Like you do. There was Nole, blowing bubbles as if nothing had happened, and it struck me that – and I restrained myself from shouting "Eureka Stockade" – with the exception of the Barlows, this hasn't been as random as it at first might seem. So I gave some thought to the Barlows and where their shop is, and the answer to that one is obvious.'

Jacquie changed gear for the next junction, cursing under her breath as it crunched ever so slightly. 'Well?'

'Left again.'

'Max, this is heading for Leighford High.'

'In a way. All roads lead there, don't they? In fact, we're heading for the Barlows' corner shop. The shop where I, and I have to admit this, dear heart, drop in on the occasional morning for a bag of sticky buns or some other comestible to keep the troops sweet in tutor meetings, or chocolate to schmooze Helen or even a nice bar of something for my good self. As the song goes, chocolate makes the world go around, the world go around, the...'

'You go to the poisoned shop?'

'You've caught the media idiom pretty well, you adman's dream. Yes, I do, or perhaps that should be did, sadly enough, go to the poisoned shop. Which leaves us with several options. Either, it is a coincidence and, as Henry would say,' and they broke into choral speaking, 'there are no such things as coincidences. Or,' he continued, solo, 'someone has a preternaturally detailed know-ledge of my lifestyle.'

'Assuming you're the target?'

'For the moment, yes.' He reached across and patted her knee. 'It's not always about you, you know,' he teased.

'So, they targeted a shop you use.' She played along, a raised eyebrow to mark the moment.

'Correct. The odd thing is that they chose to do it on a Friday night, when I wouldn't be using it for another two days.'

'It might have been done before, hoping to catch you on your way back from school. No, wait, that doesn't work. The cakes had only been delivered that afternoon; well, call it early even-ing, really. So much for bakery fresh.'

'Well, I suppose they were, once. Unless of course, your boys in blue should be out looking for that well-known Napoleon of crime Le Crust or that pair of criminal masterminds, the Brake Brothers. Um, next left, talking of brakes, and we're there. I wonder, and of course, Juliet Bravo, I bow to your superior judgement here as in all things,' he paused to wait for the light punch on the arm, 'but I wonder if Chummy is dragging it out on purpose. For his own amusement, as it were.'

'You mean he's enjoying it, like you said?'

'Yes. But also, if he makes it too obvious, we will fine down the search too quickly and we'll catch him too soon.'

Jacquie pulled up outside the dark shop and pulled on the handbrake. She turned to him. 'But surely, he doesn't want to be caught at all. He's killed someone, Max, and may well kill again. He'll be looking at a life sentence for that. No one wants one of those just to piss you off.'

'Point taken, but I think that this is some kind of game and he doesn't care what the consequences are. I think I am the ultimate target, Jacquie, because the first outbreak hit the school. Nolan came later. A sort of homing in, narrowing down, call it what you will. But if he takes out others on the way, that's fine by him. The thing is, he targeted Nolan too soon in the game. I'm already mad. Now I want to get even.'

'But what about Margaret? You hardly know her, so it can't be an attempt to get at you, well, not just you.' She didn't want the target to be Hall any more than she wanted it to be Maxwell, but straws were there to be clutched at.

He looked thoughtful. 'Yes, I know. That's the fly in my ointment. We'll have to find out where she got the cake.'

'Locally, I assume. You don't drive for miles to get a cake for your tea.'

'True, but she might have bought it when she

did a bigger shop, so we might be looking at closing supermarkets, now. Can you imagine the publicity that will bring? Asda, Tesco, Sainsbury, all like ghost towns. The press will have a field day. Stock markets will crash. Farmers will go bust. Governments will fall...' He was on a roll.

'Earth to Maxwell, Earth to Maxwell. Come in. Over.'

He gave himself a mental shake. 'Possibly I exaggerate. I'm pretty sure she bought it up the road. So, bearing in mind that the Halls live nowhere near school and nowhere near us, that means that Henry was also a specific target, since, as you say, I barely know Margaret and so her poisoning wouldn't be an attack on me personally.'

Jacquie pointed at the shop. 'Are we going in?'

'No, no. No need. I just need to get a map of some sort in my head. I'm an historian, my dear, not a...' and he shuddered gently, '...geographer. No, drive on, James, and don't spare the horses.'

'Where to?'

'To where?' he corrected automatically. 'The Halls' house.'

'Max! We can't. For a start they are probably all round at the hospital.'

'I know, that's why we're going there after the house. I just want to get the lie of the land and see where they are in relation to shops.'

'I'm sure Henry has already thought of that, Max.'

'Lie of the land, dear heart. Lie of the land. Henry may be a copper of above average intelligence, saving your presence, but he's no

220

military historian. You've got to have a feel for these things. Come on, now. Don't shilly-shally. Unless you'd rather go home and discuss the Troubridges' bridesmaidal requirements?' He glanced at her stricken expression. 'No, I thought not. Drive on.' He waved a hand towards the windscreen as a teaching aid. 'Off we go.'

And they left the sad, deserted corner shop, empty of customers for the first time in years, its stock quietly passing its sell-by date and the dust motes spiralling slowly down on newspaper and chocolate bar, on biscuits and instant coffee. The murderer had killed Mel Forman and he had also killed Barlow's Eight Till Late Corner Shop.

The lights were going out all over Leighford.

Chapter Fifteen

Henry Hall sat quietly by his wife's bedside, holding her hand. He had seen so many people, sitting just like this, victims of crime and circumstance. He had never actually put himself in their position, had never wondered what it felt like to be sitting next to the most beloved person in your life, feeling the faint flutter of a pulse in your fingers, not knowing whether it came from them or you, willing them to open their eyes. That wasn't his job. His job was to be cool, detached, professional. He couldn't help people otherwise. But he found, as all those people had found before him, that you don't need instructions for moments like these. Hope, he was finding, really does spring eternal. It wasn't in his nature to talk to her. Where some might have chatted about things, plans they would make, how things would be different if only they would turn their head, open their eyes, he found he had no regrets but one. And he didn't want to waste this moment talking about the past. All the things he hadn't done. All the times he hadn't been there. And, as an honest man, he couldn't promise things would change when she opened her eyes, when she turned her head. So he settled for squeezing her fingers every now and then and willing her to fight the poison inside her.

He was glad he had found her. It had not been

a sight he would have wanted his boys to see. She had obviously been taken ill very suddenly but had managed to make it to the bathroom. Being a policeman's wife, and knowing something was very wrong, she hadn't flushed, and he was proud of her for that. Unfortunately, the presence of umpteen different things to prevent limescale, smells and, for all he knew, infestation by termites, had made her gesture meaningless. So they were waiting for the blood toxicology and that could take too long. They were just rehydrating her and giving her various antidotes, to be sure. The problem they had was that they had to make sure that the antidotes without the antigens would do no harm.

He forced his mind back to the finding; there may yet be a clue there that he had missed. So, diarrhoea had been, as the doctors had it, present. But he had found her in her chair, in a coma from which she had shown no signs of emerging. The phone was in her hand, her hand was in her lap. It looked as though she had intended to ring, then just gave up. He had written all of these things down and now all he could do was sit here. He dropped his head onto their joined hands and muttered the nearest thing he could to a prayer. He was sure that God wouldn't mind that it included threats to dismember whoever had done this, limb from limb and slowly. An eye for an eye, after all, he thought grimly. That was God's spell too, wasn't it?

A hand came down gently on his shoulder and a voice breathed in his ear.

'Mr Hall, your sons are here. Would you like

them to come in?'

He looked up into the nurse's face. 'I don't know. Is that a good idea?'

She straightened up and said, 'Well, sometimes it helps if the patient's children come in. With no offence to you, Mr Hall, it is often their voices which bring a person round, especially a mother. And ... well, you haven't been saying much and we really do recommend...' Her voice tailed away.

Hall stood up and pushed his chair tidily away. 'Yes, nurse. Let the boys in. I'm sure she'd be pleased to see them.' He brushed past her through the curtain round his wife's bed and stalked down the ward. His sons were waiting outside the doors, brought home from their vacations by every means the police could conjure from squad car to helicopter. Even in his extremis, Hall was thinking of the paperwork it would entail.

'Dad!' His youngest put his arms round him and he patted him on the back.

'How is she?' asked his brother, ashen-faced.

Hall shrugged his shoulders and set his mouth. 'She's in the fourth bed along,' he said, gruffly. 'I'm off to the station, boys. Ring if ... if there's any change.'

The boys, as the parents still called them, big as they were, stared at him, the younger in disbelief. So, he was off to the station, was he, while their mother lay in a coma. He pre-empted them.

'It's your mother lying there. My wife. And if I *don't* go back to the station, it might be someone else's. A woman is already dead. Jacquie Carpenter's little boy had a close call this afternoon.' God, was it only this afternoon, he thought to himself? 'I want to stop it before the wards and morgues are full.' He clapped them both on the shoulder and held them tightly. 'Let me go, lads. You'll rally her round if anyone can. I can catch the bastard who did this, if anyone can. And don't eat anything, whoever offers it. Only drink from cans you buy and open yourselves. Trust me on this; I mean it.'

They nodded and turned silently towards where their mother lay. It was turning out to be a bit of a day. First, the shock news about their mother's collapse, resulting in their desperate race to get back home. Then their father showing more emotion in one minute than they had ever seen before in their whole lives. They couldn't decide on which event had surprised them more.

Hall reached the foyer of the hospital and drew a deep breath. He straightened his tie and peered round the door. The press and media had gone; his way to his car was free and clear. He stepped outside into the darkening evening and reached into his pocket for his mobile and switched it on. He would phone Jacquie first and then the nick. His phone was going through its interminable wheebling noises as it searched for a signal. He stepped further into the darkness of the car park, turning it this way and that, searching for a position, no matter how uncomfortable, that would give him more than the 'emergency calls only' message on the screen. If he had not been Henry Hall he would have thrown the thing into the bushes in frustration.

A car approaching from his left piqued his

policeman's instinct. This wasn't a road, only a car park, and so the traffic was one-way; it should have been coming from his right. He turned and saw that, not only was the car coming from the wrong direction, but it had no lights on and the driver was either very small or was crouching down behind the wheel, in what looked like a deliberate attempt to avoid being recognised. In the seconds that he had he ticked things off on the checklist in his mind. The car was a mid-range saloon or hatchback, with the maker's logo removed. It was dark, but whether blue or black or even a really dark green it was impossible to say. In the dark, it isn't only all cats which are grey, but all cars as well. The number plate had been removed. There was a screech of tyres and the machine lurched forward, the single street light flashing just once in the windscreen reflection. Time up; he leapt backwards into what he soon discovered was an extremely thorny bush, his mobile flying into the air. The car swerved up the kerb but missed him by inches as he lay there with long thorns sticking in where no long thorn should ever go. As he lay there, trying to regain his feet without moving too much, a difficult task at the best of times, let alone in the dark, he heard a scream of brakes and the sound of metal on metal.

Excellent, he thought. The bastard's hit something. Now I've got him. Spurred on, he struggled out of his bush with nothing like the aplomb of Br'er Rabbit and ran gingerly to the scene of the crash, trying to ignore the sudden pain in his ankle.

Another mid-range saloon was slewed up onto the kerb. It had a gash down one side and a large piece of bumper was trailing on the ground. Glass was glittering on the ground all around and there was a faint hiss as the punctured tyre on the front nearside let go of the last of its air. Of the other car, there was no sign.

The passenger door opened and an irate head emerged, a shock of wiry hair outlined against the light. 'Bugger that, Jacquie. That had to be deliberate. See what I mean about someone with a grudge against me?' The figure turned. 'Oh, hello, Henry. What are you doing there? How's Margaret?'

Henry straightened up as well as he was able. 'Max. Jacquie. New car?'

Jacquie was out of her seat now and was looking ruefully at the damage. 'Yes, it was. But sadly, not mine. It's my mother's. Did you get a number, Henry? It must have come straight past you. Oh, sorry, how's Margaret?'

He dealt with the most important question first. 'Still unconscious, but the boys are there and they'll let me know if there's any change. Oh, damn.' The curse sounded odd in Henry's mouth, but they understood. 'My phone went flying. They won't be able to reach me.' He started to hunt around aimlessly, hobbling over the tarmac. 'It went over here somewhere.'

Jacquie looked closer. 'Guv, you're bleeding. Did it hit you, the car?'

'No, though not for want of trying. I jumped into that bush over there. It's got really sharp thorns.'

Maxwell went over to the hedge and peered into its branches. 'Pyracantha,' he announced.

'Ouch,' Jacquie said. 'Those thorns are nasty, Henry. The tips break off and can set up an infection. And you're not walking any too chipperly. Come on, you couldn't *be* any closer to A&E than this. You need to be checked over, at the least.'

'I must find my phone, first,' the DCI said. The pain was taking over from the shock now and he knew, from careful testing, that a lot of the thorns were either still in his clothing or, rather more importantly, actually in *him*.

'I'll phone you, guv,' Jacquie said. 'Then we can track it down.'

'I'll phone,' said Maxwell. 'You move the car.'

'You? Phone?' Jacquie and Hall chorused, although it *was* more plausible than Maxwell moving the car.

'No need for sarcasm,' Maxwell said, taking Jacquie's proffered mobile. 'I *can*. I just *don't.*' He gave them a withering look. 'I usually have people.' He turned the phone to the light and then reached into his jacket pocket and took out his reading glasses. The phone in his hand made small beeping noises and he occasionally made small tutting noises. But, eventually, over in an adjacent hedge, came the sound of Henry's phone ringing. Not for Henry Hall the 'Ride of the Valkyrie', the 'William Tell Overture' or even 'What's New Pussycat?' No, Henry Hall's phone rang. Brinng brinng, Brinng, brinng. Like the man himself, boring, predictable, doing exactly what it said on the tin. Hall and Maxwell triangulated on the noise until they ran it to earth, cushioned in the topmost branches of a mercifully thorn-free shrub. Hall grabbed it, refused the call and put it in his pocket.

While some of the men in her life played hunt the mobile, Jacquie reached into the glove compartment and pulled out the can of instant puncture repair and inflator that her aunt had bought everyone in the family for Christmas. Having an unimaginative aunt was sometimes very helpful; Jacquie knew it would be there and she wasn't disappointed. It worked, as well, which was a bit more of a surprise. She got into the battered vehicle and gingerly turned over the engine.

Hall watched and listened carefully to make sure everything was working and then turned back to Maxwell. 'Right,' he said. 'While Jacquie moves the car, I will very, very slowly and even more carefully, make my way to A&E. No need for you to come. I'm sure you have places to be. But, hold on, why are you here at all?'

'We came to see you, Henry,' Maxwell told him. 'I think the poisoner is after me. We wanted to see what you thought of that theory and also, of course, to find out how Margaret is doing.'

Hall turned to his man, but rather more slowly than he would have liked, due to a particularly sharp thorn which seemed to have lodged itself where the sun don't shine. And the ache was starting to climb all the way up his leg. 'Mr Maxwell, if I may be formal for a moment. I admit that Nolan had an unpleasant experience this afternoon. But if you don't mind my saying so, my wife is on drips and various medical interventions in the hospital over there. I was almost mown down by a murderous car and even as we speak am in agony from thorns stuck in places only my flannel knows as a rule. And for some reason, you think the poisoner is after *you*. Why is this, if you don't mind telling me?'

Maxwell had the grace to look sheepish, but quickly rallied. 'I can see that you've had a bad run, but the car could be an accident, surely? He certainly didn't seem to be much of a driver, the way he ploughed into Jacquie.'

'I expect you are already aware of my views on coincidence?'

Maxwell nodded.

'Then you will realise what I have assumed from the following: logo removed from front of car; number plate, ditto, and finally, driver crouching down so as not to be seen clearly. Oh, and I forgot, going the wrong way round a car park and with his lights off. And, yes, add this in, he mounted the pavement to have a proper go at me.'

Maxwell looked into the air and mulled. 'I assume that you assume that the car driver was after you.' He knew all about 'asses' and 'you' and 'me', but this was not the time to resurrect great team-building nonsenses of our time.

'Correct. Go to the top of the class.'

Jacquie, approaching from where she had parked her mother's damaged car, heard a chill in the air. 'Is everything all right, guv? Max?'

The silence was the silence of the playground; neither one would give an inch and it was pointless waiting for a reply.

'Right then,' she said, brightly. 'Let's get you off to A&E, guv. Darling,' she looked over her shoulder at Maxwell, 'while we do this, why don't you pop on to the ward and visit your colleagues and colleague-to-be? You've probably got a few minutes of visiting time left, and if not, I rely on you to get yourself in some other way. See you in...' she glanced at her watch, '...shall we say an hour?'

Hall, standing there in agony, thought that that wouldn't be half long enough. 'Can you pop in on Margaret, please?' he asked. 'Tell the boys where I am. I'm going to have to switch my mobile off while I'm having treatment.'

'Will do,' said Maxwell, trotting off towards the main entrance. He was trying to decide whether to go for the Prince of Wales or the David Beckham approach when doing his round. This was serious stuff, but where Legs Diamond was concerned, it was hard to stop oneself having just a bit of fun.

Jacquie felt for a thorn-free area of Henry Hall to hold on to and finally found his elbow. They eased themselves slowly towards the double doors of A&E, with frequent pauses to allow Henry to adjust his clothing and manage his limp. Before they went in, Jacquie stopped.

'I'll just switch my phone off, guv. I read the other day that they don't make a ha'p'orth of difference to machines, but most places prefer to be safe than sorry.' She reached into her bag and brought out her phone. 'Look at that,' she said. 'How typical. Max has left it on the menu screen. He's really got no idea about phones.' She looked closer. 'Wait a minute. That's odd.'

'What is?' grimaced her boss. He was beginning to think he even had thorns in his teeth; everything hurt.

'Well, your number is shown as engaged. When Max rang you, it didn't go through.'

'Of course it did. It rang and we found it in the bush.'

'It may well have done. But it wasn't Max ringing you. Check.'

'Oh, God. It might have been one of the boys.' The punctured policeman tried his best to reach into his jacket, but had to admit defeat. Jacquie reached carefully inside and pulled the phone out. He inclined his head to her, asking mutely that she check. He just couldn't move fast enough, and he really *had* to know. Now.

She flicked it open and chose 'missed calls'. Her own number was there, but several down the list and not in the last ten minutes. The number at the top of the list was not one she knew and, like Hall, she was afraid it was one of his sons' mobiles. She read it out to him.

He shook his head. 'Say it again. No, not all of it. I recognise the last three digits of numbers; otherwise it takes too long.'

'Nine one seven.'

'No, that's not one of ours. Is it someone from the nick?'

'Not that I can think of. Anyway, wouldn't it come up as a name?'

'That's true. Yes, it would. Look, Jacquie, I'll be all right in here on my own. Anyway, it won't do much for our working relationship if you find out exactly where I've got these thorns sticking in me.'

She grinned, knowing that he wouldn't.

'Get off to the nick, or use your mobile from your car. Take mine as well. Find out who that phone belongs to and get a half a dozen squad cars round to his house. Take the ram. Beat the bastard's door down. Just don't kill him. I want to do that.'

'Guv!' She was genuinely shocked. He was usually so by the book.

'Sorry, Jacquie, to spoil your image of me. But I've never had thorns up my arse before, if I may be blunt, and I'm not feeling quite myself.' He turned slowly and waited for the automatic door to creak open, before allowing himself to be swallowed by the murk of the energy-saving bulbs of A&E. Fifties lighting at Two Thousand's prices.

Jacquie turned away and heard Maxwell's voice in her head. 'Never had thorns up his arse before, perhaps. That's because it's where he keeps his head.' She smiled a small smile and made her way to the car. She had a lot of phoning to do, while Maxwell enjoyed himself taking off the Prince of Wales around the sickbeds of Leighford General.

The Acting Headmaster made his way through the maze of ill-lit and worse-signposted corridors to the General High Dependency Medical Non-Emergencies Mixed Gender Bed Unit, formerly known as Tottingleigh Ward. Visiting hours were well and truly past but, as he might have expected, the Senior Night Nurse was an old Leighford Highena and so his passage was smooth.

'Hello, Louise,' he said, in that strange half-whisper that hospital visitors adopt, opening his mouth very wide and enunciating the husked vowels very clearly. 'I've come to visit Mr Diamond and the rest of the staff you have in here. Also, I have a message for Mrs Hall's visitors.'

'Well,' she replied in stentorian tones which made him wince, 'Mrs Hall is down on the left, with the curtains round. The others,' she made a sweeping gesture with her left hand, 'are spread around. Help yourself.' He turned towards Margaret Hall's shrouded bed. 'But, Mr Maxwell?'

'Yes?' he mouthed.

'You will be quiet, won't you?'

He nodded, stunned at the injustice of the reminder. Louise, it had to be said, looked different in a different uniform. But the level of inanity hadn't changed.

'You still up at the school?' she bellowed.

He grinned like a death's head – his usual rejoinder to that question.

He popped his head round the curtains and gestured one of Hall's boys to join him on the outside. In sotto voce, he sketched out the policeman's dilemma, and somehow the surroundings made it easy not to laugh. Hall Jnr – for the life of him, Maxwell couldn't remember the lad's name – nodded and slipped back behind the curtains, to keep up the droning duologue with which he and his brother were trying to rouse

234

their mother.

Further down the ward, but on the same side, were the beds containing the job hopefuls, ranged one after the other as if laid out for the choice to be made. Miss Mackenzie was first, lying back on her raised pillows in a pink nightie of such outstanding femininity that Maxwell felt it needed some kind of warning label. She was reading a book, with unlikely dark-rimmed glasses perched on the end of her nose. She looked good enough to eat and Maxwell stood at the foot of her bed, enjoying the view with one half of his brain and sending telepathic messages of apology to Jacquie with the other half.

Sensing him standing there, she looked up, over the top of her specs. 'Hello?' she said, doubtfully.

He moved round the bed and sat down on her chair, bona fide visitors for the use of. It was suitably tatty, plastic and just a soupçon Third World. 'You probably don't remember me,' he said. 'We met on Thursday at the school.'

She gave him a wan smile. 'It seems very long ago,' she said. 'But I do remember you. That boy knocked me over and you...'

He grinned. 'Yes, that was me. Maxwell. Call me Max.'

'Thank you, Max, I will. But I doubt we will be meeting again, unless your other job is as hospital visitor.'

'Now, now,' he said, patting her hand. 'The interviews still have to be held, don't forget. It's not over till the fat lady sings ... and,' he nodded behind him to where Mrs Bevell lay, a huge mound under the bedclothes, 'she seems quite quiet tonight.'

'Max, you're very naughty,' she said, smiling. 'But, no, I don't think I will be continuing with my career under Leighford's roof. I have found all this to be very unsettling.' Her eyes opened even wider than usual. 'Even if I wasn't the target, someone had a go at killing me, Max. Is that normal at an interview?'

'I've never come across it before,' Maxwell said, 'I have to admit.' He sighed. 'Still, it's not the profession I came into, in so many ways. The police are working on the case, of course, and they now think that the poisonings are random.'

'Random?' she said. 'Poisonings? Do you mean there have been more? At other schools, you mean? What *do* you mean?' Annette Mackenzie was sinking further into la-la-land with every part of the conversation. Surely, she'd wake up soon.

Maxwell looked uncomfortable. 'I'm guessing that you haven't been watching the news,' he said.

She shook her head. 'We don't have televisions in here, too much electronic gear around. Why?'

'There have been … a number of other episodes, yes,' he said, sounding horribly like Henry Hall.

'Well,' she said, throwing her hands in the air and letting them fall into her lap. 'In my opinion all the more reason *not* to come to live in Leighford. Everyone is clearly nuts.'

'Well,' Maxwell conceded, 'it appears *one* person is. Some of us would pass for normal on a dark night.'

She closed her eyes and lay back on the pillows.

236

'Possibly, Max, very possibly. But if you'll excuse me, I'll say goodnight and very possibly good-bye.' She turned her head and flashed her amazing blue eyes one more time at him. 'I'm sorry,' she said. 'I think we could have been friends.'

He patted her hand. 'I think we could have been,' he agreed. 'Goodnight. Sleep tight.'

'Don't let the bedbugs bite,' she added, reaching up and switching off her light.

He stood looking down at her for a few moments, a pale orange in the street light's glow from the window, and then moved on. Fiona Smollett was lying, not unexpectedly, flat on her back with the bedclothes immaculately tucked around her. Although not out of character, this was not all of her doing. The NHS had given her a present; not of emergency nightclothes or a free toothbrush, but of a particularly nasty dose of clostridium difficile, introduced with the needle delivering her poison antidote. Her bed was enlivened, but not by much, by a series of signs warning off the potential unwary. Maxwell hadn't much reason to touch Miss Smollett and he was quietly delighted to heed what they said and moved on across the ward to where Mrs Bevell lay, guarded ferociously by Mr Bevell, whom no nurse had been brave enough to see off.

'Good evening, Mr Bevell,' Maxwell ventured. 'How is your wife?'

'Who are you?' barked Bevell, flicking open his notepad and putting aside the bowl of fruit he had been nursing jealously on his lap.

Maxwell swallowed his natural antipathy to the horrible little man and his natural inclination to put one on him and said in his most pleasant Acting-Headmasterly voice, 'We've met, Mr Bevell. Peter Maxwell, Acting Headmaster of Leighford High School.' He leant forward helpfully. 'I believe I may be on your list.' Using his skills honed to perfection in years of waiting in front of the desk of Legs Diamond, he read the listings upside down. 'Yes, there I am.' He pointed towards the bottom of the page. 'Just below Virgin Rail and just above the Home Office.' He glanced up. 'Home Office?' he queried.

Bevell looked at him with scorn. 'Generic term,' he said, 'to cover all of the police misdemeanours.'

'Oh, I see.' Maxwell straightened up and stepped back a pace. No point in adding trespass into personal space to his list of crimes.

'Anyway,' Bevell said with a nasty edge to his voice. 'How may I help you?' As if 'help' was in the man's vocabulary.

'I'm just here to see how your wife is getting on. And the other victims of Thursday's events, of course, in my current capacity.'

'I couldn't help noticing you were speaking to that lad over there,' Bevell observed, 'the one whose mother is behind the curtains. I hope they are suing for personal distress, poking your nose in at a time like this. I am coming to the conclusion that you are morbidly curious.'

'No, no,' Maxwell said, backing away. 'Peter Maxwell, as I said. But I'll leave you now to get on with your ... jotting. Bye now. Enjoy your fruit.' And he turned and hurried away as fast as dignity would allow, past the nurses' station

238

where Louise was adjusting her nicotine patch and on to the bedside of James Diamond, erstwhile Headteacher of Leighford High School.

He looked somehow smaller even than when he was upright and trying to run the school, as he lay there under his hospital-issue covers. Maxwell had never seen the man without a tie before and it was something of a shock. Declining standards, dumbing down – it all lay there on the hospital bed. He was drip-free, but very pale and wan. The sedge had clearly withered from his lake. He turned his head and focused his eyes on his visitor. 'Hello, Max,' he said, with a ghost of a smile. 'How nice of you to come and visit.' Then his expression changed to a look of mild panic. 'Everything's all right, isn't it? At the school?'

Yet again, Maxwell found himself patting someone's hand. If he had ever had the leisure time to list potential hand pattees, Diamond's name would have been among the substitutes at best, and yet here they were, patter and pattee. 'Don't worry, Headmaster,' he said. 'Everything is absolutely running like clockwork.'

'Really?' Diamond looked a little crushed.

'Well,' Maxwell hastened to comfort the man, taking a calculated guess that he hadn't watched John Cleese in *Clockwise*. 'Not like when *you* are there, of course, Headmaster. But it is all running smoothly.' He looked down into the stressed face. 'I'm sorry,' he said. 'You're just going to have to trust me on this one. Have I *ever* let you down?'

Diamond looked as though he was going to cry. Surely, there wasn't time before lights out to even begin to list all of the times that Maxwell had

239

been suspended, absent, beaten up and all the rest. Just because his exam results were the best in the school bar the Japanese department – teacher, one; pupil cohort, one, in the shape of James Kagamoshi – it didn't mean Diamond trusted him further than he could throw him. And, in his current weakened state that wasn't very far, although he liked to tell himself that, with health and strength on his side, he could give it a go. He closed his eyes. This was all too much.

'Goodnight, Max,' he whispered. 'Thank you for dropping by.'

Dismissed, Maxwell shrugged his shoulders and went in search of Bernard Ryan. He found him in a side room, with more admonitory notices, this time on the door and small window that let visitors get a glimpse of the man within. He turned to a nurse that was hurrying past. She was not, amazingly, a Leighford Highena, but someone of the northern persuasion by her accent – perhaps Petersfield.

'Can I visit Mr Ryan?' he asked, in his hospital hush voice.

She looked him up and down with distaste. 'Are you family?'

'Er, no. A colleague.'

'Not a doctor, then?'

'No, a teacher.'

'So, not a nurse.'

'No, I'm–'

'Ancillary staff?'

'No. I–'

'Can you read?'

'Yes, I'm a–'

240

'I'll make it easy for you, shall I, then?' she said, shifting the gum to the other cheek. 'No. You can't visit Mr Ryan. If, as you claim, you can read you would be able to tell that.' And she stalked away, to bring comfort and succour to some poor damned soul.

Maxwell looked around for a trusty Highena, and finally Louise, the Senior Nurse, came round a corner, holding a bedpan at arm's length.

'Louise ... I ... oh, my word,' he said, backing away. 'Can we talk in a minute when you've...?' He waved at the pan.

'In the office,' she said, trying not to breathe, and scurried away, using the special nurse walk that was not really a run, but almost.

He went round behind the nurses' station, trying not to look at the patient charts displayed across it, and let himself into Louise's tiny glass-sided office. After a few moments, she came in and shut the door.

'Sorry about that,' she said with a smile. 'That's the trouble with having poison cases. Not only is it a bit...' she screwed up her nose, '...smellier than usual, we also have to keep it, for analysis. We're running out of shelves. Anyway, Mr Maxwell, how can I help you?' She foraged in a drawer and brought out an opened packet of ginger nuts. She loosened one with her thumb and proffered it to Maxwell. 'Biscuit?'

He drew breath to accept and then suddenly changed his mind. Where *had* that thumb been? He shook his head and smiled. 'No, thanks, Louise. I was just wondering how Mr Ryan is.'

She turned down the corners of her mouth and

241

shook her head. 'Not too well, Mr Maxwell, actually. I don't know how the poison he was given worked, but everyone seems to have had different amounts or, at least, different reactions to it. Miss Mackenzie, for example, needn't be here still, but she seems a little vulnerable and the police are also afraid to let her out. I assume in case the poisoner has another go. I can't believe she did it, can you? You know, giving herself a minor dose to cover her tracks.'

Maxwell smiled in semi-agreement. He was impressed. Louise was obviously watching a lot of *CSI*. He, for his part, couldn't help remembering the beautiful Madeleine Smith, poisoner of Glasgow– just a little before Louise's time. About one hundred and fifty years before; even Maxwell had been only a boy.

'Then, of course, Mrs Bevell was given another dose and there was hell to pay over that one, I can tell you. Plus, of course, Mr Bevell is threatening to sue.'

'Of course,' agreed Maxwell.

'I'd love it to be him, Mr Maxwell, wouldn't you?'

'I certainly would, Louise, but I've found it doesn't work like that. Professional bastards like him usually walk away scot-free. Or, in his case, a few thousand richer. Anyway, do go on. I seem to remember you had a gift for precis in the Sixth Form.'

'No, Mr Maxwell,' she smiled. 'You said that my essays were always too short by about fifty per cent.'

'Same thing. Go on.'

'Yes, Mrs Bevell. She seems to be getting on all right, despite her second dose. But you have probably noticed her robust constitution.'

This time, Maxwell threw hospital whispering to the winds and laughed out loud. The nurse grinned back. 'I certainly have, Louise. In fact, who could miss it?'

'Then, there's Mr Diamond. He's getting on all right, I suppose, given his age and condition.' She lowered her voice. 'I'm afraid he's not very fit, Mr Maxwell. He...' and here she stopped speaking at all and simply mimed the raising of a glass.

Maxwell was truly amazed. 'Does he?' This would be one for the next school newsletter.

'The liver functions were unmistakeable. Ooh, Mr Maxwell, this is in confidence, isn't it, only, I'm not supposed to discuss patients?'

'Of course it is, Louise. Of course it is. Schtum is my middle name. And what about Mr Ryan?'

'Mr Ryan is probably in renal failure.'

'Serious,' Maxwell observed.

'Well, fatal sometimes. But he'll probably die of the liver failure. Or something else, because he is in shutdown, basically. He might rally, but we're not expecting it. Meanwhile, he is compromised immunologically and so we are keeping people out.'

'And that's because of some hospital bug, is it?' Maxwell was doubly glad he hadn't taken the biscuit.

'No, no that's the poison. Yet another reaction to it, you see.' She looked at Maxwell with her head on one side. 'It's odd, isn't it, Mr Maxwell?'

'What is?' What, in all of this, could she possibly

243

pin down as particularly odd, he wondered?

'I don't get much experience of poisons in general nursing, of course. I suppose the geriatric nurses see more of that, wrong prescribing and so on.'

Maxwell decided to let that one go as a case of sufficient unto the day is the evil thereof. That, and Harold Shipman.

'But it has made us all think, having so many connected cases. The poisoner just isn't very *good* at it. The dose wasn't the same in all of the portions. That's odd. You'd think that he'd have put it in the prawn cocktail sauce, for example, but we think he must have added it later and, well, you know, just put more on one than the other. And then, he really meant to hurt people, because aconite is a very serious poison to start dishing out. You're not planning to give someone a gippy tummy when you play with that one.'

'Yes, Louise, but why is that odd?'

She shrugged her shoulders. 'Well, you'd have just thought he would be better at it, wouldn't you? Go to all that trouble to get the poison, get to where you could doctor the food and then be so ... I don't know, Mr Maxwell, what's the word I want? *Sloppy*, I suppose.'

Maxwell looked at her with new eyes. 'My goodness, Louise, you're right. He did all the difficult stuff and then messed up the simple bit, the dishing it out. And...' he shook a finger at her to keep her quiet while he gathered his thoughts, 'and he's been trying different things since then. Different poisons, but still administered in food that anyone might eat.'

She looked over his shoulder. 'Oops,' she said. 'Consultant on the ward, Mr Maxwell. I've got to go. I hope I'll see you again soon.'

But not in a professional capacity, thought Maxwell, wiggling his fingers at her in farewell. He followed her out of the office, hoping to catch sight of someone of the stature of James Robertson Justice as Sir Lancelot Spratt. Instead it was just a kid in a white coat surrounded by other kids in white coats. Eventually he found his way up to the orthopaedic ward, where Helen Maitland was making life hell for anything in a uniform. He stuck his head round the door and could hear her in full flight.

He fixed a carefree grin on his face and made his way to where she was trussed up like a chicken on traction.

'Helen! Dear heart! How the devil are you?' He bent to give her a kiss.

'Have you come to ask stupid questions, Max, or have you come to help me scratch my leg?' she said, twisting this way and that to try and reach her ankle.

'You scratch my ankle, I'll scratch yours,' he said genially, 'and by the way, we historians call them, in all modesty, nether limbs.' He extracted a biro from an inside pocket. 'Now,' he said, brandishing it, 'where do you want me to start?'

'Max, have I ever told you you are a simply wonderful man?'

'Not lately, but you can start now if you want,' he said. 'Now, tell me if this tickles.' He poked the biro gently underneath her plaster and wiggled it about. She writhed in pleasure. 'Better?'

245

'Perfect,' she breathed. 'Just perfect. How long can you stay?'

He glanced round to the end of the ward; the clock above the doors told him the horrible truth. 'Well, Helen,' he said. 'The bad news is that I can only give you another ten minutes, I'm afraid. I promised Jacquie I would be back in the car park in an hour and she worries if I'm late, for some strange reason.'

Helen laughed and lobbed a grape at him. 'I'm not surprised, Max. If you were mine, I'd keep you on a stout rope, tethered like a goat in the yard, to some immoveable object. Every time you wander off, you get into some sort of trouble.'

'Madam,' he said, drawing himself up, 'I object. After all, I am doubly your boss at the moment. As Acting Head I can fire you.'

'I simply don't know how you have the nerve,' she said, ignoring his remark completely. 'After all you've put that poor woman through over the years. Still, she must like it or I suppose she wouldn't have agreed to marry you. But, don't worry. The evening drinks trolley has just arrived, so I shall be getting outside my nightly Horlicks in a minute anyway.' She leant forward. 'Oh, bugger it. I hate it when it's him.'

'Who?' Maxwell screwed round to see better and inadvertently gave her a small stab wound with his pen.

'Ouch! Max, watch what you're doing with that.'

He looked round at her. 'Sorry,' he said, absently.

'Max? What is it?'

246

'Sorry, Helen, old chap. It's just that I recognised the trolley dolly. The wispy hair, the unkempt beard. I hadn't seen him for a while. Not since Dierdre's funeral, in fact. And just recently he seems to be everywhere.'

Helen clicked her fingers. 'Of *course!*' she said. 'I've been trying to place him. Dierdre's uncle, isn't it?'

'Yes, that's right. Oliver Lessing, as I live and breathe. First at school, now here. He's always pushing a trolley; the man's obsessed. I'll go out the other end of the ward, Helen, if that's all right with you. He's not my favourite person and he hates my guts.'

'Why?' Helen genuinely wanted to know. She loved Max dearly and, while he could be bloody annoying, she couldn't think how anyone could actually hate him.

'History, I expect.' He caught her puzzled look. 'No, no, I don't mean *History*, as in what I teach. I mean history, as in what happened in our past. He remembers the time when Dierdre and I really didn't get along and holds it against me. That and a few other things.'

'Did you ever actually *get* along with Dierdre?' Helen felt she had to ask. 'I don't really remember that.'

'Well, perhaps it would be more accurate to say that we stopped not getting along.'

'What other things?' Helen reminded him. 'Re Uncle Ollie?'

'Don't ask.' Maxwell shook his head. 'Water under the bridge. Look, darling, I must fly. I'm late anyway.' He dashed to the business end of

247

the bed and gave her a quick kiss on the forehead. 'Abyssinia. Don't take any sweeties from any nasty men.' He paused and looked thoughtfully at Oliver Lessing, struggling to move the enormous heavy trolley with his puny little legs, which scrabbled against the Flotexed floor before he finally got it moving. 'In fact, don't have your Horlicks tonight. Don't ask me why, I'd just rather you didn't.'

She followed his glance and chuckled. 'Max, don't get carried away. He's a Hospital Volunteer, not Major Armstrong.'

'Bless you for knowing the name of a random poisoner, Helen. Now indulge me by settling for your bottled water.'

She looked into his eyes. She'd been his deputy in the Sixth Form now for more years than either of them cared to remember. He had never let her down before. She gave in. 'Oh, all right. But if I have nightmares, I shall know who to blame.'

'Nick Ross,' he called as he vanished into MRSA land.

Chapter Sixteen

Jacquie reached her mother's car, and as she saw the ripped metal in the car park's lights her heart gave a little jolt as she was reminded of the task still ahead: telling her about the accident. All the memories from childhood came up and piled one on top of the other in her head. She could hear the martyred sigh, the breathy and insincere thankfulness that she, Jacquie, was unharmed and that anyway, what was a car but a chunk of metal? Then would come the head shakes, the disbelief that anyone, let alone her own daughter, could be so thoughtless as to let this happen to a poor lone widow-woman's pride and joy. The dark cloud in Jacquie's head grew large and ominous, a thunderhead with no reprieve but to burst.

She got into the car and looked around. If you just sat inside, it looked perfectly all right. She decided on that method and shook herself to get ready for the rest of the night. It was going to be a long one, she felt it in her water. She turned the radio on low, for company. Something about this case was spooking her. She had always hated poison cases and, in fact, had only personally come across two before. One had been a wife slowly feeding her husband with good old-fashioned rat poison. A sharp-eyed GP had spotted that one early enough and no one had died. The second had been the case of a daughter poisoning her elderly and increasingly demented mother. She could bond with that one, no problem. But the common strand had been that it had all been in the family. In this case, the invisible killer was using a scattergun approach. No one was immune from his deadly hobby. She sighed. She hated the random loony cases. The only light at the end of the tunnel was that, as he was so *very* random and apparently so *very* loony, it could only be a matter of time before he absent-mindedly ate one of his own doctored treats and died.

She turned her mind to the job at hand. Firstly, she checked her own phone again. She made a note in her book of the time of the call Maxwell had attempted but which had definitely not connected. She turned Hall's phone on and it flashed logos at her until she was on the verge of throwing it away. Finally, the home screen came up and she scrolled through to the call register. There, on the screen, was a call from an un-named mobile, timed literally two seconds before the call from her own phone. Next to the number was a small icon which she assumed meant that a message had been left. She indulged in a small Maxwell moment in which she longed for the days when mobile phones were the size of small suitcases and the screens were enormous, green and very, very simple. By jogging dials randomly she found herself in the voicemail menu. Trial and error finally got her to the right place and she put the phone to her ear to listen.

The voice was not one she recognised immedi-ately and it was clearly disguised, she thought, by an electronic voice changer. 'Hello, Mr Hall,' it grated metallically. 'That was a close one, wasn't it? Better luck for me next time, perhaps. I hope the wife is all right. And the little boy. I said you'd be sorry. And so will all the other hundreds of people who will be tucking into my little specialities tonight. Yum, yum, Mr Hall. Sleep tight.'

Jacquie let the phone drop to her lap. So it *was* a vendetta. And both Hall and Maxwell were right. It *was* aimed at them – both of them. She leant her head on the steering wheel for a moment and took a deep breath. Now she had to decide what to do. Did she go back into the hospital and speak to Henry Hall, thorn removal notwithstanding? Or did she ring the nick? Or did she go to the nick, leaving Maxwell stranded? Or did she wait for Maxwell? Or...

There was a knock on the window, passenger side. She jumped and turned to see who it was. A dark figure filled the window and blocked out the light. It seemed to be mouthing something. Her hand flew to her chest as her heart leapt and hammered.

'For goodness' sake, Jacquie,' the creature said, its voice muffled by the glass and the pounding of her blood in her ears. 'Let me in.'

She pinged the central-locking button and Maxwell exploded into the car on a wave of fresh air and disinfectant. He sketched a kiss at her and sat back. 'What's the matter?' he asked, peering into her face. 'You're as white as a sheet.'

Wordlessly, she held out Hall's phone to him.

'I've been visiting the hospital, sweetness,' he

251

said. 'Not having a brain transplant. The call I made to Henry was a complete fluke. You'll have to explain.'

'There's a message,' she said shortly, and pressed the required buttons and then handed the phone to him again. Unlike Maxwell, Jacquie Carpenter could remember what button did what for more than twenty seconds after the initial discovery.

He listened intently to the call, then gave her the phone back, a grim look on his face. 'A bit personal,' he said.

She nodded. 'I thought that. Then he mentioned the "little boy", Nolan, specifically. I think he must be out to get you both.' Her lip quivered. 'This one has really got to me, Max. I can cope with madmen with axes, people trying to run you over, all of that. But this is so ... sneaky.'

Maxwell leant closer and put an arm around her shoulders. She leant in, grateful for the normality of the roughness of his tweed jacket, the smell of him, even overlaid as it was by Essence of Leighford General. 'Of course it's sneaky, sweetheart,' he said, kissing the top of her head. 'You can't threaten people with poison, the way you can with a knife or a gun.' He became, briefly, every hard-boiled cop on television or cinema; Kojak meets Dirty Harry who also bumps into Booth out of *Bones*. 'Look out everybody. He's got a plant-based poison, an alkaloid by the look of it, and he's not afraid to use it!'

He felt, rather than heard, her giggle. 'Point taken,' she said into his coat. 'But, even so.'

He moved back upright and looked her in the

252

eye. 'So, are we going to stop being spooked and go out and catch this sneaky person?'

She nodded and handed him the phones from her lap. She twisted round and put on her seat belt and carefully put the car into reverse. She eased out of the parking space and drove slowly towards the exit, listening carefully for the sound of scraping metal or dragging rubber which would mean the damage was worse even than it appeared. There was just one rather faint but rhythmic clunking noise from what Jacquie thought of as the front offside and what Maxwell thought of as the driver's feet part of the car, but when Jacquie applied the brake nothing terrible happened, the noise got no louder and no sparks flew, so she decided it was safe to go, slowly, to Leighford nick and see what they could do about identifying the phone number on Hall's mobile.

'How are you going to break this bit of news to your mother?' Maxwell said, encompassing the car with one expansive gesture.

'Max, how many times must I tell you,' she said, poking him smartly in the leg, 'not to read my mind?'

'Sorry, heart,' he said. 'I'll try to keep out of your brain, but it's nice and cosy in there. But you haven't answered my question.'

She sighed. 'Oh, I don't know,' she said. 'It won't go well, that's for sure. She's a bit anal about her cars. I'll end up feeling guilty, however I play it. I've broken her car and she won't care about the circumstances.'

Maxwell looked thoughtful. 'Well, she might consider that her karmic balance has been improved by this bump.'

Jacquie laughed shortly. 'How so?'

'Well, she nearly broke our son. And I don't think even your mother would consider a car and a child to have equal value.'

'I suspect it wouldn't be as obvious as you and I might think but, yes, in principle, you're right. I still don't fancy suggesting that to her, though.' Broken children and broken cars. Images that had haunted the mind of Peter Maxwell for years. Except that now he had another child. And the loss of his first would never hurt quite so much again.

'Leave it to me,' Maxwell said, patting her shoulder. 'In fact, look, where are we?' He looked through the windscreen, getting his bearings. 'Yes, we're just coming up to the High Street. If you let me out now, I'll get a cab and get home and explain.'

'Would you?' She looked at him with big, grateful eyes. 'Max, that would be such a weight off my mind.'

'It will be my pleasure,' Maxwell said. 'You ain't seen nothing yet when it comes to guilt. She has only practised on you. I've had a million kids to iron out the glitches on. Off you go now, woman policeman, and save us from the sneaky poisoner.'

She pulled in to the side and he got out, slamming the door hard, only to have it bounce out of its distorted frame and catch him a nasty one on the shin.

'Bugger and poo!' You could tell a man with a First from Cambridge by the superior quality of his expletives.

'Try just pressing it into place,' she suggested, trying to hide a smirk.

'Oh, ha,' he said, tears in his eyes from the pain. 'We'll try that again, shall we?' And he firmly pushed the door home until he heard a click.

'That's better,' she called and drove off to the nick.

He stood there, waving extravagantly, and walked off in the general direction of the taxi rank, watching over his shoulder until she was out of sight. He had had no real plan in mind as he got out of the car, except that this sneaky killer must be out there somewhere. He knew that the Leighford Poisoner, as he was undoubtedly enshrined already in the Sunday papers winging their way to newsagents up and down the land, had not finished. His attempt on Henry Hall in the car park had been opportunistic, of that there was no doubt. His modus operandi was poison, and he still had more to share with the gentlemen (and ladies) of Leighford, now abed.

The town centre was still busy with its usual quota of binge drinkers, most of whom had teaching qualifications and who ducked smartly down side roads or into shop doorways rather than meet Mad Max face-to-face. Maxwell cut a swathe down the High Street until he smelt the unmistakeable smell that hung like an almost visible pall over the Vine, the worst pub in Leighford, and therefore the one least likely to contain either staff or pupils of Leighford High. He wondered, as he headed towards it, how it managed to still smell of an old ashtray, since no smoking was allowed within its hallowed walls. The dull

255

gleam of terminally low-wattage bulbs just made it through the nicotine-encrusted windows, and the desultory 'ping' of the arcade machine was the background music to occasional coughing and the random verbal jottings of Mad Artie, the most local of all locals.

Maxwell pushed open the door and went in. The silence became even more palpable for a few seconds as the batwing doors creaked to a stand-still and all eyes were on the dust-caked stranger, poncho slung over his shoulder, big iron on his hip. Then the game player pushed another button and Artie let fly with a particularly inventive invective.

The landlord, polishing a glass with a dirty cloth, greeted him with his own special brand of disdain. 'Help you?' he muttered.

Maxwell's usual rejoinder to that question in a pub was to ask for the best the landlord had to offer, a foaming beaker of perfectly balanced hop and malt or, perchance, a beaker of the warm south, rolled on a handmaiden's thigh. This time, he played safe. He could tell by the encrusted sugar on the optic below the Southern Comfort that no one had had one of those since his last visit. And that was in 1843.

'Southern Comfort, please. A double, I think. It's been an eventful evening.'

'Ice?'

'No, thank you,' Maxwell grimaced. 'It is meant to be comforting, after all.' A quick whack on the lip by a rock-hard misshapen lump of ice always left a nasty taste. The ice in the Vine quite literally left a nasty taste. Maxwell had always suspected that it was chipped out of gutters during the winter and stored against the day.

'Slice?'

'God, no.' It was getting worse. Had no one yet sussed that all this ice and bits was merely a way of beating Mr Disraeli's Sale of Food and Drugs Act of 1875? God alone knew what sweepings lay among the roasted peanuts on the bar. Maxwell paid and took his drink to a corner table, where he could both think and watch the world go by, if anything from the real world would risk the Vine late on a Saturday night, when the slop tray was beginning its fifteenth circuit through the unwary customer.

He knew there would be serious repercussions when he got home. There was no way he could hide this little jolly from Jacquie. She had probably already phoned home to alert her mother. Her mother, running true to form, would ring her back as soon as Maxwell failed to arrive on time. Egged on by Mrs Troubridge, who loved nothing more than death and disaster, she would be virtually hysterical and the shit would hit the fan at warp speed. He took a steadying sip. He would cross that bridge when he came to it. Meanwhile, he had a poisoner to stalk.

He reached into his inside pocket and brought out a pen and a piece of paper. He looked at the used side and smiled. It was the bottom copy of an order to the County store and he had kept it in that inside pocket since he had sent the top two copies, as per the written instructions, to County Hall. It wasn't that he didn't trust his administrative staff. He just didn't want to make them

257

accomplices after the fact. He folded it back up and put it away. He walked over to the bar.

'Do you have such a thing as a piece of paper I could borrow?'

'Borrer? Gunna lemme have it back arter?' It wasn't a bad Ray Winstone, all things considered.

'Well, no. I suppose *give* would be a better description. Do you have a piece of paper that you could give me?'

Without looking Maxwell in the eye, the barman slid across a copy of last week's pub quiz questions. Maxwell was cheered to see that he would have romped home a clear winner, had it not been for the ten questions on football teams and the twenty-five based on *EastEnders*.

'Thank you very much,' he smiled and went back to his table. Mad Artie had sidled a few places nearer but was still far enough away for his random obscenities to be part of the background noise. Maxwell smoothed out the paper and began to make a sketch map of the town centre, marking food shops with a circle. Then, he went back over the map and crossed through the two twenty-four-hour shops; although closed now, on Saturday night, they kept a large security staff and so were likely to be safe. The weigh-it-yourself shops he also crossed off, as being too random even for this particular random killer. Anything added to the enormous bins of loose raisins, currants and similar, might well go to the bottom and not see the light of day again for weeks, months or ever. This left three shops which were possibles. Of those, one faced on to the square and had huge plate glass windows down to the floor. The aisles of goods were at right angles to the glass, so any passer-by could see the whole of the shop. It was useless to consider exposing oneself near the crystallised fruits in there, he thought, concluding that he should perhaps get out more. So, that left two and those odds were fine by him.

He folded up his paper and put it in his pocket. So intent had he been on his sketch map that he had been unaware of Mad Artie creeping nearer. So his sudden cry of 'Bugger,' only inches from his ear, was bound to make the last swig of Southern Comfort go down the wrong way. Who needs a poisoner, thought Maxwell as he staggered coughing and wheezing from the Vine, when you had local colour like that to contend with? Maxwell had crossed words with Mad Artie before. Both of them called Mad and for good reason, but one of them only nor' by nor'west. Artie was barking in all directions.

Closing time was just past and the town centre was almost empty. A pair of pretend coppers were strolling along Della Street, giving a certain comfort to the populace. Those intent on drinking the night away had already moved on to the clubs on the Sea Front that stayed open virtually round the clock. The thump of an all-night bass reverberated across the square. Late eaters from the few restaurants in the centre were wandering back to their cars or throwing up into waste bins, depending on which establishment they had frequented. Gordon Ramsay would have had a field day.

Maxwell took a seat along the edge of the Councillor MacIllwain Memorial Garden, cool in the moonlight, which made much of the single remaining chrysanthemum not destroyed by the youth of Leighford. The noise from the Sea Front, only a few roads away to the south, filtered through to him as he sat there, taking the night air. The seat was hard and unforgiving, but as the human sounds died away, all he was left with was the sibilance of the sea.

Finally, he was alone. He got to his feet and made his way to the first shop indicated on his map. It was a small satellite of a large chain and, as a consequence, stocked largely items which the average town centre worker might need to stock up on on the way home: drink, mainly. Bread, butter or the many easy-spread equivalents. Cheese. Crisps and cake. Soap powder took up a large section of the retail space and that was good, thought Maxwell. A few more aisles he didn't have to keep an eye on. He chose a dark corner of the frontage, between the chained-up trolleys and the window. He could see quite a large section of the shop from there and, more importantly, both the front door and the double flaps which led into the storage section. His eyes soon became accustomed to the dark and he felt a distant empathy with Metternich, who spent large portions of any night in question patiently stalking small rodents for fun and profit.

He leant there, feeling the chill of the glass on his forehead. He tuned his ears in so that he could dimly hear the judder of freezers in the shop, switching on and off as their thermostats commanded. But there wasn't a single moving thing in there, except the slowly swinging signs exhorting him and everyone else to buy one, get one free. Whoever, he asked himself, in the strange planet of marketing, thought that BOGOF was at all inviting? He was vaguely surprised that Mr Bevell hadn't already sued for distress.

He felt an incipient cramp begin its climb up his left leg and soon could maintain the position no longer. He crept out from his hiding place and, trying to look at once casual and furtive, made his way to the other establishment on his map. This was much smaller, a family-run place not unlike the Barlows'. It was a bit of a long shot, really, but he had worked it all out. The big stores would obviously cause much more widespread panic if Chummy peppered them with his lethal droppings. But they had security, CCTV cameras and even dog patrols. The smaller stores would be less exciting for him, but much easier to break into, and Maxwell had more or less decided that this man, although ruthless and determined, was not actually very good at this crime lark. He was still thinking small.

He was at the side of the shop and pressed in to the window, inches away from the cards advertising everything from a house to a gerbil. He recognised Mrs B's semi-literate scrawl, leaping out at him from a card around halfway down. 'Cleener. Reasonabel raits. Good relaible work. Refs avialabel. Phone Leighford 626987.' Good luck to her, he thought. At least if she wrote in your dust, you'd know who had done it.

He edged round to the door, his feet sticking briefly, at every step, to the pebble-dash of old chewing gum, trodden there by generations of shoplifting children. He was sure he could hear noises from inside, but he had been listening so intently for so long he could hear the small hairs moving inside his ears, he could hear his hair growing. As he reached the angle of the building he saw, but only out of the corner of his eye, a light flash inside. He crouched down so that the National Lottery poster shielded him from anyone inside the shop. He froze as the door opened slowly and a dark-clad figure stepped out and pulled the door very quietly to, behind itself. Maxwell's breath caught in his throat. In his planning of the night's campaign, he had not really factored in the fact that he might well catch Chummy in the act. And now, here he was, just inches from him, tucking something small into the pocket of his black jacket with one hand.

Maxwell stepped forward. He brought his hand down firmly on the black-clad shoulder. 'What's going on here, then?' he boomed, sounding, even to himself, like Dixon of Dock Green on a bad day.

The ninja-like figure reacted instantly. In the hand not in his pocket, he held a large torch. The last thing that Maxwell thought as it crashed into his left temple was that he really should have taken that into account. Then the whole world went black, with wheeling stars and exploding fireworks in the far, far distance. The gum-encrusted pavement came up to meet him and was surprisingly soft, he found. He was quite comfortable as he lay there and was rather ungrateful when he felt a gentle kick in the ribs and a distant Dock Green voice boomed in his head.

'What's going on here, then?' it asked.

'Surely,' said Maxwell into the pavement, 'I just said that.' Far away on a distant planet he heard a policeman talking into his radio. He seemed to be talking about a drunk and disorderly passed out on the pavement by the paper shop. He just had time to feel smug; he must tell Henry Hall that coincidences did happen. There were *two* people passed out on the pavement by the paper shop, and he was one of them. Time did the strange thing it saves for moments – or hours – when folk are asleep, and a mere two seconds went past before he was unceremoniously hoisted to his feet by strong hands beneath his armpits.

'Hello,' said a dubious voice in his ear. 'This is Jacquie Carpenter's bloke. The old one, from up at the school.'

It would have been nice to respond to that, thought Maxwell, but his tongue seemed to have detached itself from his brain.

Then another voice chipped in. 'He doesn't really smell of drink,' it said. Then, following some sniffing noises, 'Oh, wait a minute, though. He's been in the Vine. I can smell it. Spliff alley.'

'There you are, then,' rejoined the first voice. 'You can never tell. I never had him down for a drinker. Let's get him over to that seat. He's heavier than he looks.'

Maxwell was dragged over to a handy park bench, placed there in loving memory of Jock is a Knob, if the painted legend on the back was to be believed. And it was to be believed; Maxwell had taught the boy – it was a fair characteris-

263

ation. He managed a groan and put a hand to his temple. One of the policemen brushed his hair back and looked more closely.

'Hello, look at this. He's had a hell of a whack here.'

'Got it when he fell over, I expect,' his oppo said.

'No, I don't think so. Look,' and he tilted Maxwell's head to the light, still holding back his hair. 'Look, there's an imprint there. He's been hit by something.'

'A torch,' said Maxwell's brain. 'Tch,' agreed his mouth.

'It looks like a torch or something. One of those heavy-duty rubber ones.'

'As'ri,' Maxwell said, trying to nod, but really, *really* gently.

The more sympathetic policeman bent down low so that he could make eye contact without Maxwell having to move his head. 'We'll take you to A&E,' he said, slowly and carefully.

Maxwell took a deep breath and concentrated as hard as he could. 'No,' he said, much more loudly than he had intended. 'P'lice station. Swab for DNA.'

'I'm sorry, Mr ... um, sorry, I can't remember your name.'

Maxwell was delighted that there was at least one policeman in Leighford who hadn't marked his card. 'Maxwell.'

'Yes, of course. Mr Maxwell, I'm afraid we don't do DNA on muggings. We don't have the resources.'

'Not mugging. Poisoner.'

'No, Mr Maxwell. You've been hit. With a torch. You haven't been poisoned.'

Ye Gods. Where did they get these people? He got the definite impression he was not in the presence of a fast tracker. Again, he tried to marshal thoughts and tongue simultaneously. 'I was *hit* by the poisoner. He was in the shop. I got him and he hit me.' He pointed wildly in the direction he hoped the shop lay. 'You must check that shop. He's been in there.'

He heard more radio conversation crackling nearby and then he was being addressed again. 'Mr Maxwell, we're taking you to the station. We've told DS Carpenter we're on our way.'

'Lovely,' Maxwell muttered. A welcoming committee – what could be nicer? They hefted him to his feet and propelled him to the squad car parked at the side of the road at the end of the pedestrian precinct. Pausing only for him to be sick in a flowerbed, they put him in the back and, siren wailing, they set off for the nick, which was approximately two hundred yards on foot, a mile and a half by road, courtesy of the Leighford Town Planners circa 1976.

The Nice Policeman turned round in his seat and spoke kindly to Maxwell. 'DS Carpenter said to tell you she was really looking forward to you getting to the nick,' he said.

Maxwell gave a brave-little-soldier smile. 'I'm sure she is,' he whispered and let his head loll back on the headrest. 'I'm sure she is.'

Chapter Seventeen

Jacquie was pacing the reception area, uncertain whether to give Maxwell a clip round the ear or smother him with kisses. She little realised that Nolan would present her with this dilemma on an almost daily basis, from the day he could work out how to open the front door on his own until the day she died.

After what seemed like years, she heard the squad car pull up outside and then another day passed before the little group edged their way through the doors, the policemen shouldering them open to protect their precious cargo. The scream of the door buzzer clearly went through Maxwell's addled brain like a knife.

'Hello, Jacquie,' the Nice Policeman grinned. 'This is yours, I believe.'

She stood there, shocked. He clearly had had a nasty knock and was at least semi-concussed. A clip round the ear was clearly out of the question – he had had one of those already. And perhaps the kisses could wait until later. There was blood matted in his hair and a dark trickle had run down on to his collar.

He straightened his head to the best of his ability. 'Hello,' he said, with a lopsided grin. 'I got hit with a torch, you know.'

'So I heard,' Jacquie said, then, to his escort, 'I'll take it from here, boys.'

'Are you sure? He's really heavy.'

'I know how heavy he is,' she said. 'He ain't my brother and I know where to lift,' and she slipped under his armpit and led him to a chair, where she propped him. He was glad to be sitting down again, his legs didn't really want to do stuff like standing and walking about. He slid sideways but she had thought it all through; he was wedged happily in a corner and made his own entertainment looking at the pattern in the carpet. It was all vaguely seaside, with scallop shells of quiet and blue days at sea, interspersed with the West Sussex Unit's logo.

She went over to the desk. 'Bill, who is the duty police surgeon tonight?' she asked.

Bill ran a finger down a list and checked the date. 'Astley,' he said.

Jacquie frowned and chewed her lip. 'Oh, shit,' she said. 'Max will think he's dead if Astley examines him. Never mind, I don't have time to take him to A&E and, frankly, I just want to get him horizontal. Do we have a cell empty?'

Again, Bill consulted a list. 'There's a cell that's clean, but it's the high-security one. You know, CCTV, all that. I might have to chuck him out if we get a live one in.'

'Thanks, Bill. Oh, can you ring Astley for me? And don't tell him who it is. They haven't always seen eye to eye.'

'No problem.' The desk man glanced across at Maxwell, sensing that he wouldn't be seeing eye to eye with anybody for an hour or two. He reached to the board behind him. 'Here's the key. Don't worry, I'll sign it out for you.'

'Bill, you are wonderful.' Jacquie confirmed what he knew already. 'All I need now is someone to hold open the door and we'll be set.'

'I'll do that,' said a voice behind her. It was familiar and strangely unwelcome. She turned her head, balancing Maxwell against the wall again.

'Oh,' she said, unevenly. 'Bob. Umm ... are you back?'

'No, don't worry,' he sneered. 'I've just come to get some things.' He held up a carrier bag. 'Apparently, they need my desk.'

'Thanks for holding the door,' she said. There seemed nothing else *to* say.

'You're welcome,' he said. 'What happened?' he asked, gesturing with his head towards Maxwell, who was desperately trying to focus on him, peering like a shortsighted bird of prey, first with one eye, then another.

Jacquie sighed. 'He was knocked out with a blunt instrument – a torch, we think. I'm getting the duty surgeon to have a look at him.'

Davies looked closer. 'A Maglite, I reckon,' he said.

'How on earth do you know that?' Jacquie was impressed in spite of herself.

He pointed. 'There, look. A "g" and an "l" printed backwards in the bruise. It must have been rubber cased, with raised letters. He'd look a damned sight worse if it was metal. It's broken the skin as it is.' He looked at her with feigned regret. 'Ah, Jacquie, wouldn't we have made a good team, eh? Your looks and my brains?' And with that he let the door go, knocking Maxwell

268

out of Jacquie's grasp and trapping her hand painfully in the hinge. 'Oh, sorry,' and he went out into the night, swinging his carrier bag.

'What a wanker.' Bill was out from behind his desk and helping restore Maxwell to Jacquie. The pain in her hand was so bad it had travelled right up her arm and seemed to be lodged in her head, like a migraine with no pretty lights to make it bearable. 'Are you all right? Let me see?'

She held out her hand; there was a sharply defined bruise where the edge of the door had caught it but she could move all of her fingers, though painfully. 'It's OK, Bill. Let's hope that's the last of him.'

The desk sergeant sighed. 'That would be nice. But the Federation are on to it, apparently. He might be reinstated.'

'Surely not here?' Jacquie's eyes were big with pain, tiredness and disbelief.

'They say so,' he said, shaking his head. 'Most people choose to move on, but he is saying reinstatement here or nowhere. Let's hope it's nowhere, eh?' And he held open the door until they were safely through. He didn't think that he would tell Jacquie what else Bob Davies had said. She didn't need to hear that it was, in the gospel according to Davies, either her or him.

As they lurched down the corridor, Jacquie was filled with a sudden terrible exhaustion. It wasn't just the fact that she had been up and working more hours in one day than many people did in seven. It wasn't even that she was supporting, with one arm, a fully grown man who was starting to have ideas of his own where he wanted to go. It was just that this whole thing, ever since she had seen Maxwell's jacket across the legs of a dead body, had taken less than seventy-two hours and she was in overload. Was there such a thing, she wondered, as DTS syndrome – During Traumatic Stress?

'Where am I?' Maxwell suddenly asked, rather too loudly, in her ear.

'We're in Leighford nick, Max,' she said briskly, trying to avoid the 'does-he-take-sugar' tone which was trying to insinuate itself into her voice. Mad Max didn't usually do the cliché thing.

'Why?' he asked plaintively. 'What have we done?'

'What's this "we", white man?' She muttered his ancient Lone Ranger joke instinctively. 'Nothing,' she said, wanting to kiss him on the forehead and ruffle his hair, he sounded so like Nolan. 'Nothing. It's just that you bumped your head and this was a place where you could lie down.'

'I'm not lying down,' he declared. 'I'm walking along.'

'That's right.' Please, God, let him not stick like this, she thought. Let him snap out of it soon, before I deck him with sheer frustration. 'We're going to put you to bed. Look, here we are,' and she opened the door to the cell she had been allocated. 'Oh, pooh. If this is a clean cell, I wouldn't want to smell a dirty one.'

Smelly or not, Maxwell subsided gratefully onto the bed, rolled over onto his side and began to snore almost the moment his head hit the pillow. She looked at him anxiously. She knew from her first aid that sleepiness was a bad sign. On the other hand, it was well past midnight and so he had as much right as anyone else to be tired. She was tired herself; if there had been room on the narrow bed, she would have been well away alongside him. She pushed his feet over to one side and perched on the edge. If she braced her elbows on her knees, and could just relax enough, she might just possibly manage a few minutes zizz of her own. Metternich seemed to do it with no effort required. Perhaps, she thought with a sleepy smile, if she could push her nose up her own bum, she could rest for a while.

A voice, familiar, annoying, annoyed, woke her up with a start.

'I don't understand why you people can't understand the difference between an emergency and some poxy drunk who just wants to sleep it off.' The voice paused in mid-rant. 'DS Carpenter. What's all this?'

Jacquie looked up, blearily. 'Oh, Dr Astley. Good of you to come out.'

There wasn't much chance of that. Jim Astley was as heterosexual as a die although, these days, a single malt and a round of golf had rather more appeal than creaking old, drying-out Marjorie, his better half.

He went down to the business end of the bed and stared in disbelief at Maxwell, fast asleep and snoring gently. He turned to the desk sergeant who had accompanied him down to the cells. 'Two things,' he snapped. 'First of all, why didn't you tell me it was for this man that you called me

271

out of my bed? And secondly, what's he in for? Have you got him bang to rights this time?'

Bill opened his mouth to speak, but Astley got there first.

'Don't bother,' he said. 'Off you go, back upstairs to your logic puzzles or whatever it is you do to while away the time. I'll deal with this.'

Bill turned on his heel and walked away, stiff legged with annoyance. All he said, when almost out of earshot, was, 'Sudoku, actually.' A door banged shut and the three of them were alone.

'Can I just explain...?' said Jacquie.

'No,' Astley said shortly. 'I'm annoyed and bound to take it the wrong way. It's a Saturday night thing.' He leant closer and brushed Maxwell's hair from his temple, carefully wiping away the dried blood. 'That's nasty. What was it?'

'He told the officers who found him it was a torch.'

'So he's been speaking then. Good. And I must admit I never thought I'd hear myself say that. Do we know when it happened?'

'Not precisely, no,' said Jacquie. 'But not more than three hours ago. Could be considerably less.'

'Has he been sick?'

'Yes, just once. As they were getting him into the squad car.'

'Well,' Astley said, standing up and looking down at the Head of Sixth Form turned Acting Headteacher thoughtfully. 'I think he has a concussion. How serious we can't really tell without an X-ray, but to be quite honest, by the time he reaches the front of the queue at A&E on a Saturday night, he could have recovered spontaneously from beriberi and Ebola. If I were you, I'd just cover him up and leave him to sleep. Get a chair in here and stay with him if you like, although you've got a little nipper at home, haven't you? Donald likes to keep abreast.'

For the most appalling of fleeting moments, Jacquie envisioned Astley's assistant, the Igor of Leighford, like some West Sussex Ed Gein, with body parts in his fridge. The finest breast collection in the south. She shook herself free of it.

'My mother is staying with us. She is baby-sitting.'

'Well, in that case, it's up to you.' He un-expectedly put a hand on her shoulder. 'It's been a shock. I expect you've been working on all this poison lark as well, haven't you?'

'You know about that?'

He looked hurt. 'I am the Police Pathologist,' he said. 'I get to find these things out, you know. Donald is mates with Angus at Chichester. Now there's a marriage made in heaven. It makes them sound as though they should be starring in some Hogmanay extravaganza I know, something out of *Brigadoon*, but neither of them have ever been north of Hadrian's Wall to my certain knowledge. No, Donald had a call from Angus, warning him that we're likely to be busy. Apparently, they're saving up to go on holiday to Tenerife later in the year and the overtime will come in handy. Ghoulish bastards.'

Jacquie shuddered. She wasn't surprised, but it was still a little unpleasant to hear death and disaster expressed so clearly as pounds sterling. She hardly dared ask. 'Have you been busy?'

'No. Except for that poor woman from Leighford High who, by the way, was incredibly healthy apart from being dead, we've had nothing. Chichester do all the toxicology, of course.'

'Do they have any results yet?'

'Again, no. Apart from the original poison, the aconite, they are having huge difficulty in pinning anything down. All they can say is that there seems to be a liking on the part of the poisoner for the plant-based toxins. So we'll be looking at laurel, which as you know is deadly, probably oleander, peace lily, that sort of thing.'

'My mother mentioned oleander.'

'It's not her, is it?' said Astley. He'd never had a mother to speak of and even a pathologist likes to try a joke when standing with a pretty woman, at dead of night, over the unconscious body of her husband-to-be.

'I wouldn't be surprised,' said a groggy voice from the bed.

Jacquie looked down, relief written all over her face. 'Oh, darling,' she said, reaching down to take his hand. 'Don't get up,' as she felt him starting to struggle to his feet.

'But I went to a good school,' he mumbled. 'On second thoughts, don't worry,' he muttered. 'I think I'll stay here.' He looked across and saw Astley standing over him. 'Oh, wait a minute, though. I appear to be dead. It is the Other Place after all.'

'No,' Astley said, 'Not really. No need to fear the Reaper just yet. I was just checking.' He looked up and spoke to Jacquie. 'Don't let him get up too quickly. Give him something to drink if he wants it. He'll be after a painkiller any time, I should think. Give him one of these.' He fumbled in his pocket. 'I'm sure he's had them before, with his habit of falling on fists and other people's feet. Don't let him drive or operate heavy machinery.'

'But I was going to do the ironing,' came the plaintive cry from the bed.

'If this were anyone else,' said Astley, 'I would recommend you had him checked for brain damage. As it is, I think I can give him a clean bill of health.' Astley doffed a metaphorical cap. 'DS Carpenter. Mr Maxwell. I'll bid you goodnight. Don't walk into any more torches, Mr Maxwell, will you?' And he went off down the corridor and knocked in a peremptory fashion on the double-locked door. 'Come on,' they heard him call. 'Let me out. I've got a home to go to, even if you lot haven't.' Then he was gone, in a jangle of keys and a blast of bacon-scented air from Bill's equivalent of afternoon tea.

Maxwell sniffed. 'Bacon?' he asked. 'I am rather peckish.'

'Dr Astley said you weren't to eat, just have a drink. He also left you these.' She held out her hand with the painkillers on.

'I might have just one,' Maxwell said, wincing. 'I've got the most terrible head suddenly.'

'Well, you would,' she said. 'I'm just going out into the corridor to get you some water from the cooler. Don't move.'

'Water?' Maxwell mouthed silently.

275

When she got back, he was still lying down. This sent a small shudder of fear through her body; it wasn't like him to either lie down under a setback or to obey any instruction of hers, no matter how sensible. She handed him a painkiller and he leant up on one elbow to take it.

'No, seriously, why have I got such a headache and why am I here?'

She sat down on the edge of the bed and looked into his eyes. At least his pupils were the same size as each other. 'Max, you have had, have still got I should really say, a concussion. You were hit on the head by a torch.'

'When?'

'When you disturbed the poisoner in town. I won't ask why you lied to me about where you were going when I dropped you off. I'm just glad you are all right and we'll say no more about it.'

'You're dead right there,' Maxwell said, bluntly. 'I have no idea what you're talking about. As far as I know, the last thing that happened to me was I got into your mother's car outside the hospital. By the way,' and he looked serious and clutched her wrist, 'your mother's car has had a little scrape, you know.'

'Yes, Max.' She patted his hand. 'I know. Look, if you've managed to swallow Astley's horse pill, why don't you have a go at having a sleep?'

He lay back. 'Do you know, I think I will.' He closed his eyes and pulled the blanket up to his chin. 'Can I have a lie-in, do you think? It isn't school tomorrow, is it?' His eyes suddenly flew open. 'I had a horrible dream,' he said. 'I dreamt I was Headmaster.' He closed his eyes again and chuckled softly. 'Wouldn't that be funny?'

She patted his shoulder and smiled, then bent down to kiss his cheek. 'Hilarious,' she said. 'Night, night. Sleep tight. Don't let the bedbugs bite.'

'Night, night, Miss Mackenzie,' he said, and started to snore.

'Miss Mackenzie, indeed,' she said, and went out into the corridor. 'I've a good mind to lock you in.'

Chapter Eighteen

Upstairs in her office, all was peace and quiet. Her message light was flashing on her phone, but instead of picking it up straight away, she waited, weighing her options. It was probably her mother, wound up by Mrs Troubridge to new heights of hysteria. But it might be Chichester, with a trace on the phone. She took a deep breath and picked it up, keying in her PIN.

'DS Carpenter? Angus here.' Did the man never sleep? 'How y'doing? I've had a look at your phone number and it's bad news. It's pay as you go, bought Friday off of Asda in Brighton.' Jacquie was pleased to have the detail, but it was a bit scary, she thought, that so much detail could be got so quickly. But Angus was continuing. 'It's switched off now, but I've asked the company to keep a check on it. As soon as it switches back on, they can give us a trace. Bye.'

She saved the message and pressed for the next one.

'Umm, DS Carpenter. Angus again. I've texted a mate of mine who has a voice recognition program. I sent the message as an MP3. I hope that's all right. Umm, it's a bit late now, you're probably busy. Or in bed. Ha ha. I'll ring you on your mobile in the morning.'

She put down the receiver, looking thoughtful. It wasn't like Angus to do anything off the clock.

He sounded rather nervous as well. She hoped he meant it and called; he always struck her as a bit of a slave to wine, women and song. But mostly, wine.

Before she could get up, her phone rang.

'DS Carpenter.'

'It's Bill, Jacquie. On the desk.'

'Yes, Bill?' Had he forgotten that they had spoken not fifteen minutes earlier? Had he got short-term memory loss or had she?

'Something a bit odd going on down here. I wonder if you could come down?'

'It's not Mr Maxwell, is it?' Her heart was thumping in her throat.

'No, no, not really.' There was a pause. 'I've checked the CCTV. He's fine. Still asleep.'

'I'm on my way, Bill.' She put down the phone. Bill put the phlegm in phlegmatic so it must have been odd to get him on the phone. After all, he'd been there, done that, and under his regulation blue serge, for the use of, he'd got the T-shirt.

She clattered down the steps to the front foyer, her heels echoing behind her in the cavernous stairwell. She almost burst through the doors and had to collect herself together. But there was no one there except the desk sergeant, moodily filling in his sudoku.

'Bill? What is it?'

'That was quick. It's this.' He held up a plant.

'What is it?' She was beginning to sound like one of Maxwell's broken 78s.

Bill cleared his throat. He was an avid *Gardeners' Question Time* fan and he could do a Bob Flowerdew to make your eyes water. How-

279

ever, this time, he saw the glint in Jacquie's eye and decided to be brief. 'It's a Kaffir lily. It is a border plant, really, but they force them for the supermarkets. It will flower like this for a bit and then you put it out.'

'Thanks,' Jacquie said. 'But where did it come from?'

'That's just it,' he said. 'I don't know. One minute it wasn't here, next minute, it was. I was getting something out of the file, but I can't have had my back turned for more than a minute.'

'Is there a card?'

'Yes. It's addressed to DCI Hall.'

'It's poisonous, isn't it?'

Bill looked set to propound, so Jacquie stopped him.

'If you know it's poisonous, Bill, get on the phone to Leighford General now, quickly. Tell them that Mrs Hall has been given...'

'Lycorine,' said a voice from behind her.

'Max?' she spun round. 'What are you doing up and about? And how do you know it's lycorine? You didn't seem to know much about plants when my mother was holding forth.'

Maxwell and Bill exchanged the smallest of glances. Bill had a mother-in-law too. His was an expert on TV soaps, so he reckoned that Maxwell had a slightly better deal.

Jacquie sighed. 'Yes, all right. I get it. Well, Bill, you heard the man. Lycorine.' She stepped into Maxwell's arms. 'Should you be up?'

'I've had a nap, I feel a lot better. I've still got a hell of a headache and I feel as though my head is on a bit skew-whiff, but otherwise, I'm fine.'

'How's the memory?'

'I remembered lycorine,' he said, a little miffed. 'What more do you want? I could give you a quick rundown on the reform of the Poor Law, if you're up for it.'

'I mean, of recent events.'

'I remember leaving the hospital. Your mother's car's had a bit of a bump, by the way. I remember going into a pub.' He sniffed his sleeve. 'The Vine. After that ... it's a bit hazy. There were some coppers, I remember them.' He smiled benignly at Bill. 'There was something important about a shop...'

'Don't worry about that,' she said. 'They've closed it and are searching it as we speak. Angus will be delighted with the overtime.'

'Does he never sleep?'

'I thought that. In fact, he left me a couple of messages...'

'DS Carpenter?' Bill was off the phone.

'Yes?'

'The hospital said thanks. They hadn't even thought of that one, but they are starting treatment now. Oh, and DCI Hall is out of A&E. He's on his way. May I ask, why was he in A&E?'

'He had a thorn up...' began Maxwell.

'...his thumbnail,' Jacquie quickly said. 'As a gardener, you must know how painful that is, Bill?'

The man looked puzzled. He had never had Henry Hall down for a wuss. Or for a gardener, come to that. He decided to change the subject. 'Are you waiting for the DCI?'

Jacquie chewed her lip. She wanted to see

281

Henry, to debrief, but equally, she wanted to get home, to get Maxwell home, to see her little boy and, most of all, to lie down. 'I tell you what, Bill. What time do you finish your shift?'

'Eight.'

'Eight. That's fine. Give me a ring at eight and tell me where the guv is then. I'll contact him there. I've got a few bits he ought to know.'

'Eight it is, then.' The sergeant looked at the clock. 'If you're quick you can get at least four hours of sleep.'

'Plenty,' she said, brightly. 'Night, then, Bill.'

Maxwell fell into step behind her. He leant over the desk and pointed. 'That's a nine, by the way. And you've got two twos in the bottom left-hand square.'

'Thanks,' Bill said sourly. Everyone's a critic.

'Evening, all,' added Maxwell and swung through the doors, holding his head only slightly to one side. How do you know when a door's not a door? When you've jarred yourself. Or something.

Jacquie reclaimed her Ka for the journey home. That way, she could introduce her mother gently to the fact that her car was a bit more battered and bruised than when she had last seen it. The guest bedroom faced the front and she really didn't want her to sweep open the curtains in the morning and see the devastation displayed in glorious Technicolor.

Jacquie and Maxwell travelled back to 38 Columbine in silence, broken only by the whirring of cogs in their brains. As she pulled on the handbrake, he grabbed her wrist.

'Can we agree something?' he said.

'Possibly.' She was wary. He had clearly got the sleuthing bit back firmly between his teeth and she was desperate for sleep.

'This is what we do. We go in. We go up the stairs. We go to check on Nole. We go to bed. We go to sleep. We don't discuss the case.'

'This isn't like you,' she said. 'I thought we would be up all night.'

'I need processing time,' he said. 'I think I know who we're looking for, but I also know you will disagree. I need to be sharp and my head feels full of cotton wool.'

She looked at him. Could he be getting sensible in his old age?

'Then, when we've talked it over in the morning, we can go out and catch him at it, or at least find out what he's doing and stop him doing it again.'

That would be a no, then.

Maxwell's first thought as he opened one eye was that someone was trying to prise off the top of his head. Then his giant intellect kicked in and he realised that that was very unlikely. Someone was actually trying to pull his ears off with red-hot pincers. Then he recognised the sound that was cutting through his skull like a blunt chainsaw. He kicked out randomly to rouse Jacquie and found only air.

'Max?' she appeared in the doorway, mouth full of foam, toothbrush waving. 'Can you get that?'

He grunted and flapped his hand vaguely at the

bedside table. Finally, he found the phone.

'Hello?'

'Mr Maxwell? It's Bill here. From the nick. Just ringing as arranged.'

'Is it eight o'clock already?'

'I'm afraid so, Mr Maxwell. As you can imagine, it can't come quickly enough for me.'

'I can see that,' Maxwell said, smiling. There was always a different perspective. 'Thanks for ringing. Is DCI Hall in the police station?'

'He's at the hospital, at the moment. His wife is much better, so he's just popped in to see her. He says to tell you he will come round to yours, if that's all right.'

The thought of Henry Hall phrasing it in quite those terms was a droll one and Maxwell smiled again. The top of his head stayed put; progress. 'Thanks. I'll tell ... DS Carpenter.'

The woman policeman of that name was back in the bedroom, licked and polished to perfection. She looked as if she had had a holiday, rather than three partial nights' sleep in a row. 'Is that Bill?'

'Bye, then, Bill.' Maxwell put the phone down.

'I'll take that as a yes. Where's Henry?'

'He's at the hospital.' He hurriedly calmed her worried look. 'Margaret is much better. He's coming round here, afterwards.'

'What?' Jacquie looked around frantically.

'Sweetheart, you look lovely. Your house looks lovely. Your baby looks lovely. Even your cat looks lovely. Your mother looks like a boot. I look beaten up. Everything is as it should be. And that's even without Legs Diamond being in his heaven.'

She sat on the bed and leant over to kiss him somewhere it wouldn't hurt. It was easier than it usually was when he had had an altercation with a miscreant. It had sometimes been hard, over the years, to know where to even stick a pin between bruises. A simple torch over the head was nothing. He kissed her right on back.

'Go and rally the troops,' he said. 'Your mother will need some TLC after an evening with Mrs Troubridge.'

'Oh, God, you're right,' she said. 'I'll go and start breakfast. That way, we'll have heard the worst before Henry gets here.' She hurried away.

Maxwell got up, gingerly. The room swam for a second or two, but soon righted itself and he went into the bathroom feeling quite confident. He kept returning to the last thing he could remember, trying to fill in the details. He knew that the more he fretted over it, the less likely it was to happen. He had had the same problem for years over B-feature film stars. He had once kept himself awake for night after night for weeks, trying to remember the name of... Well, it had seemed very important at the time. And now, he had at his disposal a woman who, as well as being beautiful and funny, could also use the invention of the devil, and the knowledge of the whole world of film geeks was just a click away, in what the young people called a computer. So he used the neural pathways grown dusty with neglect to recreate the minutes before the torch put his lights out. He muttered quietly to himself around his toothpaste as he cleaned his teeth.

'Who you talk to, Dadda?'

He nearly swallowed his toothbrush. If the little voice hadn't made him jump, the small ice-cold hand placed on the gap between pyjama top and bottom would certainly have done the trick.

'Hello, Nole. How're you doing, my little mate?'

'OK, Dadda. Who you talk to?'

His son had many very attractive traits, some that Maxwell even recognised as his own particular genetic input. The persistence was not necessarily one of them, and he was pretty sure it came from the maternal side.

'I was just thinking, Nole. Daddies think better out loud.' This seemed to answer the question and Maxwell got on with brushing his teeth.

'Ninja does think, Dadda.'

Maxwell pebble-dashed the mirror with foam. 'Does she, sweetheart? Well, Ninjas think better out loud as well, I suppose.'

'I s'pose,' Nolan shrugged one shoulder, then the other. Presumably, thought Maxwell, both at once was not always easy.

Maxwell fought down an urge to ask what Ninja had been thinking, but with difficulty. It would have been good to get a handle on the woman's thought processes, but he had been to a good school and so it was not to be.

'Is Ninja up yet?' Maxwell asked his son.

'Yep.'

The monosyllabic reply phase, his father thought. Oh well, it will only last for about another fifteen years. 'Is Ninja in the kitchen with Mummy?'

'Yep.'

'Let's go in there, then, shall we?' said Maxwell, walking back into the bedroom and shrugging on his bathrobe, proudly using both shoulders at once. 'We can have some breakfast.'

The boy's eyes widened. 'Not Ninja toast!'

'No, Daddy toast, or how about some Coco Pops?'

'Yep.'

'Mummy is having a visitor later,' Maxwell said in a conversational tone as he carried the boy downstairs. 'So no Coco Pops in anyone's hair.' Nolan looked downcast. 'Well, all right. Just a few in *your* hair, but no hiding them today.'

Nolan screamed with delight. A joke is no good unless people know about it and he had been wondering what the reactions had been to the case of the hidden Coco Pop. Erle Stanley Gardner and the rest of the Aristocracy would be proud of him.

'It's serious, Nole. I want you to be on your best behaviour.'

The lad nodded solemnly. 'Best 'haviour, Dadda.'

'Good.' Maxwell gave him a kiss and let him slide down to the floor. 'Let's have brekker,' and they swooped into the kitchen, where Jacquie and her mother sat opposite one another, looking like Dorian Grey and his picture.

Jacquie gave him a bright and brittle smile. 'Mum and I were just talking about today,' she said. 'Mum has a headache.'

Her mother looked at Maxwell through slitted eyes. 'I have a bit of a headache,' she repeated, in a whisper. Behind her back, Jacquie mimed lifting a bottle.

'We've been discussing how we don't really drink much when we are looking after Nole.'

Her mother buried her head in her hands. 'It's that Mrs Troubridge,' she said. 'She can really put it away, you know. I didn't realise how much I'd had until it came to standing up.'

'But, Ninj,' Maxwell said. 'Mrs Troubridge only weighs about three stone wringing wet. How can she out-drink you?'

'Are you suggesting I'm fat?' she asked, waspishly.

'No, just fatter than Mrs Troubridge. *Everybody's* fatter than Mrs Troubridge. *Nolan's* fatter than Mrs Troubridge.'

'Well, be that as it may,' said his mother-in-law-to-be, 'she can drink for England. But before it all became a blur, we discussed bridesmaids' dresses. We've decided on claret with an ecru trim.'

'Lovely,' said Maxwell. 'But isn't the ecru an endangered species? Or was that the thing on which Tony Blair promised us a referendum, but then bottled?' Before she could reply, Maxwell turned an innocent gaze on Jacquie. 'Just coffee for me, dear one, and the usual for my friend here.' He reached down and hoisted Nolan up into a chair. 'Ow. I've just discovered another thing I can't do, along with mountaineering and astrophysics.'

'And that is...?' Jacquie asked.

'Bending down,' he replied.

Betty Carpenter leant closer and peered at Maxwell's temple. 'That looks very nasty. Have you put some arnica on it? I've got some in my bag.'

'Is arnica made from plants?'

'I should imagine so, yes.'

'Then, thanks, I'll pass. Although not, hopefully, out.' Jacquie put a steaming mug in front of him. 'Ah, the cup that cheers.'

'That's tea,' Ninja said, shortly. Her temper was not improved by her blistering hangover. She had, after all, been there twenty-four hours and her visitor's manners were starting to slip.

'Actually,' Maxwell began, 'it isn't tea either. It's tar water, as drunk by teetotallers in the nineteenth century. But let's not argue.' The doorbell rang for the end of round one. 'Henry's here.'

'Oh,' Betty shrieked. 'You didn't say Henry was coming over. I must look a sight.'

'Must you?' muttered Jacquie, as her mother leapt to her feet and rushed upstairs for running repairs. Maxwell was on his way to the top of the stairs. 'I'll go,' she said. 'Watch my toast, will you? The toaster seems to be full of the bottom of a budgie's cage and it's liable to burn.' She trotted downstairs and Maxwell heard Henry's drone as she opened the door. The man's tread was heavy as he came up from street level and came into the kitchen. He looked terrible.

Maxwell pushed out a chair with one foot. 'Sit down, Henry, for God's sake, before you fall down,' he said. 'Nolan, say good morning to Mr Hall.'

'Yep,' offered Nolan.

'I apologise,' Maxwell said. 'I know he was brighter than this last night. I think the brain fairy must have been. How is Margaret?'

Hall's face brightened perceptibly. 'Much

289

better, thanks to you. I must admit the hospital wasn't very up on its poisons. It would have been all right if she had drunk bleach; after that they seemed a bit stuck. It clearly wasn't aconite again, but after that we hadn't struck lucky.' His social skills having been stretched to breaking point by this conversational sally, he turned to Jacquie. He was on firmer ground here.

'What did you get last night, on the phone number?'

'It's a pay as you go,' Jacquie said. 'Untraceable as to the buyer, but if he uses it again, we can get a position.'

'Do you think he will use it again?' Maxwell asked. 'They are so easy to get and cheap nowadays he might have dozens.'

'That's a depressing thought,' said Hall. 'We will have to accept that that might be the case, though. Anything else?'

'Well, there was the plant,' Jacquie said. 'Without it, we might not have ever got to the bottom of Margaret's poisoning and ... well, guv, you know what I mean.'

He sighed. 'Yes, I do, thanks. Who left it?'

'Bill doesn't know. He just found it there.'

'Where was he?'

'Filing, or getting a file, something, I don't know. Anyway, he says he was only gone for a minute.'

'Well, didn't he hear the door go? Check the cameras?'

'He didn't say.'

'Well, surely, he would have done if he was at the files. Ask him.'

'He's gone home by now, guv.'

'So have we. Get his number from the desk and ring him.' He sat there expectantly.

'Oh, right, guv. I'll do that now, shall I?' She went out on to the landing, taking Nolan with her, thoughts of Coco Pops on hold for now. The two men sat in silence for a few heartbeats.

Maxwell was the first to speak. 'I think I know who this poisoner is, Henry.'

Henry looked at him with the air of a man who has been waiting for hours for the other shoe to drop. 'I have no doubt that you do,' he said. The silence resumed its hold on the room, broken only by the soft hiss of the coffee maker and the ping of whole grains turning into popcorn in the toaster.

'Would you like to know who I think it is?' Maxwell asked at last.

'I don't believe I do, thank you, if it's all the same,' Hall said. 'Is there any chance of some coffee? I really am quite thirsty and I've got to take my painkillers with something.'

'I'm so sorry,' said public schoolboy Maxwell, P. 'What am I thinking?' He got up and went over to the mug rack and chose one with the word 'God' on it. His own mug said 'Genius'. 'Milk?'

'Please.'

'Sugar, or are you sweet enough?' It was a Mrs B'ism but none the worse for that.

'I'm not, but none for me, thank you.' Maxwell couldn't believe he had never thought to say that, on the thousands of occasions he could have done, over the long arches of the years.

The teacher put the mug in front of the police-

291

man and sat down again opposite him. Hall allowed himself a pleased nod at the word on the mug.

Someone had to say it, so Maxwell put himself in the frame. 'And how is your ar–?'

The door opened and Jacquie stood there, phone in hand. 'He didn't hear the door,' she said.

'Was that because he was out of earshot?' asked Maxwell. 'Or deaf?'

'I wish that was the reason,' Jacquie said, 'but he was adamant that he was just at the files and there is no reason for him to lie. Even if there was a reason, he knows how important it is. He definitely didn't hear the door. The CCTV recording is remote, as you know, so we'll have to check the hard drive later. It's not simply a matter of running the film back these days.'

'No, of course it isn't. We've had progress, I suppose, so that's why it is far less help than it used to be. So we'll assume for now that it was someone in the nick,' Hall said, definitely, throwing two painkillers into his mouth and throwing back his head to swallow them. It was typical of the man that he could take tablets sized to stun a horse with just a small sip of scalding hot coffee.

'There was hardly anyone there,' Jacquie said. 'Me, obviously. Max,' she nodded in his direction, 'out cold in a cell. The duty guy on the cell corridor. That's about it. The others were out and about, just checking in at intervals.'

'There were the two who brought me in,' offered Maxwell.

'Who?' Hall barked at Jacquie.

'Umm, Jim Edwards and ... oh, God, I can never remember the other one's name. They're both Christian names. Is it Tom Michaels?'

'No. Mike Thomas. Nice try. Did they go out after they had brought you in?' Hall asked Maxwell.

'Don't ask me,' Maxwell protested. 'I can't remember most of last night. Actually, Cowdenbeath, talking of the lost weekend, had you better check on your mother? She went up to titivate ages ago. Ray Milland might be up there with her.'

'Oh, God, yes.' Jacquie jumped up and they heard her urgent footsteps on the stairs.

'Cowdenbeath?' Hall didn't usually pry into the private lives of his staff, but sometimes, he just had to know.

'From the football results, you know. Forfar, three, Berwick, one. Hearts, two, Cowdenbeath, seven.'

'Oh,' Hall said, still puzzled. 'I see.'

'Do you?' Maxwell was amazed. 'Anyway, as I say, I can hardly remember last night. I know I was socked on the head and I am getting flashes of what happened afterwards. I remember going into the Vine and planning what shops he might target. And, of course, I got it right, because ... oh, hold on. It's coming back.'

Henry Hall grabbed a pen out of his inside pocket and had his notepad in his hand with lightning speed. There was a thorn stuck in it, which he plucked out and placed carefully on the table. A souvenir. 'Go on.'

'I was waiting outside the shop. I saw a torch

293

beam inside and I knew I had the right place. He came out...'

'Did you see his face?' Hall paused eagerly, pen aloft.

'Umm, no. He was wearing a dark thing on his head. A ... well, if I had to describe it...'

'...and you do,' responded Hall.

'...I would say he was dressed as a ninja. Which is a bit of a family joke at the moment, but nevertheless. Yes, that's what he looked like. All in black. I grabbed his shoulder...'

'What did it feel like?'

Maxwell was confused. 'A shoulder,' he said. Had those thorns done more damage than he thought? What painkillers was he on?

Hall put down his pen. 'Please, Max,' he said, sweet reason itself. 'I know you like to joke, have a laugh. I have no argument with that. We all like a laugh.' He bared his teeth to show he understood. 'But you know exactly what I mean. Did he feel fat, thin, young, old? Was he taller than you? Was he, in fact, a she? Did you smell anything? Hear anything, wheezy breathing, chewing gum, that kind of thing?' He picked up his pen again. 'Right, let's go from "What did it feel like?"'

Maxwell closed his eyes, but that made the world spin, so he opened them again. 'He was definitely a he, I think. The bones of the shoulder were quite chunky, and a woman's is usually quite fragile to hold, even a strong woman.'

'I agree. Go on.'

'He was shorter than me, shorter than average, even. Umm, he felt ... I can't describe it, really, he felt a bit out of condition. Like someone who used to be fit, but has let himself go. Which isn't to say fat, just a bit loose, if you know what I mean. Not tightly muscled.'

Hall nodded and waved him on.

'It was pretty smelly around there, just by a bin and all sorts of old chewing gum and stuff on the floor. Plus, I'd been in the Vine.'

Hall pulled a sympathetic face.

'But I think I smelt tobacco on him. Not a fresh cigarette, just ingrained smoke. Not anything untoward, you understand. Not a Barlichway crop. But I would say roll-ups.'

Hall looked up at him. 'I didn't think you smoked,' he observed.

'I don't. But I work with around about twelve hundred children on a daily basis, don't forget. And all but twelve of them smoke. And the twelve who say they don't are lying. I can tell Gold Flake from Dingo Droppings at a thousand yards.'

'Very Holmesian,' Jacquie remarked, coming back into the room.

'How is she?' Maxwell asked.

'Spark out,' she said. 'Mrs Troubridge really gave her a run for her money.'

Hall was puzzled again. 'Anything I should know about?' he asked.

'Not really,' Maxwell said. 'Essentially, two secret drinkers tried to drink each other under the table last night. Mrs Troubridge won.'

'You mean Mrs Troubridge, your next door neighbour?'

'The very same,' said Maxwell, proudly.

Hall leant back. 'I'm impressed.'

'I'm thinking of taking her out in the evenings,' said Maxwell. 'I think I could win serious money, betting on her.'

'There's probably a law against it,' said Hall.

'It would be fun, though,' mused Maxwell, wistfully.

'So, who else have you got on the list?' said Jacquie, sitting down at the table and leaning forward enthusiastically.

The men looked at her. That was so ten minutes ago.

'We've moved on,' Maxwell said.

'He's remembered something,' said Hall.

'Have you written it down?' she asked Hall, rather peremptorily.

'Yes,' he said, shortly. It might be her house he was in, her coffee he was drinking, but he was her boss, when all was said and done.

'Good. So, who else could have been in the nick?'

'We could find out from fingerprints, couldn't we?' Maxwell suddenly asked.

'Fingerprints?' said Hall. 'What on?'

'The flowerpot or the cellophane it was in. That must take prints really well.'

Hall was on his feet. 'The lilies were in a pot? In cellophane? Why did no one say?'

Jacquie looked surprised. 'I thought you'd know. They sell them in the supermarket like that.'

Henry Hall could hardly contain himself. 'Do I look like someone who does the shopping?' he shouted. 'As far as I am concerned, food just arrives on my plate, toothpaste on my brush. I don't know how they sell plants.' He let his head fall into his hands. From there, he made a Hall-style apology. 'I'm sorry. It's been rather stressful.' He ran his fingers through his hair, which was immediately tidy again. Maxwell looked at him with the jealousy a curly-haired man has for the straight. He would look as if he had been attacked had he done the same. 'Jacquie, I'm sorry to use you as a gofer. Can you ring the nick and get them to fingerprint the plant, pot and all the rest?'

'They can put it together with the DNA samples they took from me last night,' said Maxwell, excitedly.

Hall's eyes behind his lenses lit up with a new enthusiasm. Now this was *police* work. Bugger the paperwork. 'DNA! Excellent.' He turned to Jacquie. 'Did it get sent to Chichester? Is Angus on to it?'

Jacquie looked puzzled. 'DNA? I don't remember any DNA being taken.' She looked from one man to the other, her own private Wimbledon.

'But I'm sure I remembered the policemen mentioning DNA,' said Maxwell. 'Or ... that might have been me. Surely, they take DNA from a scene of violence, don't they?'

'It is procedure, certainly,' said Hall tightly. He made a terse little note in his book. 'Is it any good trying now?'

'Not really,' Jacquie said. 'He hasn't had time for a shower, but Dr Astley wiped the wound and I expect his clothes from last night are hung up on the big shelf as usual.' She sent a querying glance at Maxwell.

'Life's too short to use a coat hanger,' he said,

297

truculently. 'But surely, even with our DNA, plus a soupçon of Metternich's, Nolan's, two policemen, Jim Astley ... all right, point taken.'

Hall preferred older technology. He had more in common with Maxwell than either of them would like to admit. Fingerprints, footprints, things you could see with the naked eye; they were the kind of clues he liked. DNA may well be real, but until he found a bloodstained double helix at a crime scene, he would keep his own counsel.

Jacquie sighed. This whole thing was going pear-shaped. She tried to change tack. 'Angus said he'd phone. He's sent the message to a mate of his with voice recognition software.'

'Chichester has their own voice recognition software,' Hall said.

'I think Angus was just trying to speed things up,' she said.

'Nonsense,' Hall said. 'Angus's eyes are on his overtime. I always get an email from his line manager asking me to check his work sheet.'

'And is it wrong?'

Hall had the grace to look slightly shamefaced. 'No ... but you must admit he is mainly overtime led.'

'Maybe so,' said Jacquie. 'But in this instance, I think we all agree that speed is of the essence.' As if called out of the ether, her phone rang. 'That will be him now.' She foraged in her bag and came up with it to her ear. 'DS Carpenter.'

'Hello,' said a harsh voice. 'How are you, Jacquie?'

Her eyes flew open. 'It's him,' she mouthed.

'How's the old man?' Something about the inflection made it clear that he was using the term literally. 'Got a headache, has he?'

Jacquie stayed quiet. The best way was to goad him. She pulled Hall's notebook over and wrote in it. 'Ring Chichester. Get them to track it.' Hall went off to use the phone elsewhere. She and Maxwell could hear his urgent tones through the door. She reached out and took her man's hand.

'I fetched him one, all right. He saw stars, I'll bet. Is he there?'

Silence.

'He is, isn't he? Well, I'm sorry I didn't get a chance to slip him a little something in his hospital rice pudding. I'll hit him a bit harder, next time. See how we get on then.'

She squeezed Maxwell's hand hard, but didn't speak.

'You're not very chatty, are you? I'll say bye-bye, then. Bye-bye.' And the line went dead.

Hall came back in to the room, shaking his head. 'Check the number, Jacquie,' he said.

She punched the relevant key. 'Oh, shit,' she said. 'Another phone.'

'Criminals today just have money to burn,' said Maxwell. 'Did you recognise the voice?'

'No, it was done through one of those voice changers.' She stood there, with her phone in her hand, feeling helpless. As if to cheer her up, it rang. 'DS Carpenter.'

'Hello.' The laid-back tones of Angus filled her ear. 'How y'doing?'

'Angus, he's got another phone,' she exclaimed.

'Yeah, well, he would have. They're cheap now,

aren't they? Anyway, my mate's nearly finished your voice thing. He says it will be done by midday or so.'

'Angus, that's great news. Shall we meet you both somewhere?'

'Yeah, all right. I'm still in Leighford, I was on that shop. Oh, is...?'

'Yes, he's fine. Well, let's say the Vine at one, shall we?'

'Yeah. That sounds cool. See you there.' And he rang off.

'The Vine?' said Hall, aghast. 'Why there?'

Jacquie shrugged. 'It's Angus,' she said. No other explanation was needed.

Chapter Nineteen

And so the plans were laid. Jacquie and Hall were going to the nick in his car, to check on any progress, ring Leighford General to do a quick victim headcount and also, if time permitted, drop in on the Barlows, currently squatting at Mrs Barlow's mother's. Then, off to the dubious charms of the Vine, for something out of a sealed bottle to drink, something out of a sealed packet to eat.

Maxwell was rather mutinous when his morning was mapped out for him. When Ninja woke up, he was to take her and Nolan for a quick shop in town. She could drive the Ka. He was not to mention anything about bent bumpers, scraped side panels or any other car-related things. He was not to mention alcohol. They would buy Nolan his prize courtesy of that nice Mr Hall and then come home to await news from Jacquie. They would take drinks in cans, boxes, bottles, whatever they fancied. What they would not do was accept food or drinks from strange men.

Jacquie looked into his eyes and said, from her usual trusting stance of hope over experience, 'You won't do anything stupid, Max, will you? You won't, oh, I don't know, leave them and go chasing off or anything?'

He would have tossed his head, but he knew he would probably pass out, so he didn't.

She could tell his intention and put her hands on his chest, palms flat. 'Please.'

'Don't be silly,' he said. 'I'll have Nole with me.'

'And my mother.'

'I thought I was just listing reasons to behave,' he said, reasonably. 'Off you trot with Henry, now, and let me know as soon as you get anything. I,' and he drew himself up proudly, 'will be carrying my mobile.'

'And what good will that do? It hasn't been plugged in for weeks to my certain knowledge. No, make sure Mum has hers. I'll use that.'

'*Ja wohl, mein Fuhresse.* I will obey.' It was a first-rate Josef Goebbels.

'Well, just make sure you do. Henry's waiting in the car, so I must go.' She sketched a kiss in his direction. 'I'll see you back here, later.'

'Mwah,' he called theatrically as she flew down the stairs. He looked thoughtfully after her for a moment and then turned and went into the lounge where Nolan was watching something multicoloured on the telly. Maxwell threw himself into the chair and Nolan immediately climbed aboard and curled up in his lap. Just a whisker behind, Metternich appeared from nowhere and curled up on Nolan. They both promptly went to sleep.

Trapped, Maxwell let his mind wander and, as his son had so perspicaciously noticed, he did this best in a muttered undertone.

'Count, are you asleep?' The great beast shifted a paw and flicked an ear, which was the same as saying that, while to all intents and purposes he was sleeping, he was still awake to his master's mutter and any passing rodent. 'Right,' Maxwell said, 'pin your ears back, Watson, and see if you can pick the bones out of this one. Here we are, Sunday morning, nine-thirty and all's not very well. Particularly the Leighford High staff and wannabees in the hospital. I have been bumping into a very strange man indeed since Wednesday lunchtime. You may remember him, Count: Dierdre Lessing's Uncle Oliver. I have never been his favourite person, but he seems to be ignoring me these days. A bit of eye contact, but that's all.'

On cue, Metternich opened one eye and glared at the gabbling old fool. Did he never shut up?

'That's right,' Maxwell said, approvingly. 'That's the kind of thing. Well, it seems to me that it's a coincidence too far that he pops up and then someone at Leighford High School dies horribly. And that the occasion of the death is the interview for the replacement of his beloved niece. So, he works that out as a bit obvious, so he nicks the cocktail dishes. Although, of course, there was the one eaten by Freda which was clearly all right, unless she has the constitution of an ox. Which may in fact be the case, since she eats a lot of school dinner leftovers and is probably immune to every poison going. Hmm. But I digress. Unfortunately, he knocks Sylv over on his way out of my beloved institution and then goes home and worries about being recognised. So he starts a lot of other poisonings in the hope that he puts the police and, more importantly, *moi*, off the scent.' He smiled complacently at the cat. 'What do you think?'

Metternich squeezed his eyes shut and put a

303

paw over them for good measure.

His owner, as he rather optimistically styled himself, sighed. 'You're right. It sounds a bit unlikely, but it's all I've got. Unless...' he narrowed his eyes, 'unless we are all overlooking an even more obvious culprit, viz and to wit, not to mention to woo, Mr Sue Bevell. He had motive enough, God knows. If he can get thousands for a dodgy boiled egg in a hotel, how much more would he get for a dead wife? And someone did try again, didn't they, only on her?' He looked sternly at the cat. 'This is your fault, Count. I would have been quite clear in my mind if it wasn't for you.'

The door opened at this pivotal point in his thought process and his mother-in-law-to-be stood there, looking bright-eyed and bushy-tailed. He suspected hair of the dog, but wisely held his counsel.

'Are we ready, then?' she said, rather superfluously, since she could clearly see that Maxwell and Son were still in pyjamas and Coco Pops. 'Before I went upstairs, Jacquie mentioned a shopping trip.'

'Yes, indeed,' Maxwell said, politely. 'If you could just dislodge the cat, I'll get us both ready. We won't be more than about three hours, if memory serves. Nolan is a bit of a snappy dresser, as you know, and the right outfit can take a while.'

She reached forward to pick up Metternich.

'Take care,' Maxwell began. 'He has his claws in my ... aarghh.' He screamed quietly, but with fervour, as the steel needles of Metternich's left

304

front paw dug like lightning into the top of thigh. Nolan stirred on his lap and the mornin. was underway.

Shooing his son ahead of him up the stairs and only limping a little, he tried to marshal his thoughts of ten minutes before. In essence, it was Lessing or Bevell. Bevell or Lessing. It was no good trying to guess. He would take Nole and Ninja for a quick shop down on the Sea Front where the gift shops were still sopping up the last of the summer trade before closing tight for the winter. He would buy Nolan something that would prove to be just the first of a long and expensive set. He would send them back home for a nice lunch of tinned food from the cupboard. He would then wind up this case and be sitting, casually polishing his nails, when the police arrived to make an arrest. Then, on Monday morning, he would be all set to go back to Leighford High to complete his Plan, begun on Friday, to transform the school before Diamond's return. And all this *with* concussion.

'Your Daddy is a genius,' he remarked to Nolan, dunking him in the bath. At this rate, the child would be washed into oblivion, but there was no other way half so effective at removing errant cereal.

'Yep,' the boy agreed.

This monosyllabic lark could be quite pleasant, thought Maxwell, squeezing the shampoo lavishly on the lad's curls. Good for the ego.

Finally, they were leaving the house. Nolan was washed and brushed. Maxwell was washed but

not brushed, as the bruise on his temple made even the thought untenable. He had used to think that hair could not feel pain; he knew differently now. Ninja was looking remarkably chipper, except for possibly a little strain around the eyes. She and Nolan waited patiently while Maxwell locked the front door. As he turned to walk down the path, he was startled into an involuntary cry of alarm by Mrs Troubridge springing up from behind the hedge. He couldn't believe she could still scare him, but she managed it every time. Before he could draw breath, Ninja was in there like a ninja.

'Mrs Troubridge,' she said, airily. 'How are you this morning?'

'Marvellous, Betty,' she carolled in reply. 'And you?'

'Wonderful. We're off shopping.'

'Oh,' Mrs Troubridge feigned amazement. 'Are the off-licences open already?'

Maxwell was transfixed, but knew that this exchange could go on and on. 'Ladies, excuse me. We have a bit of a busy day ahead of us. Shall we?' And he shooed Nolan and his Ninja down the path, waggling a farewell to Mrs Troubridge with his spare hand.

At the kerb, the little procession stalled suddenly. 'Where's my car?' Betty Carpenter might have had a huge hangover, but even she could tell the difference between this tiny thing and her pride and joy.

'Oh, did Jacquie not say?' Maxwell passed the buck adroitly. 'She was a little stressed last night and just felt she would be happier driving home

in her own car. Here are the keys.' He jangled them in front of her. She felt as though the bells of St Mary's were going off in her head. But there was no Bing to sing to her.

'Well, all right,' she said, snatching them to silence the noise. She walked round to the driver's side. 'It's such a nuisance you can't drive, Max,' she said.

'Don't,' he said.

'Don't what?'

'Don't drive. Not can't.'

'Oh, I see. Isn't that rather selfish?'

He saw no reason to argue this particular toss. 'Not really.' He got into the back with his son. 'I'll be back here with Nole. The baby seat is still in your car.'

Jacquie's mother was not the most sensitive of women, but even she could tell a door shut in her face and, after some minutes of disgruntled tutting, she got the seat adjusted to her dumpy legs and off they went, in a series of kangaroo-like jerks. Maxwell wisely kept silent. He had no idea that she didn't drive either. While they made their way to the Sea Front, he kept quiet. She was clearly not much of a multi-tasker where driving was concerned and he just spoke when a turn was necessary. He was planning where to park; somewhere easy was obviously the order of the day.

'Where can I park, Max?' she asked, rather spookily reading his mind. 'Somewhere nice and easy. I'm not at all happy driving this car.'

Maxwell couldn't help himself. 'It must be two feet shorter than yours and only half as wide.'

307

'Exactly,' she said, mysteriously. 'Look, here's a car park. Is this one all right for the shops?'

Not only was it all right for the shops, it was also empty. Maxwell looked at his watch; the place should be heaving with people by now. 'This is fine, yes, great. We can either go to the High Street or the Sea Front from here.'

'Lovely,' she said, driving in and stopping randomly. This was a case not so much of parking as abandoning the car. 'Do we have to pay on a Sunday?'

Maxwell chuckled. 'Leighford Council would charge for parking on the Day of Judgement,' he said. 'Yawning graves and rivers of blood would not stop the wardens around here. You get Nole's coat on for him and I will go and get the ticket.' He strolled across to the machine and had to take a sizeable detour to avoid a gaggle of small, intense women with maps and binoculars round their necks who had just alighted from a minibus. They sounded like a flock of starlings in a roost and then, as if to complete the analogy, they suddenly wheeled in a body and headed off for the Sea Front.

Back at the car, he stuck the ticket in the windscreen and they were off, in a curious tacking route dictated by Nolan's insatiable curiosity.

'He's just like the Elephant's Child,' Betty Carpenter remarked.

'As long as he doesn't fall into the great green greasy Limpopo,' said Maxwell. 'It's a devil to get out of his clothes.'

She looked amazed. 'You know that story?' she said.

'Kipling? I should say so. You wonder how he got it all done, don't you? All those books and then the cakes. A marvel.'

She looked at him closely. If only she could tell when he was being serious, she thought, she would feel much more comfortable in his company. They walked on for a while, with the sea to their left on the other side of the coastal defences, chunks of concrete which were beginning to weather but would only ever look like chunks of concrete. To their right, the wide pavement of the Sea Front was a playground to Nolan, who ran ahead, chasing seagulls and dodging round the legs of the map-hung women.

'What a lovely child,' Maxwell heard one of them say. Then, his hackles rose and his adrenalin had him running. Her next sentence was the inevitable. 'Would you like a sweetie?'

'No!' Maxwell yelled and was among them, scooping up his astonished son in his arms. Then, remembering his manners, he yelled, 'Thank you.' He skidded to a halt and turned to face the women, now clustering together and staring at him with big eyes. One or two on the edge of the group were trying to edge further in.

The woman who had spoken turned to her friend. 'I was only going to give him a sweetie,' she said, drumming up support.

'Yes,' twittered the women, in out-of-kilter Greek chorus. 'Just a sweetie.'

'Do you watch the news?' he asked of the crowd.

'Oh, yes,' they chorused. 'That lovely Huw Edwards. Sir Trevor. Oh, yes.'

'Local news?'

They shook their collective head.

'So you don't know about our little poisoning scare, then?'

They drew one breath. 'Poison?' they whispered.

'Yes,' he said, brutally. 'A random poisoner is at large in Leighford, ladies. So offers of food are a bit off-limits at the moment, as I am sure you understand. This little chap has already had a close shave.'

'Ooh,' they cooed, increasing their bird-like appearance. Thirty hands reached out to tousle his curls. 'Poor little mite.'

Maxwell doffed his hat. 'Don't let me keep you,' he said. 'And I hope I haven't alarmed you at all.'

The sweet-offerer was pushed forward. She seemed to have become their unofficial spokesperson. 'We were going to have a fish-and-chip lunch before our walk,' she said.

'Well, ladies, that's totally up to you,' he smiled. 'But I personally wouldn't touch it with a barge pole. This man is random, as I said. You can't second-guess him at all.'

They got into a huddle. Some had brought sandwiches, it appeared, and the Tottingleigh Townswomen's Twitchers always shared everything; it was in their Constitution.

The spokesperson turned to Maxwell. 'Thank you for your warning, Mr...'

'Maxwell,' he said, redoffing his hat.

'Maxwell. We will share out our sandwiches to avoid this lunatic.'

'Well done,' he said. 'Ladies...' He stood aside

as they streamed past him.

'What a nice man, in the end,' he heard one of the tail-end Charlenes say, 'even though he does seem to have cereal in his hair.'

Maxwell raised his hat again and investigated. Sure enough, one small Coco Pop was nestling there. He removed it and threw it to a grateful seagull.

Nolan, who had remained silent throughout the experience, now spoke. 'Dadda,' he said. 'I didn't want sweetie.'

'Good boy,' Maxwell said and shooed him back to his grandmother.

'I didn't want sweetie,' he said again.

Ah, the repetitive stage. Goodie. 'That's great, old chap,' said Maxwell, absently.

'I didn't want sweetie, *becos,*' he insisted, 'the nasty man is over there.'

Maxwell's head snapped up and he instantly regretted it. 'Where?'

Nolan's little finger waved vaguely towards the shops, where the sea defence ended and the normal-width pavement began. The twitchers had gathered there and seemed to be planning a route, with much random pointing going on.

'I can't see him, sweetheart,' he said, bending down. 'Point for me again.'

The child was getting testy. *'There,'* he said, pointing in a stabbing motion. 'With the ladies.'

Betty Carpenter was standing behind them, shading her eyes with one hand and scrabbling in her bag for her distance glasses with the other.

'Ninja,' Nolan was tugging on her jacket. 'The man.'

Finally, she had her glasses on and looked hard at the group. Suddenly, she grabbed Maxwell's shoulder with surprisingly strong fingers. 'My God, Max,' she whispered. 'He's right. It is the same man. Well, it's a man who was there at the time.'

'And only Nolan knows which one gave him the lolly.' He squeezed his son hard and kissed the top of his head. 'Well done, mate,' he said, quietly. 'A chip off the old block.' He stood up.

'Yes, but which block?' Jacquie's mother said. Maxwell glanced at her and saw that she was smiling.

He smiled back. 'Indeed,' he agreed. 'Look, Betty, stay here with Nole. If I don't come back in, let's say half an hour, ring Jacquie. Tell her I'm after Oliver Lessing. Have you got that?' She nodded. 'I'll meet you here. I'm going to go and speak to the rancid old bugger. I had him in the frame all along, you know.'

'Really?' She raised an eyebrow and her daughter flitted across her face. 'Who did you tell?'

'Er ... just Metternich.'

'Oh, that's all right, then,' she said. 'At least there's someone who can bear you out. Look,' she suddenly pointed at the group, 'he's off.'

And indeed he was, running along the promenade towards the shops of the Sea Front, leaving behind the Tottingleigh Townswomen's Twitchers gesticulating wildly.

'Stay with Nolan, Ninja. Stay with Ninja, Nole,' said Maxwell, or something very like it. Neither of them would have stirred anyway; though exciting, this was also quite scary. Maxwell hared off after the fleeing poisoner, jinking, dodging and diving through the scattering women.

'He ran off when we told him about you.' The spokesperson's voice Dopplered as he hurtled past.

I bet he did, thought Maxwell, gathering speed. Lessing had an odd run, knees together and a strange gait; essentially, the quickest hobble in the world, like Mad Vince Price in the *House of Wax*. He covered the ground, though, and Maxwell, anxious not to lose him, wasn't looking at his feet, but ahead, so stumbling was the order of the day. Add to that the pounding in his head every time a foot hit the floor and he soon began to drop behind. In the maze of footpaths criss-crossing the small park between the Sea Front and the High Street, he lost him altogether. He gave up the chase reluctantly, coming to a halt in a series of long but ever slower strides. He bent down to catch his breath and put his hands on his knees. Through the blood pounding in his head, he could just hear the slap of flat feet, running in an uneven stride through the park.

He walked back to where he had left Nolan and his Ninja. His breathing became easier as he walked and, by the time he reached them, it was impossible to tell that he had been gasping for oxygen not ten minutes before.

'D'you catch the nasty man, Dadda?' Nolan asked.

'No, mate, sorry. He got away.' He looked at Ninja, willing her to comment about ancient men outrunning him, but she was silent. She was

313

privately very impressed that he would just run off like that, following into who knew what. She began to realise what her daughter saw in him. She smiled.

'Bad luck,' she said. 'But he surely couldn't have got far.'

'I should think he was just about at the end of his run,' Maxwell said. 'But the little paths through the park are tortuous and he could have gone anywhere. I'll just have to get on to Jacquie and they can pick him up at home.'

But Jacquie's mother was not her mother for nothing. 'Nonsense,' she said, briskly. 'With all this poison talk, I don't expect the folk of Leighford are exactly out and about taking the air and a coffee and cake this morning. Let's walk on into town and see if we can pick up his trail.'

'My word, Ninj,' Maxwell said, impressed. 'Let's do it. Come on, Nole, best foot forward.' And off they strode, the Three Musketeers, to catch a murderer. A small niggle in the back of Maxwell's mind was trying to get his attention, to tell him that Jacquie would have his nuts in a vice for this. He beat it down and tried to ignore it. If all else failed, he could always blame her mother. Or, at a pinch, the kid.

As they approached the recoalesced twitchers, the women backed away. It was all very well and exciting and all, but who was going to take them twitching, now that this madman had frightened away that nice Mr Lessing? Never mind, before he had run off, he had given out bottled water all round, so at least they wouldn't get dehydrated when passing the sandwiches. They twittered greetings, Maxwell doffed his hat to them one last time, and they went their separate ways.

The walk into town wasn't long, but before it was half over, Nolan was on his father's shoulders, with very explicit instructions not to hold on to ears or hair, his usual favourite balance aids. He settled instead for the collar which was only marginally more comfortable and caused momentary choking sensations every few steps.

'You really don't seem very comfortable there, Max,' Ninja observed after a while.

Maxwell struggled for breath and pointed to his collar, squeezing tight against his Adam's apple.

'Don't pull Daddy's collar, darling,' his grand-mother admonished. 'It hurts. And he's turning a funny colour.'

'I want down,' Nolan whinged. It wasn't like him to be miserable and it dawned on Maxwell that it had been a bit of a twenty-four hours for the poor little chap.

'Look, Betty, why don't you take him home?' Maxwell suggested. 'I can take it from here. I really don't want him any more involved, any-way.' That little niggle was gaining ground.

'I quite understand,' she said. 'But I can't leave you. Jacquie would never forgive me.'

Maxwell swung Nolan back to the pavement while he gathered his thoughts. There seemed no way forward except to call Jacquie and have her take over. He looked at his watch; she would be heading towards the Vine by now. He could catch her there, but then he would have to explain and, with Hall there, it was always hard to nudge them off the straight and narrow police procedure. Hell. He looked up and for a frantic, heart-stopping moment couldn't see his son. He grabbed Betty's arm and got an unpleasant handful of Bingo wing. He let go hurriedly.

'Ow,' she said, rubbing her bicep. 'Don't worry. He's over there, with that little girl.'

'Ooh,' Maxwell's schmoozing muscle gave itself a bit of a flex. He recognised the child as one from Nolan's nursery. He had often seen her and Nolan in sticky confabulation at the end of parties and the like. He headed towards them, hat at the doff, smile at the ready. The girl's mother, sitting on a nearby bench, looked up from her Sunday supplement.

'Hello,' she smiled. She looked past him. The woman she saw gave her a turn. It looked as though Jacquie had been left in the oven too long.

Maxwell followed her gaze. 'Jacquie's mother, Mrs Carpenter,' he said. He made no attempt to introduce them further, as he had no idea what the other's name was.

She was an understanding soul. She reached out her hand and said, 'Miranda, Mrs Carpenter. How are you? Down for a holiday?'

Before Ninja could start, Maxwell dived in. 'We've hit a bit of a snag, Miranda, in fact. Betty, Mrs Carpenter, isn't feeling too well, are you, Betty?'

She opened her mouth to speak but he was too quick for her.

'No, not well at all. But it's a bit difficult, with Nole, he's so excited at having his Granny down,

316

isn't he, Betty?'

Again, he beat her to it.

'Never mind, eh, Betty? Let's get you home so you can have a rest.'

Miranda cut in this time. 'Oh, Mr Maxwell, don't worry. You know how well Nolan and Florence get on together. I expect Jacquie's working, is she?' She looked sympathetically at Maxwell. She had always rather fancied the look of him; old, certainly, but at least he had the advantage of being *here*. Florence's dad was more of a serving suggestion, these days, access arrangements notwithstanding. And there was no telling where a favour might lead. If she scratched his back, who knew where he might scratch back.

'Mmm,' Maxwell said, ambiguously.

'Well, what if I have Nolan for the afternoon? We'd all enjoy it, I know.'

Maxwell feigned surprise. 'Miranda! That would be wonderful. Wouldn't it, Betty?'

She nodded. She had fallen in with the plan at last.

'Can we fetch him later? Jacquie will be back at home this afternoon. She'll call you.'

The woman stood up and called her daughter. 'We're taking Nolan home to play, Flo,' she said and the little girl jumped up and down. 'Won't that be fun?' She turned again to Maxwell. 'Does Nolan have any food fads?'

'Not really,' Maxwell said. 'But, you won't give him anything...'

'Poisoned?' she said. 'No. We're eating from the freezer and the cupboard at the moment. Like everyone else in Leighford, I should think.'

Maxwell smiled in relief. At last, someone who watched the local news. 'That's fine, then,' he said. 'Thanks so much, Miranda.' And he leant forward and gave her a kiss on each cheek. 'You are a star.'

'Really, Max,' Betty said, as they walked away towards the High Street, turning to wave at an oblivious Nolan every few steps, 'I've never seen a performance like it.'

Maxwell looked contrite and was about to apologise.

'Well done,' she added and rubbed her hands together. 'Let's catch the bastard.'

'Betty!' he said. 'I'm shocked.'

'You ain't seen nothing yet,' she said. 'Nolan isn't the only chip off the old block, you know. I didn't read all those Agatha Christies for nothing.' And off she went, setting a cracking pace, towards Oliver Lessing, Nemesis in crimplene.

Chapter Twenty

Jacquie and Hall had found Leighford nick the easy way. As they turned into the road which ended in its car park, their attention was inevitably drawn to the crowd of thousands of Leighfordians, and their noise. The flaming torches and pitchforks were missing, but they otherwise were very clearly a Mob, with a capital 'm'.

Jacquie let Hall's muttered expletive go unremarked, but explained the situation anyway, if only to clear it in her own mind. 'I expect stories of a poisoner on the loose have been somewhat exaggerated in the telling, guv,' she said.

'What do they want to exaggerate for?' he asked, reasonably. 'When I last counted, six people are in hospital, three others have had lucky escapes and one person is dead.'

'Let's check,' said Jacquie and stuck her head out of the window. 'Er, excuse me,' she said to the nearest yelling woman. 'What's going on?'

'It's this poisoner, ennit?' the woman said. Seeming glad to stop yelling for a moment, she leant down and looked in through the window. 'There's hundreds in hospital, I heard twenty people dead. They're flying casualties off all over. The General can't cope, they say. It's terrible.'

'It sounds awful,' said Jacquie. 'On the news, it just said...'

'Huh!' the woman sneered. 'The news. What's

that got to do with it? They only say what they're told to say. To stop panics and that.'

'But it hasn't stopped it, has it,' said Jacquie, sweetly. 'There must be over a thousand people here.'

The woman looked at Jacquie with suspicion. 'If you're not here to complain, why are you here?' she said. She screwed her head round and looked inside the car. The walkie-talkie was in full view, as was Hall's police pass, left out on the dash. 'You're bloody police, aintcha?' She straightened up. 'Hey, everybody. Over here. Rozzers. Senior, too, I reckon. Quick.' But Jacquie had the window up as Hall reversed, for once without his usual caution, tyres snarling.

'Careful, guv,' Jacquie said, clutching the dash. 'You'll run someone over.'

'Sounds good to me,' said Hall through gritted teeth as he reached the road. He screeched round and hared off in the direction of the town centre car park. 'This is Leighford, not Paris. We don't do mobs here.'

'I'd have thought not, guv,' said Jacquie, looking back over her shoulder. 'But that looked quite convincing to me.'

'Better radio in,' he said. 'See how they are in there.'

She picked up the walkie-talkie and pressed the button. 'Alpha Charlie Two, over.'

'Come in, Alpha Charlie Two,' said a harassed-sounding voice.

'What's going on?' she asked. 'To hell with all this "over" nonsense. Just the facts.' Maxwell would have applauded Jacquie's *Dragnet*'s Joe

Friday, but the similarity hadn't occurred to her.

'We're trapped,' the voice came back, testily. 'Was that you reversing out just then?'

'You bet,' Jacquie said. Hall nudged her. 'Hold on, DCI Hall wants a word.'

He leant in closer to the radio. 'Have you rung the media?'

'God, no,' crackled the radio.

'Do it. They won't be able to resist a man and a microphone. It'll take the pressure off. Put it out on all points. I want squad cars and a chopper in the air, just in case. Who's on duty?'

'DC Illingworth, guv.'

'Patch me through.'

Static crackled through Hall's car and Hall's head.

'Guv?'

'Rob. Looks like you've got Fort Apache, the Bronx on your hands.'

'You know how it is,' the DC told him. 'A couple of loudmouths in the front office asking what they're paying their taxes for, and suddenly you've got fucking anarchy. 'Scusing my French at all times.'

'Bill's calling for back-up,' Hall said.

'He's done that already. We've got teams coming over from Pompey and Littlehampton.'

'Mark out a perimeter for them,' Hall ordered. 'Er ... Castle Street, the Park, Della and Mapleton. Pull the cordon in. Coordinate with the chopper which should be on its way. Any actual heads broken yet?'

'No, guv.' He could hear the chuckle in Illingworth's voice. 'We've got it covered.'

'You're sure, Rob?'

'I'd rather they were here than at Leighford General. At least we can contain them.'

'OK. Keep in touch.' He sat straight again and concentrated on the turn into the car park.

'Right oh, guv.'

'It's me,' said Jacquie. 'Can I have Bill back, please?' She waited. 'How are the fingerprints coming along?'

'Bad news, Jacquie. Just nick personnel.'

'Bugger. Never mind, it was always a long shot. Thanks. We'll check back in later. Alpha Charlie Two out.'

'Roger, Alpha Charlie Two.' The crackling died abruptly as the radio went dead.

Hall pointed. 'Isn't that your car?' he asked.

Jacquie looked in the direction of his finger. 'Yes,' she said. 'It is. That means Max has actually done as I asked him and taken Mum and Nole shopping.'

'That's good, then. We know where they are. I'm always a bit suspicious when your ... Max is on the loose.'

'That makes two of us, guv. But he won't do anything when he's got Nolan with him, at least I can be sure of that.' She looked around at the almost empty car park. There was a minibus parked up near the sea defence, her own Ka and five other vehicles. Other than that, it was deserted. 'You can't usually get in here on a Sunday morning as sunny as this. Where is everyone?'

'Outside the nick, threatening mayhem,' Hall said, switching off the engine. 'Rob will be all right. If anyone can talk sense to the great British public, he can. Even so, I'm not straying far from the radio.' He got out and stretched. 'God, Jacquie, it's been a long few days, hasn't it?'

'It certainly has, guv,' said Jacquie. 'It's hard to believe that all this kicked off last Thursday.'

'I almost didn't respond, you know, to the call from Leighford High. Well, to be accurate, I didn't respond. Bob Davies took it into his own hands.'

'You would have got involved eventually,' said Jacquie, comfortingly.

Hall snorted. 'We haven't come out smelling of roses as it is, Jacquie,' he said. 'Imagine if we had taken longer even than we did. The press and that mob would have a field day.'

'We'll sort it, guv,' Jacquie patted his arm. 'Don't worry.' She knew he was thinking of Margaret, still in hospital but out of danger. He was thinking of the murdered Mel Forman, cut down because she had a weakness for prawns and an allergic teaching assistant. Randomness was the policeman's enemy; there was nothing to get a hold of, nothing to follow. Perhaps Angus would have something for them that didn't end in a no-through-road sign.

They fell into step, walking in the wake of her family, had they but known. They were West Sussex police persons, not Tonto, so they didn't know what all the signs, written clearly in the sand, meant. There was the skid mark where Maxwell had shot straight off the blocks to stop an innocent old lady giving Nolan a sweet. There was the clean area near the end of the sea defence where a flock of twitchers had milled around, waiting for their guide. There were the flat-footed, pigeon-toed marks of Oliver Lessing, approaching his ladies. Then, the spiral ground deep into the verge of his turn and flight. The marks of his passage were obliterated by the deeply marked spoor of a running man, running to save more people from death or disaster. Oblivious of the historical record being scuffed aside by their own feet, they walked along the Front and crossed the road into the park.

'We might bump into them while we're in town,' said Jacquie, for something to say.

'Hmm, yes,' said Hall absently. He was many miles away and in many different directions. He was with Margaret in the hospital, he was behind his desk, about to be crushed by teetering paperwork, he was facing a murderer, reading him his rights. Above all, he was with Rob Illingworth in Fort Apache, wondering how ugly the situation might become. The trouble was that, on the murderer front, the man had no face, no voice, nothing he could get a hold on. He was as insubstantial as air.

Jacquie knew better than to try and drag him back. When there wasn't a case to work on, he could be like this for days. But somehow, he always came out the other side, fresh and enthusiastic, as far as anyone could tell, ready for the next challenge. The thing with this case was that it was happening so fast. It was like being bombarded with missiles, each one from an unexpected direction. Some of them were ping-pong balls, others bags of shit. And, possibly, the next one could well be a grenade with the pin missing.

As they walked through the deserted town centre, they fell naturally into the regulation two and a half miles an hour, measured, automatic. Her eyes swept from side to side, taking in everything, sifting, discarding, the gaze of a policeman on the beat. Out of the left-hand corner of her eye, she saw something familiar. She looked again, but it was gone. She couldn't be sure what had caught her attention; old habits died hard.

They both heard the broken rattle of a police helicopter, droning in the distance. There was no siren to announce the reinforcements snarling into Leighford from east and west. Softly, softly, the DCI would have told them. Form your circle, park in side streets, wait. A few quiet words might still do the trick.

Maxwell and Betty Carpenter hastened through the deserted town centre, the speed as near to a run as two people who will never see fifty again could maintain. They scanned constantly, turning their heads this way and that, jumping at every blowing newspaper, dashing off in pursuit of every shadow. The helicopter drone they barely noticed. It was probably a coastguard sweep. Routine. They were certainly unaware of the squad cars prowling past the Flyover. They were alone, apart from the occasional hardened drinker heading towards the Vine, the only pub which had bothered to open in what had rapidly become a siege town. News travels fast. Bad news travels faster and the growing crowd at the police station were sending out signals on every frequency. Leighford was battening down its hatches. They could hear a measured tread behind them, but knew it wasn't their quarry. For a start, they reasoned, he was ahead of them. And his flat feet would flap on the paving stones of the pedestrian precinct they were now in like gunshots.

Maxwell suddenly stopped and triangulated like a hound on the scent. 'Betty,' he whispered. 'Can you hear that?'

She came and stood alongside him. 'Footsteps,' she said. 'Behind us.'

'No, not that. That other sound. It's got an echo; it's hard to make it out.'

She listened harder, funnelling a hand to her ear. It made her look as if she was auditioning for a role in *Macbeth*. She bent her head and closed her eyes. Then, suddenly opening them wide, she turned to Maxwell. 'It's him,' she said. 'That way.'

They dashed off down the alleyway to their left, chasing the dark elusive butterfly of death.

All too soon, Jacquie and Hall were at the Vine. No one knew how the pub had managed to survive, taking up valuable wine bar space in the middle of Leighford Town Centre. But there it was, large as life and twice as smelly. Mad Artie was noticeable by his absence. His ancient mother, who kicked him out every morning to give her space to ply her dwindling trade, had a lie-in on a Sunday, so the air in the lounge bar was merely noisome, rather than noisome and blue. The police persons walked in gingerly. It certainly wasn't wise to stand still for too long; the legend went that people who stood on one spot could be seen to sink into the soggy carpet, until they were beyond human aid.

A wordless shout called them over to the bar. Angus lounged there, with a half-drunk pint in front of him. The barman was leaning close by, fidgeting with an empty glass, its froth-flecked sides still wet with condensation.

Hall and Jacquie made their way from the door, with that sidelong look adopted by the approacher to the approachee; it was not appropriate to wave, and yet some kind of greeting was needed. Thank goodness it was a small room, thought Jacquie. There was no need to call back.

'Angus,' Hall said, shortly. 'Are we on the clock?'

'Mr Hall,' Angus said, stirring himself rather more than was usual. 'I'm not in this game for the money, you know. I'm in it for the cause of justice.'

'If you say so,' Hall said. 'Do you have the remastered voice tape?'

'Tape?' Angus laughed and moved his gum to the other side. He took another swig of his beer. 'CD-ROM, you mean.'

'For God's sake, Angus,' Hall exploded. 'What's the point of that? We need to hear it now.'

'And so you shall,' Angus said, reaching down to the side of his stool. 'I've got my laptop with me. I've come more or less straight from that shop where the poisoner was caught. Well, nearly caught; how is Mr Maxwell, Jacquie?'

'That's DS Carpenter, to you,' snapped Hall.

Oh, great, thought Jacquie. Years of schmoozing gone West. She gave Angus a rueful smile.

The boffin looked at Hall with just a hint of annoyance. Angus was not easily moved, to anger

327

or anything else, but Hall got right up his nose. He waved a plug aimlessly in the air. 'I've had this running on battery almost all night. Jeff, have we got an extension lead we can use?'

'Is it hot in here?' the barman said, a propos of nothing.

'Not especially,' Angus said. 'Do you have an extension?'

'No,' the barman said, swatting a fly only he could see. 'It is hot in here.' He threw his arms around madly, and twitched his head. 'Get off,' he cried, and fell suddenly to the floor, the thud accompanied by the sound of breaking glass.

Angus reacted with lightning speed. He leapt to his feet and put his hands on the bar, launching himself over, kicking over the glasses and a bowl of peanuts as he did so. Hall and Jacquie were both impressed and amazed and, with deference to their age and rank, dashed for the flap at the end, to let themselves through. When they reached the other side, an unexpected and unpleasant sight met their eyes. The barman, Jeff, was half sitting, half lying in a pool of alcopop, which fizzed and spluttered in a desultory way. On top of him lay Angus, retching and heaving as his system tried to rid itself of the poison inside.

Hall was on his knees, pulling the boffin off the barman, who was in a bad way, that was obvious. His colour was horrible, his eyes were rolled up, his breathing shallow. Blood trickled from glass cuts in his scalp. The DCI turned to Jacquie. 'Mind the glass. Some of it is from their glasses; we'll need that for analysis. And the peanuts, they'll need collecting up as well. That's for

SOCO, though. Call the paramedics.'

She turned to face outwards from the bar, pulling out her phone as she did so. She dialled and the seconds it took for the call to go through seemed endless.

'Police, fire or ambulance?' the disembodied voice said.

'Ambulance and police, the Vine public house, Leighford High Street.'

'Could you give me details, caller?'

'They *are* the details. Just get them here, now,' Jacquie snapped. 'I am DS Jacquie Carpenter, Leighford CID, and this is an emergency.'

'They're on their way,' replied the imperturbable voice. 'Do you need further assistance?'

'No,' Jacquie sighed, and rang off. She turned back to where Hall had turned the barman on his back and was giving mouth-to-mouth, an unlovely task on many levels. Angus was groaning, doubled up on the floor. She reached down and touched his arm.

'Angus? Angus, it's Jacquie. Can you get up?'

He shook his head and retched again.

'Come on, Angus. It's more comfy on the other side of the bar. Let's get you to a chair, or a nice bench or something. You're in Mr Hall's way. Come on,' and she coaxed him, using all the skills honed on the North Face of Nolan at bedtime, to get him to stand, to walk and finally to sit down out in the lounge.

He sat with his head on his knees, moaning faintly and sometimes giving a half-hearted heave, but he wasn't sick again. Finally, she reached into her bag and brought out a bottle of water. 'Come on, Angus. Take a sip of this.'

He backed away from it, shaking his head and rolling his eyes.

'No, come on, Angus, don't be silly. You heard me break the seal. This water has been in my fridge for over a week and then in my bag. It hasn't been poisoned, I promise you. Look,' and she took a swig. 'See?'

Reluctantly, he took the bottle from her and drank, sips at first and then great pulls until the bottle was empty. He gave it back to her and nodded his thanks. His voice was hoarse when he asked, 'How's Jeff?'

'Not too good,' Jacquie said. 'Mr Hall is working on him.'

'Hall?' Angus was surprised. 'Is he any good?'

'The best,' said Jacquie. 'He's in good hands, Angus.' It seemed almost cruel, but she had to ask. 'Was your beer from a bottle or a pump?'

'A pump,' Angus said. 'But Jeff changed the barrel and washed the lines out. In fact, it improved the taste; hygiene isn't much of a thing with old Jeff.'

'Then?'

'Then he pulled two pints.' Angus was struggling to focus, to remember. 'He drank his straight off and had another. I was feeling a bit fragile, in fact. I was working in the lab last night, when I called you. I was just going home when they called about the shop, so I came straight over. That took ages; I've only had a few hours on a mate's sofa, so I didn't really feel much like beer, to be honest.' He was getting into his stride. 'He was knocking back the peanuts as well. I

330

don't eat peanuts in bars.'

'Allergy?'

'No. I did a dissertation on the number of different organisms in a typical pub plate of peanuts for my MSc.'

If Jacquie was amazed, she managed not to show it.

'So, long story cut short, I don't eat peanuts in bars.'

'Fair comment,' she said. 'So, let's get this right. Jeff had one whole pint and you had a half; in other words, what we saw in your glass was the leavings of your first glassful.'

'That's right. But Jeff had had two; his empty glass was the second.'

'Have there been any other drinkers in here today?'

'I don't think so. But you could ask the barman from the dining room side. He would know.'

Jacquie's head came up, a deer at the waterhole. 'There's another barman? Where is he?'

'I dunno. In the other bar.'

'But, Angus,' Jacquie tried to be gentle. 'Surely, he would come round when he heard the commotion?'

'Y'd think,' said Angus, reverting to type. 'Look, Jacquie, can I lie down? I really want to lie down.' And he twisted himself round and lay awkwardly across two chairs and closed his eyes. Jacquie checked that he wouldn't fall off and, satisfied, turned back to the bar. Hall was just rising into view, like the Kraken surfacing for the last time. He was still looking down at the horror he had been dealing with at his feet. He turned his head

331

and looked Jacquie in the eyes. He shook his head slightly and turned to the flap. He was walking heavily, holding on to the bar. He slumped down on a stool.

Jacquie went over to him and righted Angus's overturned seat. She sat down and faced her boss. It was time for some straight talking. 'This isn't our fault, guv,' she said. 'It was done before we got here.'

'And you call that not our fault?' Hall said, dully. He looked at his hands for a moment, then clapped them on his knees. 'Come on, Jacquie,' he said. They could hear the squeal of the squad car outside, probably one re-routed from Rob Illingworth's back-up team. The paramedics would be with them. 'Let's get back to the nick, see what's happening there. If we can, we'll go in through smokers' corner.'

They made their way to the door and almost collided with a stream of SOCOs and green-clad paramedics. Hall didn't know the uniformed sergeant in charge. He gestured behind the bar. 'One dead, I think,' he said. 'You'll need to call it. One over there on those chairs. Arrest him. Read him his rights and take him to the hospital. Don't leave him till I get there.' He pushed past his puzzled men and went out into the fresh air. 'In fact,' he added for Jacquie's ears only. 'Don't leave him even when I get there for his own safety.'

'But, guv...' Jacquie frowned.

'No, Jacquie.' He spun round to face her. 'I know you like Angus. We all like Angus, in the sort of way that we like any strange and mildly ugly animal as invented by David Attenborough. But he's our man, make no mistake.'

'But, guv, what about the other barman?'

Hall stopped in his tracks. 'Other barman? What other barman? I didn't see another barman.'

'That's my point. There is another barman, through in the other bar. But he didn't come round when he heard the noise. Surely, an innocent man would.'

Hall pushed up his glasses and rubbed his eyes. The seat dedicated to Jock was handy and he sat down on it gratefully. Finally, he said, 'I still think Angus is our man.'

'You may be right, guv,' said Jacquie, placatingly. 'But we must find the barman as well. He may have had a drink and be unconscious somewhere.'

Hall pushed himself back to his feet. Somewhere, the little fuel gauge that monitored his brain was saying empty. Any minute, the light would come on to warn him he would stop dead within the next hundred yards. But until that happened, he must soldier on. He walked back to the pub and put his head round the door. She heard him bark orders, but couldn't hear what they were, then he was back with her and shepherding her along with a hand on the small of her back. 'Nick,' he said.

'Right you are, guv,' she said and in the same, companionable two and a half mile pace as they had arrived, they walked away. As they turned the corner towards the nick, her phone rang.

'DS Carpenter,' she said.

The town centre was still deserted, although that wouldn't be the case for long. The curious ghouls who were attuned to such things would soon be out in force, herded behind the police tape, watching every come and go of the professionals inside. Word would be on the streets. There was another one at the Vine. The sun beat down, warm and lazy as syrup and gilded the statue of Councillor MacIllwain, looking out over his Memorial Garden for eternity. Somewhere, high up above the shop fronts, a wisp of smoke rose into the air, a little hint of autumn, a warning that the year was turning. A swallow turned and dived and spiralled in the sky. A lark sang over the Dam.

And a murderer swaggered, unremarked, through the town centre of Leighford, his waiter's apron slung casually across his shoulder.

Chapter Twenty-One

Maxwell had to give Betty her due. Her turn of speed was unremarkable, but her stamina was amazing. She had fallen into the kind of dogged slog he had always imagined a Roman soldier had adopted. She tipped her weight slightly forward and let gravity do the work and he kept up with her with difficulty. He put a tick in the 'pro' box, to balance cons like budgie poo toast and ecru trims. Every little helps.

Every now and then, they would stop and listen for the flapping of their quarry. Eventually, they were close enough to hear him quite clearly, his slightly laboured breathing and the muttering under his breath. Then, they heard what they had been waiting for: the footsteps slow and stop. They looked at each other in triumph. They had him. They had worn him out. They slowed their pace to a walk and regained the power of, if not speech, then at least a kind of gasping whisper.

They came to a T-junction, where the narrow alley between the backs of shops gave way to a wider, paved walkway, where tubs of late geraniums, dusty with the lateness of the year and stunted by their diet of cigarette ends and wee, gave a brave splash of colour. They crept up to the corner and looked carefully round, one way, then the other.

'Nothing!' wheezed Maxwell. 'Where has the

old bugger gone?'

'He must live in one of these houses,' Betty said, forcing the words out with a breath. 'You know him, I thought you said. Do you know which one?'

'No,' Maxwell said. 'I knew him a year or so ago. He ... well, he left Leighford under rather a cloud and I was amazed to find him back. This isn't where Dierdre, that's his niece, from school, lived. I can only assume he bought this recently, or is renting. But, hell and damnation, Betty. We were doing so well.'

'Let's face it,' she said. 'We'll have to call Jacquie.'

Maxwell looked at her for the first time since their hunt was up. 'I don't like to say this, Betty, but she will go stark raving mad if she sees you like this.'

'Like what?' She tried to swivel her eyes round to see her own face; a good trick if successful but, yet again, she failed.

'Bright red, sweating and bug-eyed, if I may borrow a phrase from Year Nine. She'll think I have been mistreating you.'

'Why would she assume that?' she asked waspishly.

'No reason,' he said, innocently. 'But anyhoo, let's leave the call a while, shall we? He might still break cover.'

'You make him sound like a fox or something.'

'Rat, more likely. Let's just get our breath and we can plan the next move.'

They leant against the wall while the cells in their furthermost reaches waited patiently for oxygen. They both heard the voice at once.

'Mr Maxwell? Cooee.'

'What the hell was that?' Maxwell asked as they spun round trying to find the source of the call.

A gate creaked down the lane and an elderly head peeked out. 'Hello,' it called. 'Down here.'

'It's a trap,' Betty hissed. 'Don't go.'

'You can't kill with poison when the victim knows about it,' Maxwell said. 'Come on,' and he trotted off towards the gate, which Lessing had left tantalisingly ajar.

The house beyond the fence was, like Maxwell's, a tall town house, but older and very narrow. They were in the back garden, a neat little rectangle which owed much to Alan Titchmarsh and his crew. A path wound up between banks of shrubs to a small gravelled area just by the patio doors. On the gravel, his back to the house, like an animal at bay, stood Oliver Lessing. On close inspection, he was no more attractive than their fleeting impressions had led them to think. He was scrawny, his head balanced on a neck too thin for it, poking out from the collar like a Galapagos tortoise at the end of its second century. His legs stuck from his wide shorts like celery, white despite a summer's exposure whilst watching birds and anything else that took his fancy. His feet were encased in weathered Crocs, on which an incongruous bird had been buttoned. Altogether, an unappealing sight. He was wearing thick gardening gloves and appeared to be busying himself tidying up the borders around the gravel.

'Hello, Mr Maxwell,' he said. 'Welcome to my

home. And you must be...?'

'Mrs Carpenter,' Betty said, as though at a vicarage garden party.

He looked at her with his head on one side, looking for all the world like a puzzled emu. 'I thought you'd be younger,' he said. 'Late baby all round, was he, the little chap?'

'I'm his grandmother,' Nolan's grandmother said, grandly.

'Oh, I see,' the emu replied. 'That explains a lot. Did he enjoy his lolly?'

'You fiend,' Betty screamed. 'How dare you!' Maxwell held her back. No need to rush this. He needed to be sure.

Lessing looked aggrieved. 'It was only a lolly,' he said. 'Nothing to make a fuss about. Oh!' He stopped, looking horrified. 'He's not one of these little chaps with allergies, is he? Peanuts, that sort of thing. Anaphylactic shock?'

'No,' Maxwell said, beginning to get the drift. 'He's fine in that respect, but a little finicky, I suppose you could say. Comes from being an only one, I suppose. We're a little indulgent.'

'You must have more,' Lessing crowed. 'It's a terrible thing to become attached to just one child. I was the same with Dierdre. I know I was only her uncle, but ... well, you know, Mr Maxwell, what a wonderful woman my Dierdre became.'

'Um, yes, yes indeed,' Maxwell gushed. 'But, could we go back to the lolly?'

'Yes, of course. Well, there the little chap was, in his buggy, looking a bit bored. I had a lovely organic aniseed lolly in my pocket and I gave it to him. No added colours or preservatives, Mr Maxwell. Nothing to hurt the little chap.'

Betty had subsided and was looking at Lessing as if she would like to shove his head up his rather unpleasant looking shorts. Maxwell put a hand on her arm to restrain her.

'But, anyhow,' Lessing was continuing, breaking up sticks and putting them in an incinerator. 'I don't expect you chased me halfway across Leighford to hear about my little kindnesses.'

'No,' Maxwell agreed. 'Not really.'

'I expect you would like to know about the poisoned prawn cocktails.' He looked at them, cocking his head again from side to side, as if sizing them up. His busy hands continued to break up the branches, adding screwed up paper every now and again, and a slurp of meths.

'So it *was* the prawn cocktails,' Maxwell said. 'But what about Freda?'

'Freda? Oh, the dinner lady. Yes, well, surely you had that one worked out. I gave her an untampered-with one. Really, Mr Maxwell, you used to be so bright.' He strained as he broke a larger branch over his thigh. He added the bits to the bin and patted his pockets aimlessly. 'Do you have a match?'

They shook their heads.

'A lighter? Oh, no, hold on, here it is.' And he fetched out a Zippo from the depths of a pocket at the back of his shorts. 'Smoking is so bad for one, but I still like a little sneaky cigarette when I can get one,' he said.

'But why did you do it?' Maxwell said.

'Mr Maxwell, I am, again, shocked at you. To

avenge my Dierdre, of course.'

'But no one who was poisoned killed Dierdre,' Maxwell said. 'You know as well as I do who killed Dierdre. They're serving life. Mel Forman, the woman who died, she probably hadn't exchanged two words with her.'

'They were *replacing* her,' hissed Lessing, white spittle appearing at the corners of his mouth. 'My Dierdre. Replaced by someone else. Sitting in her office. Her chair. My little Dierdre.' As soon as the venom had started, so nice old Mr Lessing, purveyor of unpleasant lolly flavours, was back. 'So, come here, why don't you? Watch the bonfire.' He held his lighter to the paper in the bin and flames flew up immediately, with plumes of smoke. He disappeared in a fragrant smog. 'Come on,' his voice said, through the fumes. 'Come closer. Come closer and I'll tell you how I did it.'

Maxwell took a step towards him. 'You raving shit!' he snapped. 'I always had you down for a pervert, using your binoculars for anything other than birdwatching, but this...'

Betty suddenly pulled on the back of his jacket. 'No, Max. Don't go any nearer. Look!' She pointed to a leaf, curling over the edge of the bin.

'At what?' Even in a crisis, Maxwell couldn't be ungrammatical.

'That leaf. It's oleander he's burning, Max. It's poisonous.'

'I remember,' he said, backing away. 'Even the smoke is poisonous.' He put his arm up over his nose and mouth and, turning, pushed Betty ahead of him and through the gate.

'Come back, Mr Maxwell,' they could hear him calling. 'Come back and let me tell you all about it.'

'Call Jacquie,' Maxwell said. 'Then an ambulance. Thing is, I've no idea where we are.' He looked frantically around. This part of the town, dumb in the heat, was alien to him.

'I'll leave my phone open,' she said. 'They can do it by satellite.'

'Excellent,' said Maxwell. 'And yet, how creepy.'

She moved a few doors down and turned around to get the best signal. She punched in Jacquie's number. After a couple of rings, her daughter answered.

'DS Carpenter.'

'Darling, it's Mum.'

'Oh, hi, Mum. Good shopping trip? I can't talk, we're in a bit of a crisis right now. Can I call you back?' And the phone went dead.

Betty Carpenter was not always a patient or a very nice woman and she would be the first to admit it, but she was resourceful. She rang the emergency services and decided to leave her daughter till later. But then, she would leave no stone unturned until that girl knew what guilt was. With swift efficiency she ordered an ambulance and police back-up. She turned to tell Maxwell the news.

Where he had stood was a definitely Maxwell-shaped hole. The gate to Lessing's garden was open and she could hear falsetto screams from the other side of the fence.

'Max!' she yelled. 'Come out of there, for God's sake.'

'No need to shout,' he said, calmly, walking through the gate with an unconscious Oliver Lessing over his shoulder. He dumped him casually to the ground and neither of them minded when they heard a double thump as his head bounced on the ground. 'I wasn't letting him take that way out.'

'Well, it wouldn't be an easy way,' she said, drily. 'I believe bloody diarrhoea is one of the symptoms.'

'There's no need to blaspheme, Betty,' he said.

'I mean...' but then she caught the glint in his eye. 'Oh, I see. Well, if you will take my advice one more time, Max, I think you should strip off. The poison might be lingering in your clothes.'

He looked at her closely. Was she joking? She looked very serious, certainly, and it was better to be safe than sorry. He solemnly stripped off his jacket, trousers and shirt. His hat joined the pile and he was haggling with her over his underpants when the ambulance crew arrived. It was only when they started laughing that he realised that his mother-in-law-to-be would take some very close watching in the years ahead.

Jacquie and Hall got to the nick without further incident, noting the back-up cars parked in alleyways, waiting for the word. The mob of outraged citizens was still there, outside the station's frontage, but torn now, between giving interviews to various local news media, breaking down the doors of the nick because they had always wanted to and rushing off in search of the excitement as advertised by sirens going off all over town. The DC seemed to have it all in hand. The

342

two police people crept in by the smokers' stairs, crushing old dog ends underfoot and carrying the rank smell of old smoke with them up to the first landing.

Inside, a nervy-looking Incident Team had abandoned all pretence at following up the Incident. Instead, they were peering out of blind-drawn windows, psyching themselves up for whatever was to follow. There was glittering glass all over one end of the room where stones had crashed through windows.

'That's going to come out of the taxpayers' pockets,' Hall said and the mood lightened. 'Rob.' He shook the man's hand. 'Well done. Anything untoward?'

His DC smiled. 'Let's just say I'm glad I wore my brown trousers today,' he said. He gestured to the window. 'They're breaking up out there.' He checked his watch. 'Football's on in half an hour.'

'And there's a new crime scene at the Vine. Get through to some of your cars. Three ought to do the trick. Get them over there. Chopper still up?'

'Last time I looked,' Illingworth said.

'Keep it there for now. I want reports on crowd movements every ten minutes.'

'Got it,' and Illingworth swung into action, quietly grateful that the DCI was back. Then, he turned. 'Jacquie,' he said. 'A bit of bad news, I'm afraid.'

Her heart contracted. Her family were out there. 'Yes?'

'Your mother's car. In the car park, you know? Wrecked, I'm afraid.'

'Oh, dear,' said Jacquie, hardly able to look at

343

Hall. It was true what they said; every crowd had a silver lining.

In Hall's office, the argument that Hall and Jacquie had put on hold during their walk resumed. 'It isn't Angus,' said Jacquie. 'I can prove it if you want.'

'Well, proof would be nice.' Hall slumped into his chair.

'He rang me and left a message. It was timed at only minutes before Max was bopped on the head by a torch in Leighford.'

'What does that prove?' Hall was surly, a sure sign he was on dodgy ground.

'Well, how could he have got from Chichester to here in only minutes?'

'How do you know he was there? He could have been waiting inside the shop.'

'No. He definitely rang from the lab. I could hear that mixing thing they always have going making a noise in the background.'

Hall thought for a moment. 'He's a clever bloke. He could have taped that and used it as a background.'

'I'm sorry, guv. I don't buy that. How would he know that he would need an alibi? And, another thing. Max said he smelt of tobacco, the bloke who hit him.'

'Well, you're arguing against yourself there, Jacquie,' said Hall, pointing a triumphant finger. 'Angus smokes like a trooper.'

Jacquie crossed her arms across her chest. 'Guv, really!' she said. 'Angus is never far from a rollie, I'll agree. But since when did you know him

344

smoke anything other than something dodgy?'

Hall looked mulish. 'How would Maxwell know?' he said. 'I don't believe he could be that sure.' But he sounded less certain and Jacquie saw her advantage and took it.

'Finally,' she said, 'Max said that the man he grabbed was smaller than him, if not even below average height. Angus is like two yards of pump water. There's no way you could mistake him for a short person, unless he came out of the shop on his knees.'

Hall threw up his hands. 'I still think–'

'I know what you think,' Jacquie said, cutting him off. 'You think that Angus gave himself a smaller dose, to put us off the scent.'

Hall nodded, and poked at a piece of paper with his pen. 'Yes,' he said. 'Well spotted.'

'But, guv, that's the only reason it could be Angus, don't you see?' Really, the man was so stubborn she just wanted to scream. 'You can't just say it is Angus because we've got a mob outside. We have to get the right man, otherwise we'll be watching for poisoners for the rest of our lives. Please, guv.'

Deep down, Hall knew that Jacquie was right. If this was one of Maxwell's beloved Westerns, the mob would be waving a noose, demanding that Sheriff Hall hand the sonofabitch over. He would fire a shot in the air and they'd all go home, muttering darkly about Randolph Scott. As it was... 'All right. We'll keep looking. But we'll also keep Angus under surveillance.'

'I think we should. I think the poisoner knows he had unravelled the voicemail. He might have another go.' Please, please, listen, you cussed man; she tried to send subliminal messages to him.

He picked up the phone and dialled. 'I'll change the emphasis,' he said to her, 'from arrest to protection.'

While he made the call, she went into the corner of the room and redialled her mother's mobile number. It was switched off. Probably at home by now, Jacquie thought, sleeping off the remains of her hangover. She certainly had seemed very strange on the phone earlier. Breathless. Excited, even. A small worm of doubt started to gnaw in Jacquie's stomach.

'Jacquie,' Hall said. 'Let's get on with this then, shall we? Maxwell said he knew who had done this. Do *you* know who it is?'

'He'll have told the cat,' said Jacquie, at a tangent.

'Will the cat talk?' Hall asked, straight-faced.

'Unlikely,' she said.

'We're at square one, then,' said Hall. 'I just don't know where to go from here. The manager of the Vine had just taken on the new barman on Saturday. He could be anyone. He could be our man, but he could just be someone who, for reasons of his own, didn't want to get involved in a police investigation. Let's start again.'

'What, guv? From Leighford High?'

'Oh, God, no. I can't stand that. This lunch-time. From when we went in.'

They picked the events over into tiny pieces, and then put them all back together again. It couldn't be Angus, and yet, somehow, it had to

346

be Angus. He was always after more hours; Hall believed he had been willing to kill for the extra work. People today killed for peanuts; in this case, they could kill *with* peanuts. Jacquie couldn't believe that laconic Angus could be bothered to plan something like this and, although she knew that he wanted the cash, and liked his sleuthing and mild showing off in his lab, she knew in her heart of hearts that he was a gentle soul.

So, here they were again, whittled down to a smallish man, not too fit, smoker, homicidal maniac. Easy-peasy.

Hall's phone rang.

'Hall,' he barked. 'What? That was quick. Give me the list. Yep, right, uh huh, yes, I see. Wait a minute. Who? Are you sure? No, no, sorry, no offence. Thanks for being so fast with that. Yes, thanks. No, we don't really think it's him. No. Don't worry.' He put the phone down and looked across the desk at Jacquie. 'SOCO,' he said. 'Prints from the bar. Loads of unidentified, of course. The Vine isn't very hot on polish. But ... well, let me make another call, then we'll talk.' He picked up the phone again and dialled zero for the desk. 'Hello. Yes. DCI Hall. Just a quick question, I know you're busy. Whose fingerprints were on that plant. Yes, I know about his. And hers. Any- one else? Really? I see, thanks.' The phone went down and Hall was on his feet in one movement. 'Let's go,' he said to Jacquie over his shoulder.

'Where are we going, guv?' she asked, out of her seat and grabbing her bag.

'Do you know where Bob Davies lives?' he

asked, randomly.

'Er ... no, I don't,' she said.

'Well, you're about to find out.' And he made for the stairs.

Hall's car was parked out in the shoppers' car park so they commandeered a squad car, complete with driver and back-up. The mob had gone now, except for a small picquet of the most piqued of Leighford, DSS card-carriers to a man. And one retired colonel with shares in a supermarket. They passed the Volvo, alone now except for Jacquie's Ka, in splendid isolation in the usually busy space. They had driven about half a mile further before the impact hit Jacquie.

'Guv,' she said. 'My car is still in the car park.'

'Yes,' he said, 'I saw it. So what? They're out shopping.'

'But my mother didn't answer her phone.'

'They're in a shop. She had no signal.'

'Guv. She's with Max. He thinks he knows who did it.'

Hall looked serious. 'Call the station. See if any calls have involved them.'

'What?' Jacquie was almost climbing out of the car. 'They've got Nolan with them.'

'Well, make up your mind, Jacquie,' Hall said. 'I know Maxwell is completely crazy, but his madness stops short of anything that would hurt Nolan. So, there's no need to worry.'

'But ... my car...'

'Perhaps it wouldn't start. Perhaps your mother had a drink...'

'What do you mean by that?' Jacquie was

348

becoming very sensitive on that issue.

'Nothing.' Hall looked at her askance. Perhaps the last few days had been too much. 'Either put it out of your mind and come with me on this arrest or get out now.' He waited, tapping one finger on the back of the driver's seat. This was a habit of which he was unaware, but it drove all of his drivers almost to the point of homicide. 'Make up your mind.'

'Yes, Jacquie,' muttered his driver. 'Make up your sodding mind.'

After what seemed an eternity, she said, 'OK, guv. I'm sorry. Let's go.'

'Thank Christ,' the driver muttered and changed down for the hill that led to Davies's house.

Davies lived in a bungalow on the outskirts of Leighford. It just had a number but, had there been a scrollwork plaque outside as sported by all its neighbours, it would have read 'Screwed Over In The Divorce'. It was neglected and, even in the fag end of the loveliest summer in years, the garden was unkempt and somehow the dying flowers in the borders managed to look sinister in their damped-off death throes. The policemen all were reminded of a Tim Burton set – the whole thing was just one step to the left of normal.

The driver of Hall's car stopped, out of habit, a few doors further on. The squad car following them stopped a few doors back. There was no real need for subterfuge, they knew; Davies was well up on all their tricks, but even so, there were the neighbours to consider in this rather seedy road. It was probably the most exciting thing that had happened there since the Silver Jubilee.

'Stay here,' Hall said to his driver. 'Radio the other car and tell them to wait as well. If we need back-up, Jacquie has her radio with her and will just press alarm. Then come running.'

'I thought that poisoners couldn't hurt you, guv,' said Jacquie. 'Only by stealth.'

'That's an actual *poisoner*, Jacquie,' said Hall. 'Davies is a policeman who has chosen to poison people. He's a completely different animal.' He led the way down the path and knocked on the dusty door. An unexpected smell of a Sunday roast wafted out as Davies answered their knock.

'Guv! Jacquie! How lovely to see you both,' he said, smiling like a crocodile. 'In you come. You're just in time for lunch. Will you join me?' They didn't reply, just edged in past him into a hall that had seen better days. Every inch of the paintwork was Nicotine Yellow, a shade which even Dulux had a hard time marketing. 'No, I didn't think you would. There's plenty, if you change your minds. This is rude, but would you mind if I carried on? It's always nicer if it's hot, don't you think? Go on through. Yes, that's it, right through, into the kitchen. I eat in the conservatory at the back.'

He ushered them into the kitchen and through into what was essentially a glass-sided lean-to. They looked around with faint distaste at the green-streaked glass and lifted their feet surreptitiously to check that they hadn't stepped in anything. The initial delicious smell had become rather less pleasant the further into the house they went. Davies was behind them, a plate of dinner in his hands. He gestured to the table.

'I've only laid for one, so if I can sit there, guv? You and Jacquie sit anywhere you like.' He sat down and pulled the salt, in a red plastic drum, towards him. 'After all, you usually do just as you like, don't you?'

Hall and Jacquie sat reluctantly. Hall had had no game plan on this one, he was running on anger and adrenalin. This was one of their own, and he had tried to kill Margaret. A small part of his brain tried to weigh up which of these sins was the worst. It was a close call. 'Let's keep this pleasant, Bob, shall we?' he suggested.

Davies took a huge bite of his dinner. 'Why?' His tone was reasonable, and it was hard to see him as a mass poisoner. For the first time, Jacquie wondered whether her guv'nor had made a mistake.

'There isn't a good outcome, is there, Bob? You've killed two people, and...'

Davies waved a gravy-smeared knife at Hall. 'Hold up, now,' he said. 'I haven't killed two people. Just the barman and he was an accident.'

'And Mel Forman.'

'Who the fuck is Mel Norman when he's at home?'

'She,' said Jacquie. 'The teacher at Leighford High.'

Davies put down his knife and fork and guffawed. 'Idiots,' he said. 'I didn't do that one. I got the *idea* from that one. No,' and he resumed attacking his food, 'somebody else did that one. A nutter, I suppose. Had the right idea, though,

351

targeting Leighford High. Probably after that wanker you live with, Jacquie.' His tone was still reasonable, he was just stating facts. He held out a forkful of greens towards her. 'Go on, try some. Spinach. Lovely. Put hairs on your chest.' She shook her head. 'No? You don't know what you're missing.' He ate it in one bite.

'Bob,' said Hall, trying to get the conversation back on track. 'You're a policeman...'

'Was. Was a policeman.'

'You know the odds of two poisoners in one town are astronomic.'

'But there aren't two poisoners, are there?' he said. 'There's *one* poisoner and there's me. I just copied him. You must have already worked that out.' He looked from one to the other, smiling. 'Fuck me, you two. You won't solve anything without me. I can't believe you've been looking for just one person. You must be nuts.'

Hall and Jacquie looked at each other. All of the things that hadn't added up had been because they were doing the wrong sum. They had tied themselves in knots trying to make links between unlinked crimes. Into their minds came a simultaneous thought: that while they were here, watching Davies filling his face, another poisoner was out there, at large and able to get at his original victims, able to have another go.

Davies burped resonantly. 'Oops,' he said, and patted his chest. 'Wind in the willows. Where were we? Oh, yes. I am your *random* poisoner. I've done, ooh, I forget how many shops. And not just shops either. I've done pubs, cafes, restaurants. The casual job in the Vine was ridiculously

352

easy to get and very useful, as you already know.' He looked thoughtful. 'Shame I missed Angus, though. I really thought he'd be up for two or three pints before you got there. I was planning putting something in his stash if the beer failed, but that went a bit tits up, of course. Never mind, it's all one now.' He reached out and helped himself to some more mint sauce from a pot on the table.

'Putting aside Leighford High for a moment,' Hall said, 'did you try to poison Jacquie's son yesterday afternoon?'

Davies looked aggrieved. 'I most certainly did not. Poor little bugger, he's got enough to contend with, with those two for parents, without me slipping something in his juice. I heard about that, though. When I dropped in to the nick.' He bent a solicitous gaze on Jacquie. 'All right now, is he, young Nolan?'

'Yes, he is, thanks,' said Jacquie, tightly.

'Tell you what, though,' Davies went on, 'while young Nolan is the subject of the conversation. Two things, really. One is, don't use birthdays as your PIN. I've been listening to your messages for months. The other thing is ... well, I hardly like to say.'

'What?' Jacquie snapped, half rising from her chair.

'Where is he?'

She sat down again. 'Stop trying to scare me, Davies, you shit,' she said. 'He's with his father and grandmother.'

'His grandmother. Looks like you if you were made up to look like a boot. Short legs. Fat arse.'

It seemed disloyal, but it was accurate enough. Jacquie nodded. Hall dipped his head. Now was not the time to crack his first smile.

'When I saw them running down Silversmith Row I didn't see him. Perhaps they left him with someone, eh?'

Jacquie grabbed Hall's arm and shook it. 'I told you,' she said. 'I told you it was odd my car was still there.'

'Calm down, Jacquie,' Hall said. 'I'm sure there is a perfectly rational explanation.'

'Bugger that,' she said and dashed off towards the front door, yelling down her radio as she went. 'All units, Silversmith Row. Stat. Repeat, all units. Silversmith Row.'

'Alpha Charlie Two,' came the steady response. 'Unit November Echo already at Silversmith Row. Query send other units, over.'

'Why are they there?' she snapped. To hell with all this Alpha Charlie rubbish.

'Casualty. Elderly man. Poison. Paramedics in attendance.'

Elderly? Did Maxwell class as elderly? 'Any other casualties?'

'Negative Alpha Charlie Two. Two civilians called it in. A Mr Maxwell...'

'Thank God.'

'Query that, Alph–'

'For God's sake,' she snapped. 'Just give me the facts.'

The radio operator dropped into gossip mode. 'It's your bloke, Jacquie, and a woman.'

'My mum.'

'Makes sense. They chased this geezer to his

354

house and he tried to poison them with...' there were distant mutterings, 'smoke, it says here. Anyway, they managed to get him out of the premises and called us and ambulance control. The old bloke is OK, they're bringing him in. So, it looks as if we've got our poisoner.'

Jacquie looked over her shoulder. She could see Hall, but not Davies. She could hear his drone as he told Hall all about it. Then, suddenly, she saw Hall half rise from his chair and reach across the table. Before she could work out what was happening there was a crash of breaking crockery and a noise that went down her spine like ice water. It was a cross between a scream and a groan and it was cut off suddenly. The silence was deafening.

'What the hell was that?' asked the radio operator. 'Alpha Charlie Two, are you all right?'

She put the radio back up to her ear. 'Send paramedics to 29 Hydrangea Crescent,' she said. 'Over and out.' She turned to go through into the kitchen and then into the dirty little lean-to, but before she had taken two steps, Hall came out to meet her.

'Don't go in,' he said. 'It isn't very nice.'

'What did he do?' Jacquie asked, her eyes wide.

'He took all the poisons he had left, all mixed up in his dinner. He had had them for years, pinched from an evidence box when he was working in Birmingham. God knows why he kept them. As well as that, his "spinach" was hydrangea leaves, for good measure. His "mint sauce" was thorn apple. He really meant it, Jacquie. He would have done it, anyway. It's just our good luck that we got here while he could still tell us a few missing details.'

'Like, why?'

'Because he hated us.'

Jacquie went white. She had never had herself down as a person who other people hated. Hall put his arm round her shoulder and pulled her close. She folded into his shoulder and was still there, crying softly, when the driver put his head cautiously round the door. Hall waved him away.

'Nothing to see here,' he said, quietly. 'Nothing to see.' And he rested his cheek on the top of Jacquie's head. If she felt the single tear that dampened her hair, she said nothing, and never would.

Chapter Twenty-Two

Monday morning was on its way, but Chez Maxwell & Carpenter, Crimes Solved While You Wait,
Patent Pending, Website Under Construction,
Sunday was still the topic of conversation. The
afternoon had been exciting on so many levels.
Jacquie had explained to her mother that her car
had been trashed by an angry mob and knew
from the sparkle in her eye that she would dine
out on it for weeks.

'So, when did you first suspect Lessing?'
Jacquie asked. She and Maxwell were curled up
on the sofa, her mother had taken over Maxwell's
chair and, wonder of wonders, Metternich was
on her lap. Maxwell gave him the occasional
glance which the cat rightly interpreted as saying
'Quisling'. Nolan, safely returned by an agog
Miranda, was in bed.

'Well,' her mother piped up, although it was
Maxwell's mouth that had opened first. 'When
Nolan recognised him, really. Wasn't it?' she
appealed to Maxwell, but not much.

'I had been suspicious of him for a while,'
Maxwell said. 'I met him at school on the first
day of term. He said he was delivering as a
volunteer, so I later wondered if he had also
delivered the cocktails. But the one Freda had
had been all right. A deliberate ploy, as we now
realise, and quite clever, really.'

'Plus, of course,' Betty piped up, 'the attempt on ... you know, the great fat one you told me about...'

'Mrs Bevell,' said Jacquie, for no reason other than to stop her mouth healing up.

'So I thought then that it might be her husband, some insane litigation/insurance job. And, heaven knows, we'd all like it to be. The Leighford High incident might be a bit tricky to explain, but not impossible. Then,' he went on, 'the other poisonings began and I really didn't see Bevell having the local knowledge, although they are only from Littlehampton, so he could have sussed the ground.'

'But wasn't he at the hospital almost all the time?' Jacquie asked.

'That was the snag,' said Maxwell. 'The staff all hated him doing it, but I saw an article on the news tonight about him. Apparently, while guarding his wife, he fell asleep and, in doing so, a banana slipped off his lap. Someone trod on it and broke his arm. He's suing Bevell for loss of earnings. I really can't explain that one. I *know* I put the peel in the bin.' He smiled at the women, as innocent as the day.

'Oh, damn,' Jacquie laughed. 'That will be a drop in the ocean compared to what he has fleeced other people for.'

'You'd think so,' Maxwell said. 'Unfortunately for the Bevells, the man who slipped was a consultant surgeon visiting a patient. We're talking big, *big* money.' He sighed happily. 'I love a happy ending, don't you?'

'He couldn't stay there at night, though,' Ninja

pointed out, bringing them back to the sleuthing. She had never met Mr and Mrs Sue Bevell and didn't get the joke. 'He would have had time then.'

'True. But he wasn't free to give Nolan the lolly,' Jacquie said.

'I meant to tell you about that,' Maxwell said, ruffling her hair. 'The lolly wasn't poisoned.'

'What?' She sat up sharply, fetching Maxwell a nice one under the chin.

'You may me bye my tug,' he said, clutching his mouth.

'Never mind,' Betty continued. 'The silly old fool gave him an aniseed lolly. No wonder he cried. No child likes those.'

Jacquie laughed. 'So, he was just being finicky?'

'Well, yes. But, in a way, that solved the case. Otherwise, we wouldn't have chased him and we wouldn't have got him under guard at Leighford General as we speak.'

'True. Go on.'

'Well,' Maxwell came back into the conversation, but speaking carefully around his swollen tongue. 'That's it, really. We followed him home and he lit a fire of oleander.'

'The smoke of which is poisonous,' said Betty.

'And he tried to get us to inhale it.'

'But we're not that stupid.'

'So he stood in it himself.'

'And Max rescued him. It was terribly exciting, Jacquie. He came out through the smoke like Kurt Russell in *Backdraft*. I was so proud!'

So, there we are, thought Maxwell. It's easy to get on with your mother-in-law. Just dive through poisonous smoke to rescue a murderer and everything will be peachy.

'But, wasn't that horribly dangerous?' Jacquie asked, playing to the gallery.

'Jacquie,' her mother said, 'he was just wonderful. He soaked his scarf in the bottled water we were carrying and wrapped it round his mouth. So resourceful.'

Maxwell nodded modestly. 'I went to a good school. They taught us to be very resourceful,' he said.

Jacquie looked into his eyes. 'And tired,' she said.

'That, too.'

'And you've got to be a Headmaster in the morning.'

'So that wasn't a dream, then?' he asked, innocently.

'No.' She kissed him on the nose. 'I'll put the cocoa on. Mum?'

'May I have Horlicks?'

'You can have what you like,' her daughter said, squeezing her shoulder as she walked past.

'Horlicks?' Maxwell asked.

She winked at him. 'It goes better with the brandy,' she said, getting up and going over to the cupboard. 'Anything for yourself?'

'I'll have a small Southern Comfort, since you ask,' he said. 'I find it goes with anything.'

She handed him the glass. 'Cheers, Max.'

'Cheers, Ninj, and many of them.'

Acting Headmaster Peter Maxwell stood in the doorway of Leighford High School on Monday morning, Acting master of all he surveyed. The only slight snag in all this was that there wasn't a child to be seen and only very few staff, ostentatiously carrying packed lunches.

'They caught him, you know,' he remarked to Thingee One, who was loitering in the foyer, hoping to be given the day off.

'Yes, but, Mr Maxwell, your w ... your ... the police sergeant said on the telly yesterday – she did look lovely, by the way, I really like the way she does her hair – she said that they don't know how many shops and other places the Leighford Ripper had struck.'

'Ripper? Ripper, Thingee? Why do you call him the Ripper? He was a poisoner.'

'It's what the Leighford Advertiser are calling him on their web page, Mr Maxwell.'

'Ripper it is, then,' Maxwell sighed. 'But I still don't see why every single child has opted to stay at home today.'

'Mr Maxwell!' Thingee was surprised at him. 'He might have poisoned the water or anything. You can't be too careful.'

He looked down at her, all big eyes and willing manner. She seemed to want something else. 'Did you want something else, Thingee, old thing?'

'Umm, not really, Mr Maxwell,' she said, turning away in disappointment.

'In that case, you might as well have the day off.' He smiled at her. 'Off you bugger, now, there's a good admin person.' He smiled to himself and rubbed his hands together. 'I'll let the workmen in.' Wearing an expression that could only be described as beatifically evil, he paced his school and waited for the real fun to begin.

Eventually there came, as all things do to those who wait, peace and normality to Leighford High, its staff, students and, beyond the gates, the town. Every last piece of perishable food had been landfilled. Every bottle of milk, of orange juice, of wine had gone its diluted way far out to sea. Every lettuce, every tea bag, every egg had composted itself into a brown and indistinguishable mush. Davies had gone to his horrible end with a secret and that was how much poison he had spread through the town, and the final decision by police and council had been that you couldn't be too careful. The town's food supply had been like an unexploded bomb and it had been treated as such, the systematic clearing of the shelves of shop and house alike being carried out with military precision. Taking into account that statistics show that thirty per cent of all food bought is likely to be wasted, there was therefore a one in three chance that the packet of jelly babies with a small needle hole in it, stashed at the back of the drawer in Maxwell's temporary office, might never be eaten. Only time would tell.

Meanwhile, everything slowly maintained its equilibrium. Leighford High flourished and blossomed under Maxwell's somewhat loose rein. Paperwork happened, but not always in the right order. Uniforms were or were not worn as the fit took the individual child (although Maxwell had toyed briefly with introducing stable dress, walking-out dress and levee dress, just to add to parental expense), but nobody died. Absences fell

362

to an all-time low. Helen Maitland, learning to love her plaster, took over as temporary Assistant Headteacher for Girls' Welfare. Bernard Ryan, with a show of enthusiasm foreign to him, defied science by regaining control of his organs and James Diamond started his convalescence. Life at Leighford High was good. The workmen had been and gone. Late summer became early autumn and half-term arrived.

Maxwell was sitting quietly in his office on the first day of the holiday when the door opened and a small cough announced the presence of a visitor. He looked up and there, outlined against the light, was Legs Diamond, back to claim his school. Maxwell leapt to his feet.

'Headmaster! How lovely to see you. Sit down, do.' He ushered him round to the chair side of the desk. 'Are you back? I mean, for good? That's excellent.'

Diamond looked round slowly. Nothing seemed to have changed. He had been prepared to find changes – you could never tell with Maxwell – but everything seemed in order. There had been an odd smell in the foyer, that was all. He couldn't quite place it, it was nagging at his memory. It brought back thoughts of his first years of teaching, when he was fancy-free. It was a Proustian madeleine of a smell. He sat there, smoothing his desk, smiling at Maxwell.

'You seem to have done a good job, Max. Thank you. I've heard ... good things. Yes, very good things. Thank you.'

'Don't thank me, Headmaster. It was a pleasure. It really, really was.'

363

'Shall we walk round the school?'

Maxwell clapped him on the shoulder. 'I would only be in the way,' he said. 'I've got to get back for Nole, anyway. Enjoy your tour.'

Diamond got up slowly from behind his desk and walked into the foyer with Maxwell. He sniffed. 'What *is* that smell? It takes me back, but I can't place it.'

Maxwell breathed in through his nose, extravagantly. 'Can't say I've noticed it, Headmaster.' He turned for the door. 'Bye, now. See you next week.' And he was off, down the steps and round to the bike shed with a good turn of speed.

Diamond still stood there, sniffing. His brain cells were finally catching on and they sent him a message. Chalk! He could smell chalk! By the time he reached the first classroom along the corridor and beheld the blackboard, in all its dusty glory, where once an interactive white board had hung, Maxwell was almost too far away to hear the scream.

Chapter Twenty-Three

The weather on that Balaclava Day was perfect. In a clear blue sky, fluffy clouds scudded high and fast. The leaves were beginning to turn and, once in a while, one slowly spiralled to the ground to add its gold to the worn stones and smooth green of the country churchyard. From inside the church, a quiet, lone voice could be heard.

'...I now pronounce you man and wife. You may kiss the bride.'

Henry Hall looked fondly as the groom did just that. He had been delighted to accept when Maxwell had asked him to be his Best Man, during the mad weekend of the Leighford Ripper, as he had got used to calling him. He looked around the church and caught the eye of the other witness, Sylvia Matthews, fighting the lump in her throat. They fell into step behind the happy couple as they walked down the aisle and were ready with the confetti, strictly forbidden in a notice in the porch.

Sylvia nudged Henry and he shrugged. 'So, sue me,' he said. 'I'm a policeman. I say what goes.' And he threw handfuls of horseshoes and hearts over the couple.

'What do you think Jacquie's mother will say when she finds out about this?' Henry asked, as he took Sylvia's arm gallantly as they walked down the path away from the porch, where the vicar stood in the doorway, his back to the empty building, a tear in his eye. It had been a lovely service and they seemed such a nice couple. You'd have thought they would have more friends.

'I dread to think,' she said. 'But bags I'm the one to tell her!'

The publishers hope that this book has given you enjoyable reading. Large Print Books are especially designed to be as easy to see and hold as possible. If you wish a complete list of our books please ask at your local library or write directly to:

Magna Large Print Books
Magna House, Long Preston,
Skipton, North Yorkshire.
BD23 4ND

This Large Print Book for the partially sighted, who cannot read normal print, is published under the auspices of

THE ULVERSCROFT FOUNDATION